Lisa Farrer

MELANIE THORNE earned her MA in creative writing from the University of California, Davis, where she was awarded the Alva Englund Fellowship and the Maurice Prize in Fiction. She lives in Northern California.

Praise for *Hand Me Down*

"Melanie Thorne's debut novel is raw with emotion as she describes Liz's often futile efforts to protect her sister and herself from the predator their mother has invited into their lives. It is often hard to remember that this is, in fact, a novel and not a memoir."

—M. L. Johnson, Associated Press

"Thorne sounds utterly liberated as she describes the merits of exploring fact through fiction. . . . With the clear-eyed honesty of a Daniel Woodrell or Bonnie Jo Campbell character, Liz describes the pain of being a young person among careless, thrill-seeking men and hardworking, wounded women."   —*San Francisco Chronicle*

"*Hand Me Down* is a gritty tale of a determined young woman who really wants to make a better life for herself and protect the little sister she dearly loves. It is also a story of triumph over desperation and the ignorance of those who live in the world of selfishness. The experiences shared by Thorne have the feel of reality and propel the reader into the mind of a teen hoping to overcome the mistakes of her parents."   —*Deseret News* (Utah)

"Thorne's debut will strike an emotional chord with anyone who's ever been an overlooked child (to put it mildly), and teenage Liz—by far the most adult member of her family—is a role model for survivors."   —*East Bay Express*

"Thorne populates her pages with characters who are fascinating and sharply drawn. . . . Liz . . . a wise, wry, wonderful heroine . . . continues to narrate her journey with prose that vibrates with intelligence and passion."   —*Kirkus Reviews* (starred)

"Thorne writes convincingly from an adolescent's perspective, admitting to having mined her own experiences. The family is believably and sadly dysfunctional, and readers will empathize with each character through their highs and lows. . . . [T]his is an intriguing first outing by a talented new writer."   —*Publishers Weekly*

"Debut novelist Thorne is at her best in the evocative descriptions of place—the frozen beauty of a Utah winter, the prosaic decor of a suburban household. . . . Thorne deals sensitively with a difficult topic and the novel's adolescent perspective is sure to find popularity with YA audiences."

—*Library Journal*

"Elizabeth is a tough and tender heroine for the ages. A few pages in her voice are all it takes to make us determined to see her through."

—Pam Houston, author of *Contents May Have Shifted* and *Cowboys Are My Weakness*

"The prose here is sharp, fresh, deeply felt, and grimly funny."

—Clifford Chase, author of *Winkie*

"The novel is sad, strong, evocative as hell, and altogether terrific. Liz emerges as quite a likable and unlikely hero."

—John Lescroart, author of *The Hunter* and *Damage*

"An absorbing, sympathetic first novel."

—*Booklist*

"Compelling, heart-wrenching, and ultimately redemptive."

—Jennifer Chiaverini, *New York Times* bestselling author

HAND

ME

DOWN

A NOVEL

Melanie Thorne

A PLUME BOOK

PLUME
Published by the Penguin Group
Penguin Group (USA) Inc., 375 Hudson Street,
New York, New York 10014, U.S.A.

USA / Canada / UK / Ireland / Australia / New Zealand / India / South Africa / China
Penguin Books Ltd, Registered Offices: 80 Strand, London WC2R 0RL, England
For more information about the Penguin Group visit penguin.com

First published in the United States of America by Dutton, a member of Penguin Group (USA) Inc., 2012
First Plume Printing, April 2013

Epilogue entitled "Word Association" previously published, in slightly
different form, in *Global City Review*, 2008.

℗ REGISTERED TRADEMARK—MARCA REGISTRADA

The Library of Congress has catalogued the Dutton edition as follows:

Thorne, Melanie, 1981–
  Hand me down : a novel / Melanie Thorne.
    p. cm.
  ISBN 978-0-525-95268-8 (hc.)
  ISBN 978-0-452-29885-9 (pbk.)
  1. Sisters—Fiction.   2. Teenage girls—Fiction.   3. Dysfunctional families—Fiction.
4. Single parents—Fiction.   I. Title.
  PS3620.H7675H36 2012
  813'.6—dc22

                                                                    2011022362

Printed in the United States of America
10 9 8 7 6 5 4 3 2 1

Original hardcover design by Alissa Amell

PUBLISHER'S NOTE
This is a work of fiction. Names, characters, places, and incidents either are the product of the
author's imagination or are used fictitiously, and any resemblance to actual persons, living or
dead, businesses, companies, events, or locales is entirely coincidental.

For my mom and honorary mom

1

My mom and her husband are doing it in her bedroom. I listen to her bedsprings squeak and their hushed, heavy breathing. I need to pee, but if I get up they'll hear me, and that sudden, conscious silence would be worse than the sound of chimp squeals and hyperventilation muffled by our hollow bedroom doors and the three feet of hallway in between. At least she's not screaming, *Oh, God*, like I've seen in movies. I chew the slippery skin on the inside of my mouth and wonder if it's still a sin to take the Lord's name in vain during sex, or if then, it is like a prayer.

It is Terrance's first night out. For two years my mom has saved her nice voice for his collect calls, driven the hour and a half to Vacaville every Thursday afternoon and Saturday morning to see him, waited expectantly for his twenty-page letters full of shaded hearts pierced with arrows, poems wrought with adolescent angst, and fantasies I can never, ever, repeat out loud. His dark penciled writing is frilly with curled loops and a childlike slant. I only read the letters because Jaime made me. "Why would he want her to do that thing with the marshmallows?" she asked after she found the envelopes, dozens of them, in a pile under our mom's nightstand. I told her I'd rather not think about it.

Water sloshing and soft moaning sounds radiate from Mom's bathroom now, and I start to wonder how they can both fit in the tub but, *gross*. When Terrance arrived at the apartment today he said, "I know you don't like when I hug you, but I'm going to anyway!" He scooped me up in his arms and spun me around like I was a toddler while I stayed straight as a corpse. Mom snapped a photo and giggled. He set me down but held me close to his chest, the pressure of his splayed hands across my lower back kept my hips against him. He breathed in my ear, "I missed you."

"We're so excited you're home," Mom said, taking another picture. "Aren't we, Liz?"

"Not as excited as me," Terrance said. His fingers grazed the sides of my breasts as he released me, and if he hadn't done it before, I might have thought it was an accident. He wagged his thick black eyebrows at Mom and they haven't left her room since.

If Jaime still lived here, I'd be lying along the outer edge of her bed, singing or cracking jokes, but alone, I stuff Kleenex in my ears and fold my body until my limbs are wrapped around me like a shell.

"Check it out, Liz," Terrance says in the morning, turning his back to me. He wears only boxer shorts, his thin legs dark with long black hairs. Above the waist he looks like a bodybuilder, his back and chest divided into chunks of muscle that twitch with each of his movements. I wonder if he will continue to lift weights now that he's out of prison, and the Grape-Nuts in my mouth turn to sand.

"Very, um"—I cough, clear my throat—"muscle-y," I say, getting up.

He beams. "Thanks," he says, "but, no, look at this." He blocks my way and points at his left shoulder blade. "My tattoo." It's a six-inch King Arthur sword with detailed braiding on the gold-and-black hilt, an almost silver blade stuck through a red heart. The heart has a white ribbon running from top left to bottom right with my mom's name in delicate cursive. He says, "Don't you want to touch it?"

I have promised Mom that I will be nice. Last week she said, "This has to work, Elizabeth." After she'd bought him two new pairs of Levi's jeans and a Forty-Niners cap, after she'd gotten a second TV for her bedroom and ordered the cable package with extra sports channels, after she'd moved Noah's crib out of her bedroom, she said in a whisper, her blue-green eyes dark and too wide, "It has to work this time."

So I don't ask Terrance if one of his prison buddies inked it, or what he had to do in return, or what happened to the tattoo of his first wife's name. I don't cringe or gag at the thought of touching his bare skin. An older tattoo of a cross covers his right shoulder, this one the veiny blue-black you'd expect from BIC ballpoints and safety pins.

"Isn't it beautiful?" Mom says, coming from the kitchen carrying a plate of pancakes. She widens her eyes at me and nods at Terrance. *Please*, she mouths, her features tight. She says to Terrance, "Sit, babe." She rubs his back and pushes him into a chair, kisses his neck. "Eggs are coming."

She busted out her big ho ensemble yesterday when she went to pick him up: low-cut V-neck green tank top, black miniskirt, and black strappy heels. This morning she is wearing a new nightgown with major cleavage and I think one of her giant boobs might pop out as she follows me into the tiny kitchen with her anxious twitchiness. Her eyes plead with me while she takes my bowl and says, "I'll do that for you, honey." She hasn't called me honey since I was five. "Go, or you'll be late for school."

I walk past Terrance and roll my eyes at his back as he shovels undercooked pancakes into his mouth. Mom watches me, her face strained, frozen in that imploring smile behind his head, and I sigh. She relaxes her face, her lips quivering as they descend. She knows me too well.

"It's a pretty cool tattoo," I say, and she smiles. *Thank you*, she mouths. I grab my backpack and head out the door.

Rachel meets me for lunch at our spot by the dried-up fountain in the old courtyard near the parking lot. Blue tiles line the bottom of the pool, but it fills with brown and orange leaves as the gnarled oak trees go bare, and I brush some off the concrete edge before sitting.

"Are you going to homecoming?" Rachel asks. I just look at her. "What?" she says and pulls out her lunch. "It's our first high school dance."

"Homecoming?" I lift one eyebrow at her. "Really?" I frown at the peanut butter on bread I slapped together.

Rachel hands me a Fruit Roll-Up and some Cheetos. "I thought you might want to get out of your house for one night," she says and takes a bite of the roast beef sandwich her dad made her.

"My mom probably won't let me," I say.

"You could ask," Rachel says.

"If I can get her attention," I say. "Last night—"

"You can try," she says and scoots closer to me. "C'mon, it'll be fun."

"Dances aren't really my idea of fun," I say. I doubt Mom will buy me a dress and I don't want to find a date. "At last year's 'dance' people just head banged to Nirvana all night," I say.

"But this is high school," Rachel says. "It's different now." I scrunch my nose in disbelief. She says, "For me?"

I sigh. "Okay, I'll ask."

She hugs me. "So what happened last night?" I open my mouth and she grabs my arm. "Oh! He got out last night! I'm so sorry, how was it?"

As I tell her, deep gray clouds roll across the sun and I pray it doesn't rain. I have to walk home.

For two years Terrance called our house almost every day after school. A mechanical voice said, "You have a collect call from an inmate at a California state prison," and we pushed two to accept the call and patched Terrance through to Mom at work on three-way. I'm not sure what Mom told her coworkers at the abuse victims' organization about her husband, but she writes grants to help women assaulted by men like Terrance so I doubt anyone at her office knew the truth.

Jaime discovered early on that if we held down the mute button after we clicked Terrance and Mom together, we could hear them talk and they had no idea. Jaime listened every day. "He always asks what she's wearing," she'd tell me, or, "He gets jealous if she mentions another guy." Jaime collected information and we used it to gauge Mom's moods. If the prison went into lockdown on a Friday—which meant no visit Saturday—the dishes were done, the TV off, and dinner on the table when Mom got home.

One afternoon about a month ago, Jaime came into my room and put her head in my lap like she used to when we played house and I was the mom. "What's wrong?" I asked, putting down my book and stroking her hair.

"Terrance is getting out next month," she said and started crying. "Mom's really excited."

"Fuck," I said. "It's too soon."

"I called Dad. He said we can come live with him and Crystal."

I sighed. "He's not sober."

"So? At least he doesn't lie."

"Mom's not going to lie us into a ditch on the way to school." I touched Jaime's hairline at her right temple, where a V-shaped silvery-white scar is etched into her skin under the blond strands.

"It wasn't a ditch," she said, shaking her head and brushing off my hand. "It was an accident."

I eyed the raised and shiny reminder of the cost of letting my guard down for even a second. I said, "They're not accidents when he's drinking."

Jaime pulled her bangs over her scar the way she does when she catches me staring. She sat up. "Crystal told me this wasn't Terrance's first time in jail. That he didn't deal drugs like Mom said."

"Well, he did that, too," I said and wondered how much of the police reports Crystal had shown Jaime. Some of that stuff was not for kids. Living in Crystal's filthy two-bedroom trailer was not for kids, either.

"I'm scared, Liz."

"Scared enough to live with Dad?"

"He said he'd love to have us," she said.

"He'd love to have us take care of Crystal's daughter for him."

"You're not scared of Terrance the pervert?" She looked at me and I marveled again at how our eyes could be the exact same color blue, like seeing my eyes in her face. "Did Crystal tell you what he does?" she said. She sniffed and wiped her nose on her sleeve. "It's freaky and gross."

Crystal had seated me at her always sticky kitchen table and read me dozens of pages of eyewitness accounts, police summaries, and victim statements that provided details of his crimes I didn't need. I'd already noticed Terrance's wandering eyes carried the same restless look as cheetahs and tigers pacing in their zoo cages, instinct contained but not eliminated. "Yes, I'm scared of Terrance," I said. I've stopped wearing shorts to bed and I get dressed in the locked bathroom. "But I'm scared of Dad, too."

"Dad would never hurt us," she said and hugged me. "He loves us at least."

He hurts us all the time. "You know that doesn't matter," I said. "He loved Mom, too."

Then last week, Jaime went to school one day and didn't come home. She didn't tell me beforehand, just called from Dad's and said she wasn't coming back. Mom didn't want to talk to her. "If she'd rather be there, then fine," Mom said, smiling wide enough to show the pearl-gray tooth behind her left incisor. "No need to have a big argument about it." Her glasses reflected the light so I couldn't see her eyes, but she walked away with her hips swinging to the bass thumping from the new stereo she'd bought for Terrance.

I told Jaime that Mom was too upset to talk just yet, but I think she could hear Mom's throaty versions of Journey songs in the background. Mom sang, "You make me weep, and wanna die," her and Terrance's favorite make-out-on-the-couch tune, as she tried on outfits for his release day. Each of them was low cut, or too short, or both. All included heels. "Lovin', touchin', squeezin'." She'd had time to exercise while he was locked up, a Jazzercise tape Jaime and I did with her sometimes, and was ready to show off curves where there used to be layers.

"How long are you going to stay with Dad?" I said to Jaime.

"I think I'm moving in," she said.

A bomb detonated in my gut. "For good?"

"For a while."

"Where are you going to sleep?" I said. "How will you get to school?"

"Don't worry, Liz," she said. "I'll be okay."

"You know not to get in the car with him if—"

"Crystal says Dad has been better," Jaime said. "She makes him go to meetings."

"How does she know he's actually going?"

"How does anyone know anything?" she said, in a perfect replica of Dad's flippant responses.

"Come on, Jaime. This is serious."

She mimicked me, high-pitched and nasal, "This is serious,"

and then sighed and said, "Dad wants me here, okay? Mom only cares about her pervert husband." Jaime sniffed. "She just wants to have sex."

"Did Dad tell you that?"

"What is Mom doing right now?" Jaime said.

She was trying on a black spandex tank top with a denim miniskirt, holding Noah, and dancing around with him in her bedroom, but I didn't tell Jaime that. Noah bubbled spit as he laughed, and I wondered if Mom had smiled at us like that when we were babies.

"It was better for a while," I said. "When he was gone."

"You could come live here, too," she said.

Jaime can't always tell when Dad's been drinking. She would have kept the secret of the six-pack under his passenger seat if not for me. She cried for two hours when he forgot her last birthday, but still begged me for money so she could give him his favorite Old Spice cologne the next month for his. She doesn't know the worst of what he's done, and I've worked so hard to shelter her, she probably wouldn't accept the truth anyway.

I said, "You'll call me if he scares you? If he's mean?"

"He's been nice," she said.

"That usually means he wants something."

"He's so right that no one believes him."

I closed my eyes. *There's a reason for that.* "Just be careful."

"Yes, Mom," she said, the "o" drawn out and sarcastic. "You're so paranoid."

I looked at our mother, squeezed into a dress two sizes too small, black lined eyes and clumps in her mascara, wine-colored glossed-in lips, shaking her ass and belting out lyrics she had also sung with our dad before we were born, and said, "Well, someone around here has to be a grown-up."

Terrance can call Mom from our house for free today, but I still have to talk to him as soon as I walk in the door. "What's Mom's work number?" he says before I shrug my shoulders out of my backpack. He rests his new variable-weight bar on its base, sits up on the shiny black leather weight bench he set up in the middle of the living room. "She told me, but I forgot."

"Nice weights." I walk past the bench and try not to inhale.

"Yeah," he says, wiping sweat off his chest with a towel Mom spent a Sunday evening cross-stitching a garden scene onto. "I went shopping."

"With your money?" I say.

He scrunches up his eyebrows and says, "I don't have any money." *Duh, loser. Get a job.* Pulsing greenish veins running up his forearms to his shoulders protrude a centimeter above his skin and look ready to burst. He sees me looking and flexes his biceps. "I'm pretty ripped, huh?" he says and rubs his chest with both hands. "Wanna feel?" I tell him Mom's number and flee to my room.

I can hear his voice through the walls but I can no longer see his sweaty dark skin or big-toothed sneer and I let myself pretend he's not here. I pretend Jaime still is, and Mom is still gone Saturday mornings and I make Mickey Mouse–head pancakes and scrambled eggs and hash browns for the two of us. We play Super

Mario Brothers, and I end up giving Jaime some of my turns because she dies too fast. We sit next to each other on the floor and talk about how maybe Terrance will try to escape and he'll get shot by the guards or ravaged by German shepherds. Mom will cry but she'll get over it, Noah won't have to be raised by a pervert, and we can have our mom back. The mom who sang songs she made up with our names in them as we fell asleep, who played crazy eights and gin rummy after work, and promised she wouldn't marry anyone we didn't like.

Suddenly Terrance's voice is louder and he opens my bedroom door without knocking. "Liz, Mom said for you to order a pizza." His bare chest chunks bounce as he crosses my room.

"You can't order a pizza?" I say. Green veins still bulge under his naturally tan skin, darker for the summer spent lifting weights in the prison yard. I close my eyes and visualize his blood vessels popping.

"She said you can call in time for her to pick it up on her way home." He stops in front of my bed, extends his arm to give me the phone. "You know when she gets off work." He skims my hands with his warm, greasy fingers and leans toward me. "I just know when she gets off," he says and laughs his hyena-ish cackle. Like Dad, Terrance only makes inappropriate jokes when Mom's not around.

He puts one knee on my bed and I press my back into the plaster behind me. "You can't tell time?" I say, looking to my right, away from his sweaty skin, his sagging jersey shorts displaying his hip bones, his beady eyes that follow me like an eerie painting. He edges closer and I picture ruptured arteries, his heart shredded and leaking.

"I want pepperoni and sausage and green peppers and, mmm, how about a supreme combo or something?" He licks his lips. "Order something I'll like," he says and pats the top of my thigh. He winks at me as he turns, and his parading butt crack leaves my room.

I slam the door and call Rachel. "He doesn't wear shirts," I say. "He invades my personal space like it's his hobby."

"Isn't it?" Rachel says.

"I wish my door had a lock."

"Are you practicing your visualizations?" Rachel's mother, who lives in Reno, is an active Wiccan. She left Rachel's dad a few years ago to "pursue her destiny," but I think mostly she reads tarot cards for tourists in a casino hotel lobby. Her suggestions often work, though, and no one else is offering me any advice.

"Yes," I say. "But he doesn't seem to be bleeding yet."

"You have to really focus or it won't work," Rachel says. "My mom just won a thousand dollars."

When my mom gets home, we eat pizza from paper plates at the dining room table. We usually watch sitcoms or game shows or sports with dinner, the TV on in the living room a few feet away. Terrance taught Noah the NFL theme song and how to howl like Tim Allen in *Home Improvement*. I have kept my promise to be nice and refrained from asking if he sees anyone he knows on *COPS* or *America's Most Wanted*.

Terrance is glued to *Wheel of Fortune* tonight. "Dairy Queen!" he shouts at the screen.

"Ice cream!" Noah says, slapping his hands in the smeared cheese and tomato sauce covering his plastic high-chair tray.

I say, "Dairy Queen is not a person." I pick all the sausage off my pizza and take a small bite.

"Noah, honey, eat your food," Mom says. "More pizza, babe?"

"I sure missed pizza," Terrance says.

"Babe," Mom says. "Do you like your new workout equipment?"

He turns from the TV, his chin shiny with grease. "Yeah, babe, thanks."

"I need new shoes," I say.

"It's way nicer than the weights they had when I was in where I was at," he says.

"I'm glad," Mom says and kisses him, soaking up some of the oil from his face. She wipes her mouth on her Pizza Hut napkin as Terrance turns back to the TV.

Terrance says, "Tampon opener!"

"That's not even a thing," I say, rolling my eyes.

"Hey, Liz," Terrance says, reaching for his fifth slice. "You have a pile of turds on your plate!" He laughs and Noah laughs, and Mom chuckles, too. She laughs almost every time Terrance does.

I visualize the fake chandelier above the table falling on Terrance's head as he leans over and breathes on the little pieces of gray-brown sausage on my white plate. "Are you gonna eat them?" he says.

I lean back from his open mouth and say, "All yours." His dark hand grabs the pile of meat and shoves it into his mouth the way Noah eats Cheerios.

Terrance often takes Mom out after dinner, even on weeknights. They go to movies, to clubs, to bars, and then come home after midnight, my mom spewing sorority girl giggles that sound surreal escaping from her forty-year-old lips; scary, too, since I have never before seen her drink more than a glass of wine. Sometimes she can't hold herself up and Terrance carries her, her lipstick on his face, her skirt hiked up her thighs, once missing a shoe, both of them laughing too loud.

When they wake up Noah they ignore his cries, and eventually I lie down next to his midget-sized body covered in *Bananas in Pajamas* pajamas, and pull the bunched Barney sheets up from around his tan feet, and massage his face even though he inherited Terrance's dark skin and eyes and is sleeping in Jaime's bed. I rock Noah and sing nursery songs the way Mom used to for Jaime and me until his breathing sinks and his neck relaxes, and I always wish someone would sing to me, too.

"They're disgusting," I tell Rachel.

She says, "Sex must be great."

"Not when it's your parents," I say. "Or gross people."

"My parents never did it," she says. "I can't wait to."

"I think I'm scarred for life," I say.

"It's what I'm visualizing," Rachel says. "Sex on the beach."

I shudder. "After listening to my mom and Terrance, I don't think I can ever have sex in water."

"It's a drink, too, you know," she says. "I want to try both."

"Let's move to Mexico," I say.

"We hella should," she says. "Just you and me and all those hot guys."

Most days when I get home from school, Terrance is watching talk shows in which the woman's baby daddy is sleeping with her sister, or the transsexual comedian with anger issues apologizes for attacking a man who called him a faggot. "What a fag," Terrance says and I wonder how true the rumors about prison are. Once I painted Noah's fingernails blue and Terrance made him cry washing it off. "My son is not a homo," he yelled.

Sometimes Terrance plays the acoustic guitar he bought with Mom's money. It's a honey-colored wood, classy, and he offered to teach me to play when he found me holding it in my lap and strumming randomly. He sat next to me on the couch, scooted until his thigh lined up against mine. "I'm a good teacher," he said, tilting his head toward my neck. The iron smell of his breath, like warm blood, made my stomach churn.

"You can't really play," I said. I pushed the guitar at him, trying to force him back. "You only know two chords."

He leaned over the instrument between us. "I can play," he said. He trailed his fingers down my forearm from elbow to wrist and rested the tips on my skin like he was taking my pulse. "I'm really, really good, Liz," he said and wrapped his hand around the guitar neck right below my fist.

I retracted my arms and stood up, fighting to keep my face neutral. Our eyes met and Terrance smiled at me with his crooked mouth like he'd won something. He embraced the guitar I'd dropped, stroked the curved wood, and gazed up at me with heavy-lidded eyes. "You want to see?"

I ran and didn't breathe until I made it to my room. "He's so creepy," I told Rachel from under my covers.

"Duh," she said. "They don't send normal people to prison."

Mom is home today when I get back to the apartment and she and Terrance are giggling in the kitchen. Terrance is even wearing a shirt, though I've stopped expecting him to. They notice me and quiet. "Hi, Elizabeth," Mom says. She tries to smile but her lips spasm like little electroshocks and it just looks ugly.

"What's up?" I say, my pulse revving.

"I"— Mom says and looks at Terrance, nods her head—"we. We need to talk to you." She reaches out her left hand with the gold wedding band she paid for, but her arm drops as she touches my sweatshirt.

"Do you want a sandwich?" Terrance holds up a display of salami and jack cheese. I stare at him. He says, "Man, I missed sandwiches."

We sit at the table. "What's wrong?" I say. A thousand gerbils run treadmills in my stomach.

"Well, Terrance's parole officer called today." She glances at Terrance, who's not listening, just making smacking sounds as he chews. I imagine his face exploding. "Apparently someone called and stated their concern for the minor female living in this house given Terrance's record."

Mom takes a breath. "So the officer—what a jerk—made it a condition of Terrance's parole that he not be allowed to be near girls your age unsupervised." The gerbils hit double time. "That includes after school and sleeping in the same house." She rolls her eyes and waves her hand as if they're being ridiculous. "Since I can't supervise while I'm asleep."

"What?" Fiery tops spin in my head. I feel dizzy. "Does that mean—"

"It's silly really," she says. "There's no reason for such an extreme response, but, you know, the system stinks." She sighs.

I stare at her freshly cut and colored hair, her manicured nails. I think of all the food in the cabinets she bought for him: twelve-packs of soda and beer, doughnuts, Doritos, beef jerky, pork rinds, sunflower seeds. All the money spent on toys for him while she said she couldn't afford to buy me shoes. I think about how she's ignored me for weeks, gone to bars with Terrance and come home late, taken days off work to take him shopping, skipped church to stay in bed.

"But I was trying," I say.

"I know," she says, dropping her eyes to the tabletop.

I whisper, "For you."

She whispers back, "I'm sorry."

I think about how long she stayed with my dad; how she prayed for him every night kneeling in front of her bed, and every morning tried harder to please him through his hangover. The gerbils drop dead, and in my vacant stomach I know she's made that choice again.

Mom opens her mouth, so I try to tell her with my eyes that I know what she's going to say, that I don't need to hear it out loud. But this woman sitting in front of me with my cheekbones and small wrists and wavy hair won't look at my face. My eyes and throat burn like the room's on fire and my ribs feel shattered under the weight in my chest, but she says without flinching, "You and Terrance cannot both live here."

2

Mom swears it will be temporary. "We will file appeals," she says, sitting at the kitchen table she bought at Levitz right after she married Terrance, in one of four matching beige-and-pink cushioned chairs they've probably had sex on. "You'll be back before you know it." Her nearly translucent gray tooth gleams behind lips taut in an asymmetrical smile.

"Couple weeks," Terrance says, "tops."

Mom says, "I promise."

"It's too bad, Liz," Terrance says, staring at me as he licks mayonnaise off his fingers. "I really enjoy having you around the house." He smiles with salami in his teeth.

Little asteroids land and smolder in my throat. This can't be real. This is some kind of sick joke. "Mom," I say. "You're not serious?"

"Liz." Mom swallows and runs her fingers through her bangs. "Everyone agrees that Terrance needs a stable home during this period of reintegration."

"What about my home?"

"Pastor Ron thinks that cohabitation is essential for the survival of our marriage." She shapes her hands into fists and brings them knuckle to knuckle at her solar plexus. "Terrance and I need to rebuild our foundation, create a solid union able to endure hardship."

My mind is reeling, spooling barbed wire around my brain. "I did everything you asked."

"You were doing great." Mom starts to smile but it fades into a frown. "But Terrance needs his family. It's important that we stay together right now."

"More important than your children?"

"It's not that black and white," she says. She lowers her chin to her chest. "Noah is staying."

A noose cinches around my neck and I almost choke. "Was that supposed to make me feel better?"

"Since Jaime is already at your dad's," Mom says and sighs, "it's just you."

It's just me. My vision goes fuzzy and Mom's image turns fluid. She becomes squiggly lines and shaded circles. Her blurred lips keep moving but the water travels to my ears and I hear crackling static. I'm tumbling in the ocean, sand scraping my skin, saltwater filling my lungs and stinging my eyes.

"Liz?" Mom calls my name and slowly she comes back into focus, her face softer, her eyebrows furrowed with concern. Her head tilts to the left and her eyes look wet. "I know this seems hard," she says. "But it will only be for a little while."

"What can I do?" I say, tears spilling onto my chest. "Tell me what to do so I can stay." Every cell inside of me is clenched and heaving. Nausea swims through my gut, but I kneel in front of her and seize her hand, which I'm surprised to find is the exact same size as mine. "Please."

She looks down at me and brushes a strand of hair from my forehead. "I wish no one had to go."

I squeeze her clammy fingers. "Then don't make me," I say, my voice cracking. "Don't make me leave."

Mom takes a deep breath and as she exhales, her curly blond bangs float out from her forehead and lie flat again. She whispers, "I didn't make the rules." She slips her hand out of my grasp and looks away, her lips trembling.

I stand up, clutching my stomach. "But you picked him."

She shakes her head but her tears stream like mine. She stares at me with bulging eyes and covers her mouth with both hands to suppress a gagging sound. "I'm so sorry," she says.

"It's not like it's the end of the world," Terrance says.

I turn on him and in my head I stab his heart through his muscle-shielded chest. "You should leave," I say. He snorts. "This is because of you," I say.

"It's because of whoever called my parole officer," he says.

Mom holds up a hand. "Maybe something good will come out of this whole thing," she says and half-smiles. She inhales and releases it in uneven bursts. "God does work in mysterious ways."

"Is He punishing me?" I say. "What did I do wrong?"

"Oh, Liz, your teenage hormones are making this feel much worse than it actually is," Mom says. "Think of it as an adventure." She twists her wedding ring around her finger and closes her eyes. "That starts tomorrow night."

I gasp like she slapped me in the face. "Tomorrow?" I cough and try to inhale but it's like swallowing glass.

Terrance laughs. "Man, those parole guys are real tightwads about their rules."

There's a part of me that still thinks this can't be happening. This is a nightmare and soon I'll wake up. I pinch the inside of my wrist until it hurts. "Where am I going to go?"

Mom reaches for me. "We thought—"

"Don't touch me," I say, jerking away so fast I stumble. The barbed wire is in my blood, a million paper cuts slicing up my insides. I need to escape.

She snorts an irritated burst of air out of her nostrils and says, "In a few years, this won't seem so bad." I move toward the door, light-headed, fighting to breathe. She says, "Trust me."

Never again, I think as I bolt outside into the fresh air.

I run laps around our apartment parking lot; force my thighs to burn, my skin to sweat, my lungs to drown. When every single cell in my body feels singed and smoking and numb, I press myself into the wet earth and soak up the smell of grass and the quiet in the air, the cool softness under my back. I inhale and exhale with the wind, slowing my pulse, calming my heart. I lie there on the damp lawn and watch brown oak leaves float against the pink-orange sky and land on the concrete sidewalk with a crunch.

Mom said it's just me, but she's wrong. She may have forgotten Jaime, but I feel her absence like an amputated limb, a part of me missing but still a constant phantom presence. When I learned about binary planets in seventh grade I thought of me and Jaime, connected by proximity and gravity, relying on each other for stability so we don't shoot off into space. She's had me close by since she was born and I figured the pull I always feel when we're apart—like magnets or tides in my blood—was just as strong in her. When Jaime left, I assumed she'd come home the way salmon and turtles return to their birthplace. If I move, how will she be able to find me?

The falling leaves shift to black outlines against a shadowed blue night and the temperature drops with the sun. I shiver. What if Jaime decides, like Mom, that she doesn't need me at all?

When I return to the apartment, Noah has been picked up from day care and waddles over to me. "Liz," he says and hugs my leg. I poke his belly and pick him up, tickling his armpits. He giggles and I squeeze him close. "Good-bye, little brother," I say, snuggling my nose into his soft neck. "You be careful," I whisper and tap his tiny chin with my forefinger. He sticks out his tongue, something I taught him.

Terrance and Mom are watching pro wrestling, oiled men in Speedos screaming threats into microphones and then trying to pin each other. Terrance rests one hand on Mom's leg and holds a Budweiser in the other. I kiss Noah's forehead and set him down on his wobbly legs. Mom doesn't say a word as I walk past her to my room, just stares at the screen while Terrance rubs his thumb back and forth across the top of her thigh.

I start packing, emptying drawers and making piles. A few minutes later, Mom opens the door without knocking. She stands there silent for a full two minutes, and then she scoffs. "You don't even like living here, with Terrance, right?" She throws out her hands. "Why is this such a big deal?"

"Are you serious?"

She says, "I thought you might be glad to get away." She sounds almost hopeful.

"This is supposed to be my home." I strangle the T-shirt I'm holding and imagine strangling Terrance, my small hands around his neck, like squeezing mud through my fingers. "Anyone else would make him leave."

Mom says, "He needs me."

My throat closes around a spike. "What about us?" I say. I lower my head and let my hair fall into my face. "We need you, too." I collapse on the edge of my bed.

Mom sits next to me and uses the back of her hand to push my hair behind my shoulders. "You're always telling me you don't."

A sob rises up in my throat like a geyser, and even if I could put this sorrow into words, all my voice manages is a garbled, "You're our mom," before I'm bawling like I haven't done since I was a kid.

Mom gently draws my head toward her, and I close my eyes and surrender to my convulsing chest. I let her wrap her arms around me as I lean into her shoulder. She smells like gardenia perfume and Suave Fresh Rain shampoo just like she did years ago when she still played games with us and read us stories before bed and rented PG movies the three of us could watch together on the couch sharing a big bowl of microwave popcorn.

"Shh." She wipes tears from my cheeks and says, "I'm still your mom." She presses her hand over my ear and temple, hugs my head. "I will always be your mother," she says and I cry harder because she doesn't understand. A mother is a child's home even more than where the child sleeps, and she is forcing me to give up both.

"It's your job to take care of us," I say, wiping my eyes.

"I'm trying," she says. Mom opens her mouth like she wants to say something but doesn't. In the living room, Terrance burps like he's in a beer commercial and laughs. Mom sighs. "You always took such good care of yourself," she says. "And of Jaime. I know you can handle this." She squeezes me, and I ache to curl into her belly like I used to, sink into the safe softness of the body that made me.

But I duck out from under her warm arms and say, "That doesn't mean I should have to."

"We're all making sacrifices," Mom says. Terrance laughs again.

"He's not," I say.

She says, "How many times can I tell you I'm sorry?" She presses her forefinger and thumb to the bridge of her nose. "I don't know what else to say."

"Say you'll let me stay," I say, but I know she won't.

She looks down at my flowered bedspread, shakes her head left and right over and over like a bobble-head doll, and tears trail down her spongy cheeks. I stare at her tired skin and developing wrinkles, the gray strands at her temple, her low-cut blouse, and wonder what happened to the whirlwind of force my mom used to be: taking beatings from Dad and walking with her bruised face held high. In the silence, our heartbeats start to sound like drums, the ominous thuds in movies that signal an execution.

"I love you," Mom blurts out finally. She hugs me again and at first I remain stiff. But when she starts to pull away, I recognize this is good-bye, and I tighten my arms. Mom whimpers and holds me closer, her shoulder against my wet cheek, her strong hands rubbing my back. "I love you so much," she says.

I wipe my nose on her shirt and let go. October wind breezes through my open window and I inhale the freshness, the earthy scent of dried leaves and wet grass and pine. Chilly air settles around me like a cloak, and I try to mimic that coolness. "Okay," I say.

"Okay," she says, patting my knee and half-smiling. Her eyes are puffy. She nods once like a judge after giving his ruling, so I guess these proceedings have concluded. I close my eyes and breathe deeply in and out, ten beats each, making my lungs expand and contract inside my chest.

When I open my eyes, Mom is in my doorway with her hand on the fake brass knob. "It'll be okay, Liz," she says. "God knows what He's doing even if we don't."

She shuts the door and takes a deep breath outside my room. I picture her dolling up for Terrance, replacing her tight-lipped frown with a plastic smile, fluffing her hair, adjusting her boobs. She clears her throat and says with a cheerfulness that feels like lemons rubbed over my fresh wounds, "What's so funny, handsome?"

I cross the room in measured paces, stand at the window with squared shoulders, and face the dark. As I watch the night sketch ghostly shapes in the darkness, a draft sweeps through the room, into my cramped chest, and plants a seed of ice deep inside. I shiver and feel my skin prickle like thorns are emerging from underneath, protective spikes to ward off predators. With my eyes slowly drying, I cultivate those goose bumps across the length of my skin, and wear them like scales of armor.

For two months I've lived with Terrance's brother, Gary, and his wife in a small housing tract on the south side of town. I sleep in the bottom bed of a bunk set in their second bedroom and eat Top Ramen noodles, bagels, and once, a serving of Carol's sausage and potato casserole. "You need to eat," she said as she piled chunks of meat and starch onto my plate, a greasy heap that reflected the fluorescent lights above our heads. "You're getting so skinny," she said and covered the steaming mound in ketchup. I let their brown boxer, Rambo, eat all the sausage, and now we're good friends.

I have a TV in my room and they don't care when I turn it off so when I can't sleep I watch Leno and Conan and infomercials for electric dehydrators, skin care products, and "all natural" waxing kits with guarantees of painlessness. Sometimes I read in bed with my clip-on book light, magazines from Rachel or schoolbooks. I get sucked into the story of *Lord of the Flies*—children abandoned and forced to care for themselves—and stay up way too late reading. When the frenzied boys kill poor Simon on the beach, the words become blurry so I shove the green paperback under my pillow and remind myself that book characters are not real people. And my life could be a lot worse.

In the mornings I wait for Carol to finish her long, dark, wavy hair, which she first blow-dries straight and then re-curls with a curling iron into tight, controlled ringlets. She wears a foundation too pale for her face and a red lipstick that looks like paint against the white powder on her cheeks. She sits on the bathroom counter and leans into the mirror, her breath leaving fast-disappearing circles of fog on the glass. "Gary!" Carol yells and blots her coated lips. She smiles at her reflection, checks for red on her teeth, and unplugs the curling iron. A few minutes later they're gone.

I peer at my face in the bathroom mirror while waiting for the hot water, place my palms on the cold countertop. Dark purple-blue circles mushroom out from under my eyes and my skin hangs where there used to be cheekbones. My hair is scarecrow yellow and full of split ends. I blink, but the red still runs in jagged lines like lightning through the whites of my eyes. My eyelashes are every girl's dream, though. I could start an infomercial for crying. *New! All-day, all-natural mascara!*

After I'm dressed, I often watch TV in the living room with Rambo's brown square head and black jaw on the cushion next to me, snorting occasionally. Dad is supposed to pick me up, but most mornings he's late if he comes at all. Since he lives closer than Mom, is unemployed, and already taking Jaime to school, Mom signed me up for the impending weekday train wreck. At least Jaime and I will be together.

While I wait for the honk outside, I work on my math home-work, pushing through the equations step-by-step like assembling puzzles. Jaime and I spent hours in our shared room while our parents fought, putting together odd-shaped cardboard pieces until they formed Care Bears or forest landscapes. I taught Jaime to start with the edges and work her way to the middle, to find the joint that connects each piece to its neighbors. The concentration worked as a decent defense against Mom's self-muffled cries and Dad's screams, and algebra has a similar logic that keeps me focused.

Today when I finish, Dad's white Toyota pickup still hasn't appeared in the driveway. It's already a half-hour into my first class so I call Crystal's number. Jaime answers on the first ring.

"No school?" I say.

"Nope." She yawns. "Dad didn't even wake up this morning," she says today. Other times it's been, "He promised to take us tomorrow," or "He really is sick, I can hear him throwing up."

For two months we've talked in the mornings instead of going to school. I missed the day I was supposed to give my oral presentation on *A Tale of Two Cities* in English. I have a D in French, a C in math, and I was dismissed from my theater class project because I failed to attend required rehearsals.

"This sucks," I say.

"If you lived here, Dad would let you take his car," Jaime says.

"No he wouldn't."

"He said he would."

"Well, he shouldn't. I don't have a license."

"So? Neither does he." I hear a wet, smacking sound so she's either sucking her thumb or smoking. "He said lots of things would be easier if you just lived here."

"Easier for him."

"He's mad at you for being stubborn and selfish like Mom."

I shake my head. "He can't keep his head out of the toilet long enough to take his kids to school."

"He said if you lived here, he could afford to buy a bigger TV and he wouldn't have to go to bars to watch sports so he wouldn't stay out as late."

"That doesn't make sense," I say, but it worries me. I know inviting Jaime to live with him was not out of the goodness of his heart, but I'm not sure what he's up to.

"Wouldn't it be awesome if you could drive us to school?"

"Dad would do anything to avoid responsibility," I say.

Jaime says, "He wouldn't let me drive his car."

Jaime likes skipping school. She's done it for years but now, without having to pretend to go somewhere else, it's much simpler. She steals cigarettes from Dad's secret pack, pulls the ten-foot phone cord out to the shed in Crystal's driveway, and talks to boys named Surge or Chilly whom she met at the liquor store up the street from the trailer park, exhaling smoke into the grooves in the metal roof.

"Can you wake him up?" I say and immediately regret it. I won't risk sending Jaime into the minefield that is our hungover father, but I miss the order of school, the predictable routine, the obvious right answers. As much as I'm trying to keep up in my classes, I'm losing my teachers' trust, and know that I'm falling behind not just with assignments but with important instruction as well.

I say, "Never mind" at the same time she says, "No way." Catching up with school isn't worth her confronting a half-asleep and possibly violent man twice her size. I'd chance it if I was there, but I'm glad to hear she wouldn't.

"Are you okay?" I ask, because my other thoughts, *Don't trust him, Stay alert,* would just piss her off. She's heard it all before, and

29

I think she's enjoying being away from my mothering as much as Mom's.

"I'm fine," she says, and I hear a ding.

"Jaime," I start but she says, "Gotta go, my Eggos are ready," and then she's gone, leaving the dial tone buzzing in my hand.

I take off my shoes, pull the comforter I brought from Mom's onto the couch, and settle in for another day of watching the same movies on Gary and Carol's black box cable channels. They've been cycling *Casper*, *Apollo 13*, and the second *Ace Ventura* movie. Today will be the eighteenth time I've seen *Congo*.

Rachel calls me when she gets home from school. "Where were you?"

"Here," I say.

"Watching the telly?" Rachel says with a bad British accent and a deep voice.

I smile at her exaggeration. She's already trying to cheer me up. "Not much else to do here," I say. "Why can't I have normal parents who force their children to go to school instead of refusing to take them?"

Rachel laughs. "If you were a normal teenager, you'd love staying home all day and watching TV," she says in her regular voice.

"What did I miss in English?"

"Not a lot," she says. "We discussed *Lord of the Flies*. People said stupid things."

"I'm almost finished with it," I say. "That book has some messed-up stuff."

Rachel says, "Yeah, we talked about some of the violence."

"I had a math test today, too," I say.

"Can you make up the test?" Rachel says. "I could pick it up from your algebra teacher."

"Thanks," I say. "But my first- and second-period teachers think I'm ditching since I miss those classes so often." No school bus comes out this far. To take the public bus, I have to walk a mile and transfer twice. It takes two hours and I usually don't make it to school until third period. My first-period French teacher told me through her hot pink lipstick and thick accent that if it was true my father wouldn't drive me, I needed to tell the school counselor. She assumed I had been lying when I declined moving through "the proper channels" to get the "appropriate attention" and wouldn't take any of my late work. I sigh. "If you asked for my test, Mr. Suarez would probably think I was trying to cheat."

"My Liz Wiz would never cheat," Rachel says.

"I don't think it would even help at this point," I say. Rachel already knows that without a scholarship, there's no way I can afford college, and college is my only way out.

"My mom says the world always balances itself out," Rachel says. "When she left my dad to follow her Wiccan path in Reno, she promised someone else would come into my life as a friend, to support me. And then I met you." She sounds proud and certain, like that's proof of her mom's fortune-telling power.

"Well I hope something good happens soon." I pick at my nails. "I think the next few years are going to get worse." On the muted TV, murderous gray gorillas are bashing heads with their powerful arms.

"You are the strongest person I know," Rachel says softly. I know she admires my ability to handle obstacles, but I also know she'd never trade her safety for my strength. "You know I've got your back, right?" she says.

"I know," I say, smiling. "I don't know what I'd do without you."

We sit there for a few heartbeats, time that in person would be a hug. She says, "Enough mushy stuff." She clears her throat. "Want to spend the night this weekend?"

"Maybe Friday night," I say. "I don't think my mom will let me out of church."

"Ask, okay?" she says. "We can watch a good movie."

"Okay," I say, but I know Mom will say no. She does the exact opposite of what I want these days like she's spiting me because I didn't behave as she'd hoped.

"Righto, then," Rachel says with the English accent. "Cheerio, old chap."

I laugh. "Bye," I say.

On Saturday night I watch Ultimate Fighting with Gary on their big-screen TV. Sundays are devoted to football at this house; tomorrow he will be watching at least three games and with Picture in Picture, sometimes two at once. When Carol goes to sleep tonight, Gary will make us tumblers of Jack and Coke, and we'll watch late-night comedy sketches or movies with the lights off and surround sound on, and share a bowl of popcorn with Gary's special mix of cayenne pepper and garlic salt coating the stove-popped kernels, Rambo at our feet. A few weekends we've gone next door to play darts with Gary's neighbors after their wives also fall asleep.

The first time Gary took me, I was curled up on the couch

watching *SNL*. He unlocked the door carrying a sloshing half-full jug of whiskey and a two-liter bottle of Walmart-brand cola. When I asked where he was going, he said, "Nowhere."

I squinted at him. "Does Carol know about this?"

Gary sighed and said, "Come on if you want." I jumped up and opened the door for him. He stuck his lighter in his back pocket and flipped on the porch light. "But just this once." He didn't ask if I needed a jacket, didn't comment on my bare feet. As we stepped onto Cody's driveway he said, "You stay smart in here, okay?" I nodded.

In Cody's garage I was enveloped in clouds of cigarette and cigar smoke, white swirls circling the room like ghosts, dancing into my nose and inflating my brain until my head felt swollen and weightless. I stood in the corner sipping my cocktail, watching the giant hands tick on Cody's three-foot-tall Budweiser clock, and listened to alcohol-heavy breaths around me rally back and forth through the haze: *Hey, man, wazzup? How's the wife? How's the job? Jobs blow. Fuck yeah! Wives blow, too. Not enough, man, right?* Laughs faded in and out, the smell of motor oil mixed with smoke and cologne and my spiked soda, and Cody's hanging tools reflected the spotlights he used for fixing cars like disco balls.

"Hey, Liz, you know how to throw darts?" Cody's face crystallized right in front of mine. I blinked. "Darts?" he said and held up a blue-and-yellow-flagged metal arrow. "You ever played?" I shook my head. He took my hand. "Let me show you."

I followed Cody's Phish T-shirt to the line of dirty masking tape on the cement floor in front of the dartboard while Gary watched us with narrowed eyes. From behind me, Cody lifted my elbow and placed it in his palm. He wrapped his other hand around my wrist and jiggled. "Loosen your hand," he said in my ear. "Relax." My knees already felt mushy, my body so light, it was easy to sink into his words. He skimmed his fingers down my torso from armpit to waist, squeezed my hip, and pushed me forward. "Lean into it," he said and pressed his chest to my back. I let go of the dart. He held his breath. Bull's-eye. "Wow," he said and hugged me. "You're a natural."

I smiled and it took thirty seconds for my mouth to catch up with my brain. "Cool."

He smiled and brushed my cheek with his knuckles. "Cool," he said. He draped his arm around my shoulders and tucked me in against his ribs. I settled into his warmth, leaned my head against his chest, and closed my eyes.

Tonight, Gary and I are betting on Ultimate Fighting with Fritos and Oreo cookies. "Ante up," Gary says as Carol sits next to him on the couch. We each put two cookies on the modern off-white coffee table in front of us, shoulders bumping as we lean forward.

"That looks gruesome," Carol says and turns to me. "You like this?" Thirty seconds into the fight and the thinner wrestler is bleeding from a two-inch gash in his forehead. The blood streams into his eyes and splatters red on the white mat.

"Yeah," I say. Skull wounds may look gruesome, but it's the bruises under the skin no one can see that kill without warning. "Head wounds bleed more than they hurt," I say a half-second before Gary says the same thing—guess where I learned it?—and

Carol raises her perfectly shaped left eyebrow and dips her chin at him, or us, and I can't see his reaction. Her red lipstick has faded, and she looks less pale, her cheeks pink from the warmth of the house. The phone rings and Carol shakes her hair-sprayed curls.

"You've corrupted this girl," she says, getting up.

Gary says, "A Frito on the sumo guy," and adds a chip to the pile on the coffee table.

"Nah, the karate cowboy is kicking his ass." I pop a chip into my mouth from the bag Gary is holding.

"It doesn't matter how hard you punch if the fat blocks the pain," Gary says through a mouthful of corn. He licks his fingers. "Sumo man all the way."

"Elizabeth," Carol calls from the kitchen. "It's your mom." Rambo jumps to attention at my feet when I get up. He follows me into the kitchen, his unclipped nails clacking on the tile. I hear Gary tell Carol, "That dog really loves her."

Carol says, "Does he?"

"Hi, Mom," I say into their plastic wall-mounted phone. It's the old-fashioned kind with a rotary dial.

"I hear you're watching violent fights?"

"It's TV."

"Carol says there are no rules."

"They can't bite."

She pauses, then says, "I just wanted to make sure you would be ready for church tomorrow." Despite her refusal to pick me up for school, every Sunday morning her pastel-blue Ford Taurus pulls into Gary's driveway before he or Carol wakes up.

"I'll be ready," I say. It's the only morning I don't wait for Carol to finish in the bathroom and it's colder when I have to warm it up myself.

Mom says, "I love you."

I say, "Bye."

On the way home from church, Terrance turns up the radio when the Seal song from *Batman Forever* comes on. I know because I've see the movie twelve times. "Watch this, Liz," Terrance says. "Noah knows all the words to this song."

Noah does, and he sings in his little baby voice, having no idea what the words mean. "Kiss from rose on grave," he sings, rocking his head back and forth in his car seat. It's cute, his baby teeth like tiny diamonds in his smile, but everything Noah does is cute. He's two.

Terrance beams. "We're going to start a band," he says when the song is over.

"Won't you be a little old?" I say.

"I'm not old," he says.

"You're right," I say. "You are younger than some people in the car."

"I'm not old," Terrance says. "I'm in my mid-twenties."

"See," I say. "That's younger than late thirties."

Mom says without moving her lips, "I'd like to have a talk with you, Elizabeth." She looks at me in the rearview mirror, eyes squinted like she's trying to see through me out the window. I don't know why I baited her. Noah pulls my hair and puts it in his mouth. Mom says to me, "How about we have lunch?"

"McDonald's," Noah says, blond strands sticking to his tongue.

Mom stops at a red light and turns around to look at me, her green eyes like a cat before she springs. "Just the two of us," she says.

A few days later Terrance calls while everyone else is at school or work and says Mom wants to have lunch with me. "She felt bad about your last talk," he says.

"Why didn't she call me herself?"

"She's busy and I offered," he says. "I want my girls to get along."

Mom's blue Ford shows up in front of Gary and Carol's house right on time, but as I walk across the yard, I see dark hair above the headrest and brown hands on the wheel.

I open the door. "Where's Mom?" I say as Metallica screams from the speakers.

The smile on Terrance's face falls. "She had a last-minute meeting. She thought we might want to spend some time together instead."

"I'm not going anywhere with you."

"Not even to a bar?"

"Why would I want to go to a bar?"

He narrows his eyes. "Well if you're not interested in adult entertainment," he says, "then maybe I'll see if Jaime's up for a little fun."

He takes me to a dive bar about a mile from Gary's. It has a gravel parking lot and its weathered wooden-planked walls make up the only building in a wide field of weeds and garbage and dust. Terrance opens the solid door for me and before my eyes can adjust to the darkness, he grabs my hand and skips to a booth in the back. He tries to pull me in next to him but I shake out of his grip and sit on the opposite bench.

"I recommend the sausage plate," he says. "Nice and juicy." He nods at the bartender, a dyed redhead wearing a leather biker vest over a ragged-edged tank top that showcases the red lace top of her bra. Her arms are colorfully tattooed and as she struts toward us, I see her belly button is pierced with a silver hoop.

"What'll it be, sweets?" she says to Terrance, leaning over the table so her boobs are about three inches from his face. He doesn't bother hiding his enjoyment.

"Two brat plates," he says, slipping a twenty down into the bottom of her jean shorts pocket.

She jerks a thumb at me. "A little younger than usual."

Terrance says, "Is that a problem?"

"Does he come here a lot?" I say. "With different women?" She ignores me, but the answer is obvious. Mom is so stupid.

"Not if you make it up to me," the waitress says and I don't know if she means sex or money. She bends forward far enough that I can see her butt cheeks and whispers something in Terrance's ear. He sighs openmouthed and breathy, almost a moan, a sound I recognize from his late-night bed-rocking sessions with Mom. Redhead spins on her heels and returns to the bar.

"Did you sleep with her?" I say.

Terrance rests his head against the seat back and leaves his mouth half-open. "Cody told me about your night playing darts," he says.

"Do you cheat on Mom a lot?" I say.

He says, "I love your mom very much." He shrugs. "Cody's a

friend of mine, you know," he says. "He said you were mighty frisky that night. Drinking. Flirting."

"So you'll tell Mom about my drinking if I tell her you're having sex with slutty bartenders?"

"Cody wanted to hang out again sometime, but I told him you were off-limits."

"I can take care of myself."

"Are you sure about that?" he says. "*I* would never hurt you, Liz. You're family."

My breath catches. "Is Cody a sex offender, too?"

Terrance nods. "The best of us are so unsuspicious." He smiles.

Cody hugged me, held my hand, put his arm around my shoulders. And he's like Terrance. I say, "You guys should have to wear a scarlet letter." I think I might vomit.

The waitress plops down our food and a Budweiser. Wilted lettuce sits under three fat, pale hot dogs and a pickle spear. My already churning stomach spasms. "Two brat plates," she says. She winks at Terrance and I think of all the times he's done the same to me. "You know how I like warm sausage," she says and leaves.

Terrance grabs a fork from a plastic 7-Eleven Big Gulp cup. He squirts spicy mustard onto his plate. "How's school?" he says. I stare at him. "How's Rachel?"

My nostrils flare but I keep my voice even. "What do you know about Rachel?"

"I take an interest in my girls' lives," he says, licking mustard off his fingertips. "But I don't know if you have a boyfriend."

"And you don't need to."

"Maybe I want to get to know my stepdaughter." He dips his

sausage in mustard and bites a chunk off the end with his chip-munk teeth.

"I thought we weren't supposed to be alone together."

He sighs and puts down his fork. "I know," he says. He lays his forearms flat on the table, reaching for me, but I'm too far away for him to make contact. "It sucks."

Sweat prickles under my skin, spreading from my palms and armpits. "What if I called your parole officer right now?"

"Good luck!" He laughs. "Kayla over there knows the drill." He sucks juice off the end of his pickle spear. "She's supervising." He nods at red-haired Kayla who's drying shot glasses. "So," Terrance says, leaning back. "Talk to me. Have you made out? Been felt up? Do you like it?"

I pull my feet up onto the booth, hug my knees to my chest like I can block his voice with my shins. He says, "Sex is awesome, but there are consequences. You should wait until you're ready, and you should tell someone if you're being pressured." He eats the flesh of the pickle and leaves the dark green skin on his plate. "You can tell me anything, Liz," he says. "I'm practically your dad."

I would prefer to be here with my father, watering down his drinks and hiding his keys. At least I have tools for that scenario. Terrance lowers his voice. "You're still a virgin, right?" He chuckles to himself. "Of course you are." He raises one eyebrow and presses his lips in on each other. "I lost my virginity when I was your age." He wriggles both hands into the pockets of his shorts and leaves them there. He says, "Do you think you might try it soon?"

His words are like worms, thousands of them, slithering across my skin, tangling in my gut, filling my mouth. I need to take a shower. I can walk to Gary's from here. I can call Mom. I can call his parole officer or the police. Terrance leers at me while I somersault through my options, try to swallow the writhing mass of slime and find my voice. "You're disgusting," I say. "I can't believe Mom lets you touch her."

"She loves when I touch her," he says, tilting his head so his neck cracks. "Most women do."

"I'm out of here," I say, sliding out of the booth.

Terrance pouts. "But we just got here."

Faster than I expect, he swings his body into mine before I can stand up. He pushes in next to me and I'm forced to backpedal across the cracked leather bench to the wall. He sits and rotates his chest to face me, lifting his leg to rest it on the seat. He glares at me with eyes focused like a stalking lion. He smiles with just the right side of his mouth. "We haven't had any fun yet."

I am suddenly scared. I know what Terrance is capable of. I know public places are his hunting ground. I know he likes to put on a show and usually doesn't harm his victims, but I also know one of his assaults put a woman in the hospital. And there are probably a dozen attacks for every time he got caught.

"You think I won't tell Mom about this?"

"You think she would believe you? All I have to do is kiss her and"—he raises his hands to fondle the air—"she says yes to anything," he says. He scoots closer. "It's like I'm magic." He inhales deeply near my neck and I try to recoil, but I'm already flush with the wall and my bones won't compress any further. "You smell amazing," he says, nudging my hair with his nose. He smells like musk and rubbing alcohol.

His wet lips touch my ear as he says, "You're beautiful, Liz." I clench my eyes shut and wish I could melt into the wallpaper, become the grime that's dirtying my shirt, the tacky food-and-dust-and-booze mix that's mostly unnoticed in these dark booths where things are meant to go unnoticed, except I feel the goop sticking to my bare arms and my hair as I pretend Terrance's body is not hovering one inch from the length of mine. "Like a sexier, younger version of your mother," he says and his breath reeks of pork. "Just like Jaime will be," he says.

I tense and he's close enough to feel the contraction of my every muscle. He laughs and I wish my Achilles' heel wasn't so easy to spot. "Why are you doing this?" I whisper.

I sense his hands drifting over my waist, my thighs, close enough that I feel their heat but not their weight. I think of Jaime trying to get my attention, waving her hands a centimeter from my face and chanting, "I'm not touching you." I want to cry but I'm aware he's testing me, measuring my resistance, how much I'll do to keep Jaime from moments like this.

I feel the wind from his moving lips on my mouth as he says, "Because I can." He laughs and exits my personal space. "And I like to win."

I inhale and open my eyes. I peel myself away from the wall, shoulders slumping. "Mom never wanted to have lunch with me," I say and it's like a bee sting on burned skin.

"Your mom always talks about how smart you are," he says, sipping his beer.

I say, "What do you want?"

"Just to spend time with you, Liz." He pulls his plate closer and takes a bite of his sausage. He's smug as he wipes mustard off his chin. "Are you ready to have a nice family meal now?"

I take a deep breath and nod. "Good," he says.

Mom calls later and she sounds happy. "I'm so proud of you," she says. "Terrance said the two of you went to lunch today to try to make peace and foster a better environment for our future as a family."

"Uhh."

"He said you had a really nice talk. That you agreed to make less of a fuss, and let us have this time to restore our relationship." I shake my head, impressed by Terrance's strategy. "I really appreciate it," she says, sounding genuine. "I wanted to call and thank you for being so willing."

If she hadn't chosen this monster of a man over me, I might feel bad that he's sleeping with who knows how many skanks like Kayla. I want to crush her with the news but I know Terrance is right. She would never believe it if it came from me. "Sure," I say, glad she can't see the tightness in my jaw, the rigid line of my lips.

Mom says, "I know how hard that must have been for you and it's that kind of sacrifice that's going to make it easier for you to come home."

My heart shrivels. "I really want us to come home," I say quietly.

"I know," Mom says. She hesitates. "Was it . . . did he . . ." she stammers, and it's not like her. "Did you have an okay time?" she says and there's a hint of worry in her voice that makes me consider telling her the truth. *It was one of the worst afternoons of my life.* She twitters her nervous laugh. "I mean, not that there's any reason for you not to."

I say what she expects to hear. "It was fine."

Gary is the manager of the parts department at a car dealership and works until six on weeknights. He came home early once while I was watching *What's Eating Gilbert Grape.* That was right after I'd moved in, when cheesy Lifetime specials and Kodak commercials made me cry for hours, but that scene where Gilbert and his siblings stand thigh-deep in a field of waving grass and watch their dead mother burn up with their house ripped sounds from my throat I didn't know I could make. My face was soaked and my swollen eyes reduced my sight to slits, but I could see Gary's face when he saw me breathing in shallow gasps, red-faced but trying to calm down, and he was ashamed.

He didn't say anything, but when he sat down next to me on the beige couch with his usual Jack and Coke, he handed me a glass as well. I didn't look over at his beer gut or his round dark cheeks as I sipped my drink. The fire in my belly eased the flames in my head, and I tried to take deep breaths. When the credits rolled across Gary's big-screen television, he leaned forward, picked up the remote from the coffee table, and cleared his throat.

"You know, Liz," he said and dropped his head into his hands. His gold wedding band forced the surrounding skin to puff out around his finger. His nails were dark black under the tips. "I know my brother is a fuckup," he said, looking at the beige carpet. "I know this has got to be hard for you." He glanced at me and I was glad that aside from the coloring, he didn't look like Terrance. "You don't expect to have a flasher in the family, but . . ." Gary kind of laughed. He ran his black-tipped and calloused hands through his dark hair. "I just want you to know you have a home here," he said, and I think he meant it.

So when Mom tells me that Gary and Carol have decided to have a baby and that I am ruining their mojo—though that's not what she says exactly—I understand why Gary didn't tell me himself. This was supposed to be temporary.

3

I've been given until January to decide if I want to live with Dad or move in with Mom's sister, Tammy, in Utah. Mom thought it would be a good idea to spend Christmas with Dad to help my "decision-making process." The woman whose worst threats used to include sending me off to stay with him was now saying things like, "It will be good for you to spend more time with your father." As if I really need a weekend with Dad and Crystal to understand how impossible it would be for me to survive in their two-bedroom trailer. What I need to decide is how well Jaime will survive without me.

If not for her, I would run away. But instead, I'm sitting in between her and our father in the front seat of his pickup, with the gearshift digging into my thigh, and dreaming about my own little cottage in the woods. I'd have a fireplace and floor-to-ceiling bookshelves, big comfy chairs, and a skylight. A dog like Rambo for protection.

"You know we need to go through Vallejo, right?" I say and Dad swerves to make the turnoff. Someone honks.

"I was testing you," he says. "You think you know everything."

"I was the one who wanted to bring a map," I say.

"We'll find it," he says and puts his arm around my shoulder. The fake ocean scent of his Old Spice deodorant is sharp. "Deborah gives good directions," he says. "She's related to me."

I roll my eyes. "You didn't write them down."

"Don't need to," he says and nudges my shoulder with his hand. He pokes my temple. "I have an excellent sense of direction."

"*I* have an excellent sense of direction," I say.

"Exactly," he says. "I also have a perfect memory."

"Me, too," Jaime says.

"That's my girl," Dad says.

Jaime smiles. "I remember being born."

"You do not," I say.

Jaime turns to me and crosses her arms. "Yes, I do."

I say, "I don't even remember." Mom says I took one look at baby Jaime, pink and wrinkly, squirming and wailing in her arms, and I ran out of the room screaming. Mom had to get a nurse to chase me down because Dad didn't show up at the hospital until Jaime was seven hours old, but of course, she doesn't know that.

"So?" Jaime says. "I remember things you don't."

I think you have that backward. "Whatever," I say, crossing my arms over my chest like a shield near Dad's dangling hand. "We should have brought a map."

He says, "Don't forget, Liz," and lifts his freckled arm off me. "'We're smarter than the average bear,'" he says in his best Yogi voice. A few years ago it would have been enough to make us laugh.

I say, "That won't help us read road signs in the dark."

"Lighten up," he says to me and even though he's not holding a beer, in my head I hear the sound of the can opening, the swift hiss of pressurized air escaping, because it's what usually happens after he tells me that.

Jaime says, "Don't you know how to get there?"

Dad and I say in unison, "Of course."

I stare out the front window, the low winter sun setting behind the hills ahead, the light fractured orange, blue, purple, and pink atop the silver glassiness of the water's surface on either side of this bridge. Jaime and I made this drive with Mom every Thanksgiving I can remember until Terrance showed up. On our way to Aunt Deborah's, Dad's sister and Mom's best friend, through Vallejo and over the Mare Island Causeway, past the giant boats with rows of twinkling lights, circular portholes, and metal fixtures. We pass the marshes full of tall white cranes and egrets standing still as statues in the grass-encircled pools. Pitted and water-beaten wooden poles left over from forsaken piers pierce the water's surface. Little birds perch on top, some tucked in for the night, their feet invisible, their beaks buried under their feathered necks.

Dad clears his throat the way singers do before a performance, and I wait for his version of an apology. "Hey-a, Boo-Boo," he says and pats my thigh. "How about some Xmas tunes?" He pushes a button above my knee and the happy jingle of bells fills the cab.

We usually spend this holiday at home with Mom, enjoying our personal Christmas Eve traditions of eating a fork-optional appetizer dinner, each opening one small gift, reading from the Advent calendar we've mostly memorized, drinking eggnog sprinkled with paprika, and falling asleep under twinkling strands of colored lights to Mom singing "O Holy Night" in her soothing soprano.

But not this year. Deborah won't even have a tree since it was born out of a pagan ritual.

The radio starts a nonstop round of Christmas carols and "Frosty the Snowman" is first. Dad turns up the volume. "Frosty the Crusty," he sings, "had a big yanker up his nose."

Jaime giggles. "Dad," she says. I roll my eyes even though a few years ago I'd been proud to help him come up with new lyrics, especially if they made Jaime laugh.

"You know the words," he says and sings louder. "It was oversize and it made girls cry, so he flushed it with a hose." He elbows me and smiles. "Everybody!"

I look at Jaime and she smiles. When the chorus comes on, the three of us belt out, "Frosty the Crusty, was a fairy tale they say, but his big ol' sneeze will live in memories. He sure made that booger pay," and by the end of the song I'm smiling, too. I think of burping contests and basketball games, pitching a tent in the living room, lighting real campfires in metal buckets on the carpet when Mom was at work. I think of how before I'd understood that fathers were supposed to do more than play and make voices and be funny, my dad had been great.

We sing, "Rudolph the Fat-Assed Reindeer," and "Silent Fart." Our breaths fog up the windows and now it's black enough outside that I expect to still be able to see the stark white cranes that live here in these marshes; dark enough that it seems like they should glow.

We finally make it through Petaluma into Rohnert Park and after forty minutes of driving around random neighborhoods looking for Aunt Deborah's street I say, "Why don't we call her from a pay phone?" Crystal left with Brianna when she got off work, two hours after we left, but with the actual directions I bet she's already there. We should have just waited to go with Crystal, despite Dad's claims of road trip delights. I should have known better.

Jaime is asleep, her face pressed into the glass, her thumb in her mouth. Dad pulls into a gas station and tosses me a quarter. "I'll be right back." I glare at him. "It's none of your business," he says.

I kiss Jaime's soft forehead. "Come on, Dad. It's Christmas," I say, scooting under the steering wheel and jumping out onto the asphalt. The wind is warmer here, smells faintly briny like the beach. I unzip my jacket.

He says, "And I'm celebrating."

"Not here," I say.

His features are shadowed in the yellow light from the store, his freckles black spots on his face and arms, but I can see he's pouting. He says, "I'll let you have one."

"Like I want a beer."

He wags his finger at me. "You're more like me than you think, Liz."

"I'll tell Crystal."

This is a standoff we've had many times before. Jaime sleeps or watches TV, and Dad and I decide what compromises we are willing to make, timelines and ounces, offers and counteroffers: five blocks, one beer; five miles, half a beer. Even the cracked asphalt and gasoline perfuming the air are familiar. If Jaime was awake, we would just walk.

"Fine," he says and kicks at a Twinkies wrapper floating across the parking lot. "Not here," he says in a high-pitched mocking voice.

"Promise," I say.

"I swear on Santa Claus," he says. He taps his nose with his short pale index finger and winks. "Go get directions and stop worrying about your dad."

It's not you I worry about. "Fine," I say, my fake Converse sneakers swiveling on the pavement toward the phone booth. I don't need to watch him walk to the coolers at the back of the mini-mart, pick the cheapest beer, and take it to the counter. He'll make some joke to the cashier with under-eye circles and bad skin, who will laugh obligingly at the red-haired man who looks older than his almost forty, whose freckled fingers tremble just a little as he pulls small bills out of his wallet one by one by one.

Before Terrance, Mom was my hero. She saved us from bad dreams, left the light on in our room, let us snuggle into her bed. She rescued us from the neighbors' fighting, sang songs loud enough to drown out the woman across the landing screaming with her head out the window until her husband jerked her back inside. Mom protected us from our drunken father, stood her ground in the face of hurled beer cans and TV remotes, steered us through broken dishes on the kitchen floor and shattered windows in the carpet. She carried us past his sleeping body in bloody slippers, pulled us out of range of his raised fists more than once, and her bruises proved her loyalty. We didn't need anyone else.

Then my mom met Terrance at Friday Night Singles, a weekly, church-sponsored mixer designed to "yoke two Christians together." The metaphor said that relationships were like oxen yoked to a cart. If both beasts pulled in different directions, eventually one would give. "More often than not, it is easier for the righteous to be sucked into a secular lifestyle, simply because it is all around us," Pastor Ron said. "It becomes a daily battle with temptation." For my mom, meeting Terrance at church was like getting a thumbs-up from God.

We started picking Terrance up for church on Sunday mornings and Friday nights. He held Mom's hand during prayer. He came over for dinner and Mom cooked meals that required more than adding ground beef. Jaime liked him because he made fart jokes at the table and told stories about the three little boogers. He showed me his new shoes, his new baseball cap, his new haircut. "Liz, look at this!" he'd say, displaying a slap bracelet, a T-shirt that looked like the Coke logo but said CACA, a commercial for hemorrhoids. "Ain't it cool?" Mom sometimes cringed at his jokes or his word choice, but she always covered it quickly with her practiced smile.

On Saturdays Mom made me and Jaime clean the whole house before we could watch cartoons. Terrance came over with his laundry, and we washed his formerly white socks that were full of holes, his grimy T-shirts, and his boxers, *eww*, with the rest of our clothes while he sat on our couch, ate our food, and watched TV. Jaime dusted and I vacuumed, and together we cleaned the bathroom on our hands and knees, scrubbed the toilet, bathtub, sink, and countertops with Comet and pink sponges no longer good enough for dishes.

Sometimes we sang songs from *Cinderella* and pretended we were princesses disguised in these stained T-shirts and shorts too small to wear outside, waiting for liberation from this toil, perhaps to come in the form of cute prince brothers. Our voices blended well as we performed the harmonies we knew by heart, and Mom always said we sounded like our own choir. Until Terrance complained he couldn't hear the TV, she let us sing as loud as we wanted.

One Saturday during a commercial break in *Singled Out* on MTV—a channel that was part of the cable package Mom bought for Terrance that we were not allowed to watch—he handed his empty glass to Jaime and said, "Go be black and get me some more drink." He laughed. She looked at me and I shook my head so she just stood there, dusting rag in one hand, lemon furniture polish in the other. He said, "C'mon, now, I told you to do something."

"Are your legs broken?" I asked. Mom was at the grocery store.

"Your mom told you girls to respect me," he said, sitting up and leaning forward, narrowing his dark eyes at me.

I shot bullets from my eyes at his tiny heart. "That doesn't mean you can tell us what to do."

"Yes it does," Terrance said and shook the glass in Jaime's direction.

"No," I said and stepped toward him. "It doesn't."

He smeared his potato chip–greased finger across the freshly polished glass in the coffee table and looked at me, his nostrils flaring. "You want to be a good girl, right, Jaime?" he said and turned to her. "Only the good slaves don't got to be whooped."

Jaime hesitated, her blue eyes wide and asking me for an answer. "You don't have to," I said.

Terrance said, "I'll tell your mother." He lounged into the couch, put his feet up on the coffee table, and brushed crumbs from his tank top onto the floor we'd just vacuumed. "You'll be sorry." His tan lips curled up in a sneer.

"I don't want Mom to get mad," Jaime said and took a step forward.

Terrance stared at me as Jaime took the glass from him, his eyes gleaming with satisfaction. "That's exactly what I wanted to hear," he said and let his slimy fingers linger on Jaime's soft, pale hand, his eyebrows lifted in a silent dare. Just as Jaime started to squirm and my muscles prepared to spring, he released her with a squeeze. Inside my chest a little piece of me ignited and burned hot, seared my lungs, and crumbled like ash as he watched Jaime walk away. Someday I would find something to use against him, someday he would pay, but for now I'd have to contain the boiling urge to smash the vacuum pole into his balls and then swing it like a bat toward his thick black eyebrows and break his fucking nose.

Terrance said, "Good little servant," and patted Jaime on the head when she came back with his orange soda. His crooked teeth poked out from under his smirk.

"You look so mad," Jaime said when Terrance was in the bathroom we'd just cleaned, probably peeing on the seat. "It was okay," she said. "It only took two seconds." She sighed and wiped at the opaque smudge Terrance's dirty finger had left on the glass. "It was just soda."

I stretched my fingers and felt where they hurt from clenching the plastic vacuum attachment. I said, "It wasn't just soda."

Christmas at home usually starts with Jaime waking me up at six A.M. by pulling up my eyelids. Then we take the homemade stockings Mom cross-stitched our names onto off their ceramic angel mantel hangers and dump the contents all over the living room floor. We compare our flavored Lip Smackers, our different colored toothbrushes, sift through the pens and notepads and batteries, and pull out the traditional orange at the bottom of the sock as filler and a quick breakfast if we wanted.

Today I wake up next to Jaime on the floor of Deborah's daughter Ashley's room. I huddle under the sleeping bag and think about pulling up Jaime's eyelids, but there are no stockings hanging from the Cranleys' mantel. Nothing Santa-related, no mistletoe, limited Jesus-friendly carols, and a rule that each person gives each person one gift, though Crystal brought twelve for Brianna. We won't even see Mom this Christmas.

Jaime's hand flops out of her bag and onto my head. I swat at her pudgy fingers and at least this feels familiar. Ashley sleeps in her twin bed a few feet past Jaime, her nightgown's lacy collar rising with each inhalation. A few months younger than Jaime, Ashley still has stuffed bears and plush frogs surrounding her like pillows and they shift slightly as she breathes.

Deborah opens the door. "Cock-a-doodle-doo!" She steps over me and Jaime and opens the blinds. "Good morning, it's time to rise and shine," she sings. "Good morning, I hope you're feeling fine!"

Ashley and Jaime moan and roll over in their blankets. I reach over and tug Jaime's eyelashes. "I'm awake," she says, slapping my hand. "Geez."

"Get up, get showered, get dressed," Deborah says. "Merry Christmas, girls."

Downstairs, it's like watching a sheepherding competition in which several sheep think they're the dog. We're all wearing our Sunday best: Dad's red-and-white candy cane tie matches his red-and-white eyes, Crystal's green knit dress is belted with a gaudy gold belt, and Brianna is decked out in a green corduroy dress with white lace trim and collar. White tights end in white shoes, and a green-and-white bow sits in the orange hair that makes her look more like Dad than we do. She looks like the Christmas leprechaun.

I pat her head and say, "Merry Christmas, lassie."

"Don't mess up my hair," she says.

Deborah's hair is a darker orange than Dad's, more red, but not enough for her to look good in the burgundy dress she's wearing. Winston wears a black suit, white button-up shirt that barely contains his hanging gut, and a deep red tie. *How corporately festive.* Their seven-year-old son, Matt, looks uncomfortable in an identical outfit.

Deborah says, "Okay, coats on, everyone."

"We'll follow you," Crystal says.

"There's no reason to take two cars," Deborah says. "We're all family now." She puts her arm around Crystal's shoulder and leans in so their faces are close together, their cheeks almost touching. I hide a smile when Crystal cringes.

"I appreciate that," Crystal says. "But I'd still like to drive. David?" She walks out the door holding Brianna's hand, and Dad follows, his black Converse high-tops shuffling across the tile entryway. He turns around at the door. He says, "Girls?"

Jaime and I look at each other and know this day will be rough. Dad is rehearsing already and whatever his attention-hoarding show will be—interrupting performances at church, starting fights, prank calling our friends when we spend the night at their houses instead of his are a few previous hits—it's guaranteed to be embarrassing and unavoidable once it starts.

Jaime and I squish into the backseat of Crystal's Camaro with Brianna, wrinkling our almost matching blue dresses, Jaime's with white buttons down the front. We sit on pages ripped from coloring books, Happy Meal boxes, and crumbled Ritz crackers. I pull a plastic Garfield out from poking my butt and Brianna elbows me. On Brianna's other side Jaime says, "Ow," so I think she got a sharp little elbow in her ribs, too.

As we're leaving the Cranleys' cul-de-sac behind their shiny tan Explorer, Crystal says, "Is your sister always so bossy?"

Dad says, "She's trying to include us."

"I'm not a charity case," Crystal says. "If she'd wanted to make nice, she could have made the dog sleep outside."

"She doesn't know about your allergies."

"I told her when I got here. I bet if it were Linda"—Crystal nearly spits Mom's name—"your sister would have spent hours vacuuming and buying pillow protectors just to prevent one tiny sneeze."

Dad rolls his eyes. "Don't start."

Crystal's nostrils flare. "I also told her about Brianna's lactose intolerance and asked her to get dairy-free eggnog."

"Aren't eggs dairy?" I say.

"They put eggs in eggnog?" Jaime says. "Gross."

"Duh," I say. "Why do you think it's called eggnog?"

Dad turns to us and says, "What do you think a nog is?" His private Christmas Eve party hangover is fading. His eyes are more open and less red, and he smiles as he says, "A nog is a blow to the head, so a traditional eggnog is really served with an egg to the face."

"Mommy, can we throw eggs?" Brianna says and looks at me and Jaime with a Cheshire cat grin in baby teeth.

During the church service, Deborah leads the three-member gospel team with her acoustic guitar hooked up to an amp. As she sings, her glasses slide down her short nose. Her hair fans out like an orange dandelion tuft behind her slightly dipped head, and her eyes shoot back and forth from the music stand to her unpainted nails and pale fingers on the dark brown guitar frets. She says a quick prayer after fifteen minutes of songs and yields the floor to a man wearing a dark suit and a tie with a manger scene and glowing star of Bethlehem.

He says, "How about a round of applause for our wonderful gospel team!"

Their church is small, only a dozen or so people here today besides us, and we all sit as we clap and Deborah and her band join us in the pews. Their pastor is taller than Pastor Ron, but he's not as interesting to listen to as he spews a speech about sacrifice in a monotone that doesn't seem to register that Christmas should be celebratory.

In the row behind the adults, Matt only has eyes for his Game Boy, and Ashley, Jaime, and I play hangman on blue-lined paper I ripped from the journal that was a gift from my aunt Tammy. She said writing is a great tool for dealing with pain, but I don't write much. I carry the book with me to keep my hands busy with doodling, and because it reminds me of her. Ashley guesses "P." I draw a head dangling from the already penciled noose.

Brianna starts whining and kicking the pew in front of her when she sees Dad eating her Snickers bar. "That's my candy," she says.

"David," Crystal says. "What's wrong with you?"

"I paid for it." He shoves the last bit of chocolate into his mouth as Brianna starts to cry.

Deborah elbows Dad but he just sits there, smile on his face, chewing and staring beyond the pastor to the big wooden cross mounted on the wall and the metal crown of thorns perched on top of the dark wood at a forty-five-degree angle.

Crystal says, "Hush, baby. Listen to the preacher."

Jaime guesses "R" and I draw curled hair on the stick figure.

"You always do this," Deborah says under her breath. "Nothing is sacred to you." Dad shrugs and Deborah crosses her arms across her chest. Brianna's crying gets louder, shriller, and less authentic. "Fix this," Deborah hisses.

Dad finishes chewing and swallows. "We'll get you another

candy, lassie," he says, ruffling Brianna's hair and working his tongue to get the nougat and caramel off his teeth. Fire ignites in Brianna's eyes and she takes big gasping breaths in between cries, gearing up for full tantrum mode.

Ashley guesses "B" and I give our stick woman a shoe. Brianna gets so loud the pastor stops talking and whispers to Crystal, "That little girl might want to behave if she wants to stay on Santa's nice list."

Brianna sobs louder. Ashley plugs her ears. Deborah covers her face with her shaking hands. "No Santa?" Brianna says, standing up, her cheeks and eyebrows quaking. "No presents?" She makes little fists, opens her mouth like a bullhorn, and screams.

"Now this is a show," Dad says.

"Of course, you'll get presents, honey," Crystal says. "He didn't mean that." She squints at the pastor, but Brianna is beyond calming. She wails and stomps her white patent leather Mary Janes. She shakes her head back and forth so fast her green-and-white bow dances a jig in her flailing hair.

Dad smacks his lips and swallows the last of the candy. "I guess church can be fun." He swivels his head to look at us and grins. "Maybe we'll make this a regular thing, girls." He pats Deborah's leg twice like that makes it official.

Deborah glares at Dad with a rage I imagine is backed by memories of noogies, jagged haircuts, and countless other torments of the rotten older brother who became my father. She says, "Not everything is about fun, David." She jerks her head toward the exit and says through gritted teeth, "Maybe Brianna would calm down if she got some fresh air."

"Y," Jaime says. "Dysfunctional family!" I shush her and fill in the missing letters in our game. She whispers, "I got it."

"Damn straight," Dad says.

Deborah's jaw drops. "David!"

"Fine," Crystal says and stands on her fat-heeled sandals with stocking seams showing at the open toes. "Thanks for all your help." She grabs still-screaming-and-thrashing Brianna and says, "Some family." She marches out the back double doors, which are cheap aluminum and make a tinny clang when they close instead of the resounding boom you'd expect if this was a movie.

"I'm so sorry," Deborah says. She turns to the congregation, says she's sorry again, and then scoots so low in her seat only a tuft of red hair is visible from behind.

After the service, Crystal's Camaro is gone from the small gravel parking lot. The rest of us ride back in the Cranleys' SUV. "The nerve of your wife, David," Deborah says.

"I miss Aunt Linda," Ashley says.

Winston says, "You never should have left her, David."

Deborah says, "He didn't leave her," at the same time Dad says, "I didn't."

"He may as well have," Winston says.

"Thanks, man," Dad says. "Merry Christmas to you, too."

"A man takes responsibility for his actions," Winston says.

Dad mutters, "Walrus."

Crystal and Brianna are on the front porch playing jacks when we pull into the driveway. Deborah clears her throat and shakes her head, her orange hair fluffing out like a lion's mane. "It's Christmas," she says. "The most wonderful time of the year." She opens the passenger door, a smile stretched too wide across her face. "Okay, troops," she says, standing like a doorman at the edge of the metal frame. She sweeps her arm in a gesture for us to move out. "Let's go celebrate the birth of our Lord!" she says like an infomercial announcer.

As we file out of the SUV and walk toward the door, Crystal stands up and brushes off the butt of her dress. She props a hand on her hip and sneers. "I could have jimmied your lock, but I thought it was more polite to wait." She smiles at Dad. He smiles back. Crystal turns to Deborah. "Not that you deserved my hospitality after the way you treated us." She steps aside so Winston can unlock the door.

Deborah's eyes bulge, and she looks like a ball of wax in a lava lamp, her face growing bigger as she puffs her cheeks so big it seems painful.

"Yeah," Dad says. "What happened to 'the guest is always right'?"

"That's the customer, David," Winston says. He places his beefy hand over Deborah's and says, "My wife tried her best to make you feel included."

"Whatever," Crystal says, pushing past him into their house. "Thanks for being so accommodating. I can't wait to get the hell out of here." Her thick heels clomp on the tile as she walks away.

"I guess we're leaving," Dad says as Deborah gapes at him. "Girls, go get your stuff."

"I'm sorry," I say to Deborah as we hurry past her.

"Don't be sorry," Dad says, straightening his shoulders to stand taller. "Be strong." He raises his fist for emphasis as we head upstairs. Jaime and I collect our underwear and pajamas and tennis shoes and toothbrushes and are still shoving clothes in and zipping our packs closed as we walk out the door.

"You girls are always welcome," Deborah says. "Don't forget your Bibles." She hands us our still-wrapped gifts.

"Not us, though, right?" Crystal stomps out the door and across the driveway, carrying a bag full of presents in one hand and pulling silently crying Brianna along with the other.

"We won't be joining you next year, sis," Dad says, wobbling as he hoists two duffel bags onto his shoulders.

"Why don't you let the girls stay for today?" Deborah says. "They don't need to spend Christmas in the car." I can almost hear the unspoken ending to that sentence: *with you.* When I was six and we left Dad for good in the middle of the night, Mom knew Deborah would take us in. We lived here for over three months. Deborah babysat me and Jaime with Ashley so Mom could go to Al-Anon meetings, and she lied to Dad when he called demanding to know where we were. Deborah's loyalty to Mom bore the price of Dad's anger, but she probably helped save our lives.

Dad tosses the bags into his truck bed. "Girls, this gravy train is moving out!"

I catch Deborah's eye. "We'll be okay," I say.

"Are you sure?" she says. "I can keep you here until your mom can come."

"I'm sure," I say. At least, I'm sure he's sober, which means our odds are better than usual.

Deborah hugs me and Jaime, her perfume too sweet and fruity. She tucks a hand under each of our chins and says, "I love you, girls." She kisses the tops of our heads. "Be safe."

Dad shouts from the azalea bushes at the edge of the driveway, "I'm peeing in your flowers."

Winston says, "Grow up, David."

"I don't think he's kidding," Deborah says, rolling her eyes. "Inside, kids." Ashley and Matt wave at us as they scurry into the big house they've lived in since they were born, to their own rooms and stable lives.

I hear Dad zip his pants as Jaime and I climb into his truck. "Thanks again for your hospitality," he says loudly and laughs.

Deborah blows us a kiss and then rushes into the house, her eyes watering. Winston stands in the doorway glowering through his thick black-rimmed glasses at Dad. "Your sister loves you, David," he says. "But you are no longer welcome here." He slams the door.

Through two car windows I see Crystal smile a malicious and content, lips-curled-up-at-one-edge smile like a gloating cartoon villain. Her car starts and in two seconds she's speeding down the quiet neighborhood street.

My arm goes around Jaime's shoulders. *So much for a nice family Christmas.* I think of Mom and Noah with Terrance and his family, and my heart aches at the thought that we will never spend another Christmas morning at home with Mom just the three of us girls, eating cinnamon rolls and scrambled eggs, cuddling together on the couch to open handmade gifts like fuse bead key chains and threaded pot holders, and once, a crystal vase Jaime and I spent months coveting and secretly bought at Raley's with saved babysitting money when Mom wasn't looking. The blue glass vase still sits on her bedroom bookcase.

Dad hops into the cab and brushes off his hands. "See, Liz," he says, "how much fun life is living with your dad?"

Jaime tilts her head into my chest and sighs. "This isn't fun," I say.

"Come live with us, and join the twenty-four/seven party!" he says. "We'd have a blast."

"*You* would," I say, but he's already singing along to the radio. I hold Jaime closer like I can attach her to me if I squeeze hard enough. I press my cheek against her hair and my lungs contract. Tears well and feel heavy in the bottom of my lids, but there is no chance in hell I can make a home with my father. My one wish is that Jaime felt the same way because I'm not sure I can make a home without her.

Before Terrance, Mom and I were a team. She checked Dad's breath for booze when he came to pick us up, and I was responsible for keeping him sober until he dropped us off. My job was harder. My threats didn't pack the same punch as Mom's, and I couldn't always keep him from stopping at a gas station and cracking open one of his ice-cold Olde English 800s right there in the parking lot. Then Mom realized that sending us to Dad's was a good way to make time for Terrance, and started encouraging us to visit. She became too distracted with primping for her dates to sniff the air near Dad's face before we got in his car.

Dad liked to drive the empty farm roads near Crystal's trailer park village on the outskirts of South Sac. I imagined if I could drive, I'd like these roads, too. Not because there were fewer cops and less traffic on these dark country byways, but because the lack of lights meant deeper night skies and brighter stars. On the few nights I won the parking lot negotiations, I loved to gaze out the window at the constellations' glittering outlines: Orion and his crooked belt, the *W*-shape of Queen Cassiopeia, the Big Dipper.

One Friday night, the sky was nearly black behind churning dark gray clouds. The long stretches of green and brown fields were bathed in weak light from a white sliver moon like a scythe. Dad sang along with the Rolling Stones on the radio, "I can't get no . . ." He thumped his hands on the wheel, sometimes letting it go to do imaginary drum fills in the air while his pickup swerved left or right. ". . . Satisfaction." He bobbed his round head to the beat ringing from his tiny speakers. "Sing with me, girls."

"Can we listen to my Mariah Carey tape?" Jaime said, pulling the flowered plastic case out of her backpack.

Dad twisted the volume knob up and pretended not to hear her. "No, no, no," he sang.

"Shh," I said. "Let's just get to Crystal's alive," I whispered.

Jaime said, "Stop being so paranoid all the time."

"You should thank me, you know," I said.

"For being bossy?"

"For taking care of you."

"I can take care of myself," Jaime said. She reached across me from the passenger seat and stuffed the cassette into the tape deck.

Mariah's soprano didn't get a chance to escape before Dad pushed eject. "No fruity stuff," he said. He tossed the tape into the pile of pork rind bags, Styrofoam cups, and empty cans on the floor at our feet.

"Hey," Jaime said, bending over her seat belt and digging her short arms down into the sea of Dad's waste.

Her head dipped below the glove compartment. "Just get it later," I said. "Sit up."

"I can almost reach it," she said and unclasped her seat belt. I heard the click of the buckle just as I saw both of Dad's hands abandon the wheel to grip invisible drumsticks. He closed his eyes and we veered left into the oncoming traffic lane.

"Get up, Jaime," I said. "Now." I double-checked my seat belt out of habit. Mom had trained us from the second we left our car seats.

"When I'm driving round this world," Dad sang, still drumming in empty space.

"At least open your eyes, Ringo," I said. "Jaime, do you want your legs broken?" I tried to grab the back of her shirt but she smacked my hand away.

"Leave me alone," she said. "Let me do something without you for once."

"Getting shit from all of my girls," Dad sang as the right two tires of the truck crossed the painted yellow divider.

My fingers were millimeters from the steering wheel when Jaime sat up. "I found it," she said, shifting into a crouch and waving the cassette. She beamed at me, her dimples poking holes in her soft cheeks, and I couldn't help but smile back. "See?" she said. "You don't always have to worry."

"Put your seat belt on," I said, just as the left front tire hit something—a rock, a hole, a cat—and without hands to anchor the wheel, we swung off the road. We jolted up and then down over the hill of the shoulder, tires kicking up gravel and mud as we thumped through the grass and mucky soil of these farmers' fields.

My head snapped left, my tongue crunched between my teeth. My chest smashed against the fabric of my seat belt at each bump while my hips tested the strap across my waist. I shot out my right arm to brace Jaime, but she wasn't there. *Oh God, she's on the floor.* My knee slammed into the stick shift and I tried to force my head to the right so I could see my little sister, but my neck bounced at the mercy of the truck's worn tires over an uneven surface, and all I could make out was her shape collapsed in the darkness at my feet.

We skidded to a stop two feet away from a white wooden fence illuminated in the skewed headlights. Cows beyond lay in the damp grass, their legs under them, tags hanging from their ears like reflectors.

"Fuck," Dad said as he shook his head. "See what you did."

I took a deep breath. *I should have grabbed the wheel sooner.* I swallowed the blood in my mouth. *Why isn't Jaime moving?*

Dad opened his door and said, "I have to pee." He stumbled out and tottered away toward a bush. "Be right back."

I fumbled with my seat belt latch, my fingers shaking and clumsy. I coughed and found my voice through a swollen tongue. "Jaime?" Her body was curled on top of the garbage. White light reflected from the fence in front of our bumper glared in my eyes, but it didn't show me Jaime in the cave beneath the dashboard.

"Hey, dork face," I said, struggling under the seat belt. The ding from Dad's open door was like an alarm, shrill and persistent, pulsating at my temples. "Jaime?" She lay on her side, her knees bent near her chin, one arm limp across her legs. Her blond hair covered her face and she didn't move. I couldn't tell if she was breathing. "Jaime!" I clawed at the seat belt buckle until it unlatched.

On the floor at Jaime's side, I swept her hair off her chilly forehead, pressed two fingers to her damp neck, and found a pulse. I placed my hand on her chest and put my ear to her nose. Air moved through her nostrils and her lungs rose up and down under my sweaty palm. I patted her down for crooked limbs and open wounds, and aside from a bloody cut on her forehead, she seemed to be unhurt. "Jaime, wake up." I yanked on her eyelashes and she didn't flinch. "Okay, drama queen," I said, and shook her shoulders. "Enough already." Her head flopped to the side on a neck made of taffy.

The pulse at my temples increased to a vibration, a buzzing warning in my brain building like a swarm of bees. I tugged at her arm and pulled her face out of the trash. I cradled her head and lifted her upper body into my lap, my knee screaming at the pressure. I smoothed her clammy skin with my hand and wrapped my arms around her torso. "Hey, little sister," I said. "I'm here." I rocked us gently back and forth like I did at night when Jaime's nightmares scared her into consciousness, like I'd done when Mom's and Dad's screams burrowed through the walls.

I kissed her limp hand. "This isn't funny, Jaime," I said. I poked each of her fingertips with my nails. "Open your eyes." It looked like she was sleeping, but she was so pale. Tears streamed down my face and for the first time in years, I didn't know what to do. There was no pay phone nearby, no house with a friendly porch light. How long had it been since we'd stopped? A minute? Five?

"Jaime," I said softly. "Where'd you go?"

Raindrop pings sounded on the roof. A cow mooed. I rocked with my back against the door handle and Jaime's wilted frame against my bruised chest, swaying faster as I tried to force more air through my tightening lungs. Water splattered us from Dad's still dinging open door, and I tilted my head toward the moon but its light was shadowed in charcoal clouds. I whispered in Jaime's ear, my wet cheek pressed against her hair, "Don't leave me here alone."

I clutched my sister like she was a life raft and cried into her blond strands that were thicker, darker versions of mine, squeezed her so tight it was like we had one set of lungs, one heart pounding in my head. I hugged Jaime and closed my eyes while the rain beat a million tiny drums around us. *I don't know how to live without you*, I thought at her. *Come back*.

She murmured and opened her eyes. Her head lolled and she squinted at me. "Nerd," she said and smiled. "Why are we on the floor?" I laughed, silent tears flooding my face, and helped us up onto the wet bench seat.

"We should take you to the hospital," I said, examining the cut on her forehead.

"I hate hospitals," Dad said, sliding back into the cab and shutting his door. The shrill dinging stopped and I heard my hammering heart and Jaime's labored breathing.

"Jaime hit her head and passed out," I said. "You know, when you crashed."

Dad said, "We didn't crash," and leaned over to look into Jaime's eyes. He held up three fingers and asked her to count them. She said she didn't feel woozy, she knew her name, and her vision wasn't blurry. "She's fine," Dad said and turned the key in the ignition.

"She was unconscious," I said. "Aren't you worried?"

"I've hit my head plenty of times," Dad said.

"I'm fine," Jaime said.

"Brain trauma is serious—"

"What are you, a doctor?" Dad said and put the truck into reverse.

I quoted Mom: "It's better to be safe than sorry." I pulled Jaime's seat belt around her and made it as tight as possible.

Jaime said, "I'm okay, Liz, really."

"That's my girl," Dad said, getting back on the empty road. "Reids are too strong for hospitals."

"You can't know for sure if her—"

"We can't know anything for sure," Dad said, cutting me off. He flipped the radio knob and the voices of the Beatles filled the cab. "Chill out."

I buckled myself in and wiped at Jaime's bleeding forehead with a tissue, my muscles more tense than ever. Dad used one hand to tap drum beats on the wheel like nothing had happened, and I understood then that Jaime and I were on our own. I had to stop biding time, waiting for the relief troops to arrive. No one was mounting the rescue I'd been naive enough to hope for, and Jaime had paid for my hesitation.

Back at Crystal's trailer I cleaned and bandaged Jaime's forehead cut and called an advice nurse when Dad went to the bathroom. I observed Jaime like she instructed—though she strongly suggested we go to the ER—and Jaime was never out of arm's reach near Dad again.

All that night I replayed the memory of my little sister lifeless against me in the damp night air. I relived the guilt over my too-slow reaction, the fear that she wouldn't wake up. The fiery terror I'd felt in my gut when I thought Jaime may not return to me burned in nauseating waves, and I used the blaze to fuel my defense boot camp, my new twenty-four-hour guard. I was all Jaime had now. I needed to be tougher.

4

"You could live with me," Rachel says when I tell her I'm moving to Salt Lake City.

"Yeah, right," I say. We're sitting on the floor of her bedroom, Pearl Jam on the radio, *Cosmo* magazines open to beauty how-tos. Rachel already applied my makeup, eye shadow and lip liner in darker shades than I would have chosen, and now she's fussing with my hair.

"Why did you do this without my help?" She makes a "grrr" sound as she tries to make my too-short and uneven bangs—the result of a school-less day spent with scissors at Gary's—look stylish. "Seriously," Rachel says over the buzz of the hair dryer. "My dad loves you." She blows my jagged bangs to the side and pins them. "We could share this room," she says. "I'll give you half my closet."

I tear up. It's like Rachel offering me her kidney. I say, "If it was my choice, I would totally stay here."

"My dad could talk to your mom," she says, turning my head and brushing my hair from my scalp to the blondest tips at my shoulder blades. "He thinks you're a good influence on me. And you do the dishes and stuff."

"I think my aunt Tammy already bought a plane ticket," I say. "She's pretty cool. My mom says I'm a lot like her."

"Well then she must be cool," Rachel says. "But wouldn't it be so much cooler to live with me?" She beams. "We could be like real sisters."

"We are like real sisters," I say, leaning to nudge her with my shoulder. "Moving away won't change that."

She shoves my arm. "You can't leave," she says. "Who will explain things like symbolism to me?" Her hazel eyes fill with tears. "I can't imagine not seeing you every day."

"Me, either," I say, and scoot closer to her. "Who's going to make me laugh through all this bullshit?" I say and lay my head on her shoulder.

"No more *Cosmo* quizzes during lunch hour," she says, and half-laughs, half-sniffs.

I smile as my own eyes moisten. "No more bedroom karaoke weekends with your boom box or rainy walks in the park."

"No more baking peanut butter brownies and lemon bars and stuffing our face while watching *My So-Called Life*," she says and sighs. "Jared Leto is so hot."

I laugh a little as liquid slides out of the corners of my eyes. "No more walking the halls together singing, 'Son of a Preacher Man.'"

"But you'll be back soon, right?" Rachel says. "I mean, this is still your home."

"I don't know when I'll be back," I whisper. "I think it might be a really long time."

"What did your mom say?"

"She's acting like this isn't a big deal. Like moving to a new city by themselves is something all teenagers do in the middle of their freshman year."

Rachel puts her arms around my shoulders and squeezes. "I'm sorry, Liz Wiz," she says after a few minutes. "Will you at least be able to visit?"

"I hope so, but you have to promise to write to me."

"Or call," she says.

"*And* call," I say. "Promise."

"Of course," she says and lets me go. "Now let's fix your hair."

My aunt Tammy traveled all over the country on business trips when I was younger. She mailed me postcards from Boston and Chicago with acronyms that I had to decode, like HAGTWYWH. I made stationery pages by drawing flowery designs and curlicues as borders and stamping cats with top hats and dancing frogs in pink and purple ink, and covered them in my developing cursive. I sent her a new letter every week.

My bunny Pandy died today. It was raining and she stood shivering in her cage and then she just stopped moving. I wrote at night from my perch on the top bunk, flashlight in my mouth and Jaime asleep below me. *Mom said you might visit soon. If you come on the nineteenth you could go to my open house and see my science fair project on bean sprout growth.* I signed each letter, *Love, Elizabeth,* and added a heart above the lowercase *i.*

A few weekends each year, Tammy flew to Sacramento just to visit. She slept on the couch and woke us up early to go on Saturday outings. She took Jaime and me to Marine World where we

watched whale shows and waterskiing shows and I got chosen
from the audience to pet a sea lion which felt slick and smooth and
not like fur at all. Tammy took a picture of me and Jaime holding
baby white Bengal tigers with barely opened eyes, and we ate fun-
nel cake on a bench watching the giraffes tower above the visitors
holding out eucalyptus branches.

"Do you want kids?" Jaime asked Tammy.

"I have you girls."

"Don't you want your own?" Jaime said.

"Don't be rude," I said.

"But you have to get married first," Jaime said. White powdered
sugar dusted her lips. "God says." She licked her fingers. I handed
her a napkin.

"You could marry Sam," I said.

"Yeah," Jaime said, running sugary fingers through her hair.
"You already live together."

"We'll see," she said. "I'm not even sure I want to marry him."

"I want to marry Ryan from church," Jaime said. "He's a hunk."
As Jaime listed the names of her five future children, Tammy
smiled, but her eyes were somewhere else.

On another visit Tammy took us to San Francisco's Pier 39 and
we watched the white-faced mimes and spray-painted silver robot
men on the streets; saw the mounds of sea lions lumbering across
wooden planks anchored in the bay, barking and falling over each
other into the dark green sea where they glided through the water
like torpedoes. We ate thick clam chowder from sourdough bread
bowls bigger than our heads and tried to ignore the seagulls cir-

cling like vultures. Jaime convinced Tammy to buy her a caricature portrait, and when the artist was done drawing and Jaime saw the triangular lips and pointed nose on the picture she got grumpy. "I look ugly," she said.

I said, "It's supposed to be funny."

"It's not," she said and pouted until Tammy offered to buy us ice cream.

"How come Jaime always gets her way?" I asked Tammy while Jaime was in the bathroom washing mint chocolate chip off her hands.

"You know she doesn't."

"When I complain, Mom tells me to shut up."

Tammy squatted in front of me and looked me in the eye. Hers were bluer than Mom's, more like mine. "I know all this seems hard now," she said. "But as one eldest to another, someday you'll appreciate the struggle." I crossed my arms across my chest. "It makes us stronger," she said and stood up. "You are going to do great things."

"How do you know?"

She squeezed my shoulder and said, "Trust me." I hugged her and hoped she was right. I cried every time after she left.

Tammy came for Mom and Terrance's wedding, and her appearance was the only bright spot in a series of days full of worry-knotted muscles and fake smiles. Mom squealed with delight while I feigned excitement for what felt like a death sentence.

Pastor Ron announced at church that after a few months of dating, my mom and Terrance, two souls met and united under

God, would make the ultimate commitment to each other. I missed the service because I spent most Sunday mornings after the hymn portion ended sitting on the bathroom floor reading books starring witches and vampires. I would tell Mom I was volunteering in the nursery and hope she didn't check.

A woman who had once told me I had a beautiful singing voice came in just as I was finishing a chapter and said, "Congratulations, young lady."

"For what?" I said.

"On the engagement, of course." She tilted her head up at the mirror and brushed her rouged cheeks with the tips of her fingers. "Why aren't you in the service?"

I waved *Master of Murder* in front of me. "I can't read while Pastor Ron is talking," I said. "What engagement?"

Her fingers paused above her painted eyes. "Your mother, dear. And that nice young Hispanic man with the ponytail."

Mom apologized for not telling us sooner. "It was all so sudden," she said, like a teenage Disney princess. Even once the wedding date was set and the invitations were in the mail, the food and flowers ordered, the dress bought and honeymoon booked, I didn't think she'd really marry him until Tammy showed up.

Tammy did my hair and Jaime's while she paid for Mom to have hers done at a salon by a professional. Tammy paid for Mom to get a manicure and makeup, too, so we had the whole morning alone in our apartment.

"Can we wear makeup?" Jaime asked. She was nine and I eleven, and she was just excited to get dressed up.

"I don't see why not," Tammy said and dusted our faces with

powder. She wore a slip and a bra without wires. Her chest was freckled and tan.

"Did you know he was in prison?" I said.

Jaime said, "Shh," and elbowed me.

Tammy said, "Close your eyes." She smoothed a light peach shadow across our lids.

"He buys us ice cream," Jaime said.

"I hate him," I said.

Tammy said, "All done." She brushed her hands together. "You both look beautiful." Our long blond hair was twisted and pinned into loose buns atop our heads with freed wavy strands framing our faces.

"Wow," Jaime said, staring at her reflection. "We really do." She twirled in her pink dress, the lacy skirt spinning around her legs. "Can I watch TV?"

"Sure," Tammy said and when Jaime was gone she said, "Elizabeth."

"He really was in prison," I said.

"Do you know why?"

"Mom won't tell us," I said. "I think she's pregnant."

"She is not," Tammy said. She hesitated. "I hope she's not."

"I found prenatal pills in her bathroom," I said. "She said they want to have a baby as soon as they're married but she's been throwing up, too." Tammy's eyebrows went up and then came back down together and she was quiet for a minute. I said, "She thinks I don't know."

Tammy sighed and closed her eyes for a second. "Can you be nice today?" she said and looked at me.

"Will you move to Sacramento?"

"I'm staying until after their honeymoon."

I said, "Can't you stay longer?"

Tammy hugged me to her and rubbed my back through the slippery satin of the new dress she'd bought me. "It'll be okay, Liz."

With my face pressed into the soft skin of her stomach, I closed my eyes and pictured the way Terrance's eyes lingered on Jaime and me, the way he rested his fingers too long on our small knees and shoulders, the way he bit his lips when Mom wasn't looking. I whispered, "When you leave, we have to live with Terrance."

Mom walked down the aisle in a cream dress patterned with large maroon flowers. A gold clip with pearls held up some of her hair and some of it fell down in soft loose curls. She wore cream-colored heels and lipstick the same maroon as the flowers on her dress, held a bouquet of deep red roses, and smiled so big I was almost happy for her. A polished wooden cross spanned the back wall of the room which doubled as a gym for the Christian school attached. Terrance stood next to Gary at the altar in their brown suits, both of them wearing matching gold-and-maroon ties. Tammy stood next to Mom in her plain beige dress, her thin brown hair half up in a gold clip.

"Mom looks gorgeous," Jaime whispered in my ear. "I can't wait to get married." She sighed and put her hand on her heart when the rings came out like some of the older ladies in the audience. Pastor Ron talked about God and commitment, and like many of the women in the congregation who cried when he pronounced them man and wife, tears fell onto my lap, too, when I bowed my head for the final prayer. I didn't close my eyes but instead watched the dark spots on my purple dress ripple out across the fabric.

That weekend, during the kind of late-night conversations that made Tammy my favorite adult, she told me she believed you could choose your family, that you didn't have to love someone just because fluids had been mixed somewhere along the line. Cancer had killed Tammy and Mom's mother when Tammy was six and Mom was four, and they grew up getting beaten by their step-mother while their workaholic father sat in his leather recliner reading the newspaper.

"'Related' is biology," Tammy said. "Blood connections are on indisputable genetic levels." Mom and Terrance were honeymoon-ing in Mendocino and Jaime slept on the couch. Tammy had let me stay up and have a sip of her wine. She was on her third glass. "But love is not science," she said. "Family is more than biology."

Mom and Terrance were due back the next day and I wished they wouldn't come home. Tammy had cooked homemade maca-roni and cheese with corkscrew pasta noodles and sharp cheddar, and lasagna that had never been frozen. She gave us facials with creams that smelled like melon and apricot, put tea bags on our eyes and hot washcloths over our faces. She made pancakes that weren't from a boxed mix and eggs with chopped vegetables for breakfast. She rented movies and played Monopoly and Life with us for hours after Mom would have quit.

But what I liked best was this: after the moon rose and Jaime fell asleep, Tammy talked to me like I was a grown-up. She used adult language, and when I asked what a word meant, she told me, instead of Mom's usual, "It's kind of hard to explain."

"My friends are my family," Tammy said. "And when you get older, you can choose to have that, too."

"Mom says I have to love Terrance," I said. "That he's part of our family when they get back."

Tammy said, "You don't have to love him. You just have to be civil."

"What does that mean?"

"Polite."

"She promised not to marry someone we didn't like," I said. "She lied."

Tammy swirled the liquid in her glass and we watched as the wine coated the clear walls with a red film. "We can't always decide how we feel."

"But we can decide what we do."

"Sometimes," Tammy whispered.

"What?"

Tammy shook her head. "You're right, little girl, you're right." She reached forward and ruffled my hair. "Such a smart kid." She sighed, took a sip of her Pinot Noir, and closed her eyes.

When Mom and Terrance got back we were supposed to be asleep so I closed my eyes as she came in to check. I tried to steady my breath to match the rhythm of deep slumber in Jaime's. Terrance went to get the bags from the car and Tammy whispered right outside our bedroom door, "Are you pregnant?"

Mom sighed. "How did you know?"

"Is that why you married this guy?"

Mom's breath faltered. She said, "I do love him."

"Enough to spend the rest of your life listening to his awful jokes?"

"Is that your worst criticism?"

"Why was he in prison?"

"Why is that what everyone focuses on?"

"Are you kidding?"

"It's not like that's the only thing he's ever done," Mom said. Tammy laughed. "It's too late, okay?" Mom snapped. "He's my husband."

"What about the girls?" Tammy said. "You're hurting them."

"Oh, for heaven's sake," Mom said.

"And a baby!"

"We made a mistake," Mom said. "I made a mistake."

"So, fix it," Tammy said.

"What if this is God's plan for all of us?"

"What if it isn't?" Tammy said. "What do you actually want?"

"It doesn't matter what I want," Mom whispered so quietly I almost missed it.

Tammy sighed, her figure slumping against the door frame. "You don't have to do this," she said. "There are other options."

"Not," Mom said, "for me."

I arrive in Salt Lake City on the same gusts of wind as "the worst snowstorm of the season," the newscaster says on the radio later. Flying in heavy turbulence, my stomach drops each time we dip, but the wrenching tension in my gut is more about why I'm on this shaky plane.

"We are waiting for the parole board to respond to the appeal, but we don't know how long that could take," Mom said in the car on the way to the airport. Like she had a dozen times already, she said, "We think this is best for everyone."

Noah slept in his car seat with his head folded forward onto his chest. I looked out the window at the rain and pretended not to see my mom's blue-green eyes as they darted up to glance at me in the rearview mirror each time she spoke. "You and my sister get along so well," she said. "You guys will have fun." I bit my tongue hard enough to taste metal.

In the passenger seat, Terrance slapped his thighs as if they were drums, even with the radio off. "We'll really miss you, though," he said, turning to smirk at me. "All those good times."

Mom pulled up at the unloading zone to drop me off. "With Noah sleeping, you know. Sorry," she said as she helped me pull my duffel bags from the trunk. "You know how to check luggage, right?" Raindrops pooled in my hair and then streamed down into my face. Mom hugged me. "I love you," she said and shut the trunk. "I'm getting all wet!" she said. She hugged me again and got back in the car. Terrance pursed his lips and kissed the air near the window in a gesture that was more arrogant than sexual, like a female con artist escaping with the cash. He waved with his fingertips as they drove away, and I would have flipped him off if not for the bags in my hands packed with everything I called mine.

The man who sits next to me on the wobbling plane in seat 31B says, "Goodness, this is getting choppy," as we head over the Sierras. Out the window the clouds look like an infinite sea of thickly overlaid white feathers, fluid and solid at the same time. When I grab the armrest he pats my hand and says, "There's really nothing to worry about." He smiles wide. "God will take care of us."

My nostrils flare and I smile back without showing teeth. "I'm not on real good terms with God right now," I say. "But if he likes you, maybe we're safe."

"Where are your parents?" he says, peeking over the seats in front of us. He tilts his head toward me and leans closer. "Are you running away?" He glances at my chest.

"If I were, I wouldn't go to Utah," I say. I would go to Mexico, or Hawaii, or Greece. Somewhere warm.

"How old are you?" he says, shifting his weight toward the center armrest.

Even though his wandering eyes bother me less than Terrance's leers, I say, "Old enough to know about sexual harassment." It works; for the remaining hour of the flight the man keeps his pudgy face turned toward the aisle and lets me cry in peace. A small voice in my head chants, *Mom left me. She actually left me.* I hadn't believed it would happen until she drove away from the terminal with the newly pruned version of her family while I stood on the curb in the rain.

The clouds outside the aircraft thicken into a moving gray-white wall of swirling haze. *Tammy's great*, I think, *but she likes to travel. She has a boyfriend on another continent. She won't want me forever.* I close my eyes against the glaring white outside and try not to imagine where I'll be sent after this short-term solution fails.

My intestines tangle themselves into knots beneath my belly

as I picture Mom and Terrance and Noah getting home, rushing inside to get out of the rain, laughing at the splashes made by their feet. I picture Mom's attention to Noah and Terrance—getting them dry and warm like a mother should, rubbing shoulders and arms with firm hands, making hot chocolate and getting blankets, and a cry bubbles up my throat. What if Mom always chooses Terrance over us? What if Jaime and I never live together again? I shove my fist in between my teeth and sob with my face turned toward the churning mist outside the window.

My cheeks are still wet but I've stopped crying by the time we land in Utah. Aunt Tammy picks me up at the gate wearing khaki pants and a zip-up fleece jacket. "How ya doing?" she says and hugs me. She's warm and she holds me longer than Mom had in the rain, and I stand there frozen, squeezing my eyes tight against her shoulder. She smells like clean stream water and a hint of lavender and I inhale that freshness in the first deep breath I've taken in weeks. Tammy kisses the top of my head before she moves away and my chest tightens back up when she does.

Tammy carries my duffels to the parking garage while I keep my backpack. We step onto the moving walkway but Tammy doesn't stop like everyone else. We stride past businessmen, white men in blue suits with briefcases, four of them, one after the other. Then I put my backpack down and lean against the railing. Tammy stops and stands next to me, still lifting my bags.

Snow outside the windows floats in a light drizzle, a whirling of small spots against empty space. The mountains are huge and topped with pure white. "That's a lot of snow," I say.

"It's about right for January."

I say, "Can we make a snowman in your yard?"

"Sure," she says.

"I've never done that."

"Your mom and I grew up with snow until we moved to California," she says. "We ice-skated on the neighborhood pond, had snowball fights in the yard."

"Mom said she fell through the ice once."

"It's true," Tammy says. "I helped pull her out."

The floating snowflakes mesmerize me. On the freeway into town in the front seat of Tammy's car, I let my eyes lose focus and look past the window to the space where the white specks dance in the lights and seem to come right at me like 3-D warp tunnels on movie screens. The capitol building's white domes rise illuminated against the dark span of jagged mountains behind them. Inside the car, classical music plays on the radio, and the heater vents all point at me. Tammy's profile shows a longer nose than my mom's, thinner lips, a similar chin. The same small frame Mom carries too much weight on is more fitting on Tammy, her muscles toned and lean. Her skin is darker than Mom's, too, evidence of time spent outside on desert bike rides and mountain walks under tree-scattered sunlight, and if I live to be Tammy's age, I hope I look as fit as she does.

"I'm glad you're here," Tammy says.

"Really?"

"Really, Liz," she says and looks at me. "I was excited when your mom called. I *am* excited." Her long fingers grip the steering wheel. "You are one of my two favorite people on this planet," she says. I smile but can't hold it. I try to say thanks but my voice falters. I've never been anyone's favorite anything before.

She glances at me sideways and pats my thigh. "Are you hungry?"

At her condo I watch her pull the fold-out bed from the green-and-red plaid couch in my new room, which used to be her office. She spreads out green sheets and then puts the blue comforter she picked out at Macy's on top. "I thought you liked blue. Do you like blue?" she says. I nod. I've never owned anything from Macy's or had anyone consider purchasing what I would like before what was on sale.

Tammy folds a wool throw at the foot of the bed. She smiles. "This blanket is older than you," she says and smooths her tanned hands across the threads. "I used this to study late at night in college." She pats the fabric. "Tucked over my feet on our lumpy couch." I nod but don't say any of the jumbled thoughts bombarding my brain: *Mom left me. I need to check on Jaime. Don't get too comfortable here.*

Tammy takes a hesitant breath and clears her throat. "Anything else I can do?" she says. I shake my head. All my clothes are still packed and I just want to curl into a ball under the covers. She rubs my back lightly, and her warm hands melt a little of the day's strain from my muscles.

"Thank you," I say.

"Sure thing," Tammy says. She pats my shoulder and half-hugs me with just her right arm like I might shatter if she applies too much pressure. She leans back and smiles at me. "Make yourself at home," she says, and I believe she means it. I already feel safer than at Gary and Carol's, or Dad's, or even Mom's with Terrance there, and right now that is more than enough to be grateful for.

Before Tammy can move away, I grab her around the waist and push my face into her hard collarbone. Her back stiffens and for a fraction of a second I think she's going to pull away, but when I whisper, "Thank you so much," her athletic body relaxes and returns the hug full force like she was waiting for this chance.

Tammy squeezes me with both of her strong arms, and a tiny bit of me dares to hope that someone will finally take care of me, even if it's not permanent. She kisses my forehead, and skims her hands along my shoulders. "No problem, little girl," she says. "No problem at all."

When she leaves the room, I slip on a pair of pajama pants and slide under the crisp sheets and comforter. Tammy's welcome sprouted a kernel of optimism in my chest, and though Mom's easy release of her daughters still smolders in my gut, I fall asleep with mountains outside my window and Tammy puttering about downstairs.

It's cold in this city. So cold it's past the point of being able to see my breath because the air is already white and heavy with freezing moisture. So cold my nose and feet are always numb and it's quiet, too, like there's water in my ears and everything sounds blurry. The snow drifts in spirals beyond Tammy's windows, muffling the sounds of the outside, and inside, the chill that invaded my lungs from that first breath of frosty air in the parking lot of the airport burrows into my chest like a tick and spreads out until I worry my fingers might actually fall off.

Tammy tells me I'll acclimatize. I have teeth-chattering shivers the whole drive to school and Tammy says, "Oh, stop that," but she blasts the heater. She says, "It's not really that bad, is it?" I shove my hands deeper into my new coat pockets but can't stop shaking. She laughs. "You'll get used to it, kiddo," she says.

Tammy drops me off two blocks down from the giant redbrick building that looks like the East Coast high schools I've seen on TV, with ivy climbing up the corners, patches of snow out front, and in big brass letters, YOUNG HIGH, above heavy wooden double doors. She pats my leg before I get out of the car, says, "Good luck." She waits a minute after I start walking before she merges with moving traffic and leaves me alone. I step on the spaces between the big squares of damp concrete sidewalk. *Step on a crack, break your mother's back.*

Inside the red bricks are long tiled hallways lined with full-length lockers, expansive stairwells with portraits of historical figures on the walls, and brass spheres on the handrails. I go unnoticed until French class where I say, "Verb conjugations suck," to no one in particular and the girl I'm sitting next to asks me not to swear in her presence.

"I didn't say the *F* word," I tell her.

"I know," she says. "You said the *S* word."

"I thought *shit* was the *S* word," I say, and she doesn't look at me for the rest of class.

I eat lunch alone in one of the enclosed back stairwells. Tammy packed me Havarti cheese squares and wheat crackers, strawberry yogurt, carrot sticks, gingersnap cookies, and an orange juice box. In biology, a class way too easy to pay much attention to, I write letters. *Dear Jaime*, I write, adding a heart above the *i* in her name.

The mountains are huge. The air smells like the frozen food aisles at grocery stores and snow doesn't always melt in the sun. You'd hate the cold but my room is big enough for another bed. You know, just in case. And I can't help it, I write at the bottom, *Stay safe* next to *I love you.*

To Rachel I write, *They have off-campus lunch here. And lockers. And no black people. People say* pop *instead of* soda, flip *in place of* fuck, *and ditching class is called* sluffing. *I hate eating lunch alone. I miss you,* I write and wish there was some way to express how much.

In algebra, I sit in front of a junior who asks me where I'm from during homework time. We are supposed to trade papers and correct the other person's equations. But he hasn't done it, and I, of course, haven't, either. I'm a week behind in the semester but I'm confident I'll be in class regularly now so I'll catch up fast. "California," I say.

"You look like California," he says. His accent is delicious, like melted chocolate I want to lap up.

"What does that mean?"

He shrugs. "Beach boy, surfer girl, blond and blue eyed . . ." He holds up his hands, smiles. "You know."

"Have you been there?"

"Nope. Afraid Utah is my American experience." Mrs. Sanders asks the class to pass their homework forward. She frowns at the small stack from our row and then glances at me. I'm looking forward to starting fresh with teachers here, but it's only my first day.

I say, "You're from England?"

"How could you tell?" he says and smiles again. "Dean." He sticks out his hand. I shake it. His skin is cool and dry.

"Elizabeth," I say. I ask him what he's doing in Salt Lake and he says his dad got a job here a year ago. Mrs. Sanders asks us to face the front again. Dean puts his finger to his half-smiling lips and whispers, "Shhh," so I turn around and watch Mrs. Sanders' butt shake as she erases the chalkboard. Right before the bell rings, Dean leans forward and says into the back of my neck, "Let's talk again soon." His lips graze the tiny hairs across my skin and when I open my eyes, the classroom is almost empty.

Once bootless and inside Tammy's condo, I turn the heater up to seventy-five, put on flannel pants, two pairs of wool socks, and four shirts. I make myself hot chocolate from a packet, add some Häagen-Dazs coffee ice cream like Tammy does so it melts and forms a creamy foam layer on top. I pull the purple chenille throw over me on the couch. I wish her fireplace was real and not gas so that I could actually watch the flames eat the wood, the reds and oranges dancing with the smoky wisps of gray, and the hot logs cracking and splitting and sacrificing themselves to provide heat.

Tammy has more money than my mom, degrees instead of children. She owns stocks and bonds, buys my mom furniture for her birthday, sends us brand-name clothes and electronics for Christmas. Her house is bright and clean, like a museum filled with paintings or sculptures, and beautiful, breakable things are positioned carefully around the rooms here, too. A huge fire-glazed plate on the mantel sits next to a black wood figure of a woman with legs twice the size of the rest of her, an African stringed instrument Tammy and Sam carved their initials into lives in a glass curio along with a crystal vase and a cactus garden, a handwoven Mexican rug, and a golden Arabian urn, all collected from trips abroad. Only original artwork decorates the walls: a painting of a cow in a field with one cloud in the background; a three-foot horizontal framed picture of a birch tree forest; a watercolor of a tribal mother supporting an infant in her disproportionately large arm and hand, like she's cradling the whole earth in her little baby.

I wake up to Tammy switching on the light above where I lie on the couch huddled under the purple throw. While I slept the sky darkened and Tammy is closing the blinds in her classy dark brown business suit minus the low-heeled pumps or loafers she always slips off at the door.

"What do you want for dinner?" she says. "Salad? Homemade chili?"

"I'm not really hungry."

She says, "You have to eat something. How about some pasta at least?"

I nod, rub my hands together. "Sure, thanks."

Tammy brings me a wooden breakfast tray with a big bowl full of pasta that smells like garlic and basil. Sun-dried tomatoes glisten like rubies among the noodles. "Something simple," she says as she sets the tray on her smooth wood coffee table above her white carpet.

I am suddenly starving and it's the most delicious meal I've ever had. When I finish, Tammy refills my bowl without my even asking, and she refuses to let me help clean anything up. "I'll do it," she says, squeezing my shoulder. "You just rest."

"How was your first day?" she asks me after she's changed into her "house clothes": pink slippers and a green PJ set with frogs on the shirt and lilies on the pants.

"Okay, I guess," I say and she flips open *The Wall Street Journal*. I'm watching *Melrose Place*, which I am not allowed to watch at home. "I finished my book."

"Did you meet anyone?"

"Everybody's the same," I say. "They're all white Mormon preppy frat-boy sorority-girl idiots."

She says, "That can't be true." She turns back to her newspaper. "Did you do your homework?"

"I don't have books yet," I say. I wish I had the distraction.

A commercial with a mother and daughter laughing over a box of cookies comes on and my heart gets so big in my chest it feels like my ribs will snap. I can keep the lump in my throat as long as I don't open my mouth.

Tammy scrunches her face at me. She says, "Do you want some hot chocolate?" and gets up.

I swallow hard. "Sure," I say. "Thanks."

Later when I'm tucked under my new comforter, Tammy's old blanket, and three layers of clothing, Tammy pokes her head into my room. She sits on the edge of the bed and the metal hinges creak. She says, "How are you holding up?" I try to make a brave face, but between the cold and my attempt to keep the near-constant tears from spilling out, I think I just cringe. Tammy laughs. "That good, huh?" She leans forward and ruffles my hair. "Things will get better," she says. She takes my hand and it warms my chilled fingers. "They always do eventually."

"Always?" I say and my voice cracks.

"When your mom and I were kids," Tammy says, settling onto the mattress, "our stepmother threw things at us constantly. She locked us out of the house, sent us to bed without dinner at six P.M., refused to buy us clothes or let us go anywhere." Tammy closes her eyes and her shoulders tense. "Once Linda and I woke up with uneven bowl haircuts and a dead bolt on our bedroom door because I told our dad she wasn't feeding us."

I squeeze her hand and she flinches. "Is that when she started hitting you guys?"

Tammy nods. "She always went after Linda first." Her nostrils flare. "I fought back so she started waiting until I wasn't around." She snorts. "Coward."

I wait for Tammy to continue, to tell me how it got better, but she just sits there, wide-eyed and staring into space. "I had piano practice after school," Tammy says, still not looking at me. "I quit so I could walk her home but Linda waited so long to tell me." She drops her head and pulls her hands into her lap. "I should have noticed."

"Did you feel guilty?" I say, thinking of Jaime's scars, of Mom's, the visible surface marks and the deeper damage we can't see on their skin.

Tammy blinks and presses her lips together. "I still do," she says quietly.

"Me, too," I say. "About Jaime."

"Oh, Liz," she says. "Don't." Her shoulders relax a bit and she forces a smile. "Guilt is a useless, festering disease. Nothing that has happened to you or Jaime was your fault."

"But you just said—"

"It's harder after it becomes habit," she says.

I chew on my fingernail. "I bet Mom doesn't lose sleep feeling guilty," I say.

"Your mom made great sacrifices for you girls," Tammy says.

"Not lately." The dammed flow of tears behind my eyes threatens to burst free. "She abandoned us."

Tammy studies me and purses her lips together on the side of her mouth, considering. She says, "For a long time, I thought your mom was weak for staying with your dad. I encouraged her to get over her fear and escape, for you and Jaime. And she did, finally, but"—Tammy takes a deep breath—"now, I think it took tremendous courage for her to suffer all she did. She believed she was protecting you girls, putting your safety before hers, and she wasn't scared for herself."

I remember how secure I'd felt for the first half of my life with Mom in the next room, even if Dad was home. Without hesitation, she defended us from monsters in the closet and our rampaging father. Dad's temper needed an easy target and Mom surrendered to keep him away from us. "He hit her a lot," I say.

Tammy's jaw clenches. "I know," she says. "She's a good liar, your mom. And I was so far away."

"I used to think she was so brave," I say. She muffled her cries when Dad hit her, endured black eyes, cantaloupe-sized bruises, and sprained wrists in near silence so that her daughters could dream in peace. Jaime slept through the beatings but I often watched, powerless and furious at my tiny fists that were incapable of fighting back. "Like a superhero."

"She was brave," Tammy says with pride. She smiles, but it doesn't reach her eyes. "I think she still is. And she loves you girls so much." Tammy scoots off my bed. "You are brave, too, you know." She pats my knee and stands tall. "We are a family of warriors."

I yawn and snuggle deeper under the blankets. "What do you think we could be if we didn't have to be brave?"

Tammy's face registers anguish before she laughs. She bends and kisses my forehead. "Good night, little girl," she says and turns off my light. "Sweet dreams." The lip balm she wears leaves a sweet smell and light residue on my face, and even though I worry about pimples, I close my eyes and don't wipe the honey-scented wax from my skin.

It takes two more days of waiting for Mom to call before I finally break down and dial home while Tammy is at her aerobics class. Terrance answers the phone, "Home of the Whopper, what's your beef?"

"Can I talk to my mom please?"

"Who is this?"

"I'll give you two guesses, genius," I say.

"Well, hello to you, too, Liz," he says and snorts. "It's good to hear your voice. Hold on."

I hear a shuffle and a squeal, and then Mom breathes, "Hi, Elizabeth," into the phone. My stomach churns and I don't even want to talk to her anymore. "How are you?" she says. "How's school?"

"Okay." I hear Terrance laugh. "I didn't get to pick my elective so I ended up in technology," I say.

"That doesn't sound so bad," she says.

"My teacher can't spell and she has a mullet."

Mom says, "I hear your new room is pretty big."

"I can't put anything on the walls, but I have my own bathroom."

"Lucky you," she says. "Most teenagers don't get their own bathroom, you know."

Terrance's laughs become louder. "Babe," he says. "Babe, you gotta come see this."

Mom giggles. "Sorry, we were watching a movie."

"I'll let you go then. Don't want your daughter to interfere with your life or anything."

"Don't be a snot," she snaps. She clicks her tongue in a "tsk" sound and takes a breath like she's going to say something but then doesn't. We sit for a beat, the TV and Terrance's sniggers in the background. "Why can't we have a normal conversation anymore?" she says and now her voice is tired.

"You haven't called," I say.

"I've been busy," she says.

"Don't you miss me?"

"Of course I do, Liz," she says. "But life goes on." She sighs. "You know that."

"I thought this was supposed to be temporary."

"We still have to adjust and move forward." She clears her throat. "All of us." The subtext is like cold water flung in my face: that means you. She's not thinking about me coming home at all. She's settling into new routines, a daily life without me or Jaime.

"Hello?" Mom says.

The lump in my throat grows like a tsunami so I keep my mouth shut against the stinging grief that is quick to rise around Mom. In my memory or on the phone, all she does is remind me that I'm not as important as Terrance, that Jaime and I are not even second-string players kept on the bench. We're being replaced.

"This silent treatment is not worth the long-distance rates, Elizabeth," she says but I can't speak. "If you're not going to talk to me, why did you call?" *Because somewhere inside of you is the mother who loves us.* Mom says, "Fine, young lady, if you're not going to talk to me, then—"

I hang up. My nostrils flare, searing tears fill my eyes, flames blister in my chest, and for the first time since I arrived in this whitewashed city, I'm too warm.

Outside, the street is covered in a clean white blanket, sparkling under the almost full moon and burning stars. Icy webs dim the streetlights and the grounded moonlight stretches forever along Tammy's street. Trees are held captive by the weight of the water, animals have been caved in by layers of unique snowflakes, nothing moves. There is no sound.

Holding the silence against the ringing in my brain, I step out onto the snowy sidewalk, palaces of ice crystals cracking under my feet. I feel them break, faintly hear their crunching destruction, and suddenly I want them to crumble. I want them to explode, to shatter and burst into thousands of slivers under my devastating weight, to rupture and then vanish completely, leaving no trace of their existence. *Poof, gone.*

I smash my boots into snowdrifts, kick frozen grass, melt snow-balls in my fists. I spin and stomp on the snow in Tammy's yard until I realize I'm screaming with my mouth ripped open, my teeth and throat bared to the sky, and my chest constricting in the cold. I howl under the stars until my lungs are dry and I can't breathe, but the snow swallows my voice. The frosty white carpet and thick air absorb every resonance before it has a chance to ripple out into the night, and even as loud as I cry, no one can hear me.

5

Checking the mail has become the highlight of my weekdays. A black metal container is bolted to the red bricks of Tammy's condo next to her front door, and every day I flip through the envelopes searching for something with my name on the front, a familiar return address. I've mailed two letters to Jaime, three to Rachel, and I sent Gary and Carol a thank you card featuring a picture of a brown boxer like Rambo, but each day not one in the stack of letters is for me.

Some of the envelopes are addressed to Sam, which doesn't seem fair since in the month I've been here I haven't seen him once in real life. He lives in framed photographs around Tammy's house, mostly in her bedroom: Sam dressed in a navy-blue snowsuit doing a handstand on top of an icy mountain; Sam and Tammy in kayaks floating on a greenish brown river in South America; Sam riding a bike in the 1979 Olympic Trials.

Magazines like *Prevention* and *National Geographic* and catalogues for Eddie Bauer and L.L.Bean round out Tammy's mail, and I put it all on her wooden console table after I'm inside. I set my backpack against the stairwell, turn up the heater, and open the refrigerator. Thanks to me, a butterfly magnet full of grassy greens and bright yellows now breaks up the white of the fridge door, but Tammy's kitchen is the one room where there is nothing on the walls yet.

I pour Kashi cereal and low-fat milk into a bowl and put it on a wooden breakfast tray. I do this almost without thinking, my afternoon snack now a daily habit like so many other things have become here. This house has a routine, a schedule, even on Saturdays. Tammy lets me sleep in until she gets home from the gym, but then it's up and out of the warmth of the covers and into the gray cloudiness of winter in the Wasatch Mountains.

On weekday mornings Tammy wakes me up, "Rise and shine," and flips on the lights. If I spend more than fifteen minutes trying to heat my insides with a scalding shower, she blasts hot water from the kitchen faucet and I get shot with cold. The first few times I couldn't tell she did it on purpose. We listen to NPR in the car, and Tammy takes side streets all the way to school.

"Do you feel prepared for your biology exam?" she says. Or, "Did you finish that French assignment?" I always say yes.

Tammy and I haven't painted the walls yet, but our weekends have not been wasted. Like my mom, Tammy believes in efficiency. Sunday mornings we go grocery shopping and to Costco, and since most people here are in church the stores are almost empty. Tammy buys things like smoked salmon and Brie cheese, wholewheat bread and pasta, one percent milk instead of two, and real butter. She purchases fresh meats and vegetables and makes chile rellenos, crab cakes, and turkey burgers. She buys ingredients for pot roast, tacos, chili. She remembers that cheesecake is my favorite dessert, and she makes it with a lemon sour cream layer on top.

"Natural is always better than processed," she says. "Homemade beats restaurants for most things." I've never seen a Rice-A-Roni or Hamburger Helper anywhere in her cart, not even a box of instant oatmeal.

"I make the best blueberry muffins from scratch," she tells me one Sunday, and they are. Fresh nuggets of fruit in soft cake glazed with orange-rind-infused sugar syrup. Tammy slices one still warm from the oven, and I devour my half so fast it burns my mouth. It's like baked heaven on my taste buds and nothing else matters while I chew and swallow.

Tammy picks off small pieces of her muffin with her fingers and drops them into her mouth. She says, "During grad school, I lived off these, mocha coffees, and pasta for weeks at a time." Her eyes are far away. "I lived in a tiny studio in California with a tiny kitchen."

"Alone?"

"Sam took a job in New Mexico before I was done with school."

"You studied math, right?"

"Applied mathematics, yes," she says. "I'd come home after class or work and cook dinner every night. No matter how bad the day was, I always ate something yummy." She licks her fingers. "Has your mom told you what our evil stepmother made us eat?" I nodded—cold canned vegetables, overcooked and tough chicken innards, instant and still flakey potatoes. "As soon as your mom and I moved out, I started making things I'd never tried that were fresh and full of new flavors."

"Where did you learn to cook?"

"Betty Crocker and Julia Child cookbooks I got at a library sale," she says. "I only had one sauce pot big enough for spaghetti or fusilli or gnocchi and one skillet for sautéing veggies."

"Did you make your crab and angel hair pasta dish back then?"

"No, I couldn't afford crab," she says. "I'd cook whatever was on sale: zucchini and tomatoes, almost expired sausage with peppers and mushrooms, or sometimes just garlic, olive oil, and basil," she says. "I grew fresh basil on the tiny kitchen windowsill in an empty garbanzo bean can." She laughs and takes another muffin from the cooling rack. "I reused everything I could."

"And now you have all this," I say, gesturing to the big, light-filled kitchen. "Lots more than two pots," I say and she smiles. She hands me another fluffy blueberry treat and this half I eat in pieces, like Tammy, savoring each small crumble. We sit as trees sway outside the windows and shadows inch across the rosewood floor. The muffins cool and the bakery smell fades from the room. "I want a house like this someday," I say.

"There's no reason you can't have what you want if you work hard," she says, getting up from the table and opening a Ziploc bag she'd rinsed out and let air-dry on the dish rack.

"Is this what you wanted?" I say.

Tammy drops blue-speckled mushroom shapes into the Ziploc bag one by one until all the muffins are encased in plastic and ready to be frozen. She nods as she seals the zipper. "Some days it is, little girl." She nods again and smiles at me, showing all her teeth. Eyes crinkling at the corners, lips upturned as far as they will reach, this is Tammy's genuine grin. "Some days, like today," she says, "it's exactly what I hoped for."

Tammy thrives on taking care of the things on her to-do list.

We pick up dry-cleaning, visit antique stores, drop Tammy's car off to get an oil change while we go to yoga classes. We pick up fresh bagels from Einstein's and go to REI to buy bike parts in preparation for spring. It snows occasionally as we drive around the numbered streets of Salt Lake City's grid running errands, and I relax into the furry gray seat cover in the warm car and watch tiny spots of bright white swirl in the air. I think about home a lot, with its wide grassy fields and long freeways, lazy green rivers and level structures. There are no mountains at home, the flatness stretches for miles so the valley tempers the climate and we don't get this kind of cold. But there is more to see here.

"When it gets warmer," Tammy says one day, "we can go to the farmers' market. They have delicious fresh fruit. Do you like kiwis?"

"I don't know," I say. "I've never had one."

"And we can go hiking Sunday mornings," she says. "When the snow melts, the streams run full and we can watch the sunrise from that mountaintop right there. I promise it's better than any Sunday service you've been to."

I say, "You really hiked all the way up that mountain?" Outside the car window, snow-tipped rocky peaks surround us and it doesn't matter which one she's talking about, they are all huge.

"It's not that far," she says. "You could do it if you wanted."

Sometimes we walk down a block to the Eighth Avenue corner market to get milk or an onion, past snow stacked on the edge of the sidewalks, trees iced with layers of crystal lace. She tells me about winters in Connecticut with snowdrifts taller than me, when electricity is out for weeks, roads closed off, schools shut down. Now when I can't sleep, I wish for a storm that immense.

A blizzard so big and extensive, all of outside just fades into a gentle white void. I picture it in my mind: a whole world of blank and clean, like starting over, like this chance I've been given here with Tammy.

I balance my cereal bowl and carry the breakfast tray from the wood floor out over the carpet. I'm allowed to eat in the living room if I am careful and so far, so good. I dropped an egg on Tammy's kitchen rug last week, and when the yolk splattered against the blue weave on the twelve-foot floor runner I wondered what she'd be like angry, if she would simmer for days like Mom and then boil over. But I cleaned it up before she got home, and I don't think she knew.

I turn on the TV and punch in the cable buttons I've memorized. *Animaniacs* starts at three thirty, and I think of me and Jaime at home before Mom on weekdays after school, watching TV too loud and eating popcorn or Pringles on the couch, singing cartoon theme songs together and imitating voices during the commercials.

"What are you doing?" I look up and see Sam standing on the stairs, wearing blue jeans and a big gray sweater under a vest that looks like a life jacket. His tan is darker than Tammy's, his face has more wrinkles than in the photos, and large glasses rest on his crooked nose. We met once when I was eight, but I recognize him more from the pictures in Tammy's bedroom.

"Eating," I say through a mouthful of seven whole grains. "What are you doing?"

He cocks his hip and puts his hand over his faded brown leather belt, his elbow making a sharp *V* angle against his body. He smiles at me like I'm amusing. "I live here," he says.

Sam has spent most of the last six years in Sydney, designing a secure computer system for Australia's national health care programs. He works for their government, and makes a lot of money. He's not married to Tammy but they've been together since high school. Sam was eighteen and the manager of a diner in L.A., Tammy was sixteen and a waitress, and twentysomething years later they've lived on a ranch in New Mexico, spent two years in a flat in London, owned a house together in Connecticut, and now own a condo in Salt Lake.

His nostrils flare like I'm garbage he can't stand the smell of. He says, "I didn't expect to be bothered while working in my own home."

I don't tell him it's only his house because Tammy wants it to be. She picked the condo out by herself. "I didn't know you were here," I say. "Sorry."

"Why is the heater on?" His brown socks come down the steps and he rotates the thermostat.

"It's cold."

"It's plenty warm in this house. No reason to waste energy."

"Is Aunt Tammy here?"

"You lose most of your body heat through your head," he says. "Put a hat on."

"Inside?"

"A hat will keep you warm in most places, Elizabeth," he says. "Please turn off the television," he says when he's halfway up the stairs, his vest rustling like tent flaps or parachute pants. I push the power button and watch my reflection on the screen put spoonfuls of cereal in my mouth.

The next day in algebra, Dean tugs lightly on my ponytail and whispers two inches from my ear, "Why would a girl like you leave sunny Califor-ni-a for bloody snow-pissed Mormon central?" His voice is deep, thick, and combined with the accent that makes me feel like I'm slipping into a warm and silky bubble bath, he sounds older than his sixteen. *I could listen to him all day,* I write to Rachel.

"A girl like me?" I say. He smiles wide, showing the gap between his front teeth. He has a round pale moon face, spotted with deep brown freckles and blue eyes. His hair is long, straight, and pulled back into a ponytail at the base of his neck. I shrug. "I got kicked out."

"Whoa, tough girl," he says, circulating his fingers through the strands of hair in my ponytail. "What'd you do?"

"Nothing," I say. "It's a long story." He nods as if he knows, and I wonder about his family.

I call Jaime when I get to Tammy's after school. "What's it like living in the house that looks like nobody actually lives in it?" Jaime asks.

When Jaime and I visited during summers past, we were warned not to touch the walls. Tammy had just moved in and everything was brand new: the walls, the white carpet, the rosewood kitchen floor, the pale stone tile of the bathrooms.

Every surface was perfect, spotless. We tried hard not to touch anything—"Careful," I whispered to Jaime going up the stairs—but we would still see Tammy sometimes scrubbing our dirty little fingerprints off the otherwise unblemished white.

"Tammy's really nice," I say.

"Does she let you touch stuff?"

I say, "She makes my lunch every day."

"Crystal's taking me to school now," Jaime says.

I say, "That's great" at the same time she says, "It sucks." I chew on my fingernail. I can't tell if she's sucking her thumb or not.

"Kids here can't say things suck," I say. "They think it's cussing."

"That's stricter than Mom."

"I know." I try to think of ways to phrase all the things I want to say: *How much is Dad drinking? Are you staying attentive? Please tell me you've stopped smoking.* "I love you."

Jaime's thumb is definitely in her mouth when she says, "I miss you, too."

At dinner Tammy says, "How did your algebra test go?" while busying her hands with her napkin and the arrangement of the plates and glasses on the table. She hasn't eaten much since Sam arrived, and she's been jittery, which is not like her.

I smile. "I got an A minus."

She says, "Not an A?"

"An A minus is still pretty good," I say, my smile fading. "Isn't it?" My shoulders hunch.

"There's no reason we can't do better," she says. I gape at her with glassy eyes but she doesn't notice. She says, "Let's just try for the full A next time." She pours herself another glass of wine and refills Sam's as well.

I slump in my chair and pick up my fork to have something in my hand. "I did better than most of the class," I mutter, poking at my meat with the silver tines. Little squirts of pork juice escape the holes and mix with the applesauce.

"Was it your best effort?" Sam says and I'm forced to acknowledge his presence. His arrival had surprised Tammy, and she apologized for not telling me about his plans for a visit sooner. He was a week early, she told me, but was only staying six weeks instead of nine. "I hate when he does this," she'd said. "As if my schedule is less important." But she didn't say a word about her irritation to Sam.

Sam has been here four days and Tammy has spent all of her free time with him. They go for walks down to the mall to buy action movies on DVD that can only be watched by the two of them on Sam's laptop. Sam says DVDs will replace videos someday, so the discs are a better investment, but I think it has more to do with his desire to separate me from them. I don't complain. I don't really want to watch *Tombstone* or *Braveheart* anyway. Tammy took yesterday off work and they went skiing so early that she couldn't drive me to school, and I had to wait outside in the frozen air for the giant yellow school bus. She apologized the night before and she still made my lunch in the morning, so I haven't abandoned hope even though this whole scenario is alarmingly familiar.

Sam cuts his pork chop and asks me what I learned at school over the squeal of his knife scratching his plate.

I cringe and say, "Nothing." I push applesauce around with my fork. I don't like pork, but tonight Tammy didn't ask me what I wanted.

"Nothing at all?" he says, putting the chunk of white meat onto his tongue.

"Nothing new," I say, putting down my fork again and pushing my plate away.

"Ah-ha," he says and swallows. "That can't be true," he says and I look at Tammy. She stares at him with her chin in her palm, her pork chop barely touched, her wine gone, watching him sneer at me. His square shoulders move under the poofy orange vest he always wears, today over a brown T-shirt. His big head in its wide-brimmed Australian outback Crocodile Dundee hat casts a shadow over the table. I'm already looking forward to when he leaves.

"Can I call Jaime?" I say.

Sam says, "It's actually impossible to avoid learning anything, Elizabeth."

"Tammy?" I say. "Can I?"

Tammy sits up and clears her throat. "Of course," she says.

"It happens all the time," Sam says. "Whether you like it or not."

Tammy smiles at Sam. "After you finish your homework," she says.

"So," Sam says, turning to me. "What did you learn today?"

"I relearned how cold it is here without the heater," I say. I am wearing two of the sweaters I wore to school and still when I take my hands out of my pockets it hurts to move my fingers. Sam sets the thermostat at sixty-three degrees and won't let me turn it up.

"Where's your hat?" he says and my hands clench in the front pouch pockets of my sweater.

"Thank you for dinner," I say to Tammy and stand up.

She says, "You hardly ate."

"I'm not that hungry." I rinse my plate and wash my hands, the warm water stinging like tiny bites. "I have homework to do," I say.

"See, you might learn something yet," Sam says and turns to Tammy. She beams back at him, and I am careful not to touch the railing as I walk up the stairs.

The summer my mom and Terrance dated, she forced me and Jaime to go with them on singles group outings to beaches and carnivals and concerts in the park. We spent a weekend camping near a dried-up river where I was climbing rocks and stumbled upon Mom and Terrance, making out, his hand up her turquoise T-shirt and her hand in the butt pocket of his sandblasted jean shorts. I froze, feet unable to move and eyes glued open in horror like victims in slasher movies. Terrance noticed me over Mom's shoulder and watched me while his lips and tongue hungrily worked at my mom's mouth. His hands moved to the waist of her shorts and he winked at me as he slipped his fingers under the cloth-wrapped elastic.

I covered my eyes then my mouth as bile rushed up my throat. I spun around and sprinted as fast as I could through the dry pine needles and scratchy underbrush until my chest heaved. A dead tree had fallen across the path where I stopped and I kicked it. I kicked and bugs came out, ants, beetles, millipedes, and spiders. I kicked the tan termite tunnels and crumbling bark until my tennis shoes were brown and smothered in wood chips. I stomped and crushed and let the cracking wood and my own heavy breathing fill my ears until the log was almost sawdust. I puked into a mound of earth until my stomach was as ravaged as the tree.

"How was your walk?" Mom said when I got back to camp sweaty and coated with forest. A fine dust on my legs stuck to the soft white-blond hairs she wouldn't let me shave. She had a yellow daisy tucked behind her ear.

Terrance said, "Ours was awesome," and smiled all his crooked teeth at Mom. She blushed. I didn't eat a bite of dinner.

Jaime and I had to sleep with the rest of the children of the divorced under the flimsy picnic netting instead of a real tent, and the mosquitoes and the wind bit right through my cotton sleeping bag all night. Most of the kids had spent the day swimming or hiking, had eaten a full campfire-grilled dinner, and were excited about sleeping in the "wilderness." They lay fast asleep, their little chests rising and falling, and I would have given anything to be able to trust in the security of my parents' judgment, feel safe here in the woods because Mom was close by, like I had once upon a time. But instead, I was wide awake, spraying every bug that crawled toward my face with insecticide, and praying to a God I was still unsure about to give me back my family.

Mom was in the women's tent, maybe ten feet away, but I felt like she was miles in the distance. On the other side of the campsite sat the adult males' tent, and Terrance the enemy. Several sets of snores like semi-truck horns from men used to sleeping alone echoed out into the silence surrounding the dark towering pines. Next to me, Jaime's thumb rested between her lips, her bangs a mess across her forehead. I wiped at a little brown smear on her cheek, melted chocolate from the s'mores Terrance had made earlier. "Want one, Liz?" he'd asked me and even though I love them, as I watched his hands turning sticks of marshmallows over the fire, all I could think was that he had touched Mom's breasts, and God knew what else, a few hours ago, so no marshmallows for me, thanks.

I focused on the sky, and inhaled deep, cool breaths full of bright pine and earthy tree moss scents and asked the spotted gray moon for a sign that I wasn't going to lose Mom, that Terrance wouldn't really be able to steal the one constant I'd had my entire life. It hit me then, staring up at millions of stars, that the reverse wasn't true for Mom. While I'd never had a life without her, she'd had twenty-three years without me. I had been a surprise, the beginning of the end of her freedom, and I guessed she resented me for that. Maybe Dad did, too. I turned to Jaime's peaceful face. "We're in for a bumpy road, little sister." I kissed her sticky cheek and thought about how they'd planned to get pregnant with Jaime. She was the daughter Mom and Dad had actually wanted.

After that trip, Terrance was always around. We picked him up for church, we picked him up for dinner, we picked him up so he could pick up the laundry we'd washed for him. Mom stayed out past our bedtime even on weeknights to take him back to his apartment or give him another driving lesson in the summer twilight. She said she was teaching him to drive stick shift, but I had seen the hickeys on her neck.

The singles group spent a humid Saturday at the end of August hiking up Feather River Falls. When we got to the waterfall, a rainbow stretched across the pool where the river churned up white between granite boulders. Powdered river floated in a misty haze thick enough to blur my vision. I pretended I was alone on the planet, the first to visit this holy place where all sounds became the roar of water, all sights blurred into soft edges, and all things were impermanent. Small drops sprinkled my forehead like liquid dust and for a few minutes it felt like maybe there was a God, and maybe He was here, and maybe He does watch us and love us and want us to be happy.

On the walk down from the waterfall my mom saw graffiti on some rocks that said, *Squeeze my tits* and she whispered to Terrance, "Yeah, babe, please do." They kissed with a smacking sound, Mom moaned a little, and I realized whatever God wanted for me, it was not happiness.

By the time school started, Terrance had mastered the manual clutch enough to drive us all to church, to Taco Bell, to the unemployment office, and he let his hand rest on Mom's thigh with increasing frequency. I elbowed Jaime and pointed at his arm stretched across the two front seats. Her eyes widened. I stuck out my tongue and pretended to gag.

After one Sunday service, we sat outside Terrance's parole office.

"Mom?" I said. Jaime had fallen asleep next to me in the backseat. "Are you and Terrance having sex?"

Alarm flickered in her eyes before they narrowed. "That is absolutely none of your business," she said.

"How come he puts his hand on your leg?"

"It's to show that he cares about me."

"Is it okay to make out before you're married?"

Her hands turned to fists in her lap. "This is not an appropriate conversation for an eleven-year-old."

I said, "So it's not a sin?"

Terrance was walking across the parking lot, his white high-tops bright between his skin and the asphalt. Mom stared at his chest without blinking until Terrance waved. Mom jerked back to life and swiveled her head to look directly at me with her eyes big, her nostrils flared. She said, "I don't want you to bring this up again, okay?" I nodded. Terrance got in the car and kissed her, his black mustache covering her pink lips.

She was already pregnant with Noah.

I pull off an A on my next algebra test but my overall grade is not so good. None of my grades are up to Tammy's standards or my own. With Sam around, Tammy and I no longer run errands or go shopping or take walks. She does those things with Sam. So far, I haven't heard them having sex, though my brain often plays a radio show of Mom and Terrance's late-night rendezvous as a cruel sort of preparation.

All I do is lie in bed wrapped in my blue Macy's comforter and wool throws, reading about lives that aren't mine, preferably lives that take place in warm locales. I browse Tammy's bookshelves like they're my own personal library, choose titles like *Siddhartha*, *Like Water for Chocolate*, *Fahrenheit 451*—anything that sounds interesting—and devour each in a few days. Sometimes Dean's voice narrates the books in my head, and his soothing inflections make the stories better.

The live Dean continues to play with my hair in class, and one day I tell him I have a C. He says, "How is that possible?"

"I never do my homework."

"Why not?" he says. "This stuff is cake for you."

My eyes fill up halfway and threaten to run before I can stop them so I wipe at my left eye like I have something in it. Sam's insistence that hats can replace the heater is making my scholarship dreams harder to reach. Even in the house my fingers are too cold-stiff to write English essays or math problems, and Tammy and Sam giggling together downstairs makes it impossible to concentrate. Now that I never miss class, I'm behind on take-home assignments. It'd be funny if it weren't my future.

"Maybe we can do it together sometime," he says. I nod three times, unable to maneuver my mouth. He fidgets with his pencil. "Do you want to hang out after school tomorrow? It's discount movie day downtown."

Yes, of course, yes. The bell rings. "Yeah," I say and manage to smile at him.

"Great," he says, putting notebooks and books into his backpack.

"Great," I say.

I write to Rachel in biology, *I think I have a date. It's the British guy with the sexy accent. He's a junior and totally cute.*

Biology is the only class I have an A in right now. I got 104 percent on the last test without studying at all. Today we are learning about viruses.

"We would call viruses intelligent if they were alive," Mrs. Rayler says. She has tons of energy and a tendency to repeat herself, which is why I can only half-pay attention and still do well. She also doesn't believe in homework. Mrs. Rayler continues and I write to Rach, *Terrance is like a virus. He latches on to vulnerable cells and reproduces but we cannot call him intelligent. I can't believe I'm going out with an older guy.*

When I get to the condo, it's still early afternoon but Sam and Tammy are watching a movie. Since Sam arrived, Tammy has often rearranged her schedule.

"Hi kiddo," Tammy says as I take off my boots and coat.

"It's cold in here," I say. The fake fireplace churns little blue flames tipped with orange, but the warmth only radiates about four inches. I sit down next to Tammy on the couch and pull the throw over me. "I had a good day today." I rub my hands together. "I think I even have a date tomorrow."

"That's great," she says.

"He's British," I say and she smiles. "He has the coolest accent and he invited me to a movie." Sam turns up the sound on the TV.

"Where did you meet him?"

"He's in my math class, he's—"

"Oh, for God's sake, would you two please quit your yapping?" Sam says. He turns the sound up on the TV to almost max.

I say, "You talk all the time when I'm trying to watch TV."

Sam's eyes go wide. He says, "The difference is, I live here."

The air is ripped from my lungs like he punched me in the chest. I can't breathe for a second as I wait for Tammy's reaction.

This is it. This is when she'll have to make a choice, and my history of being in this position tells my gut to get ready to leave.

"Sam," Tammy says, surprise and irritation in her voice like a mom who witnesses her child do something she just forbade. "She lives here, too."

My ribs relax and I almost burst into tears. I didn't expect her to stand up for me. I start to smile until I see Sam glaring at me from under the dark brim of his hat. His brown eyes squint with loathing and I can't figure out what I did to earn it. He shifts his glower to Tammy and she sucks in a quick breath like she's been slapped.

Sam turns his head back to the TV, a black-and-white film I don't recognize. He says, "For now."

Tammy stays quiet this time and I'm smart enough not to say anything. I visualize Sam's giant hat-covered head bursting like a firecracker, the tattered brim floating down from the blast to rest on his bloody stump of a neck as my own throat clenches and my eyes burn.

"Let's talk later," Tammy whispers. She keeps her eyes trained down at her lily pad pajama pants. She pats my leg and her hand is icy. She says quietly, "I'm glad you had a good day." Her thin hair hides her face and she still doesn't look at me as I spread the purple blanket across her knees and disappear from the room like a ghost.

Upstairs I put my hat and gloves on and shiver under my blankets until the warmth spreads out across my skin. Tammy and Sam laugh downstairs and I know that Sam is her other favorite person on this planet and that if it came down to choosing, she would pick him. I wouldn't blame her. I am not her daughter.

When the movie ends, Tammy comes upstairs. "Hey, kiddo," she says and sits on the edge of my bed. "You warm enough?"

I stare out the window where it's getting dark outside, the gray-blue sky turning purple, shadows rolling across the red brick and white wood of the condos behind us. She says, "I want to apologize." I roll over and look at her. "For Sam's nastiness earlier." I sit up and pull my comforter around me. "He's used to having things a certain way," she says. She pauses. "He's not used to kids."

"He's condescending," I say.

"He's trying to talk to you," she says.

"He lectures."

"He's pretty smart, you know," she says.

"He always wears that stupid vest," I say.

She laughs and hugs me. When she lets go, she puts a hand on each of my shoulders and lifts them up so I'm sitting fully upright. "That vest was a gift from me for our first overnight backpacking trip together," she says, smiling. "I think it looks good on him, even if it's a little aged." She kisses my forehead. "Just like us."

She pulls her arms away and rests them in her lap. Her fingers are long, thin. Like me and Jaime, Mom and Tammy don't have many childhood photos, but there is one framed in the hallway here of Tammy playing piano. She's outside in a garden, wearing a pale green dress and a matching ribbon in her hair. At sixteen her skin is smoother and lighter but her face looks exactly the same. Her fingers look at home on the white keys, perfectly posed and just the right length.

"Elizabeth," she says. "I know Sam can be difficult. And I will talk to him about being nicer to you, but we've been together a long time and he is not used to sharing me. Since he's only here for a little while, I was hoping you—"

"I'll stay out of the way," I say.

Tammy says, "That's not necessary." But she looks relieved. "And I will talk to him about his . . ."

"Jerkiness?"

"Severity," she says. She hugs me again and smiles. "I love you," she says.

I say, "I love you, too." But I know firsthand what people do to those they love.

She tugs on the ties that hang from the earflaps of the hat I'm wearing. "Dinner soon," she says, pulling the hat down into my eyes and pushing lightly on my head. She laughs and it's a sound I haven't heard in a while.

I fall over onto the bed and lie there, wishing we could go back to before Sam showed up, when Saturday mornings were about us together, hanging out in our pajamas and eating homemade waffles, cracking up at games like Read My Lips or slapjack, when Tammy seemed lighter. Now she walks on tiptoes with her shoulders stooped, like at any moment something could jump out and attack.

"Tammy?" I say and then decide not to ask because I don't want to know the answer to a question that's still only a possibility. She stood up for me today. I haven't lost her yet.

She says, "Yes?"

I smile and push my hat up out of my eyes. "Thanks," I say. Tammy smiles back and squeezes my hand. She gets up and leaves me huddled under the blankets in the darkening grayish-purple light from the window, wondering about the day Sam forces her to answer the question I was too afraid to ask.

As I hop off the bus onto Tammy's street the next day, the mountaintops gleam like frosted cupcakes, and the sun shines so bright off the snow it hurts my eyes. I hum a Lisa Loeb song as I skip up Tammy's steps and unlock the door. I haven't stopped grinning stupidly since my bus turned a corner and Dean's waving figure and the mall where we'd spent the afternoon disappeared. We ate sour candy straws from the Sweet Factory and played Super Off Road and Zombie Attack at the arcade. We made fun of eighty-dollar T-shirts in brand-name stores and the girls who bought them, and threw pennies into the mall's basement fountain from three floors up. He didn't try to kiss me during the movie, but as we watched the scene in *Fargo* when the wife runs around in the snow in her pink jumpsuit with a bag on her head on the big screen, we both laughed so hard that someone shushed us, and it felt like a bonding moment.

"This was fun," Dean said at the bus stop, rubbing his hands together. He looked at his feet, high-top Vans sneakers in navy blue and black. Then he asked for my number. My face got so warm I took off my hat, and I wrote Tammy's number on his hand, his skin as cool as glass.

Now, as I take off my shoes I see the square blue envelope with my name on it in Mom's cursive sitting on the console table next to a note from Tammy that says, *Went for walk.*

I get under my covers with the card from Mom. I know that this envelope probably doesn't contain any of the things I wish she'd say to me, but for a few minutes I let myself imagine what it might feel like to hear them, to go home. Then I lift the baby-blue flap and pull out an invitation. A confetti-spotted, balloon-covered, store-bought invitation to Noah's third birthday party. To be held at the Delacruz residence, *Lunch will be served,* the address and relevant information written in Terrance's slanted loops that make me flash back to his letters under Mom's nightstand.

Mom's round writing in purple ink covers the opposite side of the card: *Elizabeth, I hope you'll come to your brother's birthday celebration. It won't be the same without you. Noah asks about you all the time. We miss you. Love, Mom.* My fingers tremble as I stare at the happy greens and golds of the balloons, the cobalt party hats and crimson confetti and Mom's cursive until the shades blur together like watercolors.

6

A few days later on the phone Jaime says, "This is bullshit." She received her invitation in the mail, too. "We never got parties like this."

"We never even got invitations like this," I say. "Are you going?" Tammy said I could go home for Noah's party if I want. She said she'd pay for the plane ticket, and I could stay all of spring break or just for the weekend, but I'm not sure yet. I don't want to sleep at Dad's.

"Duh," Jaime says. "He's my brother."

I hear a crash that sounds like a pile of tin cans falling on cement in the background. "Is everything okay?"

"Crystal and Dad have been fighting lately," she says. "He used her credit card at a bar."

"What an idiot," I say. "It's like he's trying to get caught."

"He says we don't need her," Jaime says and alarm bells scream warnings in my brain. He always needs someone to pick up his slack, and he's not actually an idiot. He must have a plan to take advantage of somebody. I just hope it's not Jaime. "Are you going to Noah's party?" she says.

"You know not to get in the car with him—"

"I know, I know," she says. "I'm not stupid."

"I didn't say you were stupid."

She sucks her thumb and I hear yelling behind her. The shrill in Crystal's voice is nothing like my mom's quiet pleading, but my dad's deep throaty grumbles sound exactly the same and I have to shake my head to remind myself that I am no longer five years old, shivering and afraid in a cramped apartment bathroom, holding my small hands over Jaime's tiny ears. I say, "How's school?"

There is a crash that sounds like shattering glass and cracking wood. "Shit, I gotta go," she says.

"No, wait—"

"I'll call you later," she says and hangs up.

My mind spins through possibilities for that sound: a baseball bat smashing car windows, splintering dishes and cabinets, broken lamps and bones. Dad versus Crystal is sure to be unpredictable, and even if Jaime isn't a direct target, without me, there's no one to protect her from the crossfire. I dial Crystal's number, knowing no one will answer and hoping I'm wrong. It rings and rings of course, and my hand folds into a fist around the plastic receiver.

Sam walks into the living room just as the panic in my muscles skyrockets and I hurl the phone at Tammy's couch. My eyes sting with tears and I try to go up the stairs but he stands on the bottom step, looking down at me from six inches higher than normal. I can see the little brown hairs lining his nostrils as they flare out.

He says, "I think more respect for property would be appropriate here."

"Sorry," I say.

"Especially when that property is not yours," he says and steps off the last step, forcing me back. "You should always consider the consequences of your actions, child."

"I'm sorry," I repeat and try to walk past him but he's blocking the stairs. I feel the heat in my face, the red blotchiness in my skin. I look at the floor, the tiny spots of color in the weave of the white carpet, specks of green and pink and blue scattered like tossed seeds. I think of Jaime and me tossing peanuts to squirrels once while Dad slept off a hangover on a park bench. We shelled the nuts and ate them for dinner as the sun set and all the other families went home.

"I believe a lesson in responsibility is in order. Maybe you should take notes." He smiles and launches into his lecture, and I have to bite my lips to keep the scream in my throat from escaping. He stares down at me like a judge giving bad news, his big hands in the pockets of the old orange vest, all of his tanned wrinkles and condescending brown eyes creating a barricade.

He wouldn't care that Jaime is in danger, but I have to do something. "I just want to go to my room," I say, opening my mouth as little as possible and staring at the not entirely white carpet. I'm not sure exactly how to guard Jaime from two states away, but listening to Sam is not helping.

I interrupted him, and he pauses before he says, "*Your* room?"

"Yes," I say.

"*Your* room?" He snorts. "I think maybe we also need to discuss the idea of ownership and the methods by which—"

"Please just let me go up the stairs."

"Will there be more throwing?"

I close my eyes and wish I could tap my heels together and be home. Except I'm not sure where home is right now so maybe the ruby slippers wouldn't work. If they could take me to Jaime, I'd use them in a second. I swallow the storm in my mouth. "No," I say without separating my teeth. "Can I go upstairs now?"

Sam moves a little and I squeeze past him and take the steps two at a time. I shut the door and bury myself in blankets and clothes and everything soft and warm I can find in this room that I know really isn't mine though I don't think I'd call it Sam's, either. I burrow under the pile of fabric and release silent wails into the fold-out mattress.

There were few things my dad kept good care of, but one of them was the sunset-colored Ford Pinto he had when we were little and he still lived with us. He called the car his Orange Julius and on weekends he hauled out buckets and sponges and let us help him scrub it into tip-top shape. It was the only chore he did without Mom asking, and he couldn't hold a beer at the same time. He turned up the oldies station and danced around in his flip-flops with Jaime and me. He squirted us with the hose if it was warm, and we ran around dripping with suds, slinging soapy bubbles at each other in the apartment parking lot and laughing. Together, we rinsed and polished and sang and giggled until the Pinto was shiny and we needed baths.

Late one night when I was supposed to be asleep, I heard Dad's keys jingle for five minutes outside the front door. He yelled, "Linda, God damn it," and Mom unlocked the bolt. Shaking, he told her he'd been mugged at a stoplight, that the two-inch bleeding gash on his forehead was from the carjacker's tire iron. He said he'd fought off the punk kid with a can of pork and beans.

"He got all my cash," Dad said. He grinned. "But you should see his face."

Mom stood in a blue cotton nightgown with her bare feet planted shoulder width apart, her arms crossed above her breasts. "Where's the car?" she said.

"I think I need stitches." Blood ran over the moles on his left cheek, dripped off his chin into his cupped palm. "I'm bleeding."

Mom said, "How much did you spend?"

Dad wiped at the blood in his eyes, and she plucked his faded brown wallet from the back pocket of his jeans. Mom opened the wallet and then threw the leather folds at him. "There's nothing left," she said.

Dad pressed a Wendy's napkin to his forehead. "It's my money," he said and sat at the kitchen table where I could barely see him from the crack between door and door frame. Behind me in our room, Jaime slept on her side, her thumb in her mouth, her stuffed polar bear tucked under her chin.

Mom punched her left palm with her right fist. "Tell me what you hit, David."

"I got mugged," he said. "Can't you see I'm hurt?"

Mom took two steps forward and I could only see her back, her solid feet, and thick calves. "Did you drive the car home?" she said. "You promised you wouldn't hurt your precious 'Julius.'"

Dad dabbed at his forehead with the napkin. His pale hands were trailed with drying brown blood. He sighed. "How did you know?"

"Oh, please, David," Mom said, shaking her head.

He flipped her off and slumped in his chair. "At least I didn't hurt our children," he said.

"Because I don't let them drive with you." Mom picked up Dad's keys from where he'd dropped them by the door. She turned to him. "You better hope it starts."

He scoffed at her. "Or what?"

I closed our bedroom door, tiptoed to the window, and looked out into the black night, at the black asphalt parking lot below. The Pinto sat under a streetlamp, the driver's window smashed, the front bumper crunched and facing the sky more than the road.

Then Mom appeared like a cloud, standing next to the scratched paint and twisted metal in her blue robe and white slippers. She pulled Dad's keys from her terry cloth pocket and got in the car. The engine revved for a minute in the darkness and then she rested her forehead against the steering wheel and turned it off. When she lifted her head, her face a round, white orb, silvery streaks ran down the high cheekbones I'd inherited. Then she was hitting the steering wheel with her hands open, her palms slamming the hard plastic over and over. Her body rocked in the seat, her hair whipped her closed eyes and open mouth that seemed to be screaming even though I couldn't hear her voice.

Before Dad woke up in the morning, we had packed a few changes of clothes, toothbrushes, pillows, blankets, and food, and loaded them into the car. Mom had vacuumed out the broken glass, saved the pork and beans, and even found five bucks under Dad's seat. She taped a note to the toilet lid, *David, I have to protect my girls. Please don't do anything you'll regret later. Get clean and we'll talk.* We drove away in his beloved orange car and spent the next year sleeping on couches and in guest bedrooms, wearing the same four outfits, eating whatever food was offered, and moving each time Dad found us.

I'm not sure if my dad regrets, or even remembers, the things he did: ruining mementos, photos, and other things we'd left behind, emptying their joint checking account and cancelling Mom's credit cards, threatening Mom's friends and breaking neighbors' windows, but eight years later he's still not sober, and Jaime and I are back to living in other people's houses, except this time we're separated and by ourselves. I have a million regrets.

In two hours Jaime still hasn't called and Tammy is not yet home from work. I call Crystal's number for the sixteenth time and let it ring twenty times before hanging up. Her whole life, Jaime has rarely been alone with Dad and now she lives with the man who knocked her down an escalator, broke her finger in a slammed door, and burned her with a barbecue skewer. If those things could happen while Mom or I were around, who knows what kind of "accidents" I've abandoned her to suffer without me. I need to know she's okay.

Sam is downstairs listening to NPR on the boom box in the kitchen and cooking, which means we're either having pork chops or fried eggs on English muffins. I call Mom.

"Hello?" She almost yells the word and I hear electronic buzzing and live drums in the background.

"What's going on over there?"

"Jaime?"

"It's Liz. Have you heard from Jaime?"

"Terrance and his friends are jamming," she says.

"Where's Noah?"

"He loves watching Terrance play," and the next thing she says is drowned in guitar squeal. I hear, "Let me switch phones," and then when she is back on, the ringing in my ears is louder than the background noise.

"Jamming?" I say. "What is he, fifteen?"

"What do you want, Liz?"

"Have you heard from Jaime?"

"Not for a few days."

"Crystal found out Dad's been drinking."

"That's too bad," she says.

"On the phone tonight I heard a crash and then Jaime had to go and now no one is answering."

"I'm sure everything is fine. You know your dad."

"Yeah, that's why I'm worried."

Mom sighs. "You're always worried," she says. "It's not healthy."

"Mom, please, if you could just go over to Crystal's and make sure the house isn't burning down or something—"

"Don't be so dramatic." I hear a drumroll and Terrance yells, "Awesome!" over the amped chords. Mom says, "Someone would notify me if something really bad happened."

I feel like the adult as I say, "If you went over there, you might be able to *stop* something bad from happening, so you wouldn't *have* to be notified."

"She'll be fine," Mom says. "Have a little faith."

"Faith won't make Dad sober," I say.

"Neither will giving up your sleep and your sanity to agonize over the what-ifs, Elizabeth," Mom snaps. "You can live your whole life in fear and one day you fall asleep early or go out of town and your daughter comes home with a new injury."

I'm stunned. "But what about all the times you stopped us from getting hurt?" I say. "When you were there . . ." I think of Mom's strong stance in the face of Dad's cocked fists, her solid body blockade against flung plates and glasses, her sleepless nights spent next to our beds singing soft lullabies, rubbing our backs, and stroking our faces each time he pummeled the locked door. "It would have been so much worse without you."

A squeaky guitar solo lasts too long over a bass line that loses its beat. "Liz," Mom says, her voice softer. "You can't keep a constant eye on Jaime. Just like I couldn't constantly check on you girls, even when I tried. At some point, you have to learn that no matter what you do—call his friends, drive over in the middle of the night to keep watch, demand that waitresses tell you how many drinks he's had—none of it is useful in the end." She pauses and I picture her squeezing her eyes shut, scrunching up her face, and pinching the bridge of her nose the way she does when she doesn't want to confront some fact. She must have so many memories of Dad that I can't even imagine. That she protected us from. "You can't control the world," she says. "You have to give yourself permission to let go."

"I could never let her go," I whisper.

"I'm sure everything is fine," Mom repeats, clearing her throat. "Now, did Tammy book a flight for you?" she says, her voice brighter. "I'd really like you to come visit, but with the party, I can't afford to bring you here."

"Terrance still doesn't have a job?"

She says, "I sang with him and his friends last night." She hums a little tune. "It was awesome," she says all slow and breathy like a starstruck teen. I'm just about to ask if she's been drinking when the live music jumps in volume and Terrance yells, "Babe, Noah is crying."

Mom says, "Where's Noah at?" I cringe at her use of Terrance's poor grammar, and don't hear the rest of their exchange over the vibrations. "Gotta go," she says clearly into the phone, loud enough to beat the speakers. I want to ask about Jaime again but Mom says, "Don't worry. Love you. See you soon," and hangs up. It's fine, I guess, because I would have had to scream for her to hear me, and I'm tired of putting in the effort when she doesn't listen anyway.

My bathroom at Tammy's is white and gold: gold faucets and fixtures, gold-rimmed glass shower doors. White tiles line the floor and the counter is a silvery-white marble laced with strands of gold swirl. Tammy bought me a countertop organizer to hold Q-tips and ChapStick and makeup that I use every day, but by the time I leave in the morning it's all out, covering the gold swirls. Now as I wait for the phone to ring and Jaime to tell me she's not dead, I put my deodorant and toothpaste back in the drawer, toss tissues with my glossy lip print and mascara smudges, and set my moisturizer and zit cream in the organizer.

At home I kept my stuff in my room. Jaime would steal

anything I left in the bathroom: eye shadows and compacts, perfume, my silver spider necklace. Once she asked to borrow my favorite beaded bracelet after I caught her wearing it out the door. I'd strung together little silver spheres and shiny triangular black beads that turned purple, blue, and yellow when rotated in the light. It took three hours sitting cross-legged on the floor of my room to get it perfect and Jaime lost it. She cried when she told me it was gone but I hit her anyway. She said, "I'm sorry," and put her hand up to block her face, and I shoved her shoulders hard against the wall, left her crying in the hallway, and didn't speak to her for days. I never apologized.

I hear Tammy's voice through the vent in the white tiles. If the heater isn't on, which with Sam around it hardly is, I can listen to whatever is happening downstairs. I sit on the green toilet lid cover as Tammy says, "If Liz leaves for the week, we can go to Moab."

"Or," Sam says and she makes a little "oh" noise. He's probably grabbed her ass like he does sometimes when he thinks I'm not watching. Tammy always blushes. "We could have the house to ourselves," he says. "No emotional teenagers."

She sighs. "What happened?"

"She threw the phone."

"At you?"

"At the couch."

"Was it Linda?"

Sam pounds something, a pan, a bowl. "How should I know? She practically pushed me out of the way and ran upstairs."

Tammy says, "Is she okay?" and my heart swells that she would think of my well-being first.

"Why wouldn't she be? She runs this house."

"Don't start," she says.

Sam says, "I don't want her here this summer."

"Are you even going to be here this summer?"

"That's not the point."

"Stop," Tammy says. "She's important to me."

They are so quiet I can hear sizzling. Probably pork chops.

"How long?" Sam says after a few minutes.

"As long as she needs me," she says.

"You are not her mother."

"That's right," she snaps. "Thanks to you I am not a mother."

"You're a beautiful, intelligent, successful woman," Sam says. "Why does this keep coming up?"

"What makes you think it ever leaves?"

"How many years has it been, Tammy? Isn't it enough—"

"I like having her here."

Sam sighs. "What about how I feel?"

"It's always about how you feel," Tammy whispers.

"Don't you care about our life together?" he says.

"My life is here even when you're not," she says. The heater kicks on, and the rest of their conversation is lost in a warm blast of air from the vent.

Later, I'm sitting on the bathroom floor and crying when Tammy knocks on the door. "Are you okay?" she says.

"It's warmer in the bathroom," I say. In this small space filled up with hot air from the vent I don't even need a blanket. The green bath mats are cushy and cleaner than the carpet at Mom's house.

"Can I come in?" she says and opens the door. "Liz," she says when she sees me, "get off the floor." She helps me stand, brushes off the butt of my flannel pants. She shoos me into my room. "What are you doing?"

I crawl under my blankets. "I was cleaning."

"What's wrong?" she says and sits next to me on the bed. I tuck my covers under my legs. She says, "Did you talk to your mom?"

I tell her about Jaime and Mom, and Tammy promises to fly to Sacramento herself and check on Jaime if we don't hear from her in a few days.

"Thanks," I say and hug her. "I'm really worried," I whisper in her ear.

She squeezes me tighter. "Now you know how I felt all those years your mother was with your dad," she says.

"You worried about us?"

"Yes," she says, letting go of me, her eyes fixed on a spot in space. "Your father was a dangerous man."

"He still is," I say. "That's why I need to make sure Jaime is okay."

Tammy shakes her head, her short, brown hair barely moving. "You'd feel it in your gut if something was really wrong," she says. She puts her hands on her abs.

"My gut always feels like there's something wrong," I say.

Tammy grasps my shoulders and looks at me, her shiny blue irises like I imagine mine will look in twenty years when I'm too old to cry so much. "You have to train your body to make peace with the constant wrongs," she says. "The mistakes, the regrets, the continuing reminders, you have to let them breathe or you'll go crazy." Her fingers tighten around my arms as she speaks, and I wonder how many regrets and reminders she still lives with.

I nod. "I'll try," I say and her fingers relax.

"Good." Tammy clears her throat and lets go of me with a weak half-smile. "Sam and I may be going to Moab the week you're at your mom's," she says. "You do still want to go, right?"

"I guess." I want to see Jaime and Noah.

Sam yells, "Soup's on!"

I say, "I'm not really hungry."

She stands up. "There are always going to be things in your life that you can't change," she says, her long fingers weaving together like she's tying and untying a knot. "You're going to have to learn to deal with problems, face them wearing all your armor," she says. "Wasting away under the blankets doesn't punish them." She reaches out and lifts my chin between her thumb and forefinger. "You're stronger than that, little girl," she says softly and walks across the landing to her room.

I wonder if she's crying but she flushes the toilet and runs the water in her bathroom, the same gold and white as mine but twice as big. Then she's at the edge of my bed, pulling the covers off my feet.

She says, "You'd be warmer if you ate."

"I don't want to be fat," I say. "I'd rather wear a hat in the house than look like my mother."

"I'll have to tell Sam you're taking his hat advice," Tammy says. "He'll be so proud." I narrow my eyes at her and sink into the bed. She laughs. "Just kidding," she says and yanks the whole pile of blankets off. She offers me her hands. "Now, get up."

———

We drove the sunset-orange Pinto up through Petaluma to Deborah's house the morning after Dad crashed it. Pink light shone at the horizon when Deborah answered the door in her robe and slippers. Mom said, "I'm so sorry to barge in like this."

"Nonsense, you're family," Deborah said, rubbing her eyes. "My brother is a fool."

"You should see the car," Mom said. "Thank God it still drove."

Deborah said, ushering us in, "Thank God he didn't have the girls."

For months Mom read self-help books about codependence and breaking the cycle of abuse. At Deborah's insistence, she went to three Al-Anon meetings a week and came back repeating slogans like, *Easy Does It, Courage to Change,* and *Let Go and Let God.*

Deborah taped butcher paper to the wall for the three of us kids to draw on. Jaime and I shared a bed and played with Ashley's expensive toys. She had a motorized car, an interactive computer word game, more books than I could count, and dozens of dolls. Deborah got Mom a job as a receptionist at a clinic and we were saving up money to get our own place. After a few months Mom's skin looked less gray, and Jaime didn't need me to sing to her so she could fall asleep.

One rainy afternoon Jaime and I were playing in the clinic's waiting area and Dad walked in. His orange hair was wet, his brown leather jacket spotted dark at the shoulders. He wore jeans and flip-flops and he said, "Hey, girls. Did you miss your daddy?"

"Dad!" Jaime said and flew into his arms, but I knew why Mom went to those meetings and I stayed where I was, LEGO block still in hand, poised above our growing spaceship. Mom was in the other room and all I had to do was call for her and she'd be here in a second, hair waving behind her as she stampeded over our father like Superwoman, but I just stared at him, smiling with our dimples in his cheeks, his blue eyes like falling into clear sky. He came over and hugged me and he didn't have the stale metallic scent that came with the sharp voice and yelling.

He grinned at us, turning his head from side to side to look at his daughters cradled in each of his arms. "Let's go have some fun," he said.

"We can't get in a car with you," I said.

"No problemo," he said. "We'll walk. I saw a park down the street."

"It's raining," Jaime said.

Dad said, "It just makes the slides faster," and he ran down the block. Jaime's face radiated hope as she waited for my nod and then she chased after him, laughing. I grabbed our coats from the donated plaid couch, abandoned our LEGO alien cruiser, and hoped Mom would understand.

She found us at the park a few hours later, just as the sun was glowing at the horizon. We had swung on swings and kicked up puddles, slid down wet slides into mud pits like quicksand. "Help, Dad, please," we cried. "Save us before the pirates come." He lifted us out and our feet made a sucking sound as they popped free from the sludge that made us all laugh and we scrambled onto the plastic ship.

"Scrub the deck, you scabbers," Dad said.

"Head east!" I called. "Hoist the flags!"

"Watch out for toothy, there," Dad said. "He's the captain's favorite fish."

"Land ahoy!" Jaime called. "Mom's here."

"Land ho," Dad said.

"Elizabeth? Jaime?" Mom was running now. "Girls? Are you all right?"

Dad jumped off the playground platform and said, "They're fine, Linda."

"David, I've called the police," she said. "Girls, come here."

"We're okay, Mom," I said.

"You're filthy," she said. "It's winter. David, what were you thinking?"

"I brought our coats," I said.

Mom said, "You need help, David." She took little steps back and pushed us behind her. Under all the brown on Jaime's face, her lips looked blue. I shivered and pulled Jaime close.

"They're my kids, too," he said. "I miss them."

Mom said, "I won't let you hurt them." We kept backing up.

He looked down at us. "You girls know Daddy would never hurt you, right?" He smiled but it was strained. He glared at Mom. "Why are you trying to scare them?"

"Liz, get Jaime in the car," Mom said. I put my arm around Jaime's shoulders and opened the car door, but we both stood and watched our parents.

"That's my car," Dad said, stuffing his hands into his jeans pockets. "You stole it."

"Do you want to talk about all my things you stole?" Mom said, her voice rising. "Or trashed or sold or destroyed?"

"Hey, come on," Dad said. "I just wanted to see my daughters." His blue eyes shone in the darkening afternoon light.

Mom said, "Girls, get in the car, now."

Dad's eyebrows creased. Tears slipped out of his squinted eyes. "Please, Linda," he said. "Can't I at least hug them good-bye?"

Dad begged with his eyes. Mom rolled hers and said, "Fine."

He kneeled and opened his arms. Jaime darted into him as fast as she could. Dad kissed her head and squeezed her until she groaned. "Daddy bear hug," he said. "The biggest of them all."

She wrapped her short arms around his neck and said, "Baby bear hug."

He loosened his grip on Jaime to let me into the embrace. His pungent Old Spice scent was strong, and as he held us he repeated, "I love you, girls. Don't you forget that. Daddy loves you so much."

"We love you, too, Dad," Jaime said.

"All right, that's enough," Mom said. One hot tear dripped off Dad's chin and landed on my cheek before he let us go.

Mom shut us into the backseat and got in the orange car whose bumper still faced skyward and whose tires still made a scraping sound when they turned right.

"You can't do this, you bi—" Dad said, standing up and balling his hands into fists.

She started the engine. "Good-bye, David."

"No, wait," he said and pressed his palms to the glass window. "No, please, I'm sorry," he said. Mom didn't look at him. Jaime cried as I buckled her seat belt. He moved to our window and peered in. He smiled at us. "I'll see you girls again soon," he said. Mom rolled forward. "This isn't fair." He pounded his pale fist on the hood as we moved out of his reach. "I'll find you again!"

I imagined my dad still standing there on the wet grass, rain clearing spots in the mud on his jacket and on his face long after we had rushed back to Deborah's, showered, packed our few belongings, and were driving again in the dark on unlit, two-lane country roads.

Jaime doesn't call the next day and I turn down an invitation from Dean to go to the mall after school so I can sit by Tammy's white cordless phone picking at my cuticles and thinking of all the ways Dad could hurt my sister. All the ways he already has. I peel squishy strips of flesh from around my nails and watch as red liquid fills the gullies left by the missing skin. I suck the blood from my fingers and remember four-year-old Jaime on the bank of a dark green river with a grimy silver fishhook stuck through the rose-colored sole of her foot. The damp air smelled like wet metal, mud, and rotting plants. The sky was dark sapphire in between cotton puffs of light gray clouds tumbling in the wind. Our dad held Jaime's small heel in one hand and gripped the hook with the other. His blue eyes narrowed and he said, "This is going to sting."

Jaime screamed as he twisted the barbs free and her skin broke. Blood spurted out over his hands and the grainy wet sand around them. He tied a bandana around her foot and said, "There." His face was pallid, his skin fleshy and bloated, glistening with sweat as he rinsed his hands in the slow-moving green water. On his knees he crawled toward his fire-truck-red ice chest. Jaime whimpered, her foot covered in dirt and a bloody brown do-rag, her face streaked with sandy fingerprints and salt. I reached for her shoulders and she curled into my chest and cried, wiping her face all over my Strawberry Shortcake T-shirt.

"It hurts," she said, and I squeezed her hand.

Dad opened a beer as I rocked Jaime back and forth in the mud of the riverbank, something I've done a thousand times since that day. Dad leaned his head back, exposing his soft white neck to the darkening sky to take a sip, and said one of the few true things he ever told us. "It always hurts."

Sam doesn't talk to me at dinner, even when I make slurping noises with my pasta. It's in a lemon cream sauce Tammy made from scratch and it is so good I almost don't care that I can't feel my toes. Sam doesn't say anything at all until Tammy tells me she's booked my flight home, and that I'll stay the whole week.

"Where am I going to sleep?" I say. "Is Terrance leaving?"

"I'm sure your mom will figure something out," she says and smiles at Sam. I recognize the making-nice look from Mom's face. One of the few things they have in common, apparently. "I booked us a flight, too."

"Is that so?" Sam says, raising his eyebrows. "To where?"

"Hawaii."

"You're going to Hawaii?" I say.

"Sounds perfect," Sam says. He wipes his lips with his blue

cloth napkin before he kisses her but I still want to throw up. If my napkin were paper, it would be in shreds.

After another school day of worrying I get a letter from Rachel that says she'll be in Reno for spring break. *My mom says hi, and remember to focus your breathing. She says your mom is creating major karma with you that'll even out in another life. I told her that doesn't do jack shit for you right now.* She writes about her newest boyfriend, Frank, who is seventeen and drives a brown Ford pickup in which she let him feel her up in the front seat. She writes, *Did you and Dean make out yet?* I wish.

Jaime calls as I finish reading. As soon as she says hello, I say, "Are you okay?" but it's such a relief to hear her voice.

"We might be moving out," Jaime says. "Me and Dad spent the last two nights at Steve's."

"Because Dad's drinking?"

"And 'cause he lied about a bunch of stuff." She sighs. "Crystal thought he was the one making dinner and cleaning until she came home early one day."

"Is he looking for a job?"

"Not yet."

"Then how can you move out?"

"I don't know," Jaime says. "Geez, lay off the third degree."

"Aren't you worried?"

"I have you for that."

I say, "Why are you whispering?"

"I'm not supposed to call long distance."

"I can call you back," I say. "Give me the number."

"We can talk at Noah's party," she says. "Mom said we can spend the weekend."

"You talked to her?"

"Yeah, she kept calling while we were gone so Crystal finally told her where we were. Not in a nice way though." She laughs. "Mom wouldn't repeat what she said."

"Of course not," I say, but I'm thankful. *At least she called.* "Are you really all right?"

She says, "Are you?"

I smile. She's definitely not stupid. "I love you," I say.

A few weeks later, I tell Tammy I want to go to Hawaii as she puts her toiletry bag together: Handi Wipes, Band-Aids, shampoo, toothpaste, floss. "I love the beach," I say.

"We're hiking in the jungle."

"The whole time?"

"When Sam leaves, you and I can go on a trip, okay?" Tammy seals plastic baggies around each bottle containing liquid and then puts them all in one big plastic Ziploc. Her lace-up trail shoes sit in a grocery bag, her sunscreens in another Ziploc.

I say, "Can it be a no-hiking trip?"

"Are you packed?" Tammy selects earrings from her wooden jewelry box and wraps them in a little cloth pouch.

"I don't want to go home."

She stops folding L.L.Bean T-shirts and REI khaki shorts with pockets galore, and looks at me.

I say, "Every time I think about Terrance, I get sick to my stomach." The iron smell of his breath, the slick feel of his fingers, the throaty groans he makes—things I shouldn't know at all.

Tammy finishes folding and sighs. "Me, too," she says. She sits down next to me on her bed, the leaf-print bedspread fluffing between us, and drapes her arm around my shoulders.

I lean my head into her warm chest. "And you know how Mom changes her mind," I say. "What if she won't let us stay with her?"

Tammy kisses the crown of my head and stands up. "You can't worry about things that may or may not happen." She kneels and rummages through a drawer in the side of her bed frame. "You just have to deal with whatever comes."

I wring my hands together. "How?" I say. I sound so young I'm not sure it's my voice that comes out of my mouth.

Tammy stops poking through patterned Lycra and pats my knee. "You trust your instincts," she says. "And call me if he does anything"—she pauses and stares into space like she can pluck the appropriate word from the air—"creepy," she says.

I mutter, "He's always creepy."

She cocks her head to the side. "You'd tell me, or someone, if he was ever . . . inappropriate with you, right?"

I think of all the ways he's been inappropriate, but Tammy means illegally. I nod.

"Good," she says, clearly happy to be changing subjects. "Now, which suit?" She holds up a flowery green-and-black one-piece swimsuit with the sides cut out and a racerback two-piece with orange stripes.

"Why not ask me?" Sam says, appearing in Tammy's bedroom

doorway. "Oh, definitely the black," he says and swoops Tammy up in his arms. She doesn't squeal like Mom but her long arms go around his shoulders and she smiles with all her teeth. I disappear as promised.

Sam and Tammy leave for Hawaii the next morning. They hold hands walking through the gate; just another couple on vacation in their linen pants and button-up shirts. I spend my flight to Sacramento visualizing myself with toes buried in white sand, lounging next to palm trees with the glinting sapphire blue of the ocean stretching forever in front of me.

As my plane descends into California's Central Valley, I know the grasslands and meadows, the water-soaked rice fields, the tree-lined streets, and squat foothills of home will be visible soon. The early evening sun sits low in the sky, and from the plane it looks close enough to touch. It glows a deep hazy orange, and its outline shimmers on the horizon as the pilot announces we'll be landing in ten minutes. The countryside below is sectioned off in squares of green and brown, with rivers that look like chocolate milk running across the checkerboard farmland. I already know what the air will smell like when we land: earthy dirt and fresh cut grass, silty river mud and wet tree bark, roses and cherry blossoms. Manure, car exhaust, skunk, and sometimes raw sewage are mixed in, too, but it's the smell of home.

7

Terrance's giant Mexican family shows up for Noah's party: his dad and stepmom, Gary and Carol, his aunts, uncles, cousins, and their kids of all ages, his twin half-cousins Jorge and Jose, who have also been locked up, and his grandma Lucero, a seventy-eight-year-old woman who brings her own gallon of gin and says, "No thanks, dear," when my mom offers her anything more than a glass. Terrance grills hamburgers on the barbeque and all his male relatives hold cans of Budweiser, and the women, except Lucero, nurse red plastic cups of gin and tonic. They all have black hair and Noah's tan skin, and I'm not sure how but Mom is as dark-skinned as Jaime and I used to get during summers spent at the apartment pool, and her dirty blond hair doesn't stand out as much as the gold in ours.

Kids from Noah's day care are here, too, two- to five-year-olds, some in diapers, some with parents, all running around the grassy courtyard outside our apartment building. Tablecloths cover the picnic tables and one holds buns, pickles, onions, tomatoes, plastic bottles of ketchup and mustard, and white jars of mayo. Mom's famous potato salad and Gary's special smoked wieners in barbeque sauce sit in bowls next to the sodas and beer on another table. Terrance pulls burgers and hot dogs off the flames and piles them on plates. Mom runs around, herding children, setting up the piñata, asking if anyone needs another drink, accepting invitations to family camping trips and summer concerts. She wears a low V-neck spandex T-shirt and a jean skirt, and smiles her big-toothed, small-lipped smile that looks genuine unless you know her.

We watch her from the table farthest from the barbeque and Jaime says, "When did Mom start wearing tight clothes?"

I say, "You didn't have to see her nightgowns when he first got out."

"Is this a new jacket?" She fingers the foamy black microfiber raincoat Tammy bought for me. It's not a hand-me-down and it fits well. I don't tell her it's from Gap. I shrug. "Salt Lake is cold."

"Dad won't even buy me new underwear." She picks at a hole in the vinyl checkerboard tablecloth. "Too bad Aunt Tammy hates me."

"She doesn't hate you."

"She likes you better," Jaime says. "You're just like her."

"She's your family, too," I say.

"So is Dad."

"Is he looking for a job?"

"He had an interview yesterday," she says. "And we're looking for an apartment downtown where it's cheap." Through the hole in the tablecloth, she scratches at the green paint of the picnic table. Her nails are chewed to the skin like mine. "Dad circles places he can afford, and I call and make appointments."

"How many have you looked at?"

"None yet," Jaime says. She doesn't have to tell me that Dad canceled, or didn't show up, or couldn't drive. "Some sound really cool."

"You really want to live with just him?" I say.

"He said I can have the bedroom and he'll sleep on the couch," she says.

"That's closer to the door," I say.

"You could come, too," she says. "Dad said if you live with us, we can afford a bigger place."

"Does he think I have a job or something?"

She shrugs. "He's still mad you went to Utah," she says. "He says you abandoned us." My nostrils flare. He's not even here and he knows exactly how to get to me.

I almost say, "Is that what you think?" but I don't know if I can handle the answer. I think of my room at Tammy's, my full-sized bed, my glass shower doors, the homemade dinners. After life at Tammy's, even with Sam around, TV dinners and sleeping on crumby couches wouldn't come close to tolerable.

"It wasn't my first choice," I say.

"He said he'd share the child support money with us."

"So that's what he wants," I say. I shake my head, where a little spiral of awareness is churning.

"Dad says you ruined everything," she says. "He said we could have been a family again." She lowers her head. "He says you're being selfish."

"Me?" He's telling Jaime what to say to me so I'll move in with him and he can take money he doesn't deserve from Mom to continue to not take care of his children. I wish Jaime could see how selfish he really is. "Jaime," I say, putting my arm around her shoulder. "He's manipulating you. He just wants cash so he can get away from Crystal."

She shrugs off my embrace. "It's not like I have anywhere else to go," she says, rubbing her eye.

"You could come live with us in Utah," I say. "It would be great to have you there."

"No way," Jaime says. "It's too far."

"Maybe he'll work things out with Crystal," I say. Since his plan for cash failed, there's a good chance he'll try.

"She swung a baseball bat at his head and kneed him in the balls," she says. "Dad's tired of her abuse."

I laugh and Jaime says, "What?"

"Aww," I say. "Poor Dad."

"She's really violent."

I say, "It's his karma for hitting Mom."

"He didn't hit Mom," she says. "She lies."

"She does," I say. "But Dad still beat the shit out of her."

"Whatever," Jaime says and walks toward the apartment neither of us lives in but both call home. I watch the way her hips move, how long her hair is down her back, the blond strands that are darker than mine swaying with each step. She wears makeup now, blue eyeliner and thick mascara Mom would never allow but Crystal encourages. My little sister is almost as tall as I am, her boobs have grown as big as mine in the months we've been separated, and her voice scratches in her throat enough to reveal her smoking habits. Without my protective shadow, she's sprouted like a weed and nearly closed the gap between us. I remember when she couldn't fall asleep without holding my hand; when two years felt like a chasm.

Noah is ripping bright-yellow and baby-blue wrapping paper off boxes of LEGOs and Barney videos when Jaime comes back, reeking of cigarettes. "How obvious can you be?" I say.

"Whatever," she says. "Mom's not paying attention to us." She coughs. "Half these wetbacks smoke, anyway."

My eyes go wide and I say, "Jaime, you shouldn't talk like that."

She laughs. "Dad totally said you'd freak out."

"What an ass."

"You're an ass," she says and laughs again but it turns into a hacking cough.

"That's what you get for smoking," I say.

"At least I have fun sometimes."

Noah opens books and clothes from the now tipsy aunts, a dancing chicken from Grandma Lucero, and from my mom, a lion puppet with a fuzzy mane, a two-foot tail, and big brown eyes. It wears a jean jacket with a gold star on the back and has a hole up its back for the puppeteer. Noah squeezes the furry animal to his chest. "He's into puppets right now," Mom says to the crowd.

"Simba," Noah says.

"Simba!" a few toddlers echo.

"And *The Lion King*," my mom says and laughs.

Lucero yells, "What's a Simba?"

"It's a lion, Grandma Lucero," Terrance says as he picks Noah up and sets him on his shoulders. "You know, the movie." Noah's legs hang over onto Terrance's white sleeveless T-shirt and Terrance howls something that sounds like the opening song from the Disney film, "Hiiiii, yahemaaa!! Yamheeseeshadoo." Noah joins with some "ooohing" and Mom takes a picture. Terrance bows his head and says, "The Delacruz Family Band will be performing again in ten to fifteen years." Chuckles go around the lawn chairs and picnic tables and Terrance says, "Let's eat cake."

After we sing "Happy Birthday," and Noah blows out the candles, and Mom cuts the cake and serves all of our guests before she offers a plate to me or Jaime, I'm sitting on a swing in the playground, finishing my small slice from Raley's bakery. Most of the younger kids and some of the relatives have gone home. Jaime ate her cake and said she needed a cigarette. "Those probably cost more than underwear," I said.

"I didn't say I didn't get new underwear," she said and slipped out a pack of Marlboros from inside the waistband of her jeans. "Dad doesn't pay for these, either," she said and left the sandy area for somewhere more secluded.

I didn't see him approach but suddenly Gary sits in the swing next to me and rocks his Nikes in the sand. His face is thinner; he's lost weight since I saw him last. It must be all the sex. "Hey, Liz," he says. "Good to see ya."

"You, too." I set my paper Barney plate on the ground.

"Listen," he says and I wish he wouldn't. I don't hold anything against him, I know it was Carol, but he says, "I gave your mom a few things you left at our house."

I'm glad he can't see my face. "Thanks."

"And," he says. "You know, I didn't want you to, uh, I mean . . ."

He sighs and runs his hands through his hair. He does not share Terrance's growing bald spot. "Carol is pregnant," he says.

"Congratulations."

"Carol wants a girl," he says. "And if it is, I hope she's like you."

"If I ever move back, I'll come and babysit," I say and he looks up at me, his eyebrows raised. I smile at him, an almost real smile to show him I'm okay.

He nods. "You've got a good head on your shoulders, Liz," he says and stands up. "Rambo misses you."

"I miss him, too."

"He sat outside your door and wagged his stump for days after you left," Gary says and sticks his stubby fingers in the pockets of his jeans. He says, "Well."

"Thanks, Gary," I say.

He nods again. "Yep," he says. "Take care." His head bobs up and down as he turns and walks back to Terrance, the party, his pregnant wife. I think of all the children running around in his family. The fertile Delacruz males—fed on bologna and Kraft Singles, Sunny Delight and cheap beer, the men who sag their sweatpants, who still think poop is funny, and who tell jokes that start, "What's the worst part about bangin' a nigger chick?"—they must squeeze out powerful juice.

Noah was born three years ago on a Sunday afternoon in Mercy General Hospital. Mom was calm all the way up to the maternity ward at four A.M., walking fast but steady with her feet spread wide, carrying her purse with her left hand, her right hand on her protruding belly. I carried her duffel bag and Jaime and I pushed elevator buttons and opened the doors that weren't automatic while Terrance parked Mom's Ford Taurus. When Terrance arrived, he pushed the two chairs in Mom's room together, balanced his Forty-Niners cap over his face and fell asleep behind a privacy curtain. "Wake me up when it's time," he said.

A young nurse fed Mom green Jell-O from a plastic cup. "It's not his first child, is it?" the nurse said through her pink lipstick and tight smile.

I shrugged. "With our dad, Mom had to drive herself," I said. "At least Terrance parked the car."

Five hours later Noah emerged pale and wrinkled, with white flaky skin and red spots on his face like tiny zits. Jaime said, "What's wrong with him?" Mom started crying and the nurse thought maybe we should leave her alone for a while.

Terrance had held Mom's hand during the delivery and now he stroked her forehead and told her the baby was beautiful. "He came from us," he said, tears in his eyes. "He's our perfect baby boy." He kissed her cheek. "You're beautiful," he said. "You did great." He squeezed her hand and kissed her on the lips, a gesture that for once seemed sweet rather than disgusting. "I love you," he said. "So much," he said and kissed her again.

Noah cried at night; all night most nights in the beginning. Terrance and Jaime slept through his screams but I lay awake and listened to his high-pitched wails and wondered what could possibly be so distressing at his age. Mom sang lullabies and church songs in her soft soprano, rocked him in the yellow recliner, put him in his crank-up swing. Sometimes he stopped screaming long enough to eat, which he did with his eyes closed, his mouth around Mom's nipple, his little cheek muscles working like a pulse. Mom's strong arms held him close, her free hand smoothed the downy wisps of black on his head, traced the side of his jaw with her pinky finger, tapped his round, dime-sized nose. Once, I watched him open his mud-brown eyes and gaze up at Mom as if she were the only thing he could see and she was, literally, his whole world. She grew him inside of her from nothing and I thought, *I came from that place, too.*

Noah's pale skin darkened each day, and the red spots faded, and after a few weeks he looked less like a big creased worm with arms and more like a baby. Jaime and I did extra chores and whatever Mom asked without arguing. We washed piles of spit-up towels, baby onesies, and Terrance's new work jumpsuits. We washed Mom's pajamas and sweatpants and our own laundry. We took poopy diapers to the dump; cleaned bottles, hospital-green nose plungers, and tiny thermometers. We walked to the liquor store four blocks away to buy milk, eggs, toilet paper. I cooked spaghetti and fish sticks and frozen pizzas for dinner. Mom said thank you for almost everything we did, but her voice was robotic, and she didn't say much else except her quiet cooing to Noah.

After a while, Mom went back to work. Noah started smiling, but he still cried at night. I listened to Mom tell him about her day, her coworkers, her grant-writing projects advocating assistance for abused women. She talked to him as if he were a normal person while he screamed like it hurt his throat. One night I got up to pee and saw Mom standing at the kitchen window with all the lights off, silhouetted in the moonlight, swaying her hips and shoulders with Noah in her arms, her heels planted two feet apart. She stared out the window at the starless sky and rocked.

"Mom?"

She turned and whispered, "I think he's asleep," without interrupting her swaying. Black rings made caves around her eyes and dried tears glinted on her droopy grayish skin. "But I have to keep moving."

I whispered, "Want me to wake Terrance up?"

"He has to work tomorrow."

"So do you."

She turned back to the window. "I did this for you, too, you know," she said, her eyes wide open in their caverns. "Rocked you, took you for drives. You cried all the time except in the car. Worse than this, worse than Jaime, but it was night when your dad couldn't stand it so I'd wrap you in a blanket, put you in the car seat, and drive around the neighborhood playing Joni Mitchell until you fell asleep." She rocked her hips and swung her arms, stared through the glass at the night.

"At least Terrance doesn't do that," she said. "He doesn't yell like your dad if I couldn't get you to be quiet. I hear him still, in my head sometimes. He'd yell with his voice scratchy and he'd throw things and I'd say, 'Shh, baby,' over and over, but you wouldn't stop and he hadn't hit you, I never saw him hit you, but you could fall if he hit me and I was always tired, too tired to drive, so sometimes I'd just sit in the car in the apartment parking lot and let you scream."

Goose bumps moved up my arms and mostly bare legs, covered to midthigh by one of Mom's old T-shirts. I took a step toward her.

She was crying. "I'm sorry I let you scream," she said, staring straight out the window. A few distant stars looked like tiny blemishes in dark paint. "You were never afraid of him, and I was so scared," she said, still moving to her own rhythm. "I'm so scared," she said.

I wrapped my arms around her soft waist, under where she held Noah, and she kept rocking so we swayed there together until the sky was spotted with twinkling white defects.

Jaime and I are sleeping on the couches tonight and since Jaime is still shorter, even if only a little, she gets the love seat. These slate-blue sofas have been around longer than Terrance and with him gone we try to pretend he never existed. Jaime says, "The house smells funny now."

"Yeah," I say. It smells like musty sweat and hot metal. I say, "It smells like Terrance." We are eating microwave popcorn and watching *Twister*.

Mom comes in from the hallway. "Noah is finally asleep," she says. "All that sugar." She laughs. "Did you see him hit the piñata?"

"He had fun," I say.

Jaime says, "It was good cake." We all sigh and watch the screen: cows floating in front of Bill Paxton's brand-new red truck, mud spraying the windshield, Helen Hunt's hair still flawless despite tornado wind speeds.

Mom says, "I need to talk to you girls about something."

I pause the movie and we both look at her and then at each other. We know how these talks go. She sits in one of the beige-

and-pink-cushioned chairs at the table and faces us, now wearing cotton pajama pants and a big yellow T-shirt. Her hair is in a ponytail for the first time I've seen since Terrance was released. She has a hickey on her neck. "We are buying a house."

Jaime says, "A real house?"

"I thought you couldn't afford a plane ticket," I say.

Mom says, "We got evicted."

"What's that?" Jaime says.

"Because of Terrance?" I say.

"Someone called the landlord and told them about Terrance's record," Mom says and shakes her head. "Like people can't change."

I say, "Who called the landlord?" but I have a guess after today's talk with Jaime.

"Terrance wants to raise Noah in a house."

Jaime says, "I want to live in a house."

"We'd like you to come live with us," Mom says and Jaime and I both freeze. We look at each other with eyebrows cocked and heads tilted. Mom says, "This second appeal is going well, and we should know by the time the house is ready, but I think God has answered our prayers."

"What if the appeal is denied?"

"It's in God's hands."

I say, "But will you make Terrance leave?"

She takes a deep breath, closes her eyes. She stands up. "You girls are my blood. Nothing is more important than that." She kisses each of our foreheads and stands in her bedroom doorway. "You can come home in June, I promise." She smiles and I think she believes it. She says, "Good night," and closes her hollow door.

Jaime and I lean toward each other across the coffee table. Jaime whispers, "I don't want to live with Terrance."

"The appeal will get denied," I say. "She'll never make him leave."

"If we live with Dad, we can do whatever we want."

"Except relax."

"He's not that bad," she says. "He doesn't drink in the car anymore."

"Without Crystal, he can do whatever he wants, too," I say.

"At least he's trying," she says. She frowns and pulls away from whispering distance. "We can't all be perfect like you," she says, and it stings more than I would have guessed for a line both my parents have said to me before.

I turn off the TV, my throat tightening. I know Jaime's memories don't include the beatings I remember. I know she never hears Mom's pleading in her head—*Please, David, think of the girls*—or the thuds of hard knuckles against soft flesh. It wasn't Jaime who cleaned tobacco spit out of Mom's hair, or knelt on the bathroom floor to remove glass shards from the soles of her feet with tweezers, hands slipping down metal slick with blood until my fingertips were bleeding, too. Jaime doesn't remember the look on Dad's face as he punched his wife, eyes wide and unseeing, his jaw fixed, teeth grinding millimeters to the left and right as he swung. She's never had to watch her father come at her with that face or his fists, see that he doesn't care who she is in that moment, and know that she can't defend herself.

Jaime doesn't remember because Mom and I worked hard to shelter her. Until today I was proud to have done such a good job. Now, I have to make her see that Dad is dangerous without deepening the divide that's grown between us. If I lose her, it was all for nothing.

We spend Sunday packing our stuff. "Or I'll do it for you," Mom says as she's putting on nylons and a dress without cleavage for church. When she leaves to pick up Terrance at Gary's, Jaime and I make pancakes and eggs in our pajamas, and watch the rest of *Twister* together on the floor.

Later, in the nine-by-nine-foot room that used to be mine, Terrance's leather weight bench and his dumbbells have forced my bookcase and dresser to the corners. My bed, part of a bunk that Jaime and I shared when we shared a room, is back on top in Noah's room. Dust coats the few books and knickknacks I left behind, and I put everything in one box. My journals and favorite books and clock radio are already at Tammy's.

In my room at Tammy's, Alanis Morissette and The Beatles look down at me from either side of the fold-out bed. She rigged a string system so I could hang posters without putting holes in the wall, and I also have an Escher sketch and a Picasso print Tammy bought for me at a gallery in Park City. And even after I heard Sam tell her it would decrease their property value, Tammy let me stick plastic glow-in-the-dark stars to my ceiling.

In this room where I used to sleep, Terrance has redecorated the walls with Metallica and Black Sabbath posters, a dartboard, and pictures of shiny hairless men showing off chests as big as tractors, arms carved and tight, oiled up and flexed. His guitar stands in front of my dresser, the light wood backlit by the dark green paint on the drawers. His fingerless leather weight gloves sit on top where my makeup used to live.

I move his guitar and open the top drawer. Most of what is left I put in a Goodwill pile. I have a whole closet full of nice, first hand, and hole-less outfits at Tammy's. I no longer need these hand-me-downs, flood jeans, and stretch pants. There are a few nice dresses in the closet, a few pairs of summer shoes worth keeping, and sleep shorts I can wear if Terrance moves out. I stick them in another box along with stuffed animals I don't want to take but can't bring myself to throw away. I move Terrance's guitar back in front of my dresser but I turn all the tuning pegs in different directions, one so tight the string snaps. I stand there picturing all the parts of him that could snap like that with the right pressure: bones, tendons, windpipe.

Jaime comes in and sees me staring. She says, "Let's break it."

"Mom would know."

"So?" Jaime picks up the wooden neck and lets the body dangle. "How else can she punish us?"

"What if we can actually come back?" I say.

Jaime rolls her eyes but puts the guitar back on its metal stand. "Did you hear them on the phone this morning? It was like déjà vu."

"Tammy was the same before Sam came to visit," I say. "He called every Sunday at five A.M."

"Dad calls Crystal a psycho bitch," Jaime says. "And then they make up and have really loud sex."

"Mom and the idiot, too."

"It's nasty."

"I try not to think about it," I say and she nods. We stand there quietly for a minute, the sun shining through the blinds on the window, making shadow stripes across our feet and the brown carpet. Jaime plucks the thickest strings on the guitar and they vibrate like footsteps in the empty apartment. She puts her thumb in her mouth and sighs, and I wish I could offer her more than this instability, something better than our parents. All the things in my head sound like Hallmark cards, but I want her to know that I will never let her down. I decide on, *You can always talk to me*, as a starting point, but before I get it out she pulls her thumb from between her lips and says, "You've French-kissed a guy before, right?"

Our talk is better than shredding Terrance's Forty-Niners cap or scratching his CDs would have been, and by the time Mom comes home I know that if Jaime and Dad actually get an apartment and she asks me to, I will move in with them.

I let Dad hug me before Jaime gets in his pickup. His dark orange beard is rough against my cheek but he doesn't smell like beer. "You look weird," he says to me.

I say, "You look unemployed."

He smiles and wags a finger at me. "You got that cleverness from me."

"I was being serious."

"A serious pain." He laughs.

Jaime says, "Dad."

"I know, I know," he says. "She's always serious."

"You're so clever," I say. "Why don't you go into advertising?"

"Good night, Liz," Jaime says, tossing her backpack into the black bed of his pickup. "Thanks," she says and gets in the cab. We smile at each other.

"You could come have fun with us, Liz," he says.

"You mean drink too much?" I stand on tiptoe and check in the truck bed for alcohol.

"Just as frigid as your mom," Dad says, shaking his head. "Where are you spending the night?"

I put my hands on my hips. "Why do you care?"

"You could still come back to our place," he says. "We've got a couch with your name on it."

"No, thanks," I say. "I'd like to sleep without shoes on."

"Fine, hoity-toity." He gets back in the cab. "But you better not be staying at your mom's if Terrance is there," he says. "You know the rules."

Suddenly all the signs click in my head. Dad inviting Jaime to live at Crystal's. The call to Terrance's parole officer. Dad and Jaime encouraging me to move in with them. I stare at him, taking in his freckles and blue eyes, thinking back to all his little comments. "Why didn't I figure it out before?" I say.

"What?" he says, mocking. "That us *real* Reids like to enjoy ourselves?"

"It was you," I say. Trying to collect child support money was not him taking advantage of the situation. It was the reason the situation was created. "You called Terrance's P.O." My hands form fists at my side. "This whole thing started because of you."

"I don't know what you're talking about," he says, looking away from me and slamming the door shut.

"I can't believe you would rip our lives apart like that for money,"

I say. My nostrils flare and I think of all the times he forgot to pick us up, or spent our dinner cash on booze, or made us sleep on the floor of some passed-out friend's house. "You selfish prick."

"Liz!" Jaime says.

"He set this in motion, Jaime," I say. "You can't trust him."

"Things are in motion," Dad says, his voice harsh. He looks directly at me through his open window and lifts his eyebrows. "Maybe you should think about which direction you want them to move."

I bite the inside of my lip until I taste blood. "Is that some kind of threat?" I say, leaning forward so Jaime can't hear.

"I'm simply suggesting you carefully consider your options here, Liz," he says, his lips turning up at the corners. He glances at Jaime. "Make family a priority."

My jaw tenses enough to make my ears ring. "I will never forgive you for this," I say through gritted teeth.

"Well," he says. "No one can live up to your high-and-mighty expectations." He turns the key and the engine roars to life. He sticks his head out the rolled-down window and smiles with an air of victory. "Not even you."

"Please don't kill my sister," I say.

"I'll do my best," he says. "But accidents do happen."

"You're mad at me, not her," I say.

"Call us when you lighten up," he says. He puts the truck in gear. "Or if you decide to put someone's needs before your own for once."

It takes all my muscle control to keep my feet on the asphalt, to not pull Jaime out of her seat, to not run after the truck bed where we spent more than one night half-asleep on the hard plastic parked behind Dad's bar of choice. My body is screaming for me to give in and say yes, okay, I'll come live with you, you win, I'll do what you want. But I just stand there, watching Jaime drive away with one of the two most terrifying people I've ever met, and feel ashamed.

"Be safe, Jaime," I say to the parking lot.

Back inside, Mom says if we're discreet, both Terrance and I can spend the week here. I can't tell Jaime or Dad, but lying is better than sleeping at Tabatha's, a woman who lives on the other end of the apartment complex with two teenage sons over six feet tall with no exposed skin un-tattooed. Mom met her in the prison visiting room, "How convenient!" she'd said, and they often carpooled to Vacaville until Terrance got out. Tabatha's husband has ten years left on his sentence.

"She's supposed to be gone," Terrance says when he gets back from drinking with his cousins and I'm still here. "I could get arrested."

"So what else is new?" I say and Mom snaps, "Elizabeth." Then she says to Terrance, "No one will know."

He points at me, glowering. "She wants me to go back," he says. "She'll call my P.O."

"I thought you two were getting along?" Mom says. She eyes Terrance. "Why would she do that?"

Yeah, Terrance, I think, remembering the stickiness of that dive bar booth, him smelling my hair, threatening to torment Jaime. *Why would I do that?*

A cloud of fury bursts in his eyes, but he transforms it to desire faster than should be possible. "Babe," he says, running his hands up her torso. "I need to lay next to you tonight." He caresses her cheek. "I missed you." He lowers his mouth and kisses her neck, still glaring at me.

Mom closes her eyes and says, "I missed you, too." The anger in Terrance's eyes fades to triumph as he nibbles at her skin. I am wondering how many layers I would need to sleep outside when Mom says, "But it's Liz's turn."

I'm shocked and grateful, and while Terrance also looks surprised, his face hardens and his eyes narrow into slits. He jerks away from her so fast it's almost like a slap, and no matter what she's done to me, the second he hurts her I am free to claw out his eyes and scratch off his skin. "She ruins everything," he says.

"I told her she could," Mom says. "I promised."

"You could sleep at Tabatha's," I say, shrugging.

"Go to bed, Elizabeth," Mom says. "Now, before I change my mind."

Terrance doesn't leave, but I think I ruined their mojo. Terrance isn't as magic as he thought, I guess. Their bedroom stays quiet all night and while I appreciate the silence, I still can't sleep. I think of Dad's plan to get Jaime and me to live with him, his self-serving obliviousness to what that one phone call would do to his daughters. More cash means more booze without more work, and I have no doubt that Dad would be like a frat kid with a fake ID if he succeeded. Of course, he was banking on Mom's faulty parenting to back him up, and he won that bet. Jaime and I just keep losing.

I wanted to hate the baby. I'd planned on it all those months as Mom's belly grew, tried to ignore the instinctual response to coo and cuddle the tiny crying bundle wrapped in soft white blankets, reminded myself he was half enemy blood, and as long as I wasn't alone with the little guy, it worked.

At four months old, Noah was still crying all night but Mom never yelled at him. She screamed at Terrance for leaving the bathroom light on, for leaving his boots in the hallway for her to trip on, for not putting the toilet seat down. She yelled at us if our rooms were messy, yelled at me if dishes were piled in the sink or if the carpet looked dirty. The woman who normally waited until telemarketers finished talking to politely say, "No, thanks," was now saying things like, "I don't have time for this crap." Her eyes were hardly open at dinner but she still got up for church each Sunday, she managed to drive safely, and she never yelled at Noah.

It was summer. Noah could hold his head up and grabbed at plastic toys, dolls, faces, and our hair. His little hands were surprisingly strong. In the mornings while Mom got ready for work, Jaime and I watched him along with *Saved by the Bell* and *Sweet Valley High* on TV. During commercials for games like Crossfire and Mouse Trap, we pushed the skin of Noah's forehead into his eyes so he looked like a shar-pei puppy. We sang along with the Tootsie Roll and Mentos jingles during commercials, made Noah's chubby legs dance, molded his baby hand into a fist, and then pulled up his middle finger.

"Look at his big ears," Jaime said. Sometimes we called him Dumbo.

"He'll probably get Terrance's buck teeth," I said.

"He doesn't look like Mom," she said and poked Noah in the belly. He made more sounds now than just screams. Giggles and nothing words poured out of his mouth. Jaime said, "What if he's not really our brother?" He stared at us with the same wide brown eyes he absorbed everything with, darker coffee colored in the center and muddy brown at the edges, and always alert, examining. I pulled the skin from Noah's cheeks and watched his lips stretch into a twisted clown smile.

"Half-brother," I said. "And we saw him come out." He bounced and waved his chubby arms, and I thought if someone replaced his eyes with blue and lightened his complexion, he looked a bit like Jaime. Same round face, pudgy cheeks, soft chin.

After Mom left for work with Noah to drop off at day care, Jaime and I were free until five P.M. We lazed in front of the TV for more than the allotted three hours and sometimes didn't get dressed until four thirty. We did our hair and makeup like the Glamour Shots photos some of our friends had done at the mall, and pranced around the living room in our pajamas, making up dance moves and singing as loud as we could along with the blaring radio. We lounged at the pool in ninety-degree sun, listened to tapes I'd ordered from Columbia House for free: Ace of Base, Stone Temple Pilots, and Boyz II Men. We applied tanning oil and remembered to turn frequently. Sometimes we put lemon juice in our hair for highlights, or cucumber slices over our eyes to "banish bags," practices I'd read about in the *Cosmo* magazines I bought with babysitting money and hid under my bed.

A few weeks before school started Jaime and I walked home from the pool with our towels wrapped around our waists, rubber flip-flops wet from our dripping bodies and squeaking with each step. We were arguing about whose turn it was to make lunch as I unlocked the door.

"I made sandwiches yesterday," I said.

Jaime shrugged. "You're older." She smiled and pushed me and then we both saw Mom's purse on the kitchen table. At two thirty, it should not have been there.

We knocked on her closed bedroom door. "Mom?" She didn't answer but I heard sniffs so I turned the knob.

Mom sat on the mattress with her back to the door. "Mom?" An overturned plastic hamper spilled clothes onto the floor, pants and collared shirts were on the bed, something like a dark T-shirt hung from the lamp, cutting the light in half.

She said, "I'm okay." Her fingers twisted a white cloth in her lap but she didn't lift her head. "It'll be okay," she said. "Please shut the door."

I made tuna sandwiches and fruit punch Kool-Aid and by the time we were fed and in dry shorts and T-shirts Mom said she needed to talk to us. Her eyes were red rimmed and bloodshot, but her face was dry.

She took a deep breath. "Terrance was arrested this morning."

"For what?" I said.

"He's in jail again?" Jaime said.

"He didn't mean any harm," Mom said.

I said, "What did he do?"

"He was just flirting," Mom said. "What do women expect when their butt cheeks hang out of their shorts?" She pressed her fingertips to her eyebrows and covered her face.

"When's he getting out?" I said.

She released a huge sigh. "I don't know," she said and started crying in big heaving sobs. Jaime looked at me with wide eyes, but I didn't know what to say. Mom said, "They don't believe him. He wouldn't do what she said he did, but with his record." She wiped at her eyes. "He could do time."

Mom looked down at her blouse, at the daisy-size wet spots mushrooming out from her breasts. "Damn, I'm leaking." She went into her bathroom, dripping all over, tears adding moisture to her shirt.

"Time for what?" Jaime said.

"Prison time," I said.

"So Terrance is gone?"

"Maybe," I said. "I hope so."

Mom yelled, "Can one of you bring me a bottle?"

When I handed her one of the dozen bottles I'd hand washed in hot soapy water that morning, I saw that the white garment she'd been clutching earlier was in her bathroom trash. Her bed was made and carpet cleared, most of the clothes were back in the hamper. Mom sat on the toilet with her breast-feeding bra unhooked and hanging open under her left breast, the yellow suction cup of the pump attached to her nipple. "I don't know what we'll do, Liz," she said. "He didn't make much, but it helped and with the car payments and Noah's day care . . ." She finished pumping and capped the bottle top. She rehooked her bra, pulled a clean shirt from her closet, and slipped her arms through the sleeves.

"He's never coming back?"

"It'll be okay," she said.

She came out of her bathroom and hugged me. Jaime appeared in the bedroom doorway and Mom pulled her close, too, and squeezed us both hard. "We'll be fine," she said, but she wasn't blinking.

When she left to pick up Noah, I dug out the clothing she'd thrown away: a pair of the white basketball shorts Terrance wore loose and baggy. They were made of slippery synthetic jersey material and these were ripped near the crotch so no wonder she trashed them. I felt stupid for trying to play Nancy Drew. But later, when Crystal read me the police reports, I understood why Mom had destroyed her room that day. A waitress at a Denny's in Lodi claimed that Terrance had made "suggestive comments" and "obscene gestures" at her. The waitress then claimed that Terrance had followed her into the bathroom, unzipped his work jumpsuit, and popped his penis out of a hole in his baggy white shorts.

8

Sam barges into my room without knocking. He used to share this office space with Tammy before it became my room, and he acts like I'm a squatter he can't get rid of. He walks to the ceiling-high bookcases against the wall and clears his throat. I turn up the volume on my CD player. Sam clears his throat again and hefts a huge textbook off one of the lower shelves. I hum and open my math book. Sam walks to my desk and stands with his free hand on his hip. He bends over so his mouth is level with my ear and says with his bran muffin breath, "I meant for you to turn your music down, Elizabeth."

I don't look up from solving for x. I say, "That's what words are for."

Sam isn't wearing his Crocodile Dundee hat today, the weather has warmed up enough, I guess, though I still wear sweatshirts in the house most of the time. "Well then let these words clarify my meaning for you," he says, creating a gun with his thumb and fore-finger and pointing at his lips. "Turn. Your. Music. Off." I reach up and turn the volume way down so only the faintest hints of drums and guitars float out of the palm-sized speakers. "I said, 'off,'" he says.

"With my door closed you won't hear a thing," I say.

He slams his heavy book onto my desk. "Tammy asked me to help you with your homework," he says. "But with that attitude, you'd be insufferable."

"I don't need your help."

"I agree," he says. "I think your best is just mediocre." My eyes narrow and my lips fold around my teeth. "Tammy worries your grades are not high enough for acceptance at a quality university," he says. "I told her, 'Like mother, like daughter.'" He scoffs. "She should be overjoyed if you are able to enroll in a state school."

"I am not like my mother," I say. "The last few weeks it's been your fault I'm too cold to do homework."

"You can't blame others for your shortcomings, Elizabeth."

"At least I admit I have shortcomings," I say, dropping my pencil and standing up. "A successful life doesn't just mean money, you know."

"What would you know about success?" He laughs. "The uneducated rarely achieve it—and with your background, well." He picks up his book and starts to walk away. "Tammy's blindness with regard to you is apparent." *You, too, buddy.* He says, "It's no surprise to me that your aspirations are rather low."

I frown at the bald spot on the back of his head and wonder what Tammy sees in him. I think of her nervous hands at dinners since he showed up, her jumping up at his slightest mention of a drink or a snack, how they always watch, eat, and do what he wants. I think of their weekly phone calls while he's in Australia, his presence felt in stored possessions and displayed photos for most of the year. When they returned from Hawaii they were tanner, but didn't seem any closer. I say to his back, "I would want my partner to be happy."

He shakes his head. "Happiness isn't giggles and rainbows, child," he says. He stands taller in the doorway and adjusts his shoulders. "We're both satisfied."

I say with the voice Mom calls snotty, "I thought you were supposed to be a genius or something." I raise my eyebrows.

He sighs. "You'd better get back to work," he says. "With how long it will take you to riddle out those equations, only two pork chop plates may be necessary."

My face heats up. "I hate your pork chops," I say as he goes down the stairs. I slam the door, turn the volume on my Counting Crows CD back up, and dive into my math homework. Unlike my issues with Sam, my math problems have a right answer I can double-check in the back of the book. *I'll show you, jerk.* Without frostbitten fingers, I finish the equations in record time with every answer correct on the first try.

At school, Dean's luscious red lips stick out and fold into a dramatic pout when I tell him I'm moving home at the end of the year. "How will I survive without you?" he says.

Dean and I have been eating lunch together on the grass behind the art building when the weather is nice like today, with the mid-May sun melting the chill from the air, the mountains on all sides sparkling like polished teeth. We sit cross-legged, leaning on hands propped behind us, the knees of our jeans touching.

I smile and poke his ribs with my index finger. "Are you saying you need a girl to protect you from the big bad LDS gangs?"

"The Mormon regime is afraid of independent women," he says. "You're like their Kryptonite." He tilts his head back and gazes at one puffy white cloud as it drifts across the baby-blue sky. I close my eyes and let my skin soak up the warmth.

Dean says, "Are you sure you want to move back?" I've told him enough about my situation for him to ask.

"It's home," I say.

"Won't it be a new house?"

"It's still home in the bigger sense," I say and shove his shoulder. He smiles. I say, "You can write me letters."

"I'll write you a book."

"We can do math over the phone," I say. I'm determined to show Sam that I will rise above my parents' examples, without his help, so I recruited Dean as an after-school homework partner. Both of our grades have improved.

Dean nudges my knee with his and says, "We can do other things over the phone." He grins at me, revealing the gap between his teeth, and lifts an eyebrow.

"Um." I think I might be blushing.

Dean removes his hands from the damp grass and leans sideways toward me. I flash back to Mom and Terrance, the steps from making out on a camping trip to marriage and a baby, and then Mom's teary complicity in his latest crime, and while my body may want to respond, my brain isn't ready for Dean to kiss me just yet. I prepare to back away as his cute face comes closer, but he reaches past me and snags a cracker off my wrinkled paper lunch bag. I exhale as his body moves past mine again to settle back into his grassy seat. I shake my head.

He grins again. "What?" He pops the cracker into his mouth. My cheeks are definitely pink. He tugs on my ponytail and opens his mouth to say something just as the bell rings. He groans and I wonder what he almost said. "Better get back to the cages."

Dean walks me to class like a gentleman, and while I'm relieved there's no pressure from him, my cheeks stay flushed for hours.

I spend the bus ride up to Tammy's imagining what life would be like if I stayed in Utah. I'd go out on dates with Dean, to movies and parties and maybe even prom. We'd hold hands in the hall-ways and homework sessions might include "other things." Tammy and I would hike in the canyons and play games and stay up late talking over bowls of ice cream. Sam's not around for very long at a time, and at least I never feel his probing eyes on the spots where my skin meets my clothes. Also unlike Terrance, Sam seems to like his personal space as much as I relish mine. Part of me thinks I could be okay here.

At the condo there's an envelope from Rachel waiting in the mailbox along with Tammy's catalogues and the neighborhood newsletter. The Sacramento return address makes my eyes burn. Rachel writes, *Spring Break was awesome. My mom taught me how to banish negative energies and do a soul cleansing. Plus, she gave me a bunch of R-rated movies. I miss you! I can't wait for you to come back. No one else will let me do their hair.*

I miss Rachel, and I miss Jaime—who still hasn't written me a single letter—even more. It was so hard to say good-bye to Jaime after our Spring Break talks, and it's been hard to track her whereabouts since. For days at a time while I wait to hear from her I do homework with the phone by my books, put the phone on the bathroom counter when I shower, beg Tammy to get call-waiting since Sam is regularly on business calls. Not that he would answer. I call Crystal's every twenty-four hours, but they're only sometimes at her house. Jaime and Dad often stay at Steve's and sometimes Jaime spends a night at Mom's in exchange for babysitting. "They come home drunk," she tells me. "It's almost like being at Dad's."

She calls when she can. Dad thinks I'm a bad influence. "After she talks to you she starts asking to go to school and stuff," he said once when he answered Steve's phone. "We're not like you," he said. "Leave us alone." I know he bad-mouths me the way he did our mom when we were little and I have to trust that Jaime sees what he's doing. She keeps telling me she's not stupid.

Then Jaime calls one night and says, "Guess where I am."

"Did you find an apartment?"

"Better," she says. She's not whispering or speaking in one-word sentences, and I can't think of why she might be so excited. "It's foggy here. It makes me think of turkey," she says with a levity in her voice that's been missing for months. "Or maybe, drama over a Snickers bar?"

"Aunt Deborah's?"

"Yep," she says and I sense she's smiling.

Jaime tells me that Deborah, not having heard from any of us for a while, tracked Dad to Steve's house. Jaime answered the phone and told Deborah she didn't know where Dad was. Yes, he's still drinking, still not working, still in denial. Deborah didn't think that was a "suitable environment for a child."

"She was all like, 'I'm coming to get you. I'll be right there,' and hung up like Batman or something," Jaime says. She laughs, which is a sound I haven't heard recently, and it makes me smile. "Dad didn't come back before Deborah showed up so I left him a note."

"What about school?"

"She's going to homeschool me for the rest of this year," Jaime says.

"What did Mom say?"

"Dad's pissed," she says. "He said I betrayed him."

"He deserves it."

"He yelled at me until Deborah hung up on him," she says, sighing. "Mom thinks it's better for me here."

"We agree about that," I say. "How do you feel about everything?"

"Time for dinner," she says. "Gotta go. Aunt Deborah made meatloaf. Everyone says hi." She pauses. "I'm good, Liz." Then she's gone, again, but at least now I know she'll be safe.

When the six weeks are up and Sam is heading back to Australia, he pats me on the head and says, "Don't let me discourage you, kid. You're smarter than you want to admit."

I say, "I'm even smarter than you think," and Sam laughs from his gut, a deep sound I've never heard. It makes Tammy jump.

He says, "It's not what I think that matters." He winks at me and nods his head toward Tammy. Then he turns to her and grins. "Shall we go?" He holds out his hand and bows slightly from the waist like a suitor in one of the old movies they like to watch together.

Tammy puts her hand over her heart and bats her eyelashes. "My dear Samuel," she says. "That's mighty bold of you."

"I'm a bold man, young lady," Sam says, taking Tammy's hand. She does a little curtsy. Sam says, "I do believe you're blushing."

"Am I?" she says. "Oh, dear." She twitter-laughs, and it turns into a real giggle.

Sam leads her down the stairs to the garage and I smile as they move out of sight. I bet it's these little moments that keep their relationship alive, and I'm glad I got to witness this side of him. He loves her, even if I can't always see it.

Tammy returns from the airport red-eyed and tense. She spends days scrubbing floors, dusting the mantel and its decor, the curio cabinet with its artifacts, washing walls and counters, vacuuming the carpet that nobody wears shoes on, humming, "I'm Gonna Wash that Man Right Outta My Hair." She goes to work but then comes home early and washes sheets, blankets, towels, and place mats without looking at any of them. She Windexes all the windows, mirrors, glass cabinets, and framed art. She doesn't ask about my homework, and doesn't interrupt my twenty-minute shower. She makes chocolate chip cookies, brownies, cornbread, carrot cake, and scones instead of dinners, and washes down her fresh-baked goods with hot chocolate. She eats in the living room and watches movies she just watched with Sam.

Sunday morning the phone doesn't ring on cue and Tammy lies in bed past noon, staring at her starless ceiling. I ask if she wants me to bring her breakfast. "Those banana muffins you made yesterday haven't even been frozen yet. Want one?"

"I'm fine," she says.

"Some hot chocolate?"

"Just worry about yourself, please," she says and I think she must have forgotten who she's talking to.

But on Monday morning she's up before me, my lunch has more than pastries, and she walks to work for the first time in weeks. "It's time to start moving," she says and breathes deep. The almost-spring air is crisp like a waterfall and smells sweet like flowers. She says, "The streams are full of runoff, the columbine and forget-me-nots are blooming, rainbow-colored birds are everywhere." She sighs. "The mountains are alive and full of things I want to show you," she says, her blue eyes clear and fully open.

I smile. "I can't wait."

Without much waiting at all, the ground shifts from brown to green and spring officially settles in the Wasatch Valley. The warm air and bright sun make my muscles ache for movement and the knowledge that Dad can't hurt Jaime makes each deep breath and sun-kissed step even better. Tammy and I hike in Little and Big Cottonwood Canyons, creek-filled valleys full of bushy, leaf-heavy branches bursting with shades of green and just-opening flower buds that show off slivers of the color that will fully bloom in a few weeks. We do yoga and play badminton in the condo's shared grassy area and ride bikes along the stone wall that edges the cemetery on Eleventh Avenue at sunset with paper-white mountain-tops highlighted against the hazy pink-tinged sky beyond the headstones. The wind whips my hair against my chilled face, but it's worth it because when I pedal fast enough this high above the valley, it feels like flying.

We attend the first of the outdoor concerts at the neighborhood library—a Celtic instrumental band with flutes and a bagpipe. Tammy grabs my arm and pulls me up to dance with the three elementary school kids doing *Riverdance* moves and the white-haired couple swaying and clapping their wrinkled hands. She twirls me around with the beat, our hair floating in the breeze. Tammy laughs and does an Irish jig move with her elbows bent, and I kick my feet, and we giggle and move until we're out of breath and the musicians take a break. We sit on the rim of a planter box full of sprouting greenery, trying to catch our breaths while still laughing. The old couple stares at us. Tammy puts her arm around my shoulder and says, "Thank you."

I wrap my arm around her waist and lay my head on her collarbone. "For what?"

"This is fun," she says.

We take walks at Red Butte Garden, bring sketch pads and watercolors, carrot sticks and apple slices. We find a sunny spot to sit and spread out an orange blanket Tammy keeps in the trunk of her car and outline shimmering dragonflies and pastel-yellow baby ducks in charcoal, draw water lilies and cattails rising from the deep green pond. Brown rock peaks decorated with grass tufts and green trees stand watch above us, the air is sweet and clean and fresh, and I have never felt so full. The color comes back to my cheeks, my hair gets lighter with each day outside, and I even notice extra freckles on my face and newly tanned arms.

One weekend Tammy and I paint the kitchen a pale sage green we picked out together after careful swatch consideration and three failed test colors. She doesn't watch my every stroke, and when she leaves the room to answer the phone I don't eavesdrop once I know it's Sam. Tammy hasn't mentioned him since he left and she hasn't cooked any of the pork chops in the freezer, but after talking to Sam, Tammy almost always places the handset in the base and stares at her fingers resting on top of it for a few minutes before saying, "What did you say?" when I haven't said a word.

Today, as usual after she hangs up, I want to ask if she's okay but she'd say yes, and I want to ask if it's because of me but she'd say no, so instead I tell her a story I know she won't like about the biker I saw the other day on my walk who fell over. I laughed after he fell and I laugh again now telling her about it and picturing his legs stuck to the pedals, kicking in horizontal circles on the pavement.

Tammy says, "That's not funny," but I keep laughing. It is funny to me, but more importantly I know she needs something else to focus on, something to pull her out of the head space she retreats into after talking to Sam. It works. She picks up her roller brush, dips and slides it through the thick green liquid with excessive force, and lectures me on bike safety until it's time for lunch. I only half-listen, but Tammy's jaw loosens as she talks, her paint strokes become slower and more deliberate and her eyebrows relax. I know I can't solve her problems, but at least I can help take her mind off the worst of it, even if only temporarily. And as I'm starting to understand, sometimes the temporary things are the most significant.

When the kitchen walls dry, the room looks like a page from one of Tammy's *Sunset* magazines, with the hints of green undertones in the rosewood cabinets accented by the sage walls, her antique table as a dark anchor for the room's center, and white doors full of windows leading to the awakening plants on the patio beyond.

We decorate, too, retrieve a painting Tammy had stashed away in her garage, get it framed and hung above the telephone table. The painting of an oversized striped teapot full of lavender stalks—an original, of course, from an art festival a few years ago—is full of rich purples and maroons, dark blues and blended gray-greens. We choose a deep slate-colored frame and a white mat, and the teapot stands out so much it looks like it might come to life and walk off the canvas. "Sam hated that painting," Tammy says once it's perfectly aligned and secure on the wall.

We gaze at the detail of the paint strokes, the intricate lines of the lavender's silvery-green leaves and gray-purple buds. "Of course, he wasn't around when I bought it."

"I love it," I say.

"Me, too," she says. "I had forgotten how much."

We place a blue-and-white patterned trivet on the tabletop, and I fill one of her clear glass vases with real lavender I pick from the library's garden and set it on the raised porcelain tile. She switches out her plain white fruit bowl for a faded burgundy piece of pottery shaped like a tulip, and we buy a dark blue ceramic pump soap dispenser at Macy's that costs fifteen dollars to replace the three-year-old plastic drugstore soap container she'd been reusing.

When we're done, we stand together and survey the fruits of our labor. Tammy says, "It's lovely." Her face shines as she smiles at me, and I think about what a difference a little color makes. It's like all the ruby-red and Valentine-pink tulips popping up in people's yards around town, the summer yellow of daffodil blooms in roadside beds, and forsythia flowers appearing on branches. The kitchen looks like a new room.

Tammy hugs me and says, "Thanks for helping." She leaves her arm around my shoulders and walks me to the patio doors. No bulbs bloom in her garden, but bright spots of green peek through the flattened gray plants, and pale new shoots rise up from the brown earth. "That's next," she says, squeezing my upper arm and smiling at me. "I hope you like digging and pulling weeds," she says and I'm surprised to find I'm excited about more work.

One night after a delicious dinner of spinach salad with chicken and feta cheese, and a few rounds of Mastermind that Tammy wins, Mom calls. She asks how things are going, how the packing's coming along, what the weather is like. I've lived here four months now and not once has she called to chat, but I really know something is wrong when she asks to speak to Tammy. "What happened?" I say. "Did the appeal get denied?"

Mom says, "We haven't heard yet."

"But I can still come home?"

"Of course," she says, but the brightness in her voice gives her away.

While I wait for Tammy to pick up the phone downstairs, my stomach cramps. Mom's changed her mind. Jaime and I will never live together again. Sam will come back and say he didn't sign up for my return. He'll threaten to leave if I stay and Tammy will keep me because she feels like she has to and she'll resent me for Sam dumping her. Or, like my mother, she'll give in to her man and I'll have to live with Dad.

I hold down the mute button when Tammy yells, "I got it."

I press the phone to my ear, heart thumping frantically like Pandy the bunny's tiny heart. I remember her constant panic, the way she clawed at my chest with her hind legs, a fur ball fighting to get away like her life depended on it.

"Linda?" Tammy's voice knocks me back from memory lane, and as much as I hurt when Pandy died, I would trade that pain for the current ache in the space of a terrified heartbeat.

"Hi, Tammy," Mom says.

"What's wrong?"

"Geez, you sound like Elizabeth." Mom sighs. "I do want her to come home."

"She is coming home."

"Well, yes," Mom says, "but—"

Tammy says, "No buts, Linda. I already bought the plane ticket. It's all she talks about."

"I'm not saying she can't come home," my mom says. "It's just that the parole decision won't be made until the end of June, and Terrance has nowhere to go, so . . ." She nearly sings the word "so," turning it into three syllables, and then takes a deep breath.

"Are you kidding?" Tammy sounds as outraged as I feel.

"I thought maybe the ticket could be changed to a later date," Mom says.

"What about Liz?"

Mom says, "You don't have plans, do you?"

"What if the appeal is denied again?"

"If you can't switch the ticket, it's okay," Mom says. "We'll figure something else out."

Tammy says, "You know that's not the point." It's almost exactly what I would have said.

"I know children have never been your first priority," Mom says.

Tammy lowers her voice. "Excuse me?"

Mom says, "I just know how busy your life is, and how a child can sometimes be an inconvenience and I know you never wanted—"

"Stop it, Linda, just stop."

"You're right. I'm sorry," Mom says and clears her throat.

"You know how much I love that kid," Tammy says quietly. "She won't tell you, but she's hurting." I hear the tightness in Tammy's throat and realize this is hard for her, too. We're a team now, and I wish she really was my mother. How different life would be.

"She's tough," Mom says. "She can handle it."

"She's still a kid," Tammy says.

"Try telling her that," Mom says, and I wonder again at how two sisters can have such different perceptions. Tammy understands that my wanting to be an adult is not the same as being one.

Mom and Tammy sit silent on the line for a moment, their breathing heavy and deliberate. I try to picture them as kids, like me and Jaime, laughing at nothing and playing made-up games together, pledging solidarity against their stepmom, sharing whispered secrets across the dark space between bunk beds, but I can't. Protective instincts don't necessarily create closeness, and I know Tammy did her best to keep Mom safe, but if they were ever friends, I can't see it now in their separate lives, their distance, their conversations. Sisters connected by genes and the survival of a shared history they don't like to talk about. I hope Jaime and I don't end up like that.

Mom finally says too cheerfully, "Okay, well, tell Liz we'll see her on the sixteenth as planned."

"She deserves better than this, Linda."

"Well, we can't all live up to your expectations," Mom says and hangs up. I hear Tammy slam the phone into its base, and I know it's something she's been told before. My heart aches to sprint down the stairs and hug Tammy until my arms hurt.

Later, Tammy makes a simple basil, tomato, and asparagus pasta dinner and we eat in near silence in front of the season finale of *Melrose Place.* She avoids my eyes and I know she is debating whether or not to tell me that Mom is likely to send me off again as soon as my plane lands. Tammy serves me seconds, and then brings out bowls of rocky road ice cream. I raise my eyebrows at her. Dessert is usually reserved for high-calorie-burning days.

"I thought you might like a treat," she says, her eyes bright with too much liquid. If I didn't already know what was wrong, I would be suspicious now. She dips her spoon into her bowl. "Besides," she says, licking chocolate off her lips. "You have to help me finish the ice cream before you leave, or I'll eat it all and get fat."

Later that night, I lie awake and stare at my starry ceiling as it loses its luster. The energy absorbed by the plastic fades after the lights go out, and when I try to look at one star directly, it disappears from view like it doesn't want to be studied. I run my eyes over the shapes I've found and named during weeks of falling asleep to these glowing points, La Pomme, Baby Unicorn Head, Bigfoot. Tonight a guillotine appears in the starry outlines and the game stops being fun. I roll over and squash my eyes shut just as Tammy walks in. The angled line of the blade I saw burns neon green against my closed lids.

The mattress shifts as Tammy settles next to me on the bed. "I'll bring home some boxes so you can pack up the stuff you want me to ship."

I say without opening my eyes, "Will you move to California?"

Tammy takes a deep breath and lets it out with one long exhalation. "Maybe someday," she says. She picks up my hand. "But I want you to know that you can always come back here. If things don't work out." She squeezes my hand with her long fingers and I squeeze back. "There's always room for you in my house," she says.

"Thank you," I say. I sneak a peek at Tammy's face and think I see shiny lines trailing down her cheeks. We lie there for a few minutes, the distant laughter from the TV downstairs or a bus opening its doors across the street occasionally breaking through the silence. "I heard what Mom said today," I say. "On the phone."

Tammy's eyes pop open. "Your mom loves you," she says and rolls onto her side so she can look at me. "She's dealing with some things right now, I think."

"It's still not right to break a promise."

"You know we moved out when we were just a little older than you?" she says, and I nod. "We got jobs. We worked on weekends and while our friends were at football games and class trips to Disneyland. We didn't really get to date." Tammy clucks her tongue. "I think your mom sees Terrance as a chance to be a teenager, to have the fun she didn't get to experience." Tammy shakes her head. "She's rebelling at the same time you are."

"You didn't get to be a teenager, either," I say. "How come you haven't escaped into a fantasy world?"

"I was older," she says. "And your mom and I have very different needs." Tammy smiles and looks up at my stars. "She was so good with you guys when you were little," she says. "Amazing, really. Patient and gentle. Modeling correct behavior, teaching without punishing. Making you laugh." My eyes tear up. Tammy sighs. "I used to watch her, the way you girls looked at her, and think I'd never be as good with kids as my sister."

"I miss that mom," I whisper.

Tammy says, "One day when Terrance stops being such a novelty, she'll realize the mistake she made."

"You think?" I say.

"I know," she says. "Linda is too good a person not to." Tammy scoots to the edge of my bed and stands up. She looks down at me, her body outlined in shadow from the hall light behind her. "In the meantime, remember that your mom's issues are her own. Don't use her stupid choices as an excuse to give up." She bends over and kisses my forehead. "Just like I've said since you first came out from behind Linda's leg and shook my hand when we met. You are only going to get stronger."

Tammy and I continue to keep busy during our last few weekends together. We hike, we garden, we shop. She buys me a pair of Birkenstocks like hers. She makes salads with homemade vinaigrette dressings and fruits like pears and strawberries. She puts fresh berries in Saturday morning whole-wheat pancakes and serves them with powdered sugar and turkey sausage. She grills salmon on a barbeque on her back patio and we peel the pink meat from the silver skin with our fingers under the stars, accompanied by a cricket orchestra. It could be romantic, and I bet Tammy wishes Sam were here, and I wonder if loving someone means you are never happy unless they're around and sometimes not even then.

Dean and I keep flirting in class and after school. Our hands find each other's forearms, knees, and waists with increasing frequency, and my skin tingles every time. We take walks at lunch under Utah's blazing sun, sit shoulder to shoulder on shady benches after school to do homework, and laugh a lot. When I imagine him kissing me, which I do often, in great detail, his voice doesn't have to stop just because his lips are occupied. Tammy and even my teachers have caught me with a dreamy smile on my face more than once. It's embarrassing, but not enough that I won't indulge the fantasy.

"Those geraniums we planted are coming in nicely," Tammy says, and I shift my thoughts from Dean to the two-foot clay pots we hauled from the nursery, filled with dirt and roots, watered, and fertilized. We brought life to this cement patio with tall, deep urns of hanging vines and trailing flowers and wide shallow pots of bushy silver-tinted leaves and spiky blue-green shrubbery.

I smile at our blooming garden. "The parsley seeds finally sprouted," I say. At the edges of the pavement, we dug holes, picked weeds, tilled the soil, formed evenly spaced rows. We sowed seeds and fluffed compacted roots, estimated sizes and distances, transferred ferns into the shady corners, planted a rosebush in the sunny corner, and placed the five-herb garden on the side near the sliding glass door: basil, dill, cilantro, mint, and parsley.

191

"Next year we can do peppers and tomatoes," she'd said as we worked together, backs bent and knees bruised. I felt my hands swell and expand in the dirt. I rolled mud and worms and soil through my fingers and smelled the earth before it bloomed, the deep, moist scent that fades when summer dries the ground. I watered our garden each day when I got back from school, weeded the beds and pinched off dried leaves. I've spent hours out here with the mix of warm sun and cool air on my bared skin, the soft dirt in my hands.

"We make a good team," she says. "I'll miss your help."

For a minute I wonder why she thinks I'd stop gardening and then I realize that she means I won't be here. She will stay when I fly back to Sacramento. My eyes burn and my throat swells and Tammy's eyes look wet, too, and we make eye contact and smile and exhale air in that self-conscious half-laugh, half-sob release. We don't say anything, but we cry together. We sit on her cushioned patio furniture, under stars brighter than they ever are at home, inhaling damp earth and smoky fish on this thin mountain air, and we cry.

I go to the last day of school mainly so Dean can sign my yearbook and we can say good-bye. I find him leaning on a small birch tree near our lunch spot, smoking a clove cigarette. "You smoke now?" I say, waving at the gray wisps he exhales.

"My first one in months." He puts the cigarette out on the tree trunk. "But I'll quit if you stay."

"You're not even addicted," I say.

"Utah needs you."

"I blend in too easily."

"You can infiltrate their system," he says.

"I'll miss you, too," I say.

He grumbles, "Whatever," and snatches at my yearbook tucked under my arm. He tugs hard and it comes loose but I jerk forward and am almost standing on his Doc Martens.

He smiles down at me from a few inches up, his blue eyes and pale skin washed out in the June sun. I lift my heels and press my lips to his chin, which feels a tiny bit scratchy. My eyes are still closed as he drops my yearbook in the grass and wraps his arms around my waist. He leans me against the tree and kisses me slow and deep, one hand in my hair, one hand on my hip, his tongue kneading my mouth like the best massage ever. He tastes sweet like chocolate and mint, and slightly spicy like burnt cloves. He pulls back so he can look me in the eye and smiles. His hand slides out of my hair and lingers against my cheek. He says, "I've been wanting to do that since you turned around your first day and smiled at me."

I find my breath and say, "Really?"

He nods and slides a finger down my jawline. "I really wish you weren't leaving."

"I'm not leaving right now," I say and Dean's smile spreads wide enough to show all his teeth and the gap in front. He wraps his fingers in my hair and pulls. He lifts my chin and brings my face to his, his fingers curled in my blond strands. I inhale his air, his smoky scent, and let myself forget everything else.

When I get to Tammy's later I flip through pages of people I half-recognize but don't really know, sports teams, academic clubs, row upon row of smiling white faces. On the big two-page aerial photo spread of the senior class lined up to spell YOUNG with their bodies, Dean drew speech bubbles from some of them saying things like, *I've got a bug up my ass and I love it,* or, *God help me, I've been asked to think!*

To me, he'd written, *For my sunny CA girl, My life was a bowl of shit with Mormons in it before you. Please come back and save me from drowning.* He signed, *Dean, The English Guy* and wrote his address. *P.S. Maybe you'll take pity on a Utah man and send him a photo of a beautiful woman wearing a bikini? He promises to return the favor.*

"He kissed me," I say to Tammy at the airport. "Dean, the British guy."

She raises her eyebrows. "How was it?"

"You can't ask that." I'm sure my cheeks are pink and the silly grin keeps breaking loose so I look out the window. Outside sits the red, white, and blue plane that will carry me home, the swaying green grass fields beyond the runways, the still-white-capped mountains at the horizon, the blue sky background. Dean is out there, too, I think, and realize I've been smiling.

"Wow." Tammy chuckles. "Is your heart pitter-pattering?"

I say, "Forget I told you."

She pats her hand against her chest. "Ba bum, ba bum, ba bum."

I roll my eyes, but we both laugh. I say, "You're still going to come visit, right?"

She nods. "When we get back from Africa."

"What about after that?"

"Well, I think I'm going to Mexico and a little bird told me there's a lounge chair reserved for you, too."

I jump up and hug her. "Mexico!" I hug her again. "Thank you, Tammy, for everything." My eyes start to water and Tammy pulls me close. I rest my cheek on her shoulder, her clavicle sharp under my cheek. I hold my tears in, but let out a small whine with the effort.

She squeezes her arms around my shoulders and whispers, "I know." She lets go of me and tousles my hair. "It was my pleasure, kiddo." She sniffs.

"Sorry I caused problems with Sam."

"Oh, stop."

"You were a great mom," I say and the speakers announce that I can board now. Tammy squeezes me so hard I can't breathe so I don't until she lets go. I fill my lungs with her clean lavender and herbal scent, which lingers in my nose even after I've found my seat and buckled myself in for the turbulence that's sure to come.

By the time we land I've blown my nose into a whole pack of tissues, and I can't smell anything. My eyes hurt. As we roll up to the ramp, the woman next to me who asked about a dozen times if I wanted to talk about what was wrong hands me a card. *Church of Jesus Christ of Latter-day Saints Troubled Teen Center.* "We have some excellent resources," she says as the seat belt light flicks off.

A female flight attendant asks me if there is anything she can do and I realize I'm alone on the aircraft. I miss Tammy already. I wonder what it would be like to own a plane. Go anywhere, anytime. "Does this plane go back to Salt Lake?"

"No, this is our last stop," she says and glances back at the other women standing near the cockpit. "Do you live here?" she asks. Out the tiny windows tall green-and-yellow grass stalks stand tall in the lack of wind.

I'm not sure. "I'm fine," I say. "My mom lives here." I pick up my backpack and walk up the ramp to the gate.

Terrance's bald head is the first thing I see, and then his bald lip. Mom is holding Noah and they are both waving. She sets Noah down and he runs in tiny steps over to me saying, "Liz, Liz." I pick him up and swing him over my head and then down onto my hip. Two years ago my hip wouldn't have supported him. "God, you're getting heavy, little man."

"Gosh," Mom says.

Noah curls his arms around my neck and wedges his face under my chin. I lean my cheek to his still-baby-soft black hair and rock him on my hip, his legs around my waist.

"It hasn't been *that* long," Terrance says and steps closer. "But we're all glad you're back."

"What happened to your hair?" I say. "You look like a Nazi." I set Noah down. "Or a serial killer."

"Good to see you, too," Terrance says and tries to hug me.

I raise my duffel bag to chest level as a buffer. "Please don't," I say, my eyes pleading with Mom, but she pinches the tender flesh above my elbow and pulls me aside. "What is wrong with you?" she hisses, crushing my skin between her fingers.

"Can't you go anywhere without him?" I jerk my arm away and rub the red thumbprint with my left hand. "Did they deny the appeal?"

"Let's not make a scene," she says and tries to put her arm around my shoulders. I sidestep her reach.

I say, "He's not leaving, is he?"

She sighs, drops the hand she'd raised to touch me, and presses it to her forehead. "I thought we'd at least make it to the car," she mumbles.

"Why did you let me come here?"

"It's just a small problem," she says.

"I hoped you wouldn't really do this."

"You may not have to leave. There are options—"

"Stop it."

"You're right. We should discuss this at home."

"I want to go back."

"To Tammy's?" She almost laughs. "Don't be ridiculous," she says. "Let's get out of the airport and we'll figure something out." A new flight number is up on the screen and people are arriving for check-in. The flight attendant lied. This plane is going to Houston.

"I'm not sleeping at Tabatha's," I say, but where can I go?

Mom says, "You will sleep wherever I tell you to."

"No." This is my fault really, for believing her, for having faith.

"Move it. Now, Elizabeth." She extends her arm again, but I swat at her wrist and turn away.

"No," I say, louder, my back to her, my feet moving forward.

"Elizabeth," she warns, but I keep walking. "Elizabeth!"

A few people are staring. A tornado swells in my chest and roars in my ears but I keep walking through the bright lights of the terminal. It's like I'm seven and Dad has passed out in a gas station parking lot four blocks from our apartment and it's getting dark but I hold Jaime's hand and just keep walking. It's like last fall and I'm wrapped in a towel, headed from shower to bedroom while Terrance watches from the hall, his mouth slack, his eyes sliding all over my skin, but I keep moving forward.

Mom doesn't follow me. She says, "You'll be back." She snort laughs and calls out, "You have nowhere else to go."

She's right. But I square my shoulders and keep walking.

9

Mom and Terrance's new house has a front yard with bright green grass, rosebushes along the walkway, and a six-foot tree sapling ringed by rocks in the middle of the yard, wilting in the sun. They live in a housing tract on the north side of town where all the street names are trees, Birch, Willow, Cedar, which makes it sound like a lush green area full of mature vegetation and thick canopies of foliage, but the sun bakes the tiny plants that stand in the middle of all the other yards, too. Each house stands against a leafless sky and looks the same except for its color. Mom's is a pale gray.

Their garage door opens and Noah says, "Angel!"

Mom says, "Oh, yeah, we got a dog."

"You'll love her, Liz. Everyone does," Terrance says. "Worth every penny, right, babe?"

"How much was it?" I say.

"She," Terrance says proudly, "was two hundred bucks."

My jaw drops. "Does she lay golden eggs or find truffles or something?"

"Purebred boxer," Terrance says. "She's going to be a show dog. She'll pull her weight." *Unlike you*, I think, but Mom's priorities are clear.

Mom unbuckles Noah and he and Terrance go into the house. I get my new duffel bags—matching, blue, water-resistant nylon from Eddie Bauer—out of Mom's trunk and set them on the ground next to a pile of boxes with my and Jaime's names written in black ink. I stare at the pile, arranged neatly in a corner of the garage. Jaime wrote NERD STUFF on one of my boxes. I smile, but not so Mom can see. Mom says, "Let me give you the tour."

It seems like torture to be shown a home where Mom has a happy new family, and in which Jaime and I will probably never live, but I follow her into the house. Three small bedrooms, two bathrooms, a family and living room and lots of windows later, and we're standing in the backyard watching Terrance prance around a little boxer puppy that looks like a miniature Rambo without clipped ears. She chases a tennis ball too big for her mouth and licks Noah's entire face with her bright pink tongue.

I say, "Gross."

"It's actually very clean," Mom says.

Terrance says, "Cleaner than human spit."

"Dogs eat poo," I say.

"Let's go inside," Mom says to me and we go back through the sliding glass door and sit at her kitchen table, the same beige-and-pink cushions we'd sat in when all this shit started. She inhales, opens her mouth, and then closes it.

I look around her new kitchen: honey-colored cabinets, white counter, and raised bar area with room for stools underneath, high slanted ceiling with a fake chandelier light fixture above the table. I sigh. It looks like it would be a nice place to live.

"It's a big house," I say. Bigger than all the apartments we've ever lived in, with luxuries like a backyard and a garage that Jaime and I never had.

"I know there's room for you here, Liz," Mom says, "but that's not the issue."

"I know." I know that even if they had nine bedrooms, space wouldn't be the issue.

She takes a deep breath and exhales. "You were right at the airport before you stomped off," she says. "Our appeal was denied."

"I bet Dad helped with that."

Mom looks angry for a minute as she thinks, but then she sighs. "Well, there's not much we can do about that now," she says. "We have to deal with what we're given." Outside, Terrance has turned on the hose and he squirts Noah and Angel as they run around in the grass. Mom sighs again. "I've been racking my brain trying to figure out a way for us to all be together," she says, and I wait for the "but" that will send me somewhere new, but she just stares off into space.

Terrance makes a rainbow of water and Noah runs back and forth under it with his arms above his head. Angel barks at the stream of water and tries to catch it in her mouth every few seconds, but jumps away and snorts as water goes up her nose. Terrance picks laughing Noah up and spins him around. Noah laughs harder, water dripping from his chubby and tan chest and arms.

Mom lets air out of her nose in that "hmf" sound that's actually a small laugh in our family. "We talked about Terrance getting his own place, and about moving you into an apartment nearby where we could watch you."

"That would be so cool," I say.

"I'm going to talk to Pastor Ron, too," she says, "to see if maybe someone at church has an extra bedroom."

"Please don't make me live with people I don't know again."

"Beggars can't be choosers," she says, and rests her forehead on the table. But it's her fault I'm in this mess and I refuse to beg.

While Mom is "racking her brain" for a solution, I spend most nights at Rachel's. We stay up late and watch R-rated movies with all the lights off, giggling, rewinding and rewatching sex scenes. We light candles and cast spells from the books Rachel's mom gave her. I recite an incantation for independence and Rachel mixes cayenne pepper and bay leaf for an increased eroticism spell.

"Remember, you have to really want it to work," Rachel says before we read the chants. She holds my right hand with her left and we each light a white candle on our other side. "Visualize your goal," she says and closes her eyes.

I close my eyes and see myself sitting on cement steps in front of a college campus library under a blooming, sweet-scented cherry tree, laughing with a few smart classmates, on my way to an advanced literature class, or heading home to my loft apartment. I have a job, make my own money, and need nothing from my parents. *I will be free*, I repeat in my head. *I will be free.*

We also smoke weed almost every day. She leads me up to her balding, skinny, and single father's room after he leaves for work in his brown slacks carrying his worn leather briefcase. "Bye, Maple-y Rachel-y," he usually calls from the bottom of the stairs in a silly cartoon voice. Rachel rolls her eyes every time, but I know she'd miss it if he stopped. Lately she seems to be more aware of how lucky she really is. Her dad provides for his family even if he dabbles in old habits from his teen years in the sixties. He may be eccentric and a little bitter, but he's a real father, and I'd choose him over mine any day.

"Bye, Dad," she says, and then she grabs my arm and heads across the hall as soon as his key clicks in the lock. In his musty closet on the top shelf in a faded yellow cigar box, Rachel's dad keeps a plastic bag of drugs wrapped inside a paper lunch sack. All his clothes are brown, and a green suit jacket with elbow pads hangs in yellowed plastic. Rachel steals a nug or two of his weed every couple of days. She says, "Even if he noticed, what would he say?"

"My dad would make me pay for the stuff I took."

"My mom said he'll just think he's doing more," she says. Her mom told her where to look for the box. "And if he suspected, he'd blame my mom before he confronted me so he'd have an excuse to call her." Like my father, Rachel's dad is still in love with the woman who left him. Unlike my father, Rachel's dad is a good person and married a woman who never wanted to settle down. I feel bad for him in the evenings after dinner when he sits in his recliner with his slippers on and a glass of wine, watching cable news channels or episodes of *MASH*, and it makes me wonder if anyone has a functional relationship with the person they love.

Sometimes Rachel and I watch cartoons, or read *Cosmo* articles out loud to each other. "Energize Your Life: In and Out of Bed" or,

"How to Please Your Man." Rachel occasionally asks me to repeat certain instructions and advice, and she writes it down in her journal.

"You don't even take notes at school," I say.

"I don't want Frank to think I'm inexperienced."

Sometimes we put swimsuits on and go over the levee to the river, lie out on a small sand bank or a big log. We talk about sex, since she's probably going to do it soon, and who is going out with whom, and who is doing it, or at least almost, and about starting our second year of high school.

"Where you gonna be?" Rachel asks. "Maybe we can get our lockers together," she says, stretching out across a log wider than our shoulders, chest to the sun.

"I wish I could tell you."

"How much longer you going to be back and forth?" she asks. "Not that I don't like having you here or anything." She pokes me with her pink-nailed toes.

I dip my feet in the river and watch them disappear under chocolate-colored mud. "Maybe my mom'll let me get my own place," I say. It was more likely than Terrance getting his own apartment. "But she'll probably make me live with one of the old ladies at church. Our pastor made an announcement at the end of the service last week." To Pastor Ron's credit, he seemed reluctant to bring it up with me sitting right there in front of him. "Even though Pastor Ron didn't say my name, the whole church knows it's me who needs a room, and everyone knows why." I curl my toes deeper into the brown-black silt. "I'm now a cause for all these Christian do-gooders who want to help. The same ladies who give me sad eyes when they see me in the foyer and ask how I'm 'holding up' if my mom isn't with me."

"At least you'd get to stay in town," Rachel says as she dangles her long, tan leg in the water.

"It's so embarrassing," I say. "I hate my mom."

"My dad said she called last night while we were on our walk," Rachel says.

"He told me, too, but I didn't call her back," I say. "She doesn't want me to live with her, but she wants to run my life."

"I'm sure she missed you," Rachel says.

"I doubt it," I say, though I continue to nurse a small hope that she did.

Rachel says, "It'd be so rad if you got your own place."

I shake my head and brush a fly off my knee. "She can't afford it," I say.

"Hey." She sits up and adjusts her bikini top. Her boobs are much larger than mine. "Maybe you could emancipate yourself like Drew Barrymore. Divorce your parents. They're totally fucked anyway." She looks at me. "No offense."

I shrug. "It's true." The wind picks up and goose bumps run up my arms and legs. I pull my feet from the mud and swish them around in the cool green water until they're clean.

Rachel says, "I'm sorry, Liz Wiz." She pulls her long brown hair into a ponytail and adjusts her square sunglasses.

The sun hangs low in the sky and mosquitoes buzz where the air is still. A breeze pushes clouds across the horizon, disturbs the biting swarms, and mixes the heavy heat with river cooled drafts. I say, "Can you get welfare if you're emancipated?"

She stops fiddling with her hair and looks at me. "You'd really do it?" she says.

The clouds move faster, tumbling in white drifts above our heads. "Maybe Jaime could come with me," I say, picking sand out from under my chewed nails. "We would do better on our own."

"Everyone needs a family, Liz," she says.

"What if your family sucks?"

"I was joking," she says. "About the emancipation thing."

I say, "Good joke."

I ask Rachel to take the bus with me downtown the next day. A homeless man who reeks of stale booze asks us "pretty ladies" if he can have our shoes. We're both wearing flip-flops. He says, "I can pay," and pulls from his pocket two pennies, a Ping-Pong ball–size wad of multicolored chewed gum, and a dead cockroach. He shoves his hand under Rachel's nose. "Your choice," he says. "But the roach'll keep you company."

Rachel's eyes bulge and she starts shaking. I grab her hand and we stand together. "No, thanks," I say, nudging his outstretched hand aside. "We like our shoes. Excuse us." We walk past him out into the midmorning sun, jumping off the bus steps and onto the sidewalk. The air smells of exhaust and the rumbling traffic is constant on these busy streets. I triple-check the directions I wrote down last night and turn left.

Rachel says, "I've never been down here by myself." She clutches my arm.

I pat her hand. "You're not by yourself," I say.

"That dude on the bus was scary."

"He wasn't that bad," I say, thinking of my dad, of Terrance. "I wonder what he would have done with our shoes."

We sweat as we walk past crumbling brick buildings and grimy storefronts for old-fashioned tailors and appliance repairs and a barber shop with the red-and-white candy cane pole out front. It's not noon yet but the sun is high enough that the heat has settled in the air and feels thick and heavy. The courthouse steps are spotted with a rainbow variety of pigeon poop, and Rachel and I both look up and then duck our heads as the blue-green birds circle above us. There's a metal detector, but it doesn't seem to work since it beeps at everyone, and Rachel and I both have to step to the side and lift our arms to be personally wand scanned by a burly guy sweating through his khaki polyester guard uniform.

After a half-hour of waiting in line at the self-help center behind a tattooed pregnant girl who can't be much older than us, we finally get to talk to the "facilitator," a large black woman with sparkly purple fingernails that extend an inch above her fingertips.

"Hi," I say. "How are you?"

Her brown eyes barely glance up from her computer screen. Solitaire. She makes a noise like "Humpf."

I say, "I was hoping to get some information about filing for emancipation?"

She doesn't say a word, but points to the wall next to her booth where there is a six-foot panel of probably fifty plastic slots for papers.

"Um," I say, eyeing the rows of brightly colored forms, some a foot or more above my head. "I have to fill out some forms?"

She rolls her eyes and moves an ace to the top of her board. "And you said you needed help."

I say, "Could you please tell me which ones?"

She reaches out a fat hand with skin rolls and, barely looking away from her game, pulls out four little booklets, a pamphlet, and a single sheet of paper, and plops it all down on the six-inch counter in between us. "There," she says. She looks past me to the line and opens her mouth, but I say, "Is there any way you could help me? With these?" I put my hand on the pile of papers.

"I can't give legal advice," she says. "I can't help you fill out forms." She opens her mouth to call the next person again, but I say, "Wait. Please? Isn't there someone I could talk to?"

The woman must hear the tremor in my voice because she looks at me for the first time. She eyes me up and down, taking in my blond ponytail, my height, my T-shirt with a unicorn on it. "You trying to be on your own, little thing?" She raises a pierced eyebrow.

Rachel says, "Her parents suck."

The facilitator snort laughs. "Oh, honey. Don't everybody's?" She sighs and clicks her fingernails across her desk. "Look, there's a court mediator. Put your name and information on this list." She hands me a clipboard. "Someone will call you. Next!"

On the air-conditioned bus, I make sure Rachel takes the window seat and I flip through the three-inch stack of paperwork the woman gave me. I immediately see a problem. "You have to get your parents' permission to be emancipated?" I say.

Rachel says, "Doesn't that defeat the purpose of being emancipated?"

I say, "You also have to be able to prove financial independence."

"What bullshit," Rachel says.

I lean back against the seat and watch men and women in suits and dresses walk in small groups, laughing, talking, some eating sandwiches or burritos as they move. They probably complain about their jobs, but I'd work fifty hours a week to get away from Terrance and the mother who doesn't act like one. At least adults have freedom. I sigh. "Well, so much for that plan."

"It'll be okay, Liz," Rachel says, but I'm not so sure.

A few weeks later Mom's car is parked in Rachel's shady driveway on a Monday afternoon just as we get back from the river. Sun-lazy and still high, I don't understand what's happening as she starts screaming at me before we reach the house.

"Get in the car!" she yells. "Get in the car now!" She punches my arm as I move past her toward Rachel's front door, and then she raises her hands above her head like she's going to pound me with both her fists. Rachel flinches and jumps away. I stand my ground and stare at Mom, her eyes narrowed and teeth gritted, and wait for the blow to come. I almost want it, want an excuse to take a swing at her face, break her jaw, and shatter her glasses. But instead of hitting me, she presses her clamped fingers to her own temples and screeches. Rachel gapes at me with bulging, tear-filled eyes.

"What's going on?" I say when Mom quiets. I haven't seen her this pissed off in a long time.

"You! I've had it with you."

"What did I do?" I say.

"Get in the car," Mom says even-toned and low-pitched, pressing down her hair with her palms and then smoothing under her eyes with her fingertips. "You're leaving."

My stomach clenches. She can't be taking me away again already. "Why?"

She looks me in the eyes for the first time since she arrived. Her green eyes look glassy for the split second before they harden and she says, "You know why." She gets back in her Ford Taurus. "You think you're so smart," she says, her hand on the armrest, her leg hanging out the door. "Emancipation is not a freakin' joke, Elizabeth."

"I wasn't joking," I say. "I wanted to talk to you about it."

Her eyes burn holes in my cheeks from five feet away. "You're going to wish you were joking," she says and swings her leg into the car.

"But I didn't even file," I say. "How did you find out?"

"Go get your stuff," she says.

"Can we at least talk about this?" I say. "Don't you want to know why I thought I'd be safer on my own?"

Her eyes show fear for a split second before they narrow again. "Would you like me to call that court mediator for our talk?" she says and her voice is full of venom. She slams the metal door and starts the car. A Rod Stewart song drifts out of the window. "If you're not back down here in ten minutes, I will come upstairs and drag you out by your hair, you ungrateful snot."

In her room, Rachel cries while I shove shirts and underwear into my backpack, which has become a familiar task. "I am so sorry for you," she says.

"I'm sorry you had to see that," I say as I roll up a pair of shorts. "Do you want your swimsuit back?" I say. "I can change really fast."

"You can keep it," she says. She paces the room and tears keep sliding down her face.

Rachel watches me pack my toiletries and tie my shoes to my backpack strap by their laces. She doesn't blink. "Your mom is fucking crazy," she says suddenly, and sobs harder. "How come you're so normal?" she says.

"I'm not," I say. My hands tremble and tears blur my sight as I try to zip up all my clothes crammed into the big pocket of my pack. *In some ways I'm just like her.* I inhale a shaky breath and slump onto Rachel's bed.

"Why aren't you freaking out?" Rachel says.

I look up at her. Her mascara is smeared in black smudges around her hazel eyes and gray lines stain her cheeks. "I am," I say. "But I've told you about my mom before, right?"

She snorts air out of her nose in an almost laugh. "I kind of always thought you exaggerated for effect." She wipes at her eyes. "You should call social services, or something. Seriously."

"She's not that bad," I say.

Rachel stares at me. "I would be balled up and shivering in a corner right now if I were you," she says and sits next to me. "Where do you think she's taking you?"

"I have no idea," I say, the perpetual lump in my throat scratching its way to the surface. "And that's really scary," I say, my voice shaking. Rachel puts her arm around me and I turn into her shoulder and release the tears I didn't want Mom to see. "What if she sends me somewhere far away from everyone?"

We both jump when Mom honks the horn. Rachel's eyes widen. The horn blares again, and Rachel looks afraid and younger than me in this moment.

Rachel says, "Would she really come up and drag you out by your hair?"

"Probably not," I say, but I don't want to test it.

Rachel squeezes me again and cries into my neck. "I love you," she says.

"I love you, too."

"I wish you really were one of my sisters."

"Me, too," I say.

In the car Mom barks, "Buckle your seat belt," and doesn't say another word for miles. Images of teenage boot camps invade my mind, and I imagine endless push-ups and group showers. I picture a mental institution where I'll be medicated for my attitude, and not allowed to use real silverware at mealtimes. I might have pushed too far this time, and I'm not sure what Mom is capable of these days. I keep the swelling mass in my throat down by convincing myself she can't afford any excessive forms of punishment, but I can't keep my lungs from their rapid inhalations.

After forty silent minutes in the car I know where we're headed, and my breath starts to slow to normal. No Christmas lights shimmer on the boats lining the causeway into Sonoma County this evening, no black abyss to cross in the dark without directions. Mom's tan fingers squeeze the wheel like a coiled python, and her eyes never leave the road ahead. I sit as close to my door as I can manage, my thigh pressed against the armrest, my shoulder touching the cool glass. I'm jealous of the moving air outside, wafting through the tall green grasses, brushing the rusty-brown cattails, soaring above the wetland, free to go anywhere it wants.

Where Mom is taking me is the only place left, and Jaime's already there so it makes sense. Whatever happens next, at least we'll be together.

10

Mom grips my wrist with her strong-boned hands and jerks me from her light blue sedan toward the Cranleys' house like I'm a criminal. She pushes me into a painted white chair at Deborah's kitchen table, tells me not to move, and whacks the back of my head with her palm while Deborah gets tea.

"You better freakin' behave yourself here," she says and pinches my forearm. "This is your last option."

"What about Tammy's?"

"She won't want you back," Mom says. "Not after I talk to her."

"You'll lie," I say and know she would.

Deborah returns with a tray carrying two mugs painted with little roosters, and sugar in a white ceramic serving piece. Mom sips her tea and talks about my future like I'm not right here.

"She needs better influences," Mom says to Deborah. "More stability." Mom's eyes shine with tears that weren't there when she hit me two minutes ago. "I don't know what's wrong with her." She leans forward and whispers, "She went to the courthouse to talk to someone about emancipating herself."

Deborah puts down her mug. "What?"

"Like Drew Barrymore," I say.

Deborah's blue eyes scrunch with concern behind her glasses. "You're still growing, Liz," she says. "There's plenty of time to be an adult."

"I'm more mature than Mom," I say.

"See?" Mom says. "Listen to that disrespect—"

"Respect is something you earn—"

"Not when you're a child," Mom says, and smacks the back of my head a little softer this time with just the tips of her fingers. It makes me wonder if Dad hit her harder when we weren't around. Deborah clears her throat. "Liz, things won't be so bad here." She smiles and pats my hand, her nails a soft peach color that clashes with her orange hair.

"Parents are supposed to take care of their children," I say, my chest prickling with familiar pain.

"Enough, Liz," Mom says, sighing like she's bored. "We've been over this." She positions her fingers in a pyramid above her nose, her thumbs under her chin, and shakes her head with her eyes closed. For a second I think she might cry; that maybe she's realized that Terrance isn't worth giving us up. For just a sliver of a minute, hope sneaks into my gut like it's not sure it belongs, and I want so much to invite it to stay.

But Mom opens her eyes and spreads her arms out, gesturing to Deborah's suburban-housewife kitchen. "This isn't the worst thing that could possibly happen to you," she says. "It's not like you're homeless or hungry or dying. Nobody is beating you. You're not a Third World slave child," she says. "Stop complaining."

"Mom?" Jaime's voice is suddenly in my ears and she appears, rubbing her eyes, her hair frizzy at her forehead and temples. "Liz? What are you doing here?"

Deborah widens her eyes at me and Mom, and puts an arm around Jaime's shoulders. "Did we wake you?" Deborah says and leads Jaime away from us.

Jaime's tangled blond ponytail rounds the corner and I think of all the times I brushed her hair. All the times I made her laugh, cooked her dinner, helped her with her homework, kissed her scraped knees or cut fingers. I threatened her bullies at school, walked her home, and tucked her into clean sheets. I smothered my fear during Dad's rampages so I could sing her to sleep without my voice shaking. To be close to her, I will try to accept this new home and she's not even my daughter. I don't understand how Mom can walk away.

"How could you leave us?" I say, sinking down into my chair, a vise closing around my throat. My lungs squeeze in my chest near my pounding heart and my palms bead with sweat. "You said we were your blood."

"When you're older and married, all of this will make sense," Mom says. I hang my head. "You'll see," she says, but the words are strained.

I say, "I guess we will," but I'm certain she's wrong.

After Mom leaves, I lie awake in Deborah's guest room on top of the perfectly made twin bed and stare at the empty ceiling. I'm still wearing Rachel's bikini under my clothes because it's the most familiar thing in this house besides Jaime's breathing in her bed a few feet away. I clench and relax my shaking hands, grind the river silt between my toes, and inhale deep, unsteady breaths.

Jaime's cold toes are suddenly pressed against my shins and her nose is inches from mine as she curls up facing me on the bed. Her thumb rests loosely in her mouth and without taking it out she says, "Don't cry. Now we can live together again without our stupid parents."

I hadn't meant to cry. "You like living here?" I say.

She shrugs. "It's not as scary as Dad's." Jaime pulls her thumb out of her mouth and wipes the shriveled skin on her shirt. "It's safe to sleep here, Liz." She hugs me. "I promise." She climbs into her own bed and I hear the rustle of sheets as she wraps herself like a mummy. She says with her thumb back in her mouth, "You don't have to keep watch."

My aunt Deborah and her husband, Winston, have a bread machine. It has a timer. At night you can put all the bread ingredients into its rectangular tin pan: the flour, milk, salt, yeast, and whatever you want for flavor, and then put the pan into the white plastic machine, set the clock and voila, fresh bread is ready in the morning.

I watch Deborah close the lid and set the timer. "We always have homemade cinnamon bread hot and fresh Saturday mornings," she says as she wipes off the white-tiled countertops and puts the perishables back in the refrigerator. Deborah's kitchen is done in a "French country style," she told me earlier, pale yellow, deep blue, and white. White cabinets have rooster knickknacks on top, a wallpaper border displays blue-ribbon-wrapped straw hats. "Right out of the machine, the butter melts down into the bread

and it gets all smushy and yummy, and so good, Liz, I promise."
Deborah says, "I promise," the same way my dad does, and my gut
warns me not to trust her.

It is my fifth night here, but I know enough not to ask to watch
TV. It's past ten P.M. and technically, I should be in bed. Winston
is a computer programmer who spends his weekends researching
military history and combat procedures for his future novels, and
this house runs on rules: bedtimes for school nights and weekends; TV, computer, phone, and video game time limits; a rotating chore calendar for the kids, to which Jaime's name has been
added, I notice. She is supposed to vacuum tomorrow.

Deborah says, "It's time for bed, Liz."

"Okay," I say, but I don't move.

She hugs me. "Try to get some rest," she says. "Good night."
Deborah disappears up the stairs. Her soft socks on soft carpet
make a nearly silent exit.

I doubt I'll sleep tonight, either, but standing in the kitchen in
the dark by myself doesn't help, so I head toward the guest bedroom off the side of the family room, where Jaime has been living
the past few months. Two twin beds with matching sky-blue com-
forters awash with sunshine-yellow flowers rest against white
headboards with carved white daisies. A sunflower wallpaper border coats the top foot of wall space around the room, two white
nightstands and a white dresser sit near the beds, with a blue lamp
on the dresser top. It looks like a stage set or a model home and
feels just as phony.

I hover over Jaime in the moonlight, her thumb tucked in her
mouth, her hair a knotted mess behind her head. It's July and still

she wraps the blankets tightly around her, cocoon style. Only her face sticks out, which looks less like mine than ever. I listen to her heavy breathing, the same sound she made when we were little and shared a bed. Not snoring, just the sound of full lungs expanding and contracting, air forced through small nostrils. Her jaws are loose, her eyebrows relaxed. It's like when I held her hand so she'd sleep through breaking dishes, slamming doors, our mother's crying, and just like then I am jealous of her closed lids and deep breaths and dreamland, but also glad that at least one of us feels secure enough to rest.

I haven't slept through the night since leaving Rachel's. During daylight my eyes can close without the panic that comes after the sun goes down, and while everyone goes about their busy summer lives just like they did before I showed up, I take naps curled like a cat on the carpet or the couch, wherever there's a warm red glow on the back of my eyelids. When I lie still in the dark, my mind releases armies of memories that tramp across my closed eyes and churn the acid in my stomach into white-water fists. Snapshot images play in loop tracks like slideshows: Mom's pale face shoving screaming toddler Jaime into my arms as Dad's fist collides with her jaw; Jaime's unmoving figure on the floor of Dad's pickup, blood trickling down her cheek; Terrance licking his lips as his sagging shorts and bare chest lean over me; Mom's hard eyes as she left me here like I'd been dismissed.

I'm sure Mom thought this would work. That I'd want to rebuild my life around Jaime, go back to being defined as the big sister, and part of me thinks it would be easy. I could slip into my old role, my lines memorized, my act perfected over the years. There is no room for originality or deviation from the standards here; the point is to shape me back into the obedient and compliant child Mom needs me to be. In exchange for stability and a chance to live with Jaime, I am supposed to surrender myself. I understand the trade-off. I'm just not sure it's worth it. I think I might be ready for a different function in this family, a new part, like a starring role in my own life and a fresh location. Even with Deborah's good intentions, she'll never understand me the way Tammy does.

I kiss Jaime's forehead and feel my way through the dark hallway to the bathroom, my nighttime refuge. I paint my toenails with some cranberry-colored polish I find in a back cabinet and sing to myself. I envy Jaime's ability to ignore the "reminders" Tammy talked about, the constant weight of past wrongs. Tammy said I should try to make peace with the hurts, but if they keep repeating, how can I move on? In the mirror I notice a string of red bumps running down my left cheek. In my head I hear Jaime call me pimple face, which she did when she wanted to be mean. My shoulders slump in my reflection. We don't even spend enough time together to fight anymore.

Out in the family room I step gently on my newly painted toes, the tan carpet spongy like short-clipped grass under my feet. The quarter moon shines through the locked windows and lights up the space enough for me to see the furniture in the family room: the gray sectional couch, the recliner by the fireplace. This fireplace burns real wood, though, since Winston says it's a "fire hazard," it never gets used. The dark timber mantel displays a ship in a bottle, and a gold-framed painting in pastels of three women wearing bonnets and laughing in a grassy meadow that is definitely not an original.

The light from the windows increases as I survey things that don't belong to me: Ashley's *Tiger Beat* and *Teen Vogue* magazines on the floor, Matt's handheld video console, a pair of his little socks bunched up by the TV, Jaime's pink plastic Hello Kitty makeup case and scrunchie on the couch. Outside, the sky is gray-blue and hazy. Lingering fog filters the rising sun and it figures that even during summer I can't get away from the gray.

I pick up one of Ashley's girly magazines just as Matt comes down wearing *Bananas in Pajamas* pajamas. I smile. "My brother loves that show," I say and picture Noah singing along with the talking bananas, clapping his small hands. "He has those same pajamas," I say. "A few sizes smaller."

"I didn't choose them," Matt says and plops down next to me. "Mom buys all my clothes." He yawns, and with his eyes half-closed shoves a cartridge into his SEGA console. "Want to play?"

I shrug and take the controller he hands me. The game is Primal Rage, dinosaur combat. I control a red, fire-breathing T. rex named Diablo and as soon as I learn the maneuvers, I pretend Matt's bluish-purple velociraptor is Terrance and attack it with a vengeance. I think of his damp lips on my ear and deliver a spray of fire. I think of his heavy-lidded stare and stomp on the velociraptor's head.

"Do your parents let you play this violent death match stuff?"

Matt leans toward me. "I convinced Dad it was a prehistoric learning game." My eyebrows jump and he grins. "It does teach survival skills," he says. "So it wasn't really a lie."

I laugh as his aggressive dinosaur leaps at me with teeth bared. "What if you get caught?"

"They trust me," Matt says. "It's you guys they think will lie."

"That's good to know."

"Mom says it's not your fault. That you and Jaime were in bad situations," Matt says, his fingers clicking away on his controller as his dinosaur completes flying kicks and underbelly attacks on my much slower T. rex. "She said you had bad influences."

I sigh. "What does your dad think of us?"

Matt hesitates, and that's enough confirmation for me. Deborah can be as charming and convincing as my dad, and I bet Winston doesn't have much of a chance to say no when she puts her mind to something.

I say, "Do you ever read?"

"Sure," Matt says, "I read science books about flying and space engineering and entomology and—"

"Are you into guns?"

"My dad has guns," he says. I know. I also know he keeps them loaded in a safe in his office, a safe taller than me.

"Does he let you use them?"

"Not here." Matt's birdlike dinosaur pecks at Diablo's neck and rips off a strip of red flesh. Blood sprays everywhere but fades before hitting the pixilated background grass. "But sometimes he takes us to the shooting range. He says it's important for our safety." My neon-green life box at the top of the screen runs out, and I die. Too bad Terrance doesn't have a life meter that's running low. "You're better than Ashley," Matt says.

"Thanks," I tell him and pat his head, which has yet to outgrow that baby phase of being twice the size of his body. He looks like a giant doll no one would ever buy. When Matt was little, he pounded his head repeatedly against walls, floors, doorknobs, and once, the concrete driveway. These days, I understand the impulse and I wonder if he remembers what was so horrible he wouldn't stop until he was tied down or passed out.

Matt sniffs and says, "Mmm. Saturday morning bread." It does smell good, and it reminds me of waking up in Connecticut the first time we visited Tammy. Each morning she toasted cinnamon-raisin bagels and scraped real butter across the top. The fog rolled away from the surface of the pond behind her house, revealing jungle-green plants and trees growing at the water's edges near cattails and lily fields, their lush, thick canopies stretching out over the moss-coated surface. We sat on bar stools at Tammy's kitchen counter and watched the humid stillness, sometimes broken by a lethargic dragonfly or a leaf too heavy with sweat dropping its puddle. She asked us questions like, "If you could go anywhere in the world, where would it be?" and promised to take us there when we were older. "When you graduate from college," she told us, "I'll take you anywhere you want."

The cinnamon smell draws me from the dinosaur battles on-screen to stare through the clear plastic square on the bread machine designed for viewing, but all I see is gray. "How do you tell when the bread is done?" I ask Matt, who is on level twelve with his velociraptor.

Deborah answers from the stairway. "It beeps. It's supposed to be done at eight, but then it needs to sit for a minute."

It's too early to listen to Deborah's list of things she thinks she can do to cheer me up. She won't talk about what happened, she'll only say things like, "Try to look on the bright side," or, "Positive attitudes put problems in their place," as if I'm depressed because my favorite TV show got canceled. She says things like, "Oh, come on, Liz, it's not so bad. If you come to the mall I'll buy you a new outfit." As if presents and cinnamon bread can protect me from the real dangers she doesn't want to address.

The bread machine beeps while I am looking through the window in the top and I jump. Deborah presses her hand against my back for a second and I jump again. She says, "So, what do you want to do today?" I shrug. "I thought maybe we'd go shopping," she says.

"You don't need to buy me anything."

"Do you have a dress for church?"

My nostrils flare out, but I bite my tongue, literally, and taste blood. "I'm sure I can find something."

"I want you and Jaime to sing with me on the worship team," she says and my eyes go wide. "Oh, don't worry, not tomorrow of course, but soon. Jaime already agreed. You two have such heavenly voices; I can't wait to hear you in practice."

"Um." My face feels stiff, my tongue is swollen, and I can't make my mouth form words.

"So you'll need something pretty to wear, and we might as well start looking today." My brain is overloading with things I can't say, filling like a balloon and ramming my skull from the inside. "The early bird gets the worm," she says.

"I feel ill," I say.

"You just need to eat," she says. "You hardly touched my famous meatloaf last night." She slices me a big piece of squared cinnamon goodness and slathers it in butter. I have to admit it is delicious. She cuts and butters slices for Matt and herself and we stand in the kitchen eating fresh bread and staring out the window at the azalea bushes near the driveway.

After my second piece Deborah says, "So, should we get going?"

"Going where?" Ashley says as she staggers into the kitchen like she's drunk.

"I don't know if I'm up for the mall," I say.

Deborah huffs her lips together and sounds like an unhappy horse. She lifts her hands and says, "What teenager turns down new clothes?" Those of us who have sex offender stepdads who don't need any encouragement.

Ashley says, "You said you'd buy me a new swimsuit."

Deborah says to me, "Do you need a swimsuit?" and Ashley gives me the evil eye behind her mother's red hair. She makes an *L* with her thumb and index finger and raises it to her forehead.

"I have one," I tell Deborah, and wonder what Rachel is doing today without me. "Thanks, though." What I wouldn't give to be lying out by the river, coconut tanning oil on my skin, drugs blurring my thoughts, talking with Rachel and laughing at her jokes.

"You must need something," Deborah says and it's true, but she can't provide the things I need.

I say, "Sleeping pills?"

Deborah frowns. "That's not funny, Liz."

"Sorry," I say. "Did my mom tell you how long she plans to leave me here?" I ask and my voice strains just a little.

Deborah reaches over to hug me and I let her. She smells like laundry detergent and artificial fruitiness. "Let's talk about that later," she says. Deborah puts a bread crumb in her mouth and then licks her fingers. "Okay, troop," she says and claps her hands together. "Time to start the day."

Ashley groans, but my days and nights and naps blend into each other without clear stops or starts and I wasn't kidding about the sleeping pills. I can feel myself slipping deeper into a pit of quicksand, being swallowed bit by bit. Every day it's harder to move my feet so I stop struggling and don't bother to scream, even when I'm trapped up to my waist and can't move my hands, even as my mouth fills with thick, grainy mud. No one has noticed yet that I'm sinking.

At dinner, Deborah spoons more mashed potatoes onto my plate even though I haven't eaten any from the pile already there. Fried chicken and peas also sit untouched in front of me while Winston is on his second serving. After prayer, this family dives into their food, shoveling like stable boys until their plates reflect their faces.

"Matt," Deborah says. "Tell us your Bible verse for tomorrow."

He clears his throat and swallows his chicken. "'Seek ye first the kingdom of God and his righteousness.'"

"Very nice," Deborah says and Winston nods, still chewing. She says, "Girls?"

Jaime and Ashley look at each other, take a breath, and say simultaneously, "'For God so loved the world that he gave his only begotten son that whosoever believeth in him shall not perish but have everlasting life.'" They take deep breaths and giggle.

"Good job, girls," Deborah says.

Ashley says, "What about Liz?"

"That's okay," I say, pressing drifts of potato through the tines of my fork.

"If you learn, you won't feel left out in Sunday school," Matt says. I smile at him, but this is something I do want to be left out of.

"I don't think I'll go to Sunday school," I say and the table goes silent. Winston stops chewing. Jaime cringes. Ashley smirks. "We all go to Sunday school," Winston says.

I'd gotten spoiled living with Tammy. Sunday mornings we hiked on wildflower-coated foothill trails humming with singing birds while the sun rose, biked up City Creek Canyon and sketched pine trees or the brook skipping over water-smoothed rocks, took naps under the swishing sound of waving birch and oak branches and broken rays of sunshine. Nature is Tammy's church, and if I had a choice, it'd be mine, too.

"Your mom would like you to attend church," Deborah says.

"This family goes to church," Winston says.

Even Jaime, "It's a pretty cool church, Liz." She nods at me like *shut up*, and just like that, I know she'd choose to stay here even if Mom said we could come home.

Ashley says, "So, Liz, you want to learn our verse now?" and smiles wide in challenge, her braces full of green and white flecks.

"Actually," I say, "I remember that one."

"Prove it," Ashley says, so I do. I repeat the Bible verse I've said a thousand times before and it means no more to me now than it did when my Sunday school teacher gave out candy to the kids who could memorize a few lines after a half-hour of repetition.

"'For God so loved the world . . .'" I say, but wish I could say that it doesn't matter how cool a church is if you don't believe in God, that worshipping something without proof is insane, that I think Christians are hypocrites. Ashley pouts and crosses her arms over her chest when I finish, but Jaime smiles and Matt applauds.

"Wonderful," Deborah says and Winston nods. "Just wonderful." She claps her hands together. "Liz, have you ever thought of playing guitar?"

I shake my head, fill my mouth with five peas and a piece of chicken, and chew.

The clothes Mom brought in my never-unpacked duffel bags still smell like lavender and rain, or at least that clean smell after rain has rinsed the air, and also something else that's just the smell of Tammy's house. I miss her every time I take out a clean shirt and they are almost gone. I sent her letters from Rachel's house, but her six-week safari has thirteen days left.

I am looking for something "appropriate" to wear to church tomorrow. One of the skirts Tammy bought me or the thin white linen pants might work. I'm holding up a brown cotton A-line skirt when Deborah comes in. "Oh, honey, don't you have anything less somber?" She glances at the neutrals and dark colors in my bag. "Something pastel?" she says. "Maybe a light pink?"

I don't move but my eyes won't stop blinking. She puts a hand on my shoulder, gives it a quick squeeze. "Don't fret," she says. She takes the skirt from my hand, squints at it. "As long as you don't wear a black top, it'll do for tomorrow," she says and hands me the clothing. "But we are definitely going shopping, missy."

Jaime comes in as Deborah is leaving. Deborah says, "Jaime, show Liz your church dresses."

Jaime waits until Deborah is outside around the corner and says, "You're not going to like them."

I cross my arms over my chest and frown. "I'm not going."

"I'm sleeping in Ashley's room tonight," Jaime says. "We only get to do it on Saturdays. She has a TV in her room, we rented *Clueless*. You could come, too," she says, but I know her too well.

"Thanks," I say. "I have my book." I'm reading *The Last Vampire* again and wishing I were a five-thousand-year-old vampire with powers. If I had super strength or could manipulate people with my gaze, Mom and Dad and Terrance would lose their authority over me.

Jaime says, "Church will be okay tomorrow."

"What if I don't go?" I say, feeling like the pouty younger sister.

"Please just come," she says.

I can see in her blue eyes that she means she likes it here better than anywhere else, that finally something good has happened, that she still believes in God and He brought her here and gave her a new family and a home where she feels safe, and I realize if I ruin all of that for her, I would be as selfish as my mother. "Okay." I sigh and she hugs me.

"You're the best sister ever," she says. She takes her blanket off her bed. "You gonna be lonely without me?" she says as she heads out the door.

"Of course," I say. I smile so she knows it's okay to leave, but it's impossible not to feel lonely when you're the only person awake in a house before the sun has fully set and the only person afraid of the loaded guns in the six-foot safe upstairs; when you start to feel closer to your geeky eight-year-old cousin than to the sister you grew up protecting and you can't forget the feeling of a man twice your size pressed against you in a dark bar; when you can't listen to rock music or read interesting books or say what you actually think or witnessed or talk honestly to anyone and all I want to do is sleep but I bet that doesn't happen tonight, either, and if God does exist then I fucking hate Him.

In the morning I'm sitting at the breakfast table counting roosters in the kitchen—twenty so far—when Ashley comes in. "What's wrong with your face?" she says to me after she's poured herself some orange juice, licked the rim of the plastic jug, halfway twisted the cap back on, and left it on the counter.

"Ashley," Deborah says, but I catch Ashley's smirk behind her juice glass. The small line of red bumps on my cheek has turned into a full-blown rash. They are definitely not pimples.

"I think it's from your dog," I say. "He licked my face."

"I'll get you some cream," Deborah says to me, pats my shoulder, and goes up the stairs. I appreciate the thought, but Deborah's thing is saving people. Church clothes and rash creams are just the beginning of her Elizabeth outreach program.

Ashley says to me, "So why does your mom hate you so much she kicked you out again?" Matt's eyes go wide but he doesn't say anything. Ashley takes a sip of her juice and puts one hand on her hip. "Loser."

My hands grip the plate in front of me—"Everyone loads their own dishes here," Deborah says in my head—but I think I might smash it into Ashley's face so I leave it and start to walk away. Ashley says, "You need to clear your place."

Matt says, "That was mean, Ash."

She says, "Can it, nerd."

I keep walking and I hear Deborah as I round the corner into Jaime's room. "What happened to Elizabeth? I brought her something for that rash."

Ashley says, "She didn't load her plate."

In the guest room we share, Jaime's bed is empty, her blanket missing, her sheets tossed to the side of the mattress, a dent in the pillow where her head would be. It's like crime-drama shots of missing children's rooms, possibly what it could look like if Terrance made good on his threats and came after her. Like he told me, he likes to win, and Jaime, who may not fight back, would be an easy conquest. *What would I do if she actually disappeared?* Maybe it isn't just her who needs me.

I imagine hibernating, going to sleep and waking up to a new layer of earth, a clean landscape and fresh air, inside and out having grown into new skins. I crawl under the comforter with the brown A-line skirt that smells like Tammy's house and build myself a cocoon.

11

"Don't let them watch this channel," Winston says to me, coming up behind where Ashley and I sit on the *L*-shaped gray couch in the family room. He adjusts his tie and yells, "Deborah!" his voice like a foghorn.

Her red hair appears behind Winston's wide shoulders. She's wearing a flowery dress, shapeless and flowing, and her Just Peachy perfume fills my nostrils. I have my own bottle of the orange-ish liquid Deborah gave me so I could "feel peachy every day." It doesn't work.

Deborah says, "The number of the restaurant is on the counter, Linda, and I left money so you can order a pizza. Make sure Matt gets to bed by ten. The girls can sleep in Ashley's room but they need to keep it down so Matt can sleep." Deborah waves to me, and leans over the back of the couch to kiss Ashley on the head. "Thanks!" she says, and I try to ignore the fact that she just called me my mom's name.

Winston puts his hand on Deborah's back, his computer-programmer belly hanging over his brown slacks stretches a little with the extension of his arm. "Kitten? Shall we?"

Deborah calls, "Be safe, kids," as they round the corner into the entryway. I hear Winston say, "Are you sure we shouldn't get a real babysitter?" just as the door shuts and the security alarm beeps on.

Ashley changes the channel back to MTV, and I ignore Winston's last command. He already doesn't trust me, and if I irritate Ashley too much, she'll make up something I did that's much worse than allowing her to watch music videos and convince her parents it's the truth.

"Just talked to Mom," Jaime says to me as she comes out of the guest room. "She wanted to talk to you." Jaime sits next to Ashley's bare legs on the couch in her matching blue lace tank top and tiny cotton pajama shorts, like they're Barbies dressed for bed. "You haven't talked to her in weeks," Jaime says. "She thinks you hate her."

"She's perceptive," I say. "When did you stop?"

"You don't really hate her," Jaime says. "She's your mom."

"She let a pervert into our house," I say. "Doesn't that bother you?"

"Hey, it's our song," Ashley says. Jaime turns away from me, and she and Ashley sing and snap their fingers, bop their shoulders, and weave their necks Stevie Wonder–style along with the MTV video.

A few weeks ago I saw them make up a dance to this same Mariah Carey tune. I peeked through the small window in the guest bedroom and watched them gyrating in the driveway like the half-clothed women currently shaking their butts at the cameras. I thought about how Jaime and I used to make up dances to Prince and Janet Jackson songs, counted out steps in beats of eight, swirled and jumped and sang along to the radio when Mom wasn't home. Back when Mom was a common enemy and as sisters we held hands and faced the firing squad together.

"You're not supposed to watch this," I say, getting up.

"Whatever," Ashley says.

Jaime says, "You watch this all the time."

"I'm older," I say. "What kind of pizza do you want?"

"Pepperoni and pineapple!" they say together and burst into giggles.

"Gross," I say, but it doesn't matter. I'm not going to eat any of it. "Will Matt eat that?"

"Who cares?" Ashley says. I figure he can pick it off.

When I get off the phone with Round Table, Ashley and Jaime are giggling. They try to hush as I get closer, but can't, and I remember one year at the state fair on the Zipper adventure ride when Jaime and I screamed from the gut, throats open and heads thrown back, we laughed so loud that the conductor stopped the spinning metal cages and told us if we didn't quiet down he'd make us get off. We tried to say we were sorry but he unbuckled our straps and we fell out of the sticky vinyl seats wiping tears from eyes still narrowed with laughter. We clung to each other as we stumbled down the rickety metal plank lined with aluminum folding fences, smiling, snorting, and trying to breathe.

"You want to call Darin?" Ashley asks Jaime.

"Who's Darin?" I ask and they giggle again. "Seriously," I say, thinking of Cody's charm, Terrance's confidence in his talent for blending in. "You shouldn't be calling boys you know nothing about."

"He's nice," Jaime says. "He's from church."

"Terrance goes to church, and think about what else he does," I say, longing to tell her all of it: what it feels like to have his skin so close, have him look at you with lusty eyes that should only be for his wife. But like with Dad, if Jaime knows the truth, I haven't done my job.

Ashley says, "It's none of your business," and they get up to go to Ashley's room, snickering and whispering to each other. Matt is coming down the stairs and Ashley pushes him as he jumps off the last step. He whines, "Ash," and runs into the family room.

"Why are you so mean to him?" I say.

"Why do you care?" She makes a *W* with her hands, her wanna-be French-manicured nail tips like little horns at the tops of her index fingers. Sneering at me, she says, "Get it?" and walks up the carpeted staircase, wagging her ass like a hooker.

Matt sits in his legless chair in front of the screen. "Want to play Sonic?" he asks. I sit next to him on the floor and with his help, make it past the first few levels. He likes explaining things. Some days when I hibernate in my shell he sits next to my bed and I listen to him talk about planes or space or biology for hours, and it helps take my mind off the things that aren't so easily spelled out. Thanks to him, I've learned that some cicadas spend seventeen years underground and then emerge with wings, that ants live in tunnels where they build rooms to store food and raise young. The colony cannot survive without the queen. She has to lick each egg before it hatches; the larvae eat her saliva as they emerge.

"You don't have to do that," Matt says. "She doesn't bother me."

"It doesn't matter," I say. "Older sisters are supposed to look out for you, not push you around. They should help you with your homework, and keep your secrets, and let you have a vote in pizza toppings."

He says, "Pepperoni and pineapple?"

"Yeah," I say, "but I got root beer for you."

"Ashley hates that," he says.

"I know."

"You're my favorite babysitter," Matt says. We watch a hedgehog run and spin and absorb hovering golden hoops with a jingling coin sound until the doorbell rings.

The pizza guy is cute in a generic sort of way with plain sandy-blond hair and brown eyes. After I've paid him and set the alarm back to paranoid, I can feel Dean's full red mouth on mine and imagine his white face and blue eyes as he leans in toward me. . . . I sigh and wonder if Dean imagines running his hands over my skin and kissing me as much as I think about him.

A week after arriving here, I pulled out my yearbook where Dean had written his address and blushed again at his request for a picture of a "beautiful woman wearing a bikini." I wrote to him, *This part of California isn't always that sunny, and while I have escaped the Mormon regime, my current household is still religious. Phones here offer no privacy, so I hope you'll write me back.* I signed my letter, *I wish you were here,* with a heart and my name.

He wrote me back quickly, answered all my questions, and asked me a few. The letter was pen pal–ish—in a good way—except the last line which read, *Any news about those beautiful young women posing for a photo—in the clothing of their choice?* He signed off, *I wish I was there, too. Or better, yet, that you were here. I hope you come back.* I carry the letter in my pocket, and more and more I hope the same thing.

I wrote letters to Rachel and Tammy, too, when I first moved in. To Rachel I wrote, *My uncle keeps loaded guns in a safe the size of a closet. My aunt Deborah only buys pink clothes and wants me to sing in the church worship team. Did you do it with Frank yet?*

To Tammy I wrote, *Jaime is best friends with Ashley. We eat a lot of chicken pot pie. I'm not allowed to walk outside by myself after dusk and they make me go to church on Sundays. I miss the mountains.*

I told Tammy I missed her fancy cheeses and sour plain yogurt, her whole-wheat bread and natural, sugar-free peanut butter, her waking me up early and forcing me to hike and even her nitpicking about my grades. I miss Tammy asking about my day and actually listening, her holding me and not trying to fix it. I called her the day she should have gotten back from Africa, but I just got the machine. I didn't even get to hear Tammy, just Sam's voice, "We're not available at the moment. Please leave a brief message." I left Deborah's number but it's been three days. When I try to focus on the positive of Tammy and her house, it just makes me miss everything more, and with Jaime slipping further and further away, I don't know if there's a reason for me to stay here.

I notice an envelope with my name on it on the small mail organizer near the door as I juggle the pizza and soda. I get excited until I realize it's not Rachel or Tammy or Dean's handwriting, even though the intense slant and girly loops are familiar. Lava bubbles in my stomach while I wait for the kids to eat their slices and clear their plates and go up to their rooms, and then I open the letter before the gurgling fire can completely scald my guts.

Terrance wrote, *Dearest Liz, Your mom is upset you won't talk to her, and that upsets me because I want my girls to get along. I thought I'd write to make sure there was nothing I had done to offend you, and that you weren't taking something that happened between us out on your mom. You know how much I care about you, and I hate worrying that I somehow ruined our relationship. I enjoy our conversations very, very much, so if you ever want to talk, about anything, feel free to call me. And remember, if I don't hear from you, I'll have to call Jaime to make sure things are okay. I miss you. Love, Terrance.* Under the word "love," he drew the same heart he'd used on his letters to Mom and I gag on the bile that shoots up my throat.

I lie spooned against the curve of the couch for the next hour, my eyes wide and watering and my heart hammering, unable to watch TV or focus on anything except Terrance's thinly veiled threats. Once again I marvel at his aptitude for manipulation. Deborah or Mom would say that he is trying to be nice, but they don't know how often he winks at me or makes inappropriate jokes, how often I've seen his butt crack and hip bones, and once his shorts hung so low I saw the tips of his black pubic hairs. It's these images that batter my brain over and over, and the fact that if I share them with anyone, Jaime will be in the same sinking boat.

Deborah and Winston come home a little after eleven. I hear the door open, the alarm beep, and Winston going up the stairs. I get up because I know he'll be back down soon. He never goes to sleep without checking that all the windows and doors are locked, the alarm is set, and the dog is in the house, but none of his security measures make me feel any safer.

I sit up, yawning, and wave to Deborah as she sits in a pile of dog hair. "How did things go?" she says, her hand swooshing at the floating tufts of fur.

I try to calm the churning in my stomach, swallow acid. "Fine."

She takes a deep breath. "Are you okay, Elizabeth?" Her brows crease in that same look of concern I imagine on her face when she leaves the house in the middle of the day and shows up at the houses of the hurt or suffering, the unwed mothers or pregnant teens, her neighbor whose son she thinks is gay, the old lady who wants to die alone.

"I'm fine," I say and start to get up. Deborah stands up, too, and puts one hand on each of my upper arms.

"Let me help you," she says. Her elbows bend and suddenly she's hugging me. "You're hurting. I can see it," she says.

I inch my body back far enough that my calves hit the couch, my balance is thrown, and I fall into a cushion. "You can't help," I whisper. She has no idea what's really wrong, and doesn't want to know.

"Maybe not, but God can. He's here for you, Liz."

I've spent the last four Sundays at church in a pink dress Deborah bought me that is edged with white lace and sports a pink bow at the center of the collar, listening to sermons about forgiveness and the power of God's love preached by a middle-aged man who checks out my legs when I sit in the front row beside Deborah. God isn't even in the building.

"He's not," I say.

"It may not seem like it, but He's chosen this path for you for a reason."

"If that's true, then I'll be fine."

Deborah says, "Jaime says sometimes she wakes up in the middle of the night and hears you crying."

"I can't sleep at night," I say.

"Probably because you read such morbid books," she says.

"Vampires aren't morbid."

"They're dead."

I say, "They're immortal."

"You hardly ever smile."

"I'm a discriminating audience."

"And you never eat," Deborah says. "You're turning into skin and bones."

"Maybe then I won't look like my mom," I say.

"Elizabeth!" She throws up her hands and her blue eyes get wide, her cheeks puff out, and I think of my father's face one time he hit me. He wasn't supposed to see me standing over the stainless steel sink in Crystal's trailer, pouring his forty-ounce bottles of Olde English 800 down the drain. He was supposed to drive us here, to Deborah's, a two-hour drive through unlit, two-lane country roads, and lots of fast freeways. I'd already taken the cash from his wallet.

His eyes bulged, his jaw set, and it was like slow motion as he charged me in his bare feet and ripped jeans. He punched my stomach and when I bent to breathe, he shoved me down against the plywood cabinet under the sink, jammed his knee into my chest, and pressed the cupboard handle into my back so deep I had a four-inch arch outlined in black and blue for weeks. I didn't make a sound, just gritted my teeth and waited. I never showed anyone the bruises.

Deborah's energy deflates and she plops down next to me in her linen dress. "The vibrant little girl who used to bounce around and ask questions about everything and who sang and played and laughed . . ." She sighs so deep dog hair swirls in the air around my head. Deborah shakes her head. "That light I used to see in you is gone, Liz," she says. "It's gone and that makes me sad."

I don't remember the girl she thinks I was.

"I scheduled an appointment for you to talk to a counselor," she says. Her eyes are closed so I lean my head against the couch and close mine. In the silence I think of rivers running into oceans, tides ruled by moon rhythms, the security of instinct. Water doesn't get sad and slow down; animals don't get lost after a bad night, their emotions don't impede their survival. No matter how many scout ants never return to the colony, the queen sends out more of her children without hesitation.

"Good night," I tell her, getting up. She looks at me, those orange-brown eyebrows angled in, her translucent pink-rimmed glasses lifted slightly.

"You'll talk to her?" she says.

"I'll go," I say.

"Elizabeth!" Winston doesn't need to yell. His voice carries deep and loud, his laugh like a truck horn blast. It's so bad Ashley refuses to sit near him when we go to the movies. "Elizabeth!"

He never calls me Liz. I am wearing Rachel's bikini—and, I have to say, filling it out more than when I'd left Rachel's, so much that I'm starting to almost consider Dean's photo request—and lying on the concrete on the edge of the pool. Six feet at the deepest end, it has a waterfall with dark porous rocks and tropical foliage and a black bottom for solar heating, but with Jaime all buddy-buddy with Ashley and "adult supervised swimming only," this pool is not the perk it could be.

But I can still lie on my back beside the shimmering surface, listen to the babble of the waterfall, look at the sky, and pretend that my location isn't this conservative nothing-to-do-town, but simply, poolside, anywhere, USA. I am getting pretty tan.

Winston appears through my sunglasses. "Elizabeth," he breathes, winded from the walk outside. "There you are."

"Here I am," I say.

"You're too close to the pool," he says. I scoot two inches. He says, "I'm going out." Pause. "Deborah is shopping." He looks uncomfortable, his belly tilting from side to side as he shifts his feet.

"Okay," I say and close my eyes. Fat men try to talk to cute girls anywhere. I could still be anywhere.

"I need you to watch Matthew."

I stand up, wrap my towel around me, and tuck the end under my armpit. The atmosphere is ruined anyway. Winston stops averting his eyes. I say, "Isn't he just playing SEGA?"

"He needs to be supervised."

"I think I'll hear him if he starts crying from finger cramps," I say and Winston doesn't even smile.

Inside, Matt sits on his legless chair in front of the screen, closer than usual. "So, I heard you need to be watched," I say.

He shakes his head, which looks even bigger without his glasses. "My dad worries too much," he says. He's playing a puzzle game that looks like Tetris. Colored blocks float down the screen like neon raindrops.

"No kidding."

"He went to get my new glasses. He's blind without his, so . . ." Matt shrugs.

"Where's Jaime?"

"Mom took the girls to the mall."

"'The girls?'" I say. Not so long ago that term referred to different girls.

"Yeah, Jaime and Ashley wanted to go shopping." He rolls his eyes.

"They didn't even invite me."

"I thought you hate shopping."

"I guess they've really bonded."

Matt says, "Like carbon and oxygen," and I laugh out loud. I sit down next to him on the carpet. He squints at me. "What?" he says.

"Do kids make fun of you at school?" I say.

He looks at his bare feet and his light brown bowl cut flops forward. "Sometimes," he says. His head pops up and he looks at me the way Jaime used to when I said I had good news or told her I'd let her have control of the remote. He says, "Do you know why?"

He can't throw a ball, he's afraid of birds, he has little spotted scars on his forehead from the years he pounded his head into rough surfaces. He still goes to therapy. I shrug. "Kids are mean," I say.

"My dad says small people pick on others to make themselves feel big."

"That's some of it," I say. As if Winston's guns aren't proof enough that he was bullied. "I bet you're also the smartest kid in your class, and that's some of it, too."

Matt looks up at me with raised eyebrows. "Can you teach me how to play a sport?"

"Which one?"

"It doesn't matter," he says. "One with a ball?"

On the way to the therapist's office Deborah tells me I could be part of the family if I wanted to, if I stopped isolating myself. "Jaime is already one of the Cranley crew," she says. As if I needed to be reminded. Deborah says, "We want to see you smile again."

Every week it gets harder to dodge her requests for me to sing at worship practice. I picked up her guitar once when she wasn't home and strummed the strings. I pushed the memory of Terrance's offer to teach me how to play from my mind and felt the vibration of the wood, the humming between my ears and in my fingers, and if they weren't songs to praise the god who was on my short list, I might have tried to learn.

Deborah says, "You have a home here, Liz, if you want it." She looks at me so I nod. "But you have to put a little effort in."

I know she wants me to eat more than cereal and smile at

church and pray like I mean it and curtail my sarcasm and sing with her praise group and pet the dog and get used to the guns and the rules and the roosters and even though I remember how to play along, I feel like I shouldn't have to. "Okay," I say.

Deborah smiles at me like something has changed. "Great," she says. I wonder how long I'll last.

"How are you feeling, Elizabeth?" The counselor is a short, round woman, almost as tall as I am and twice as wide. She has straight black hair cut in a bob that stops just below her ears.

"Fine," I say.

"Can we try for more specifics?" A thick, dark wooden cross hangs on the wall above her desk. Under it is her psychologist's certificate, as if God had some say in her credentials.

"I'd rather not be here, but I'd rather not be anywhere, so here is good enough I guess." I shrug.

She writes something down on her little pad. Her feet cross at the ankles. She says, "Do you mean you'd rather be dead?"

I play with a rip in the fabric of the couch. Not leather. "Not dead," I say. "Just, nowhere."

She scribbles something else. "Do you have suicidal thoughts, Elizabeth?"

"Don't we all?"

"Are you depressed?"

"Only when I'm thinking," I say and she sighs. She leans forward in her cushy leather desk chair. Neat piles of paper sit on top of the cherrywood cabinets behind her. Perhaps they're other patients' files, notes from sessions with people who are having affairs, or fantasizing about someone of the same sex. People who are damaged and in need of repair. After I leave, she'll add me to that pile.

"Elizabeth," she says and adjusts her notepad on her lap so she can clasp her hands together. "I can't help you if you won't open up to me."

"Who says I need help?"

"Your aunt is worried about you."

"She worries about everyone."

"Do you worry about yourself?"

Sometimes. I stare at the carpet. Brown, a little darker and less faded at the edges of the office. How many other people have sat in this seat and been asked the same questions? She doesn't really care about me. And she can't help, either. The one person who could is literally sleeping with the enemy.

Ms. Counselor stretches into the high black back of her chair. "Everyone worries about something," she says. "It's perfectly natural."

Cicadas chirp in my head and I understand why they never shut up. After years of living underground, they surface, bursting, winged, free but doomed, and they spend two weeks singing—or maybe they're screaming—in the trees before they die. I feel like I'm doomed, too, and I'm scared I'll never even get to be free.

She says, "Why don't you tell me what worries you."

When I was little, I worried that my parents would never get back together, that we wouldn't have a family again, that Jaime and I would be separated. The years we eluded my father I worried he would find us, I worried when he yelled and hit Mom, worried

Jaime would wake up, worried we'd have to go to the hospital or the police station again. I worried that Dad was too drunk to drive, worried that Jaime wouldn't notice, worried that she'd be thrown headfirst out the window and Dad would be unharmed.

I worry that Tammy will choose Sam and move to Australia, that she won't want me back, that I won't be able to leave Jaime, that she won't care if I do, that I won't be given a choice. I worry Mom will never change her mind, that Terrance will get tired of almost assaulting me, or fed up with my begrudging compliance and turn his creepy eyes and poisonous words on Jaime. I worry about this jittery inertia, this contained fear and anger, circling like whirlpools in my chest, weighing down my lungs all the time, but I know without it I might not make it on my own and that worries me even more.

"Elizabeth?" Counselor lady is handing me a blurry tissue. I take it from her but it just sits in my hand. I clear my throat and she becomes clean, in focus, and I am so fucking tired of the angled eyebrows of temporary concern that are completely useless. No one can make a difference but me. "I'm done worrying," I whisper.

She lifts her head from whatever she was writing on her yellow notepad and says, "What was that?"

Enough cowering. I force the swelling in my throat to subside, brace my ribs against the panicked vibrations in my lungs, and slide my armored exoskeleton back over my chest. The heaviness is familiar, comforting, but no longer strong enough. It needs thicker panels, arm extensions, a higher collar. I tighten the straps on my shields and imagine the improvements and increased protection. I take a deep breath and exhale in one long steady stream of air. *It's time to fight.*

"Elizabeth?"

I swallow and clear my throat, square my shoulders against the couch. "I'm fine," I say and almost smile.

12

After more than a month of not talking to my mother, Deborah insists it's time. I swore I was done with her, but I suppose that wasn't very practical. She is my mom.

Deborah hands me the phone when she and Mom finish their weekly Liz's attitude and behavior update. I say, "Have you heard from Tammy?"

"Hi to you, too," Mom says. She sighs. "It's good to hear your voice, Liz. I've missed you."

"Apparently so has your husband."

"What does that mean?"

"He wrote me a letter."

She hesitates. "Well, that's nice."

I shake my head. "Tammy was supposed to be back from Africa but she hasn't called me."

"Didn't Jaime tell you?" Mom says. "Tammy and Sam are in Australia."

"Australia?" I suddenly feel itchy, like baby ants are hatching under my skin.

"Then they're going to Ireland. She said she'd call when she got back to the States."

I scratch my forearm and my eyes burn. "Okay, thanks," I say. "Bye."

"Liz, wait, please," Mom says. "I understand why you're angry."

"Congratulations."

"If I come visit, will you talk to me?"

"Will you admit you married a creep?"

"Liz," she says.

"You want to talk?" I say. "Let's talk about how dangerous Terrance is."

"He's not dangerous." I can almost see her roll her eyes as she draws out "dangerous" in a mocking tone that sounds like a teenager mad at her parents.

"You know exactly what he is," I say and realize as soon as the words are out of my mouth that she must, and she's still standing up for him. "You work every day to protect the world from men like him, and yet you gave him free rein to prey on your daughters."

"Stop exaggerating," she says. "He's not violent like your dad."

"He's worse," I say, the baby ants now crawling and squirming over my body like Terrance's words. "And you're blind."

"It's that attitude that's keeping you at Deborah's, young lady."

"I thought it was your husband showing his penis to strangers."

She hangs up.

We arrive late to Jed Smith Middle School's Back to School Night and speed walk across the parking lot and through the long, slat-roofed hallways. Deborah's arms are full of signed permission slips: flute for Ashley, drama club for Jaime, cheerleading for them both. My sister, six months ago smoking cigarettes and ditching school, now chatters nonstop about dance moves and pom-poms.

I sit in one of dozens of yellow plastic chairs next to Deborah in her flowered jumper dress and listen to the principal discuss the new lunch menu, explain the locker assignment system, and introduce the teachers up on stage while Jaime and Ashley giggle and whisper and look around the auditorium for other kids they know, their soft features overwhelmed by bright lip gloss and shiny eye shadow.

I watch them and think about how they spend so much time together these days, I hardly recognize Jaime. She's given up her dark flared jeans and blue eyeliner for frilly pastel skirts and pink eyelids. She and Ashley brush each side of their long hair one hundred times each night and apply creams and rinses and masques to their flawless skin. They tell each other they look beautiful, that Darin likes Ashley, that Bobby likes Jaime, that their boobs are bigger than they were yesterday, "for sure."

I listen outside Ashley's bedroom door sometimes, sit with my back against the wall, knees hugged to my chest like they might provide some comfort.

"Of course Kelly is uglier than you."

"Amanda is totally not his type."

"Is this zit totally obvious?"

"Does this skirt look good?"

Often, I can't distinguish Jaime's voice from Ashley's, both high-pitched and breathy like they're always excited. I remember when Jaime sounded just like me and wonder when she'll start to sound like herself.

I ask Deborah if I can go outside and Matt says, "Me too?" so we head out the green double doors into the late-afternoon fog and muddled orange light. We find a place to sit outside on the bleachers that edge the school's deep green football field. The sun has begun its descent into the west, and I stretch my legs onto the bench below and bask in the glow.

To my right, Matt plays his Game Boy, some kind of alien shooting adventure. We've been throwing a football around in the backyard and kicking a soccer ball in the Cranleys' driveway the last few weeks. It's good for both of us to get outside and stretch our wings. Once, Matt kicked the soccer ball right into Ashley's ass as she danced around in her Daisy Dukes and she lost her balance and fell forward into her vacated lawn chair. I high-fived him and we laughed until she screamed, "I hate you both!" and ran inside. Jaime wavered for just a second before following Ashley up the porch steps to the big brown door, but I understood: she can't play for both sides. At least now Matt can kick and throw. We're still working on the catching.

The delicate fog drifts are getting thicker, the sun darker orange-red and lower on the horizon like a giant, perfectly round nectarine. Goose bumps start at my sandaled feet and run up my tan legs and I shiver. Summer is ending and I still don't know where I'll be starting school. Deborah has signed me up for the local high school and everyone seems to think I'll be staying here, sharing a room and feeling like it's unsafe to be honest. Soon they'll add my name to the chore list, and I'll have to start a new school again. I'd get to live with Jaime, but even so, I'm pretty sure it's not what I want.

Mom's voice lectures in my head: "clear rules," she says, "regular church attendance." She paces and wags her finger at me. "You need to learn about making the right choices," she says with a straight face, the engagement ring she bought twinkling on her hand as a reminder of who she chose. Not only did she ditch her own daughters for a sex offender, but she allowed him to touch us, hug us, spend time alone with us, all the while knowing, probably better than anyone, his inexhaustible lust. I think of the occasional hints of worry in her voice, her hesitation and chirping laughs full of nerves when she asked about our lunch together last fall, and I know she suspected. But she did nothing.

In my head she reprimands me for my attitude, tells me I need to treat Terrance with respect and kindness, accept him as family. She invited a lion into our den of lambs, turned her back on the slaughter, and then has the gall to say, "I am still your mother."

"Then act like it, you stupid bitch, or I'll stab your fucking eyes out," I say out loud. I think for a second that Matt might tell on me despite our recent bonding. "I wasn't talking to you," I say, releasing my fingers from their grip on my knees, nails leaving crescent moons in my bare skin.

Matt smiles, his newly emerged adult teeth big between his chapped lips. "Well if you do that, I'll have to saw off your ears with a butter knife."

"Okay," I say. *Huh.* "Then I'll chop off your feet and glue them to your back so you have to walk like a cockroach."

"Fine," he says, fingers still tapping away at his red-and-black buttons. "I'll cut off your fingers, fry them up, and make you eat them like sausage."

"Gross," I say. "I'll throw up the finger sausages and make you lick it off the dirt and then I'll slice out your tongue and make you swallow that, too."

He laughs. "I'll pull off your arms and stuff them up your butt so your guts explode with poop." He hunches farther over his screen.

I picture Mom's cheekbones, her blue-green eyes, her rounded chin. I think of her snapping photographs as Terrance pressed his hips against mine. "I'll shave off your face with a cheese grater and feed the gooey mess to Biscuit."

"Eww." He giggles an evil giggle and rubs his hands together. I smile at him. "Okay," he says and pauses his game. He takes a deep breath. "I'm going to shove your hair down your throat so you can't scream and then rip open your belly, pull out your intestines, and tie your feet together. And when you fall, I'll wrap the rest of your slimy entrails around your fat neck and squeeze until you freakin' choke." Matt's hands clench into fists, his little fingers red and white on top of his khaki shorts.

Matt's eyes are focused somewhere past the grass, on the trees at the opposite end of the field, huge maple trees, their broad, five-fingered leaves catching the wind and rocking their dark branches, waving like coral arms against a backdrop sea of blue-orange sky. He's not blinking.

"You want to talk about it?" I say. I get it, I do. All the anger, all the fire shooting around inside. "Sometimes it's good to let things out." I think of my recent increase in recording my thoughts, the pages of rants in my journal.

Matt lets out a long breath and says, "Did you know the small intestine is twenty feet long?"

I say, "You are such a boy."

"So are you sometimes," he says. He unclenches his fists a little and peels his brown eyes away from the swaying trees. "That's why you're cool," he says and punches my shoulder. He looks a little taller, a little thinner in the face than when I first moved in; some of his baby fat has melted away. If he learns to come out of his shell, he'll do fine.

"You think I'm cool?" I say.

"Well, yeah," he says and shrugs. "But consider the source." I laugh.

In the growing dusk the fog is thick and gray-yellow, the sun's outline no longer visible beyond the clouds. The trees are like charcoal shadows on a swirling pencil-sketch sky. I hope Jaime still thinks I'm cool, but I also think if she doesn't, it'll be okay.

Winston leaves for work at seven A.M. and after the alarm beeps but before Deborah gets up I call Tammy's number. I hop around on the tan carpet in my bare feet. I cross my fingers. I visualize Tammy in her leapfrog and lily pad pajamas, walking across her wood floors in her pink house slippers, picking up the white cordless handset, and saying, "Hello?" but it's just Sam again on the machine.

A letter comes from Rachel. She writes, *I did it!! Frank took me camping and we did it under the stars and it was so romantic and I can't wait for you to visit so I can tell you all about it. With details.* A smiley face winks at me next to the period and "details" is underlined twice. *My mom said she had a dream that you were going on a long journey and came to her for new shoes. She told you to follow your heart, not your feet, and you grew wings and flew away.*

I wonder if Rachel's mom really does have a kind of gift. One sleepless night I'd repeated Jenny's prayer from *Forrest Gump,* which we'd watched as a family with Deborah fast-forwarding drug and sex scenes. I whispered from on top of the yellow-flowered comforter three feet from sleeping Jaime, "Dear God, Make me a bird. So I can fly far, far away from here," over and over. Emancipation didn't work, but if I could fly away, that would be a fine alternative. I imagined my toes turning into claws, my nose lengthening, feathered wings unfurling from my back. I pictured the ground miles below and the infinite sky ahead until the rising sun made any chance of transformation seem impossible.

Deborah sits next to me at the edge of the pool and I angle the letter so she can't read it. "Juicy stuff?" she says. I fold the letter and put it in the pocket of the baggy shorts I've been wearing all summer that have grown baggier each week. "Oh, Liz," she says and sighs. "Who knew life could get this complicated?" I think of one night when we lived here and Mom's Al-Anon meeting ran late. I was curled on the floor in our room upstairs, holding Jaime's Snuggly and crying. Deborah wrapped me in a blanket and made me warm milk. She watched TV with my head in her lap and I fell asleep to the rise and fall of her chest, the sweet smell of her perfume. "I'd like to respect your mom's wishes and make peace with you if that's possible," she says.

"I appreciate the offer," I say. "But if Tammy will let me, I'd like to move back in with her."

"Your mom thinks our place is a better environment."

"It's perfect for Jaime," I say. "I'm thankful that she has you."

Deborah leans back on her pale freckled arms, like Dad's without tattoos. The sun shines dark yellow behind gray clouds tumbling violently in the wind that only feels like a light breeze down here. "Your father's not speaking to me," she says. "He says I robbed him of a golden opportunity."

"It was him, you know," I say. "He called Terrance's parole officer. He thought he'd be able to get child support money from Mom."

Deborah cocks her head to the side and frowns. "He's not that good at strategy."

"Crystal is conniving," I say. "I bet it was her idea."

"It does sound like his brand of selfishness," Deborah says.

"Talk about a plan backfiring," I say. It would almost be funny that he got the opposite of what he'd been aiming for, except he set this snowball of bad decisions in motion, and even now, the effects of this shit storm keep piling up on me despite the fact that he lost. "Jerk."

"Liz," Deborah says. "He may not be the best father, but there's no need for that kind of language."

"You should hear the things I say to myself," I say. Deborah shakes her head but doesn't say anything. The breeze picks up as the clouds darken to wet-concrete-gray above us. The wind is cool and moist, like it just left the ocean, and smells like seaweed and sage. I wish beachfront property was one of my housing options. "You'll keep Dad away from Jaime?" I say. She doesn't need to know Dad used her. She's safe from him for now.

"Yes," Deborah says. "I think I can manage to protect you both."

"Jaime is lucky to have you," I say.

Deborah brushes off her hands and places one on my knee. "I'm afraid you're stuck with us, too, Liz."

"What about what I want?"

She pats my knee with her fingertips and stands up, her brown sandals slapping the cement. She kisses the top of my head but it's not the gesture of comfort it is when Tammy does it, and my chest burns so hot I want to dive into the pool and inhale all that cool water.

"Dinner's almost ready," Deborah says and smiles down at me. "We'll fatten you up, yet." Dinner is probably meatloaf and canned green beans, or chicken baked in condensed mushroom soup next to iceberg lettuce coated with bottled ranch dressing. It's the food I grew up eating, but after my exposure to Chez Tammy, it has become less appetizing.

"Thanks," I call as she walks away. "Be there in a minute." I know feeding six on a single income is hard, and that I was spoiled with Tammy's love of food, but I yearn for halibut tacos with mango salsa, Tammy's garden-grown herb and goat cheese salads and homemade dressings, her roasted-veggie pasta. I smell chicken pot pie and imagine inhaling the spices in Tammy's kitchen instead: curry, cumin, cardamom, saffron, the scents of distant lands stirring up travel fantasies. I know Deborah is trying to help in all the ways she can, but I also know this place will never feel like home to me even if I wished it would.

Tammy calls Deborah's the next day while I'm out by the pool, but Ashley tells her I don't have phone privileges. Hours later when I come inside, I rip the phone from Ashley's hand as she smirks, but I restrain myself from elbowing her in the ribs or punching her braces and coating the inside of her mouth with tiny cuts. "You can't use the phone," she says. "You're not allowed."

"I'm not trying to steal your mom," I say. Ashley stares at me. "I'm sorry she ignores you, but it's not my fault."

Ashley says, "My mom feels sorry for your pathetic family."

I sigh. "I know."

"Because you're losers."

"Some of us are trying to change that," I say. "You have something in your teeth." She jumps up and runs into the bathroom.

I dial Tammy's number as I walk into Jaime's room and pace back and forth on my toes, bath towel wrapped around my waist, a T-shirt thrown on over Rachel's bikini top. My throat is dry, my hands tremble. I put my tongue between my teeth to keep them from rattling. *Please be there.* The phone rings three times and I can see the white base and handset sitting on her phone table in the kitchen next to her Georgia O'Keeffe address book and pile of grocery coupons. *Pick up, pick up.* Four times and I can see the rosewood floors and cabinets, the antique table and green place mats to match the green walls we painted. Five times and Sam's voice says to leave a message.

I say, "Tammy? It's me, Liz, and I miss you so much. I just wanted to talk to you. There have been some big changes here and I heard you went to Ireland and . . ." I start crying. When her answering machine beeps I throw the phone at Jaime's bed and cry until the acid rivers have been drained.

At dinner, the doorbell rings as Winston is saying grace. He ignores it until we say, "Amen." Biscuit barks when it rings again, a quick, shrill ding-dong, and Deborah jumps up like she was waiting for a package. She says, "I'll get it," and glances at me. I pretend not to notice, but wonder what she has up her "Project Elizabeth" sleeve for this evening.

"Probably a salesman," Winston says. "We don't need a new vacuum!" He flaps his flowered paper napkin open and tucks it into the collar of his blue work shirt, now unbuttoned at the top.

"What if they're selling Bibles?" I say.

"We don't need any more of those, either," he says.

Matt says, "Dad, can we get a basketball hoop?" His napkin is also tucked into the neck of his T-shirt, though he never makes a mess.

"Whatever for?" Winston says.

"For playing basketball."

Ashley says, "How about a karaoke machine?" She turns to Jaime. "Wouldn't that be awesome?"

"So awesome," Jaime says.

Winston says, "Kids, we're not buying anything. It costs enough to feed this house."

Deborah says, "Liz," from the door just as Winston says, "Who was it?" and stands up. We both walk toward the entryway.

Mom stands near the door in too-tight jeans with Noah on her hip. I guess she was serious about visiting. "See, I told you I would come to see my girls," she says and sets Noah down on the white and tan tile. He rubs his eyes and clings to Mom's knee. "Don't I get a hug?" she says and moves toward me, arms out in front of her.

I stand there, frozen and scowling, so she settles for rubbing my shoulder, her smile fading.

"Hi, Mom," Jaime says, coming up behind me. She hugs her and Mom's smile perks back up, but her shiny, grayish tooth peeks through her lips and I know she's faking it.

I pick Noah up and kiss his cheek. He smells like corn chips and Johnson's Baby Shampoo. "Hey, little man."

"Linda, what a surprise," Winston says, glancing at Deborah and hooking his thumbs under his black belt.

I put Noah down and he whines so I pick him back up. "Liz!" he says and snuggles his baby face into my neck. "Come home." Rubber bands snap in my chest, but I will not cry.

Deborah says, "Linda, would you like to join us for dinner?" She leads Mom into the dining room. We all follow, Biscuit jumping as high as Mom's cleavage and her swatting at his pointy nose each time.

"Oh, no, I don't want to impose," Mom says. "We already ate."

"We're almost finished," Deborah says. "Liz, would you like to skip doing your dishes to spend some time with your mother?"

Ashley glares at me as I set Noah down and kiss the top of his head. "No, thanks," I say and sit at the table.

"Give her a little while," Deborah tells Mom. "She'll come around."

I stare at my tuna macaroni casserole; stab a couple of peas with my fork. I imagine they're little green bullets, bullets I could load into one of Winston's guns. I visualize the shots piercing Mom's chest, splintering her skin, and in my mind I squeeze the trigger until it clicks empty.

13

Later that night, Mom knocks on the guest bedroom door where I'm writing in my journal. I haven't gone back to the counselor with her prominently hung wooden cross, but I consider this release of thoughts my own private therapy.

"Can I talk to you without getting verbally abused?" Mom says. I shrug, but mentally I am donning my armor, the exoskeleton made of silver shields and chain mail, and a thick helmet that protects my eyes. "That was a joke," she says.

"Ha-ha." I sit up.

"You look pink," Mom says and I know I've gotten sunburned, all that time lying out by the pool.

"It'll turn tan," I say. "Remember how brown we used to get?"

She smiles. "Like little Indians."

Mom sits on the edge of Jaime's bed. She jumps a little and then pulls a pager from her pocket. Her face tenses as she checks the screen. "You have a pager?" I say. "Didn't you say those were for drug dealers?"

"It's nothing," Mom says, slipping the black plastic square back into her jeans. She crosses her legs and clasps her hands on top of her knee. "Things are okay here, right?" I stare at her. "And it's not that far from home," she says.

I still have boxes at Tammy's, boxes at Mom's, and am living out of duffel bags here. "I don't have a home," I say. "Thanks to you."

"I'm sorry, Liz, okay?" She grabs Snuggly from Jaime's pillow and wrings his neck.

"It doesn't matter if you're sorry," I say and close the journal that Tammy put in my Easter basket. We'd taken our decorated hard-boiled eggs to the top of City Creek Canyon instead of going to church, lay with the sun's warmth on our faces and the creek's clinking in our ears. I take a deep breath and prepare my shields. "I want to go back to Tammy's."

"That was temporary," Mom says.

"I want to ask Tammy if I can live there longer."

"What about asking me?" she says.

I say, "Can I live with you?" Mom makes an "uh" sound in her throat and shuts her eyes. "I didn't think so."

She sighs and drops her chin to her chest. "If it makes you feel any better, I'm pretty unhappy right now, too."

I roll my eyes. "You married a flasher."

"He made a mistake."

"He shows other women his penis."

"He has a disease," she says. "An addiction."

"If I start doing heroin, can I come home?"

"Watch your smart mouth," she says, her head snapping up.

"Did you ever think that he might scare us?" I say, my heart starting to rev up. "That maybe he's been inappropriate with your adolescent daughters?"

She stares at me for a full thirty seconds without blinking. Then shakes her head like she's trying to erase what's inside. "He would never hurt you girls," she says. "He loves you."

I scoff. "Love is not the word I would use."

"He's your stepfather," she says.

"No, he's your husband," I say.

She opens her mouth, closes it, and pinches the bridge of her nose. She eyes me. "Do you want to tell me something?"

I consider opening up, liberating all the images of Terrance's behavior from their flimsy cage in my mind, but she would never believe me. She can't, because to admit the truth would be to admit she made the same mistake she'd made with Dad and endangered her children again for a man unwilling to change.

"Please just let me go back to Tammy's," I say, looking into her eyes, trying to make her see that this is what I want, what I need.

She turns away and stands up next to the bed, wiggles to adjust the waist of her jeans. "I'd prefer you stay close to home, with Jaime—"

"And her best friend Ashley."

"In a family environment, with Christian influences—"

I say, "Don't forget the guns."

"Deborah said she'd love to have you."

"So she can fix me." I gather my knees to my chest, anchor my back to the wall behind me. "Tammy just wants me to be myself. To be happy."

Mom straightens her glasses. "I know, I know. Tammy is soo great," she says, mocking. "Did she bribe you or something?"

"You said you thought we'd get along," I say and shrug. "You were right." And Tammy would never let a pervert into her house, or her bed, or her children's lives.

"Liz," she says, her voice sinking into her lecture tone. "I know how hard this must be."

I try to clear the rising ache in my throat. "You don't," I say.

"I do," she says and I think of her and Tammy moving out of their abusive stepmom's place as teenagers, receiving money as the only form of support from their inattentive father, and I wonder why she's doing this to me if she knows. "But I also know you need stricter guidelines," she says.

I almost laugh. "Terrance can't even keep his pants on."

"Don't you talk to me like that," she says. She takes a breath. "I am still your mother."

I say, "Not if I could choose."

I think I see hurt flare in her eyes for a split second before she shoots out her arm and grips my chin with one hand. She squeezes my cheeks with her poorly painted nails.

"You're not as smart as you think you are, and you are not an adult," she says and digs her fingers deeper into my face. "I deserve your respect and this back talk stops now." She releases my chin with a jerk and throws my head back.

I taste blood in my mouth and I have no snappy comeback. She smooths the thighs of her jeans with her palms and exhales. She says, "You will live here, where I know you're being monitored."

My shields feel cracked, but I can't give up yet. "I don't want to stay here," I say quietly. In my head I'm mending all my armor, restacking my fortress.

"You don't have a choice," Mom says. I test my defenses, my battle weapons: weakened but not useless. I shoot poison-tipped arrows from my eyes at her back. She turns to me, her hand on the knob. "This is for your own good," she says. Her wrist rotates. I spring.

I throw my journal at her head and when she ducks, eyes reflected shock-wide in her glasses, I leap forward and slam the door shut so she's trapped with me. I smash my palm against the white door. "You want to know why I don't respect you?"

Mom spins faster than I thought she could move. She grabs my hand and twists me around, away from the door. "Because you're a mouthy teenager who needs a good spanking," she says and shoves me toward the bed.

Her hands feel like clamps and she's twice my weight but I don't stop struggling. "Because you're a selfish bitch in denial!" I'm rammed face-first into the comforter, and I wait for the blow. I remember other spankings with long wooden spoons or plastic hairbrushes, Jaime and I lined up against our beds, butts out and eyes clenched, waiting for the slap sound that comes before the sting, but Deborah opens the door before Mom can whack me.

Deborah says, "What on earth is going on in here?"

"Elizabeth attacked me," Mom says, loosening her grip. "She's completely out of control."

I jump up off the mattress, my hair in my face, my ears ringing. "You're out of control!" My heartbeat throbs in my temples, blood pulses in my fingertips. I feel like I could breathe fire. I say, "I hate you."

Mom takes a step toward me but I raise my clenched fists, let the lightning that's always just below the surface flash in my eyes and she backs off. "What is wrong with you?" she says.

"This is my life." I don't blink, don't take my eyes off hers, the greenish tint we share, our wavy hair, those cheeks worth showing off. I remember when she said she'd die for us.

Mom says, "You need to calm down."

My fists, still raised to my shoulders, quake in the air. My skin itches over muscles ready to burst. Mom puts her hand to her mouth and her face crumples like a frameless paper lamp. She takes a step back. She whispers, "Just like David."

I think of my father's indiscriminate blows, his face vacant, his eyes bright and pupils huge, and I know it's not the same. But it's too close. Instead of the punch I want to launch I say through gritted teeth, "Maybe you deserved to get hit then, too." It feels good for a second, satisfying, like breaking my fingers against her chin. Mom lunges and slaps my cheek.

Deborah gasps. "Elizabeth," she says. "This is your mother."

I cradle my face, look away from Mom's glowing eyes. I wonder if mine look the same, evenly matched arsenals of rage in our round faces. "She's doing a bang-up job, too," I say, rubbing my jaw.

Mom says, "I'm doing the best I can."

"Nothing you do anymore is for us," I say.

"It's all for you girls," she says. "I've been trying to keep you safe."

"You unleashed a predator," I say.

"He never hurt you," she says, her eyes wide.

I feel the fire in my face again, barbed wire in my blood. I say, "If that's what you think, then Terrance's stupidity really has rubbed off on you."

Jaime and Ashley come into the room in their nightgowns:

shiny yellow and skimming the tops of their knees. Ashley says, "Who was screaming?"

Jaime says, "What happened?"

"Girls," Deborah says. "Why don't you head back to your room."

Jaime says, "I'm not leaving Liz."

Ashley says, "I don't want to miss the action."

Deborah says, "Now, both of you."

I stand taller, still kneading my cheek with my fingers, but proud of Jaime's strength and glad to be on the same side again. "This is Jaime's fight, too," I say. "Mom abandoned both of us."

Mom presses both hands to her stomach. "I didn't abandon you."

"You love Terrance more than us," Jaime says.

"You girls don't understand," Mom says, her eyes shining. "I—"

Winston's booming voice says, "Excuse me?" and raised voices filter into the guest room from the front of the house. We all look out the door as Winston says, "No," and another angry male voice responds. Mom's eyes stretch in their sockets, but then she shakes her head and pats her pocket.

Winston says, "I don't think—no, wait—" and then I hear a female voice say my name. *Tammy?*

I sprint past Mom, Deborah, Ashley, and Jaime, around the corner and past the sectional couch and see Tammy walking past the refrigerator. I stop. It's true, she's really here. She's tanner and her hair is lighter and she's smiling at me, her honey lip balm reflecting the light.

"Hey, kiddo," she says, and I am in her arms in two seconds.

"You came," I say.

I hear Mom's heels click on the kitchen tile, but the sound stops short when she sees me and Tammy hugging. "No one needs you here," Mom says to Tammy, her eyes narrowed.

"I do," I say.

Tammy's cheek muscles twitch. "Liz sounded so scared and lonely on my machine," Tammy says and squeezes me closer.

"You don't get to swoop in and be the hero," Mom says. "Stop trying to take control."

"But she's here to save me," I say.

Mom squints her eyes so much they're almost closed. "You can't have everything. Not anymore."

Tammy sighs. "I just wanted to help."

Deborah enters the room in her fuzzy socks, followed by Ashley and Jaime. Deborah looks at Mom's shoulder-width stance, her clenched fists, and then at Tammy. Deborah says, "Um, hello, you must be—"

Mom interrupts her. "You can't take my daughter just because you don't have one."

Tammy's torso tightens and she glares at Mom. "You don't want to start this, Linda," she says through gritted teeth. Her lavender smell is faint but detectable in the deep breath I take before she lets me go, and it makes me feel secure, calms some of the burning in my chest. Until I see Terrance standing ten feet away. Tammy waves a hand in front of her and says to Mom, "Grow up."

The anger drains from Mom's features when she notices Terrance behind us. "Babe," he says, coming toward her. She cringes. "Babe, I needed to see you, and this dude"—Terrance nods at

Winston who is walking into the kitchen, scowling—"didn't want to let me in."

I stare at Terrance in his cutoff sweat shorts and green racer-back tank top, trying not to think of his meaty breath in my ear or his slick fingers on my skin and failing. "What are you doing here?" I say.

"I'm her husband," Terrance says, his wide nostrils flaring. "I'm a part of this family."

Deborah rolls her eyes, and for the first time I wonder if she's not entirely supportive of Mom's decision. "We don't really have space for any more guests," she says.

"Linda," Winston says. "I'm sorry, but I don't want this man in my house. Or around my daughter." He turns to Ashley. "Upstairs, now."

"But, Dad—"

"Now!" Winston barks like a sergeant and everyone jumps. His pudgy fingers grip Ashley's petite shoulders and he herds her toward the stairs.

"How come Liz gets to stay?" Ashley says.

Winston says, "You, too, Jaime," and she looks to me first and then Mom for confirmation, but he is not waiting. Jaime's big, wet eyes meet mine as she's propelled past me.

As Winston marches Ashley and Jaime in their tiny night-gowns up the stairs to Ashley's room, Terrance says, "What's his problem?"

Mom steps toward the entryway and says, "Why don't we go outside and talk?" She tips her chin down and widens her eyes at him but he misses the hint.

"What for?" he says and she looks at the floor. His eyebrows shoot up and stay there, dark arches on his face. His jaw flops open as he makes the connection. "Are you ashamed of me?"

Deborah busies herself with adjusting a fake potted plant. Tammy presses her lips together like she's trying to seal her mouth shut.

"You were supposed to stay at the motel," Mom says, quietly, barely moving her face.

He says, "You were supposed to come right back."

I say, "You brought him?"

"For God's sake," Tammy says. "Can't you go anywhere without him?"

Mom swivels her head to Tammy, her hair spinning out around her head. "Just stay out of it," she says. "This is none of your business."

Deborah drops a plastic palm frond and takes a hesitant step toward Mom. "Linda—"

"I know," Mom snaps and Deborah blinks in surprise. Mom softens her voice and says to Terrance, "Let's just talk outside for a minute." She lays her hand on his forearm but he brushes her off like she's a fly.

Terrance says, "So I'm not welcome here?"

I smile at him without showing teeth. "Way to figure it out," I say. Mom gives me a look that says *shut up*, but I'm done listening to her. I put my hands on my hips and face them both. "If only you could figure out how to keep your shorts on."

Terrance points a finger at me and steps forward in his sneakers. "You little bi—"

Mom grabs his arm and pulls. "Enough," she says, but he pries her fingers open and escapes her grasp.

He says, "You're damn right it's enough." He shakes his head back and forth and glowers at me. "I deserve your respect."

I laugh. I can't help it. Cold hatred radiates from his eyes, and my heart flutters with panic, but I'm prepared to stand my ground. I say, "You don't deserve anyone's respect."

Terrance jabs his finger in the air at me. "I'm sick of your smug mouth, girl." He strides forward and in my head I start checking my armor, but Tammy moves toward me, and so does Deborah. I push my shoulder blades together and stand straight. He says, "Maybe you need a good spanking."

"Watch it," Tammy says, shooting Mom a sideways look. "You have no right to speak to her that way."

He sneers. "I'm her father."

Tammy says, "You're a project," and Terrance looks wounded for a second before turning on Mom. "Are you going to let *her* speak to *me* like that?" he says.

Tammy's voice is even, but I can see her long fingers trembling a little at her sides. "Why don't you just go," she says. "Can't you see no one wants you here?"

Winston comes back down the stairs and stands by Deborah, his hands in the pockets of his blue robe. He says, "Yes, we would appreciate if you would leave." He shifts his feet and his right hand contracts around a weight under the navy terry cloth. "Before things get out of control."

Terrance scoffs and flexes his muscles under his tank top. "Are you threatening me?" he says, puffing out his pecs and clenching his fists. He looks Winston up and down. "You?" His hyena laugh is shrill and eerie.

Winston lifts his chest and his belly bulges forward, and I think if Terrance knew what was in Winston's pocket, he might not be so snide. "Fine," Terrance says. "We'll get out of here. Who needs you jackasses anyway, right, babe?"

Mom closes her eyes and her shoulders droop. "This is why I didn't want you to come," she says, her face wilting. She sighs heavily and opens her eyes. "I'm so sorry," she says to Winston and Deborah.

"You're not going to stand up for me?" Terrance says to Mom, ripples of shock spreading across his face. "Pastor Ron says you're supposed to back me up."

"I do," Mom says. "I am." She tries to pull Terrance's arm again, but the effort is futile. With Terrance's bulk, he doesn't budge unless he wants to, and he's planted his feet on the carpet. "Let's just go for now, okay?" she says. He crosses his arms over his solid chest.

Winston steps forward, the blue-green veins in his right arm raised and pulsing. "We would like you to go, Terrance," he says, his voice firm but quieter than usual. "Don't make me ask you again."

Mom's face is red. "Please, babe," she says and there's an insistent pleading in her voice. "We can talk back at the motel."

Terrance whirls to face me. "This is your fault," he says, hardly parting his crooked teeth.

"Mine?" I say.

"You turned her against me," Terrance says, raising his fists to waist level. "You've been planting lies in her head for months."

"I never told her anything," I say and narrow my eyes at him. "Not even the truth."

Terrance's eyes bulge at the same time as Mom's, and her hands clasp over her mouth while Terrance's nostrils spread. He shakes his head again and bares his teeth like a dog preparing for attack. "Don't forget who you're dealing with," he says, his voice low and harsh.

Tammy's eyes are wide, too, but they're full of fire, and she says to Terrance, "If you hurt my niece—"

Terrance says, "I never touched her."

Deborah's face is full of concern and she peeks at Mom before saying, "What truth, Liz?"

My heart feels like it's going to beat through my rib cage, but I tuck it behind my steel breastplate. *It's now or never.* I take a deep breath. "Does Mom know about Kayla?"

Fury smolders in Terrance's eyes as he looks at me, but this time I'm not alone. It's not just me in a dark back booth with his mouth near my neck and his muscles blocking me in. This time I have witnesses.

Mom says, "Who's Kayla?"

"No one," Terrance says.

"She's a waitress at the bar he took me to," I say.

Tammy says, "He took you to a bar?"

I say, "He said Mom wanted to have lunch with me and he picked me up instead."

Mom is terrified. Her palms cup her cheeks and she digs her

275

fingers into her temples. "No," she whispers. Her eyes are fixed on some point in space, stretched open so far it seems like they should pop out. Her head wobbles side to side, and she mutters, "No, no, no, no."

"What else happened, Liz?" Tammy says, and everyone looks at me.

Mom tangles her fingers together in her hair, still staring wide-eyed. "Nonononono."

But it's time for her to hear the truth about the man she married. There's nothing he can hold over me anymore. Jaime is out of his reach. I inhale and say, "He flirts with me. He makes inappropriate jokes and asks about making out with boys and tries to talk to me about sex." I feel tears building and I close my eyes. "He winks at me. He breathes on me. He hugs me too long and too close and his hands graze my thighs and my boobs and my hair." I pause in the stunned silence and open my eyes to a sea of distressed faces. I say, "He threatened to do it to Jaime if I told."

Tears slide down my cheeks and I stand there while everyone processes what I said. Tammy's eyes are wet and Deborah looks horrified, her hand over her open mouth. Winston doesn't look at me. Mom doesn't, either, still shaking her head and repeating no over and over under her breath.

"I didn't know what to do," I whisper and lower my head.

"Oh, Liz," Tammy says and rushes forward to hug me. "I knew this creep wasn't rehabilitated," she says. She holds me against her. "Why didn't you tell me?" I relax into her arms and let myself be cradled.

"She's a liar," Terrance yells. He turns to Mom, his muscled arms outstretched and palms open. "Babe, she's lying. I didn't do anything wrong." He flings a hand toward me but doesn't take his eyes off Mom's frozen face. "She asked me to take her to that bar. She tempted me!" His hands ball into fists. "Your daughter's a tease!"

Mom snaps back to life and ends her useless mantra. "You're a liar," she says through tight lips, her voice hoarse. Her eyes flash with rage and her knuckles vibrate near her frenzied face. "You said you were going to your support group. You said you were looking for a job. You said you had stopped flirting and going to strip clubs." Mom's whole body shudders and everyone stands back from her gyrating arms. "You're not even trying! You were supposed to be getting better!" Her glasses sit skewed on her nose and her cheeks are splotched deep red.

"There's nothing wrong with me!" Terrance says.

Mom turns her back to him. "I'm so sorry, Liz," she says. "His counselor suggested you not live together, but I thought he would be fine. I thought he was trying to be a good father, to get to know you, be a part of your life. I wanted us to be a family."

Tammy is outraged. "You knew there was a chance he'd go after your daughters and you let him into your house?" Heat radiates from her torso and arms.

"I thought he would get better. I thought I could make him better," Mom says, the words spilling out of her mouth. "But then I noticed he wasn't improving. And when David called the P.O. I thought it was a good chance to take temptation away from him and keep you girls safe." She clutches her gut and makes a sobbing sound.

Tears sting my eyes. "You knew?" I say, and my stomach churns bile into caustic waves. "You knew what he was doing to me?"

"Of course not," she says, but she looks at the ground.

Razors carve up my lungs and I cough. "You knew and didn't stop him."

"I swear I didn't know," she whispers, pressing her hands deeper into her belly and folding forward.

Tammy frowns at Mom, and pulls me closer. "How could you?" she says, her voice straining.

Mom sighs. "He's my husband."

Tammy says, "You're supposed to protect your kids."

"I was trying to protect them," Mom says. Her wide eyes scan the room, but no one is coming to her rescue. "I honestly thought he would get better with counseling and time and then you could come home when it was safer." Mom's face breaks and tears carry inky-gray mascara trails down her cheeks. "I thought he would get better and I wanted us to be together, all of us, a family, and I thought, I thought . . ." Mom stutters and takes deep quaking breaths like she's going to hyperventilate. She drops to the floor, her jeans squeezing at her hips, her low-cut top sagging with her breasts as she crosses her legs and slumps against the banister, weeping.

Tammy says, "Liz is never living with this waste of life again." She looks at Deborah, who nods. "Jaime, either," Tammy says. She points at Terrance who has been watching Mom with his beady eyes hardened and a fixed jaw. "You need to get the hell away from this repulsive piece of shit you married before—"

"Fuck you, you stuck up bitch," Terrance says calmly, his voice cocky.

"Hey," I say. Deborah sucks in a gasp. Winston tightens his pocketed grip.

"What a big man you are," Tammy says, letting me go. "Picking on women." He struts toward us slowly, like he's in control. Tammy moves in front of me. "You're a coward," she says.

He tsk tsk tsks. "You're just like Liz," he says. "Trying to turn my wife against me." He smirks and runs his tongue under his upper lip. "Didn't work though, did it?"

Tammy shakes her head. "You're done hurting my family," she says, a menace in her voice I've never heard before. "I will make sure of that."

Winston hasn't taken his eyes off Terrance and now he steps forward, too, his fingers stiff inside his robe pocket. "You need to leave this house," he says.

Terrance grits his buck teeth and cracks his knuckles. "I'm not leaving without my family."

Winston draws his shoulders back and puffs up his chest. "Indeed you are."

"They're not going with you," Tammy says.

"I'm not leaving without my son," Terrance says. "Where is he?"

"You're not taking him," I say, shifting my feet toward the stairs. Terrance looks up to the second-floor landing. "Noah!"

"No more," Mom says, standing up. She turns on Terrance. "I'm not doing this again." I wonder if she means fight with Terrance or if she means trying to save a husband who doesn't want to be saved at the expense of all of us. Tears are still drying on her face, but her eyes are decided. She says, "Go back to the motel room. I need to think."

"Not without my boy," he says. "Daddy's here!"

Mom says, "He's sleeping."

"Please don't yell," Deborah says, putting her fingers to her forehead.

Mom says, "Terrance, stop."

"He's the only one who hasn't betrayed me," Terrance says, progressing forward.

Winston inches around the side of the staircase. He says, "I will call the cops if I have to."

Terrance is at the bottom of the steps now. "I don't give a shit about your threats, fatty."

Mom says, "Do you want to go back to jail?"

"Without you and Noah, I have nothing," he says.

"You can't go up there," I say, almost at the stairs. "I won't let you hurt him, either."

Terrance scoffs. "What do you think you can do against me, you little piece of ass?" he says.

Mom gasps. "Terrance!"

"None of you can stop me," he says, sneering at all of us like a movie demon. He looks at me and his grin widens. "I always win."

"This is ridiculous," Tammy says. "I'll call the police. Where's the phone?"

"You'll just scare him," Mom says, facing Terrance from where she stands near the banister.

"Noah!" Terrance shouts and starts to run.

As he lifts his foot, Mom, Tammy, and I all move toward him. He doesn't stop even when Mom positions herself in front of him and he knocks her over onto the steps with his momentum. They both make "oh" sounds of surprise as they go down.

I reach for the back of Terrance's tank top and get ahold of the fabric just as he falls over Mom. The cloth rips but my balance is thrown and I topple onto the bottom stair near their flailing feet. Terrance struggles on top of my writhing, screaming mother and her blue-jeaned calves kick under Terrance's hairy legs. One of her heels flies off and hits a cabinet in the kitchen with a bang. Deborah says, "Oh, dear Lord."

Tammy says, "Get off my sister!" and lunges for Terrance. She steps over me and grabs his arm, but he whips his fist behind him without looking. She ducks and shrieks and falls on me.

"Bitch," Terrance spits. Mom is still screaming. Not words, just throaty wails. Terrance finds his balance and pins Mom to the stairs with one hand. "Stop," he says, but she keeps shouting and thrashing. "Shut up!" he says and pushes on her shoulders.

Tammy gets back on her feet and tries to pull Terrance off Mom, groaning with the effort. I am trying to sit up, to see Mom's face, to make sure she's okay, to understand what's happening. I'm wondering why Winston hasn't pulled out his gun when I hear a voice that stabs me in the gut.

Jaime yells, "Stop!" louder than Mom's howling, louder than

Terrance's and Tammy's grunting noises. "Stop it! Stop it! Stop it!" Jaime screams and there is so much raw power in her voice we all freeze and look up.

She stands at the top of the stairs holding a gun. *Oh, shit.* She grips a brown handle in her small white-knuckled fists; a stubby black barrel protrudes four inches past her tightly wrapped fingers. She points the gun at Terrance, her arms fully extended and already wobbling. "Get off my mom," she says, punctuating each word like a bomb. Her finger is not on the trigger, but the sliver of space could be closed in a fraction of a second.

Terrance lifts his hands slowly, Tammy plops onto the carpet, and Mom rolls onto her stomach, wheezing. Jaime's nightgown vibrates around her legs and her cheeks quiver, but her eyes are resolute. "Leave them alone," she says.

"Jaime," I whisper, my eyes watering. The gun barrel bobs left and right as she looks at me, the dark round hole at the tip jiggling in space. "Jaime, what are you doing?"

Tears stream down her face. "Liz," she says, and her voice cracks. "I wanted to save you." She glances at Terrance, who stands on the bottom step with his hands in the air. "From him." Her arms drop a bit with the weight of the gun and it shifts in her hands as she struggles to keep her aim level. "I heard what you said. I heard what he did to you." She jerks her arms forward and retrains the barrel at Terrance's chest. "What he wanted to do to me."

There are claws in my throat and I fight to keep my voice even. "This isn't the answer, Jaime," I say. "He's not worth it."

She says, "But he ruined everything! He stole our mom and

made us leave. He hurts women." Her blue eyes squint at him. "He deserves it."

"I know he does," I say, taking a small step forward.

"If he's gone, he can't ever hurt you again," Jaime says, her shoulders starting to twitch. "Or me or Mom or Noah or anyone else."

"I know," I say. "But it's not your job to protect us." Mom gags and covers her mouth with her hands. I say, "I'm supposed to take care of you, remember?"

Jaime's whole body shakes now, and I don't know if she can see through her tears. "I love you too much to let you ruin your life over him," I say. "So put down the gun, okay?" She's nodding and crying and the gun trembles with her. "Terrance will leave, and we'll be fine," I say. She bows her head and her arms collapse at her side. Faster than I would have thought possible, Winston is up the stairs, jumping over Mom, and taking the gun from Jaime's limp hand.

I rush toward Jaime and swoop her into my arms on the landing as her knees buckle. "It's okay," I say as she folds into me, blubbering. I say, "We're all okay." I wrap my body around Jaime's like a shield as she dissolves into giant heaving sobs, and we sink down onto the tan carpet and cry.

Winston holds the gun he took from Jaime at his side, his other firearm deserted in his pocket. "Terrance," he says. "I am a crack shot. Do I have to ask you again to get the hell out of my house?"

I close my eyes and hug Jaime's head to my chest. I hear shoes on tile, rustling clothes, hushed voices, doors opening and closing, but I tighten my arms around my little sister and she squeezes me back and we press so close together I can't separate our tears or breaths or hearts and I don't want to. It's like we've crawled back into each other's skins, which is exactly where we're supposed to be. It feels like returning home.

14

Jaime sleeps next to me in the dark, her face nestled into the green nylon of her sleeping bag. I lie awake, staring at a starless ceiling and listening to her familiar breathing, deep inhalations through her small nose, a consistent in and out of flowing air. I memorize the rhythm; try to match my breaths to the rise and fall of her lungs. I've watched her sleep so many times that even though I can only see the outline of her face, I know her skin and muscles are relaxed, her jaw loose, her hair mussed. When she has a bad dream her face contracts, but if I kiss her forehead, the tension in her body releases. When Jaime smiles in her sleep, I always smile, too.

We're on the floor of Ashley's room, using the same squishy sleeping bags we used at Christmas. Dad isn't here, Terrance has left, and the guns have been locked back in their metal box, but I don't feel safe yet. As usual, Jaime gets to rest while my brain refuses to take a break from worrying, churning what-if scenarios into thick knots inside my head. Tammy and Mom are staying in the flowery guest room, "talking things out," and I chew my fingernails into ragged stumps for hours while I imagine the decisions they're making "in my best interest." I suck the blood that pools in my shredded cuticles and try to convince myself that Tammy is my biggest ally and won't let me down.

I blow a kiss at Jaime's face as I pull my green journal from one of the big pockets in my cargo shorts and stand up. I whisper, "Sweet dreams, little sister," as I head out to the bathroom.

I sit cross-legged on top of the terry cloth–covered toilet lid and unclip my favorite pen from a small inside pocket of my shorts. I know going back to Tammy's was my decision, but I still feel like my life isn't really mine yet. *Mom was right though,* I write. *I am stronger than her.* I fill fifteen pages of my journal with my small, tightly curled green-inked cursive until my fingers and wrist ache and weak purple-blue sunlight starts to filter in through the bathroom window. I write, *You are not your parents,* and promise myself I never will be.

"Liz?" Jaime says, knocking. I uncross my legs and close my book. My knees crack as I move. "What are you doing?" she says as I let her in and shut the door behind her.

"Writing," I say.

She yawns. "I have to pee."

"I can get out," I say. Her sleep-lazy eyelids droop and her skin shines faintly in the low light. I say, "How are you feeling?"

She shrugs. "I think I'm probably in big trouble."

"Thanks for standing up for me," I say.

"It was my turn," she says and my lungs pinch.

Thousands of questions run through my head. I want to ask if she understands the magnitude of her actions, what it felt like to hold the power of Terrance's life in her hands, if she thought she could really pull the trigger. As much as I wish Terrance would disappear from our lives, I'm almost certain I couldn't.

"I'm proud of you," I say. "That took courage."

"I wish I could have helped more," she says, running her fingers through her bangs and showing off her scar.

"You did great," I say, and smile.

"I'm glad you get to go back to Tammy's," she says. She turns to the mirror, checking her chin for blemishes under the surface of her perfect skin. "Now we'll both be okay."

I nod. "I think things are better for me there." I look at her. "And you don't need me anymore."

Jaime stops scrutinizing her face. "I'll always need you, Liz," she says and my chest constricts like a tiny bird clenched in snake coils. Our ocean-blue eyes lock in the mirror, our faces reflected back like two interpretations of the same portrait. When we were little, people thought we were twins.

Our likeness smears in my sight and Jaime leans over and hugs me, plunks her chin on my shoulder. I lay my face against her head and we anchor our forearms around each other's backs. We stand on the bathroom floor as the sun rises outside and hold each other, rocking back and forth in the semidark like we've done so many times before it feels like habit, like a tradition that may be over.

I kiss the top of her head and let her go. "I will always be here for you," I say and she rolls her eyes like *of course*. "I love you," I say.

"I know," she says. "I love you, too." She pushes at my shoulders with a stronger force than I remember. "Now get out."

————

White clouds glide past the windows as our plane starts its descent into Utah. The Great Salt Lake is the color of baby-blue spring skies in the gold of the setting sun and in this bird's-eye view it's ringed by green-and-yellow hillsides with orange-dusted earth peeking through the vegetation like solid sand dunes on a beach of grasses. The plants fade into coffee-with-cream-colored stretches of muddy shorelines against the ancient lake. The mountains are muddled black-brown peaks in the distance, but I can still see their white caps, and I feel sorry for the parts of the rocky summits that never get warm.

Tammy tells me what she and Mom discussed last night at Deborah's. "I promised not to let you run wild and to more carefully observe your book choices," she says. "But I wouldn't promise to take you to church."

"Thank God," I say.

"She says you're harboring uncontrollable rage." Tammy looks at me, her blue eyes squinted, the skin at the corners wrinkling. "But you look controlled to me."

I think about the whirlpools in my chest, the storms that grow in my throat. "I might have said some things," I say, but there is no reason to rehash them. Putting thoughts and events into words in my journal is working I guess. It seems easier for me to look forward.

"Your mom wants you to come back for Christmas," Tammy says. "She invited both of us." I try to imagine our traditional Christmas Eve finger-food dinner with all of us together. It'd be a chance to share stocking finds with Jaime again, to spend time with Mom and Tammy, to start new holiday rituals with Noah.

"Will you come?" I ask and Tammy nods. I say, "What about Terrance?"

"She said she missed you two last year."

"She's not going to leave him, is she?" I say. "Even after what happened."

Tammy purses her lips. "I guess we'll cross that bridge when we get to it," she says, but we both know Mom stayed with my dad for ten years. At least Terrance doesn't hit her.

"Thanks for letting me come back," I say.

"I was kind of hoping you would want to," she says.

"I was worried you would say no."

"Why would I do that?" she says and hugs me. Her clean lavender scent fills my nose and I collapse into her shoulder and take deep breaths like I've been starved of oxygen for months. I close my eyes and tighten my arms. "I missed you," she says. "The house was too quiet while you were gone."

"I missed you so much," I say, letting go of her and leaning back into my polyester seat cover. I almost feel secure, like things are finally going to change in the right ways. There's just one thing left. I say, "What about Sam?"

"He's not, um"—she clears her throat and shifts in her narrow chair—"jumping for joy at the moment," she says. My pulse starts to speed up until Tammy says, "But I'm tired of sacrificing my happiness for his."

"Really?"

"I told him if he wasn't going to live here permanently, he

couldn't expect to get his way," she says. Aside from wringing her hands in her lap, she seems relaxed. "I need to start making decisions and building a life without him since he doesn't seem interested in giving up his job anytime soon, and he agreed."

"He's missing out," I say, and Tammy smiles at me in that sad way you see on TV when someone feels nostalgic for something they realize they can never get back. "If he was really as smart as he thinks he is, he would come back for you."

She laughs. "That's sweet," she says. "But I don't think it's a question of intelligence."

"Is it me?" I say. "I don't want to cause problems for you."

"It's him." She squeezes my knee and shakes her head. "We've been through worse," she says, and even though I know that's probably true, I also know how quickly the women in this family can change their minds. She takes a deep breath and lets it out slowly. "I'm willing to take the risks."

The hum of the jet engines and circulating air buzz across my skin, and the seat belt light flashes back on with a ding from the overhead speakers. I hope Tammy won't regret her choice as much as I hope I won't regret mine. I say, "So this is definitely more than temporary?"

"Why not?" she says. "Your stuff is already at my house and there's a ceiling with your name on it."

"Thank you," I say.

She says, "Thank you."

"For what?"

She nudges my arm with her elbow. "You make me happy, little girl," she says. She puts her arm around my shoulders and turns me toward the window and both our smiles reflect in the plastic oval that frames our destination.

This house still has a routine, and I am happy to slip back into it over the next few weeks. Tammy leaves for work in the mornings after she opens my blinds and invites rays of sun directly into my eyes. She usually says, "Rise and shine, little girl," like she used to, and I have been so glad to wake up here I don't remind her that it's summer.

I eat Kashi cereal and steel-cut oatmeal, farmers' market strawberries and nectarines for breakfasts, make Caprese salads with fresh heirloom tomatoes, basil leaves plucked from our garden, soft mozzarella, and crunchy sourdough bread for lunch. I carry my meals on trays to the lounge chairs on Tammy's patio, and eat al fresco to soak up as much sunlight as possible. I revel in the lack of gray.

I choose new books from the wooden shelves in my room—*The Chosen, Kindred, The Bean Trees*—and read for hours in the natural light, butt sunk into big, patterned cushions, body wrapped in the radiant warmth from heated cement. Out here in Tammy's garden—our garden—I'm amazed by the growth of the ferns, the blooming power of the rosebush, the now two-foot-tall herbs that give off their strong and spicy scents without even being touched. Reading, tanning, watering the plants, I spend hours each day under the open bowl of a sky in this city edged with stone summits, well-rested, belly full, and muscles loose.

I even call Dean to tell him I've returned. "For good?" he says.

I smile that silly, wide-open, teeth-revealing grin that infects my face whenever I hear his deliciously accented voice. It's too early to tell him I missed him, but I think we'll get there soon. "For a while at least," I say. "Depends on what this town has to offer."

"What made you come back?" he says, and I tell him it's kind of complicated. I cried when I hugged Jaime good-bye, but my first night here I slept for nine hours straight sprawled out on the queen-size mattress, and I knew this was the right choice. Tammy left my glow-in-the-dark constellations on the ceiling, and it's nice to sleep under stars again, even if they're plastic.

Dean asks if he can come over and kiss me for the whole afternoon. I almost say, "Sure, why not?" but remember my promise to be stronger than my mother, to make smart decisions, and invite him to the movies instead. "It'll be like that first time we hung out," I say.

"Hopefully not *exactly* like that time," he says. I roll my eyes but the goofy grin attacks my face again, and I think maybe romance doesn't have to sabotage my quest for independence, doesn't have to be an addiction like Terrance's, or create the destructive submission I saw in Mom. I think of Dean's careful words, his shy smiles and cool skin, and know it won't be the same for me.

He says, "I'm really glad you came back."

"Me, too," I say. "See you soon." I place the white cordless handset back in its base, smiling, and twirl on the ball of my foot on the hardwood floor.

I finger the wooden railing as I climb the white-carpeted stairs, flip the light switch in my room without looking for it. I play

Journey's *Greatest Hits* album, which I stole from Tammy's collection, and sing "Don't Stop Believin'" at the top of my lungs as I finish situating my room. I hang Alanis and the Fab Four back on the walls, rearrange the framed photos of me and Jaime, me and Noah, and a new one of me and Rachel at the river on one of the tables next to my fold-out bed.

I belt out "Be Good to Yourself," as I unpack my toiletries and put them back in their countertop organizer, where they'll stay for all of five minutes once school starts. My clothes go back in my nightstand drawers and in the closet, the pink church dress gets squished into the back in case I visit the Cranleys on some weekend in the future, and since Jaime's there, I'll have to visit.

So far, Tammy has asked what I want for dinner each night, and I've lapped up my old favorites and also new delicacies like curried potatoes and saffron ginger lamb. We take walks up into the Avenues past ivy-coated houses, down tree-lined streets above the Salt Lake Valley, the city lights twinkling gold, yellow, red, and white below us in the still-balmy end-of-summer air, the sky periwinkle-blue. We inhale the scents of dusty soil and sun-wilted leaves and listen to the crickets strum their creaky songs. We talk about our approaching trip to Mexico, and where we should travel next. We talk about the future, starting school, what universities I might want to attend. I registered for classes last spring because we had to in homeroom, but now I'm glad I'll be taking classes I chose: playwriting, choir, and honors English. I imagine hanging out with Dean and doing homework together, holding hands in the hallways, elbowing through the jocks in their red-and-black letter jackets as a team. I'm looking forward to bringing home A's so colleges will want me and Tammy will be proud. I want to be proud of myself again, too.

One night we get back from a walk and as Tammy fills two glasses with water, I push the blinking red button on her answering machine. The tape clicks and Mom's voice drifts out of the speaker.

"Hi, Tammy and Liz, it's Mom." Pause. "Um, Linda." I roll my eyes but her formality makes my chest contract. I haven't talked to her since returning to Utah even though she said she'd call. I glance at Tammy, who stands at the pristine white ceramic sink with her back to me, her head down. Mom continues, "I have good news," she says, her voice too high to be genuinely cheerful. "You can come home just like you wanted!" she says and my breath catches. Tammy sighs.

Mom says, "Call me when you get this so we can work things out and you can come back before school starts. Thanks!" The answering machine beeps and the red button becomes a steady glow.

I pick up the phone without waiting for the shock to subside. Did she finally get rid of Terrance? What about Jaime? If I could remember Mom's number right now I would dial, but my mind is full of tumbleweeds. The plastic receiver is cold, but warm hands close around mine and lift the handset from my grasp. Tammy says, "Let's talk for a minute before you make any calls." She puts the phone back in its base.

I look at her, eyebrows raised. "What do you know?"

Tammy pulls out a chair for me. I sit and she walks to the freezer, selects a gallon-size Ziploc bag full of brownies. She places a brownie in each of two bowls and sticks them in the microwave. While the dessert rotates, Tammy says, "That night at Deborah's, your mom got a pager message that led her to make a private phone call." The microwave beeps and the smell of chocolate fills the kitchen.

Tammy hands me a bowl. "After the call, she said she needed to leave, even though it was late. She wouldn't say why."

Tammy puts the bag of brownies back in the freezer and sits across from me at the table with her treat. "It's been almost a year since Terrance was released," Tammy says, and I am surprised to hear it's been that long since I left Mom's house. "With his record and the statistics about sex offenders . . ." She shrugs and licks her fingers. "I had a hunch. After we got back here, I made some calls and filled out some forms. It turns out it's pretty easy to request copies of police reports." She leans back in her chair, looking pleased. "I even paid extra for rush delivery, thinking Linda might do something like this."

"Terrance exposed himself again?" I say.

A hint of a smile twitches Tammy's upper lip. "Not exactly."

From the police reports and the victim statement, we know that Terrance went to a Target about a half-hour away from Deborah's house. Security cameras show he entered at 9:22 P.M. The victim, Shari Knowles, twenty-six, noticed a "dark-skinned man with tattoos and a shaved head," browsing greeting cards down the aisle from where she stood trying to pick out a new clock for the house she shares with policeman, Brady Knowles. The man, who turned out to be Terrance of course, spent the next ten minutes inching closer, picking up a card every few steps and glancing at her. As Shari chose her clock and turned to leave, Terrance moved to the middle of the aisle.

"Hi," he said.

Shari hesitated but returned the hello. "Nice clock," Terrance said. He put his hands in the pockets of his red Forty-Niners jersey shorts, and the look on his face made Shari uncomfortable. The store intercom clicked on, and Shari instinctively looked up at the voice announcing twenty minutes until closing, which made her realize if she wanted to pee, and she did, she should go soon. Terrance shifted his weight into her personal space. He leered at her, his hands moving in his pockets. "You have the most—"

"Stop," she interrupted, not sure exactly what was going on, but still creeped out. "I'm married, and I'm not interested." He looked surprised, but she walked away and didn't look back. She headed toward the aspirin and vitamin aisle and the doors that led to the bathrooms. She didn't notice anyone following her.

Shari walked through the swinging doors into the warehouse section of the store. Stacked columns of crates and boxes faded out of view into the darkness of the storage area, but the doors of the individual male and female restrooms were lit by a hanging bulb. Shari heard the swish sound of the double doors opening behind her as she fumbled for the light switch just inside the women's restroom, one foot propping the door open. She smelled Terrance before she felt his hands on her hips, a metallic scent mixed with cheap cologne. It's a stench I remember well.

When he grabbed her, she dropped her purse and the clock and jerked her right elbow into Terrance's chest in the reflexive self-defense move her husband had taught her. Terrance grunted, but pushed her into the bathroom. He called her a bitch, but she felt his excitement pressed against her butt. Shari thought of her husband, the kids she still wanted to have, and her self-defense lessons came roaring back. As Terrance shoved her face-first into the wall, she twisted away, clawed at his jaw and cheek, and kicked him in the balls as hard as she could. Terrance howled with pain and Shari punched his Adam's apple. Terrance choked and she was out the doors and screaming for security.

I envision Terrance before the attack: buck teeth protruding from his cocky smirk, following a girl he thought was as helpless as all the others. I like to believe he was swaggering and confident, following old habits, sure of his perverted fix like who knows how many times before. I imagine his certainty when he pounced, his shock when Shari fought back and got away, and his frustration at being caught. I imagine him gasping for breath on the dirty bathroom floor, and picture his injuries — bruised testicles, swollen throat, and bloody scabs down his ugly face.

It's late when we finish reading all the material that came in the packet from the police, but I still want to call Mom. A million questions ping-pong in my brain and I know I won't be able to sleep without addressing some of them.

Mom answers on the third ring. I say, "Are you going to tell me why I can suddenly come back?"

"Terrance violated his parole," she says. "No big deal, but he'll be back in jail for a while."

She's still lying to me. It's not a surprise, just disappointing. "Mom, I know Terrance got arrested again." Silence echoes across the line. "For assaulting the wife of a cop."

"How do you know that?"

"Are you going to stay with him?"

"This was our fault," she says. She clears her throat. "My fault. I wasn't there for him that night. He needed me and I deserted him."

I roll my eyes. "He chose to ignore the help he was offered," I say. "Just like Dad."

She sighs. "He can't help himself."

"He's getting worse."

"I can't give up on him," Mom says. "People deserve second chances."

"He's had more than two chances," I say. Mom sniffs and I wonder if she's crying. Maybe she realizes she's lying to herself, too, and doesn't know how to stop.

But I made a vow to take care of me. "What happens if I come home and Terrance gets released with the same condition as before?"

She says, "We have a new lawyer who may be able to get Terrance a reduced sentence since it's that woman's word against his and she hurt him so badly."

"He attacked her," I say.

"So she says," Mom says.

"She's married to a cop and Terrance has a record," I say. "People will believe her."

"Anyway," Mom says, and I picture her waving her hand in dismissal. "It's possible you'll both be home soon enough."

"Even after what he did, you'd let us live together?"

Mom says, "I could really use your help."

"Have you told Jaime?"

"You're such a good big sister," she says. "Noah and Jaime need you." I hear the stiffness in her voice and my heart hurts. It would be so easy to go home. To let myself believe the fantasy that we'd all be happy living together. "We all need you," Mom says. "And I truly do miss you, Elizabeth. You're so far away now."

My eyes fill. I've been exposed to a better life here, but it's so hard to refuse her offer. My throat swells like it's trying to tell me to shut up, but I say, "I don't think I can come back."

"I don't understand," Mom says.

"I'm sorry."

"Isn't this what you've wanted all year?" Mom says. "To live with your family?"

"I do live with family," I say quietly. "I miss you though."

"Well then come home," Mom says, frustration edging into her voice. "I thought you'd be more excited about this. You were so upset when you had to leave."

This makes me want to stay with Tammy even more. I shake my head. "I have a life here now," I say. A life where I'm a priority to someone else, not a backup plan. "I don't want to have to worry about being uprooted if you're forced to choose again." As long as Terrance needs fixing, he'll be Mom's number one concern.

She whispers, "But this is your home." Her speech is soft and stilted, a sound I recognize from all the times I held back bubbling tears.

I exhale deeply and realize, even though it wrenches my body like a shock wave, Mom's isn't really my home. "Not anymore," I say. I will probably never live with her again.

I call Jaime the next day to see if Mom gave her the same option to go back. She hasn't even heard that Terrance is in jail again. "That's awesome," she says.

"I know," I say. "He even got his ass kicked by the woman he assaulted."

"Good," she says. "I hope it really hurt."

"Me, too," I say. "Mom said we could live with her again."

Jaime says, "For how long?" and I half-smile. She's learning. It's kind of sad to hear her so distrustful, but I'm glad she's upped her guard. She has to grow up, too, and I can't always be there.

"I told her I wanted to stay here," I say. "I figured you'd want to stay at Deborah's."

"Yeah," Jaime says. "Even though Ashley's a total brat sometimes."

"Just make fun of her braces."

"And Aunt Deborah wants me to learn guitar."

"Well, you like to sing," I say.

"I wish I could sing with you," she says. "Our harmonies sound better."

"I'll come visit soon," I say. I think of Ashley and her rude faces and Winston's behind-my-back digs that he thinks I can't hear. "Or maybe you can come here."

"Not when it's snowing."

"Whenever you want," I say. "Maybe for the summer."

Jaime says, "Will Tammy make us eat health food?"

I laugh. "We can cook whatever you want," I say. "Either way, we'll see each other soon, okay?"

Jaime says, "It's been, like, a week," and I realize the ache I usually feel when we're apart is muted. Our orbits are still connected, they always will be, but now our bond seems able to withstand greater distances.

"Call anytime," I say. "And write me back for once."

"Writing is boring," she says.

"You can write anything," I say. "Tell me what's going on."

"Yesterday Aunt Deborah said maybe I need to start therapy," Jaime says, her voice a little lower. "As if there aren't other people in this house who need a shrink."

"What did you do?" I ask, thinking of my visit to the church counselor's office, her neat stacks of files on her cherrywood bookcases, those of us with damaged minds described on paper and categorized into nameable ills.

She says, "I picked out a black T-shirt at the mall."

I laugh. Jaime's crime isn't the same as my sinking consciousness over the summer, and I don't think Deborah will actually make her go sit on that fake leather couch and answer vague questions from the small woman in her fancy chair.

"It's not funny," Jaime says.

"But you're still okay, right?" I say. "And you know you can call me if you need me?"

"I'm fine," she says, and I don't ask her again.

That night, after Tammy and I play badminton and watch a movie with bowls of fresh fruit and whipped cream, I get under my green sheets with my blue comforter folded at the foot of my bed. The crickets have kicked their melodies into high gear, and cool breezes waft in through the open windows. I write in my journal for as long as my brain needs to vent like I've been doing every night. Sometimes I make future plans in the gold-lined pages: *play guitar and sing in a band, write a book, visit the Parthenon.* When I turn off the light and my fake stars cast green shadows that mingle with the white glow from the real stars outside, I often pray for Jaime, for Noah and Matt, for Mom and Deborah, and even Dad. I ask the universe to keep them safe, and I don't think it matters where the ideas go exactly, as long as I send them out into the world.

"Hey," Tammy says, sitting on the edge of my bed, the lines of her strong bones and lean limbs smudged and backlit by the hall bulb. "I wanted to say good night."

I smile. "Good night," I say, rolling onto my side to face her and snuggling into my crisp sheets. I breathe in and let out the air slowly, savoring this moment, this place I never expected to end up but am so thankful for.

"So," Tammy says. "Can I wake you up early tomorrow for a hike?"

"Totally." I missed our Sunday morning rituals, sanctuary without church, support without conditions. I'm looking forward to walking mountain trails, watching plant shadows move like living paintings on the uneven dirt as our feet beat in harmony with the birds and bugs. When I close my eyes in the dark now, I visualize nature. Images with echoes I can almost hear of rushing rivers and lakes lapping grainy shores lull me to sleep.

"We should bring our sketchbooks," I say. "And the watercolors." Tammy raises an eyebrow at me. "I'll even wear one of your nerdy fanny packs to help carry everything," I say. I can't wait to witness the leaves starting their descents from tall branches, watch the tree-lined hillsides fade from shades of green to yellow and orange. I want to capture the beauty beyond what I can hold in my memory.

Tammy laughs. "For the last time, lots of hikers wear them." She pushes at my shoulder with her fingertips. "But, sure, let's make a day of it." She looks down at me, her blue eyes shadowed, and tilts her head. "You must not have gotten outside much at the Cranleys'."

"You have no idea." I missed the fresh air, the elevation, the open sky, the smell and sound of snow runoff rushing over mossy stones, floating through fields of wildflowers and groves of pines, birch, and oak, and diving under logs. The water doesn't complain about where it ends up or how it gets there; it just continues on its way, absorbing little pieces of everything it touches as it rides the current. I want to learn to cultivate peace like that, to worry less about what's around the bend. "I missed our hikes," I say. "And our talks."

Tammy's eyes shine and she smiles. "Me, too." Her hands fuss with the creases in the linens for a minute, and then she rests her right hand on my knee. "It's great to have you back," she says, squeezing my leg.

My heart swells. I would choose Tammy to be my family even if she wasn't my blood relative, and I know she feels the same way about me. I smile a genuine grin, show all my teeth. "It's good to be here."

Tammy lies down next to me on her back. "There was an emptiness without you." I move closer to her warmth and close my eyes. She sighs. "Even when Sam was here."

In our peaceful silence, I listen to Tammy breathe. It's not as familiar as the higher-pitched whine of air through Jaime's small nose, but it's comforting, a chanting rhythm of air in and out through lungs and nostrils, the reassuring sound that proves I am not alone. Someone I love is close.

Tammy breaks the pulse of her breathing and says, "I think I got so used to your footsteps, your socks and hair clips all over the house, your silly TV shows . . ." She takes my hand. "I liked being a part of your everyday life."

"I liked that, too," I say, and think about my anxiety on that first plane to Utah. I never thought I'd find a home here, but it feels like this was the path I was meant to take. I say, "Do you believe in fate?"

Wind stirs the trees outside and the bushes we planted on the patio below, and the whooshing sound of rustling leaves quiets the crickets. An owl hoots and the crickets begin their chirping at a lower volume, like some of them are now too scared to sing.

Tammy shifts on my fold-out bed, and I peek at her. Her eyes are open and she's staring at my mostly faded green stars.

"I believe in choices," she says. "What's great about life is that other people's choices can surprise you, make you realize things you might not have known otherwise."

"Like how Mom's mistakes brought me here?"

She nods. "But if we're happy, why worry about how we ended up where we are?"

"Are you happy?"

"Are you?"

"Sort of," I say. "Mostly. Now."

"Me, too."

"When I think about the future," I say. "All the things I can still do."

She smiles at me. "Me, too," she says.

An herb-scented breeze fills the room and shuffles the papers on my desk. I shiver. Tammy sits up and pulls my comforter up to my neck. She kisses the top of my head and smooths my hair behind my ear. She says, "I think this is exactly where we're both supposed to be." She brushes my chin with her forefinger and thumb.

It feels good to be the one getting tucked in, to let someone else stand guard. She says, "Sweet dreams," and I think that might finally be possible. Tammy moves away, but I know she's not going far.

I say, "I love you," as she closes my door partway and leaves the hall light on without me even asking. Soon, I may not need the glow behind my eyelids to fall asleep. It gets easier each night here. "You're a great mom," I mumble and close my eyes.

"I really thought I could be," she whispers. I feel the air shift above my skin and then a kiss on my forehead, and the scent of Tammy's honey lip balm wafts into my nose. Her voice, "I love you, little girl," carries me through the night.

After our morning hike, Tammy goes to aerobics and I take a long shower in my private golden bathroom. Clean and dressed, I walk the borders of Tammy's house slowly, soaking in the stability of the sameness. Tammy's art still tempers the white of the walls in the living room; the dustless glass curio cabinet still stands proudly as protector of Tammy's international souvenirs and mementos from her travels. I hope someday I can fill my own house with beautiful reminders of the places I've visited, the adventures I've experienced.

My bare feet slide across the white carpet to the couch, where the cushions are plumped and clean. The purple chenille throw is folded and draped across a pile of floor pillows in the corner. The TV still hides behind the wood cabinet with sliding doors, the fake logs sit ready for burning in her gas fireplace, the recessed lights above my head cast soft glows across the spotless surfaces of Tammy's possessions. The kitchen walls are the same sage green Tammy and I painted together, the purple and blue-green teapot painting is as dramatic as the day we hung it. The room still looks lovely, as glossy and fresh as a magazine spread.

I breathe in the smell of this house: the herbal freshness, the clean, rain-washed scent of her laundry detergent. I bask in the quiet. No SEGA video game beeps or hip-hop music, no barking dog, pep talks from Deborah, or bellowing requests from Winston. Just the hum of the refrigerator and the twitter of birds outside. I step onto the patio under the bright blue sky and stand in the shadow of the brick building Tammy and I share, surrounded by growing evidence of our garden labors. Somewhere a dog barks, and a lone cricket impatient for dusk strums its legs.

I know life here won't be perfect. I know that soon winter will arrive and dust the world with ice. The frost will invade my chest again, my fingers will freeze inside my gloves, and my body will want to hibernate beneath a nest of soft wool blankets until I learn to thaw myself out, figure a way to keep my blood pumping against the cold. I know Sam will return and spout speeches about the merits of hat wearing, cook pork chops, and glare at me when Tammy's not looking. I know his presence will remind me that this arrangement is not quite solid, that nothing here is really mine, including Tammy.

But in this moment, I stand tall and focus on the slack in my shoulder blades, the loose muscles in my arms and back that have been freed from the flexed tension of a persistently active fight-or-flight response. My neck feels longer, my jaw relaxed, and I haven't chewed on my nails in days. I focus on little things like the church bells singing in the distance, the jug of hibiscus sun tea brewing on the patio table, the letter from Rachel sitting upstairs on my desk awaiting my reply.

I exhale in one long, even release, smiling at no one and stretching my hands above my head in a yoga sun salutation. The air is thick with heat and smells like dry grass and dusty rock. At the horizon, the sun dazzles the mountaintops with a white-gold sheen, like they're jewels too big to harvest. Soft breezes stir aromas of creek water and tree sap into my nose and swirl the hair around my head. A hummingbird flits by our climbing vines, close enough that I can hear the thrumming of its beating wings, the sound of constant motion against the wind, and then it flies away, its feathers catching the sunlight and shimmering pink, green, and gold as it disappears.

I breathe the earth-perfumed air, bare feet planted solid on bumpy and still-warm concrete, lift my face to the heavens, and feel grounded.

Elizabeth Reid

lizreid@ucsc.edu

Nonfiction Seminar

Fall Quarter 2005

WORD ASSOCIATION

Beauty

Jaime is the pretty one. Both of us blond and blue eyed, I'm thinner, but sometimes not by much, and she's always been more willing to flaunt things. She hasn't not had a boyfriend since she was eleven. Like most pretty girls, she knows how to wiggle her ass and lean over the desk just so, and is then convincingly surprised and appropriately grateful when her boss lets her have two Fridays off in a row or the guy at the vending machine gives her the last Coke.

At fourteen, she and her friends flashed a group of bearded men in the parking lot of a Tool concert for a keg of beer. She lost her virginity that same year to a guy named Spike with our mom asleep a few feet down the hall. The first time a guy grabbed her ass without her permission she was working at Java City. She was sixteen and almost always stoned, and she giggled instead of kicking him in the balls. He gave her rides to and from work for weeks. There might have been more between them, but she doesn't tell me everything.

She's quit three jobs because of some sort of sexual harassment. I once asked her why she didn't just wear less revealing clothes. "I have a right to express myself, Liz," she said, like I was stupid. "They're all perverts, anyway."

I said, "Even I can't help but look at your cleavage when you wear that red V-neck spandex top with a lacy black bow at the center and a push-up bra underneath."

"I don't wear a push-up," she said. "I can't help it if I have big boobs."

"Small shirts don't help, either."

"Whatever," she said. "At least I have a chest."

Jaime still takes particular pleasure in calling me a "late bloomer." Two years older, I hit puberty first, but it hit her much harder and at thirteen, her breasts were about as big as mine are now and hers kept growing. I was taller, but she wore more makeup and used her body in a way my self-consciousness would never allow. People thought she was older. Guys bought her drinks at bars way before she was twenty-one. A flip of her long blond hair, a shining smile, and her little-girl-being-tickled laugh and she'd get into a show for free, or snag the cute waiter's number and a free glass of wine, or receive a complimentary bobble-head doll from a vendor at Great America.

Intelligence

Since we're labeling things, let's call me the smart one. I read faster than anyone I know and retain almost everything. I have excellent recall and a near photographic memory. My mom is still amazed when I can recite specifics she's forgotten: her old work address, her husband's prison I.D., the names of people I only met once at a birthday party when I was six.

When I was in first grade, a woman with braided pigtails pulled me out of Mrs. Petersen's class and asked me to put together puzzles in her office. Her name was Carol, and she let me drink my apple juice box as I studied the angles and holes in each shape, rotating the blocks in my hands so I could see all the lines and indentations. I set the juice box on her desk and arranged the blocks into the 3-D structure I'd seen in my mind. All those curves and edges molded into a wooden horse; later, flat plastic shapes made a sunflower; a different set of wooden blocks became a ship. Carol smiled wide at me when I handed her each finished whole, showing all her white teeth. She made a note on her yellow legal pad, nodded her head like she'd proved something, and beamed at me. Carol also gave me math problems and reading tests, and after two days of this she told me if I wanted to, I could be in the advanced second-grade class next year.

Jaime called me smarty-pants. She still does sometimes, though I try not to correct her grammar as much these days.

Hope

My dad hit my mom with anything he could find when he wanted to hit her, but every time he started AA, she thought, this time he'd really do it. This time would be different. He sounded so sincere in his promises.

They even renewed their vows when I was five, did a whole

wedding set-up with the white dress, white balloons, three-tiered white-frosted cake with little plastic bride and groom, the stuff they hadn't done when they got married. They look so happy in the pictures, both thin and healthy, sunlit and framed by blue sky. My mom is wearing makeup, my dad is clean-shaven and sober, and they are both wearing smiles I haven't seen since. There are some shots of the four of us: me and Jaime in little white dresses with bows and ribbons, white flowers in our blond hair, dimples in our cheeks. We look like a family.

Fifteen years later when my dad went to jail for drunk driving and asked me to clean out his apartment and hold his stuff for six months, I found a whole box of these photos next to his bed. He still asks how Mom's doing when we see him, even before he asks about us.

Faith

My mom's mother died when she was a toddler, and her stepmom beat the crap out of her and my aunts. She dragged them around by their hair and threw things at them: books, butter knives, hot curling irons.

I know my mom was scared. I know she cowered years later when Dad raised his arm, too, but was used to covering the bruises. I know she was afraid to be alone, too afraid to leave, and in her heart and at her church, voices were saying she had made a promise to my father and the one in heaven. And she loved them both.

Friends took us in immediately when they saw her swelling lip or black eye, let us stay the night on their living room floor. They gave us money, sent cards at Christmas with checks that made Mom cry. They brought us turkeys at Thanksgiving and coats from the donation pile at church. God provided when my dad couldn't get off the couch. She trusted Him with all our lives because she didn't have a choice.

I remind myself every day: there is always a choice.

Compassion

My dad always gives money to bums. Even the ones who hold signs that say, "Why lie? I need a beer." He says that might be him someday.

"If I was on the streets, Liz," he asked once, "if I came to your house some afternoon and knocked on your door, you'd buy me a sandwich, right?"

Fear

Jaime would say I tortured her. She'd cite the general: that I was mean and bossy and condescending. She'd give some specifics too: the time I threw a pen at her head and made her bleed, the time I kicked a hole in her bedroom door, the time I shoved a piece of bread up her nose. She'd say I called her fat and corrected her grammar and laughed when she mispronounced words like "ordament," or "skullitin." She'd say I pinned her down and spit in her eyes, sat on her chest with my knees on her arms, leaned over her face and let the bubbly white spit fall slowly over my lips while she struggled. She might say more than that, because there is definitely more, and worse, and while she would absolutely exaggerate, it's also mostly true, even though I wish it weren't.

How much of our behavior is inescapable? If violence begets violence, how many times will I lash out? As often as I watched my father beat my mother? Should I count her split lips or broken ribs, her black eyes?

I worry that no matter how much I channel my emotions into productive artistic expression, the traits carried in my body and absorbed from my upbringing and the decades-running family tapes in my head will eventually override my best efforts at a better life.

I really want a better life.

Miscommunication

My dad offered me money at the beginning of the summer. "I got some extra right now, Liz, and I know I didn't help much before, so I could probably let you have about three hundred dollars."

I was moving south in September to attend UC Santa Cruz and said that'd be great. "I could really use your help with a deposit when I find an apartment," I said. I swear that's what I said.

In August, Jaime and I went to where he had just moved in with his girlfriend to celebrate his birthday. He held a Budweiser and Peg looked sixty years old, all the wrinkles on her face. Packs of cigarettes, all open and most half empty, sat in each room not even next to the overflowing ashtrays. My dad barbecued and I stayed outside where the air was clean. Peg's seven-year-old son sat next to me on the grass. He talked about rabbits.

Jaime bummed a cigarette from Peg, took one of my dad's beers from the fridge, and sat in the lawn chair next to the grill. A stack of Costco frozen burger patties stood on the table, and flies and bees buzzed around the meat. Peg came out and her smoke mixed with charcoal smoke, and my head throbbed in the sun. She slipped her arms around my dad's waist.

"Peg works as a guard at Folsom Prison," he said to us.

"Terrance was there for a while," Jaime said.

"No he wasn't," I said.

"He's in prison now," my dad said to Peg.

"For what?" she asked, the creases around her mouth like caverns when she puckered for a drag.

"Flashing!" he said, and laughed so hard he spilled beer down the front of his Grateful Dead tank top. "Their mom married a flasher," he said, and shook his head. "That's got to be worse than me, right?" He flipped a burger.

After the burgers and the cake Peg bought that said, *Happy Birthday Stud*, we gave him his presents: a box of Jordan Almonds, some Old Spice aftershave, and soap on a rope. Later, after all that and when it was almost time to go, I asked him about the money.

"You said you didn't want it," he said.

"What?"

"You said you didn't need it."

"I said I could use it later," I said.

"I don't have it anymore," he said. "I spent it."

"Can you give me anything?" I asked. "I have a nine-hundred-dollar deposit due on the first. Even fifty bucks would help."

"You said you didn't want any money."

"I didn't, but if—"

"No, I don't have fifty bucks." He opened a new can. "It's my goddamn birthday."

When I got home, there were three messages from him. They were mostly just slurred swear words and name calling and "you ruined my fucking birthday" in various forms, some with "bitch" tagged on either side of the sentence, but the words that stand out the most when I think about that day are "money grubbing whore."

No matter how much you think you hate your father, things will change after that.

Optimism

My mom believes in God's plan. She believes there's a reason. My mom stayed with my dad for thirteen years.

Growth

In college I wrote an essay about how my mother's second husband, convicted multiple times of indecent exposure, was "inappropriate" with teenage me. I wrote about his lustful glances, his sexual comments, a lingering hug that ended with all ten of his fingers spread and resting across my ass in a not-quite squeeze. None of it was obvious enough for my mother to intervene, even when I told her I didn't want him touching me. "I asked him not to hug you anymore," Mom said, shrugging. "I don't know why he still does it."

I gave her a copy of the story to read when she came to visit me at UCSC and she folded it and put it in her faux leather purse from

Kmart. She took me out to dinner for my birthday and we ate at a seafood restaurant on the pier with seagulls flapping in the breeze and sea lions barking occasionally from below. We both ordered the lobster special and after we finished eating we sat and soaked up the setting sun sparkling on the slate-blue water. I loved living in a beach town because it always smelled like the sea, but on the water I also got the mist, the salty breeze in my hair, the taste of the ocean in each breath.

"Are you still trying to make me feel guilty, Elizabeth?"

I glanced down. A corner of my hastily refolded essay stuck out from her purse. "I forgot how fast you read," I said.

She shook her napkin and smoothed it out again. "I wish we could all move on from that whole situation."

"I didn't mean to hurt you," I said. "I just wanted to tell my story."

"It's not just *your* story."

"Those experiences belong to me."

She cleared her throat. "Ignoring the"—she rolled her eyes— "exaggerations, I could still see that you are a talented writer."

"Really?" Something like pride bubbled in my chest, an unfamiliar effervescence that lifted me up. I sat straighter in my seat.

Mom said, "Just as long as everyone knows he wasn't really like that."

"Terrance?" I said, the little bubbles of confidence popping like firecrackers against my ribs. "Yes he was."

"Oh, Liz." She laughed. Still, again, like she had all those years ago when I'd begged her to keep him away from me, begged her to let me stay, she actually laughed.

Suddenly I was fourteen again, leaving my home while he took my place, separated from my sister and bouncing between temporary beds in other people's houses. Her dismissal poured saltwater on wounds that had just begun to heal. "He touched my breasts right in front of you," I whispered. "I know you tried not to see."

The shock exploded on her face in bulging eyes and an open mouth and for just a second, a tiny, tiny flash of a second, I thought she might be ready to hear the truth. But she chuckled and shook her head. "Oh, Liz," she said again. "You're such a good storyteller."

I sighed, unsurprised, but this time I didn't let her delusions crush me. I swallowed my protests, tucked the truth away for later. It got a little easier each time. I forced a smile. "Thank you for dinner."

"Happy birthday."

Identity

Jaime has gained close to a hundred pounds in less than two years. She says it's because she quit smoking. She says she knows she's fat and she wants to do something about it, but it seems like recently she's just gotten bigger. When it got warm, I saw her giant calves, and she doesn't even wear jeans anymore, just pants with elastic waists. I worry about her health.

But she still photographs well, knows exactly when to smile. Her blue eyes look blue in pictures whereas mine are always red and my face is doing something weird because I'm uncomfortable. She still has long blond hair that she wants to grow to her butt, and I want to say something about how if she keeps growing her butt, too, they might meet in the middle, but that would be mean. And it doesn't matter anyway because the waiter still brings her a free margarita when we go to Ernesto's, and she is currently sleeping with two of her best friends, though not officially with anyone. "It's called benefits, Liz," she says, and sips her drink.

I've spent two years pining for the guy I thought was the one I couldn't get tired of wanting, but the not having is getting old. I never give the guys who try to talk to me a chance; I never shake my ass for a free drink; and what I miss most is being held. Jaime doesn't have to sleep alone if she doesn't want to. She would never admit that's why she brings men home, but I would never admit that I understand; that sometimes I wish I could pretend, too.

"I get what I want," she says, and she does. She smirks at me. "Smarty-pants."

All my years of advanced classes and creative learning and she started ditching school in fifth grade, and look at us now. Her skills are much more practical.

Justice

I heard this on the news: A man is in the process of robbing a woman's house. It's raining; he slips on the roof tiles and falls through the glass skylights in the woman's kitchen and breaks his leg. Now he is suing her for the medical costs plus damages for "psychological wounds."

My dad thinks it's great. "Good for him," he says. "He was just trying to make a living."

"Could that be you someday, too?"

"Nah," my dad says, and shakes his head. "I'd just bust the door in."

Regret

My mom stayed over at my apartment a few years ago. She'd fought with Terrance and showed up unexpectedly, wanted to sleep on my futon and watch *Evita*. She'd found out Terrance had been cheating, which was a surprise only to her, but I let her cry in peace. I got her a ginger ale and some crackers, stole a chunk of chocolate from my roommate's stash. I turned off all the lights and spread a blanket over my messy-haired, pale, and droopy-skinned mother while she stared at the screen with glassy eyes. I rubbed her back like she'd done for me when I was sick, but I wasn't sure it helped. The one thing I knew wouldn't help was to say I told you so, so I kept my mouth shut.

In the yellow haze of pre-dawn I woke to the sound of sobbing. Mom was sitting on my bed, holding my hand, crying. "I'm sorry," she said when she saw my eyes open. "I'm so sorry." She reached out to push a loose strand of sweaty hair behind my ear. "Mom?" I said, my sleepy brain reminding me I wasn't a little girl waking up from a nightmare with Mom to stroke my back and tell me it was all going to be okay. She didn't know I had nightmares almost every single night. She couldn't be there to comfort me.

"I couldn't see it before. He's . . I wish . . ." she said, hiccupping and sniffling. "If I could go back and do it again, I'd pick you." She leaned over and hugged me, her tears hot drops on my collarbone, her gardenia perfume sweet in my nose. She was soft and warm and I hugged her back and knew that what she'd said was untrue, but it was nice to finally hear. "I love you," she whispered. "I'm so proud of you. I wish I had your strength."

A few weeks later when she told me she was pregnant, she was folding Terrance's laundry while he went out "drinking with the guys." She started crying and apologizing to me again, but I think she was really sorry for the child she was carrying, guilt-ridden over bringing a new person whose father she might be leaving into a home she could no longer pretend was happy.

My realization was different: I was going to have another little sister and I would do anything to protect her just like I'd done for Jaime. I loved her already.

Relief

Jaime has a scar across her arm about two and half inches long and a quarter inch wide. It's a shiny white band between her shoulder and elbow, visible just below the hem of her T-shirt sleeve. The scar tissue is pale and puckered and looks like her wrinkled right thumb, which she still sucks at age twenty-two. I notice similar scars on the arms of others girls at the coffee shop on campus or the bus sometimes, thin white lines across their biceps, none as big or as thick as Jaime's. She told me she did hers with a safety pin. I think about all the time that took, the patience.

Acceptance

My mother's husband was on the news last December. Grainy security camera footage from a Walmart showing an "unidentified

Hispanic male" who had been exposing himself to women trying to do their holiday shopping. His face wasn't visible in the shot, but it was unmistakably him. The swagger, the baggy pants, the Forty-Niners cap. Seeing him onscreen conjured his coppery sweat smell in my nostrils and the feel of his greasy fingers on my skin.

I shuddered and then watched, frozen, as the footage looped and local newscasters gave instructions for contacting the police with any information about this man, shook their heads and said something about how sick people can be. "And at Christmas!" the woman said with her red-lipsticked lips and her eyes wide under her shellacked bangs. The man and his hair helmet nodded.

Ten minutes later I hadn't moved. *Ohmygod.* I had the remote in one hand and the phone in the other. I jumped when it rang. "Did you see it?" my mom said. I nodded. There are things you think you know, things you might have vaguely imagined even if you try not to, but you don't really know until you see them broadcasted live on TV. Terrance seemed so happy, strutting through those double glass doors. "I turned him in," Mom said.

My throat was caked with dust. "Good."

She said, "I'm supposed to get some reward money." She twitter-laughed.

"And he'll go back to jail?" I started to relax.

"I'm finally going to divorce him, Liz." She took a deep breath. "I promise," my mom said. I'd heard that line before, but maybe for this new daughter, she'd fight harder. Maybe she'd love my little sister enough to make the choice she should have made for me.

Independence

One of the first things I did when I got my own apartment last year was buy a chain lock and install it on my front door. I finally had a place that could only be opened by me and me alone, so I wanted the extra security, but more than that, I wanted a daily ritual that would say *this is mine.* A tangible, audible, satisfyingly obvious reminder that others were not allowed in unless I let them, and no one could make me leave without just cause. Mine.

I slid the lock through the metal groove after I'd also locked the dead bolt and cried for two hours. Then I made myself broiled salmon with balsamic and honey glaze, sautéed garlic zucchini and lemon rice pilaf, and savored everything: the fresh fish and sun-kissed produce; my freshly watered and thriving houseplants; the artwork I'd picked out and hung on the walls. Family photos on the table tops: of my athletic aunt—my honorary mom for years, tan and lean—and me standing in front of a waterfall with the sun cresting the treetops around us; of me and Jaime at her high school graduation, me so proud I'm beaming, but her smile is still a million times brighter; of my baby brother who's almost as tall as I am kicking ass on the soccer field; of my mom and me and Jaime, arms around each other's shoulders standing in front of a vineyard we visited for Mom's birthday, laughing, all of us, our high cheekbones pink, our blond hair shining in the golden afternoon light, our blue-green eyes clear and unguarded. I actually look happy. We all do.

Jaime comes over sometimes when she needs a place to "chill," and I let her eat my food and laze around in my pajamas, and we talk until two in the morning about boys and clothes and movies like we did when we shared a room, back when the only thing we had in this world was each other.

But mostly, I relish my solitude. I turn on the TV after school or work and settle in to enjoy whatever the hell I want to watch without anyone to complain or judge, to eat a delicious dinner that's exactly what I wanted at this exact moment, to relax in this safe space, to be in a home—to be home—like I've never experienced, a chance to be myself completely and fully explore what that means.

I whisper, "This is mine," and my body sinks down, centers. I say it again, just to feel the word on my lips. "Mine." That release happens a little faster each day.

Freedom

I'm not afraid of anything anymore. I mean, that's a total lie, I'm scared shitless by many things, but what I meant, what I mean, is that I know I can handle the fear. I know I can take it. I know I'll survive unless I don't want to, and sometimes even then.

I can only keep moving.

Happiness

The summer I was eleven my mom left us alone when she went to work. Jaime and I would take our Barbies, each with its own specific name—Cindy, Carmen, Joanna—to the apartment pool nearly every day. We didn't go to the one by the complex office because kids were supposed to be fifteen or supervised to swim. But no one watched at the small pool on the far end of the housing blocks near the freeway, so we went there. Sometimes we brought a boom box, blasted Ace of Base or Boyz II Men, sang the harmonies together while we smeared on coconut-scented tanning oil from bronze bottles of Banana Boat.

We played mermaids searching for treasure underwater, kicked our feet in one swoop like tails, threw rocks in the deep end and dove for them. We made Joanna and Carmen go on dangerous boat trips in their hot pink plastic Cadillac, through shark-infested waters with pirate attacks and thunderstorms and deserted islands. We had tea parties underwater, perfected below the surface flips and acrobatic maneuvers holding hands. We did handstands and little dance moves like synchronized swimmers we'd seen on the Olympics. We jumped from the Jacuzzi into the pool and back again. We dove through inner tubes and pushed each other off them. We had contests to see who could hold their breath the longest, who could swim mermaid style the fastest, who could find the white rock at the bottom of the white pool first.

We were just sun-bleached, brown-skinned little girls, playing in the water.

ACKNOWLEDGMENTS

I want to thank my agent, Trena Keating, for believing in me and this book wholeheartedly from the start, and for her expertise, patience, and enthusiasm each step of the way. I lucked out when you agreed to represent me. I also want to thank the tremendously talented Denise Roy, for helping to make this book the best it could be and being an absolute joy to work with. I knew after our first call we would be a great team. I could not have asked for a better editor.

I'm indebted to Pam Houston for suggesting I apply to graduate creative writing programs and essentially altering the course of my life, and for shaping me into a better writer by being one of the best teachers I know. Thank you for inspiring me with your writing and your kind words about mine.

Thanks to John Lescroart, whose generosity, support, and praise changed the way I saw my future, and gave me hope that a career as a writer might be possible; and to my writing teachers at UC Davis, particularly Lynn Freed and Fenton Johnson.

I owe so much to my fellow fiction workshoppers at UC Davis, who read the earliest pages of this novel and also became friends: Carola Strassburg Valdez, Ben Kamper, Krista Keyes, Melinda

Moustakis, Aimee Whitenack, and especially Liz Chamberlin, Adam Scott, Reema Rajbanshi, and Juli Case, who continue to read my work, nudge me to keep at it, and help me with writing (and life) dilemmas. I would not have made it this far without you guys cheering me on.

A special thank you goes out to Susan Scott, my self-proclaimed number one fan, for her unwavering faith that I would publish this book, and for her encouragement, friendship, and fantastic sense of humor. To all my friends, students, and colleagues who expressed interest in this project before it was finished: thank you for motivating me with your contagious excitement.

Words can't fully express my gratitude to my family: Bethany, Joshua, Bonnie, Nancy, and my mom, Sue, for listening, putting up with me, making me laugh, and above all else, loving me no matter what.

And, most importantly, Will. Thank you for reading scenes over and over, cooking delicious food, keeping me sane, understanding the writing life (and me), and all the other wonderful things you do. Thank you for your confidence in me, your endless support, and your love. None of this would be possible without you.